ENTICE

EXQUISITE SERIES #2

ELLA FRANK

ELLA FRANK, LLC

Copyright © 2014 Ella Frank - The Exquisite Series

Cover Design: Jay Aheer, Simply Defined Art

All rights reserved. No part of this book may be reproduced, scanned, or distributed in any print or electronic form without permission. Please do not participate in or encourage piracy of copyrighted materials in violation to the author's rights. Purchase only authorized editions.

This is a work of fiction. The names, people, places and incidents are products of the author's imagination or have been used fictitiously. Any resemblance to actual persons, living or dead, events, or locales is entirely coincidental.

ALSO BY ELLA FRANK

The Exquisite Series
Exquisite

The Temptation Series
Try
Take
Trust
Tease
Tate

Sunset Cove Series
Finley
Devil's Kiss

Masters Among Monsters Series
Alasdair
Isadora
Thanos

Standalones
Blind Obsession
Veiled Innocence

Co-Authored with Brooke Blaine

Sex Addict

Shiver

PresLocke Series
Co-Authored with Brooke Blaine

Aced

Locked

Wedlocked

DEDICATION

To my husband, as always, because every time I sat down to write, edit, or work on my blog, you never once asked me not to. You were just happy to be in the same room.

I love you and us for that.

CHAPTER 1

Past

"I can't believe you just asked me that," Shelly fumed, hands on hips, mouth open.

Adam sat on the couch, looking at her. "Why? Come on, Shel, it's not like you don't have the money. Three thousand dollars is nothing."

Shelly took a deep breath and turned around to walk into the kitchen. When she got there, she spotted the knife block—*better not tempt myself*—and made her way to the window instead. After two years of bailing out her wannabe-entrepreneur-slash-inventor boyfriend, she'd finally snapped at his latest idiotic idea.

Up until now, most of his "inventions" had been semi-plausible, and she'd been able to convince herself that he'd make enough money to pay her back. However, several thousands of dollars later, she was still out the cash, and he was *still* sitting on *her* couch, cooking up the next million-dollar idea. According to Adam, the latest and greatest was "The Auto-Toss," a moronic invention with "Want your salad tossed for you?" as the catchy slogan.

Really? Is he serious? Does he even realize the double entendre there? Shelly raised her hand, squeezing the bridge of her nose. *Honestly, who needs an automatic salad-tosser?* Okay, even thinking about that made her want to laugh at him. *More to the point, is this who I want to share DNA with and raise my children? Is this who I want to support for the rest of my life?*

The immediate and obvious answer was *hell no*.

"I can't do this anymore," she said, shaking her head.

"Do what?" Adam demanded.

Shelly turned to face him. He was now standing and glaring at her.

"This." She motioned back and forth between them.

Adam arched a brow and crossed his arms.

She tried to look at him objectively, from top to bottom, as though she'd never met him. He was standing in her living room dressed in unlaced Doc Martens. He had on scruffy blue jeans that had a rip across his left butt cheek—which she knew from staring at his ass one too many times—and a blue flannel shirt.

She wanted to like what she was looking at. She wanted to remember why entering into this relationship had been a good idea, but as he stood there glaring at her, she couldn't see it—and didn't that just piss her off.

"You don't like the new idea? I mean, come on. It's great—"

"Stop. Please, God, just stop. I'm done with this—as in us. It's not working anymore. I've been thinking about it for weeks. And now this, well, this whole salad-tosser thing? It's a *ridiculous* idea. I'm not even remotely interested in giving you more money."

His face contorted in anger. In all honesty, she couldn't tell if he was more pissed off about her breaking up with him or for telling him his idea essentially, well, sucked.

"You're such a snob," he yelled, pointing at her as if to punctuate his point.

"Excuse me? I'm not a snob."

"Yeah, you are. The whole time we've been together, you've looked down your nose at me."

Shelly blinked slowly, feeling her temperature rise quickly. In fact, if she had to guess, she'd wager her fair skin was probably turning a nice purple shade of pissed off and steam was probably starting to leak out of her ears.

This fight wasn't a new one. Throughout their whole relationship, Adam had always accused her of being a snob, and up until this moment, she'd never even entertained the thought he might be right.

Up until this *exact* moment.

"You know what? For once, you're right. I'm sick and tired of giving you money to sit at home—*my* home—and come up with these stupid dead-end ideas that you never follow through with. I've got to admit, up until now, *most* have had an inkling of making it. But this one? Wow, this one really blows. So yeah, I guess you can call me a snob because I want a man who'll go out and get a job. Oh, and here's a novel idea—keep it."

For a moment, Shelly thought about the main example of a man in her life—her father. All of a sudden, she saw her mother sitting in their kitchen, waiting for him to come home, only to find he had been held up for some reason or another.

Yeah, some reason in a skirt.

Nope, Shelly swore she wouldn't be *that* woman either.

"But I'll tell you one thing," she said. "The man *I* end up with will be honest, he'll be hardworking, and he will *not* sit on his ass while I'm out busting mine."

Adam came around the table and stopped right in front of her. Looking down, he sneered. "You've always been such a fucking princess."

Shelly felt as though he'd slapped her. Her father called her that, and honestly, he hadn't meant it in an endearing manner either.

"I think you need to leave," she told him through clenched teeth.

"What about all my stuff?"

Shelly glared at him, not one to be intimidated. "You can come and pick up your *one* suitcase tomorrow."

"Well, Dr. Monroe, I'd love to say it's been a pleasure, but hey, even the sex these last few months hasn't been." With that, he turned and grabbed his cell phone from the table.

Shelly glared holes in his back as he walked to the door. *Asshole. Like the five minutes he spent on top of me was the highlight of my week.*

Without a backward glance, he walked out, slamming the door. It crashed shut with a resonating boom.

As Shelly stood in her empty living room, she made a promise to herself. *No man will ever use me again.* She vowed to only date a man who could give her what she needed and did *not* look to her to be their sole provider.

It was a promise she intended to keep.

∽

Present

SHELLY KNOCKED on the back door of Exquisite and waited in the chilly February air. Coming from a hectic Monday at the hospital, she thought she'd be late, but she'd managed to arrive by seven thirty.

Mason's mother, Catherine, had always hosted the traditional Langley dinner on Monday nights. But shortly after she died, the Langley family decided that it didn't feel right to go back to her cottage without her there. So they'd switched to the restaurant, which worked out well since Exquisite was closed on Mondays. Somehow, ever since Lena had been welcomed back into the Langley family unit, Shelly too had found herself adopted.

Hearing the click of the lock, Shelly turned to see Mason pushing open the door.

"Shelly." Mason pulled her into a tight hug.

Shelly gladly returned his embrace. After all, he was Mason Langley, and she wasn't going to pass up a chance to get her hands on his sexy body, even if he was engaged to her best friend. "Mason. How are you tonight?"

"Great, just great. Get in here. The food's cooking, the wine's open, and Lena's at the bar, making margaritas."

Shelly smirked as he tugged her through the door. She walked down the main kitchen aisle and out to the dining area. Shelly looked to her left and saw her friend behind the huge mahogany bar that ran down the side of the restaurant. Lena waved at her.

Shrugging out of her coat, Shelly smiled as Mason took it from her. "Full service tonight, chef?"

When he grinned, matching dimples appeared. "Nothing but the best here at Exquisite." He winked.

Nodding, Shelly tugged at her tight little red skirt. "That's actually true, including your alcohol. So I'm going to go over to your woman and grab some."

"Let her know I'll be in the kitchen if she needs me."

Already moving toward the bar, Shelly called over her shoulder, "Will do." She stopped in front of her friend and colleague. "Where's my usual cosmo, huh?"

Lena arched a brow. "Sit down. Tonight, you're trying Lena's Margarita."

"Oh, am I?" Shelly watched as Lena salted the four large glasses in front of her.

"Yep. You, Rach, and Wendy are my guinea pigs."

"Lucky us." Sighing, Shelly looked around at the now-familiar bar and dining room.

"Hey, what's up?" Lena asked.

She shrugged then shook her head. "Nothing. I'm just feeling sorry for myself."

Lena frowned and reached over the bar to grip Shelly's hand. "Well, you shouldn't. You're wonderful, and we all love you."

"I know you do, but I can't have sex with you."

Lena laughed, pulling her hand back to pick up the pitcher of margaritas. "Oh. I see. It's *that* kind of feeling sorry for ourselves."

Picking up a straw from the container on the bar, Shelly twirled it between her fingers. She blew out a breath and felt her blond hair ruffle against her cheek. "Yeah, it's that kind of 'I feel sorry for myself.' I hate being sexually frustrated. It sucks. Well, not literally obviously, but you know what I mean."

Lena rested a hip against the bar and pushed a margarita toward her. "Actually, no, I don't. I've never felt like that."

"What about before your sex god turned up?" Shelly asked with a huge grin as Lena predictably stiffened slightly.

"Sex god? Really? Please don't say that around him. The man already has a huge ego. You don't need to feed it."

Shelly took a sip of her drink and nodded. "Okay, but I'm right, aren't I?"

Grinning, Lena took a sip from her own glass and looked over the rim at Shelly. "Oh yeah. He's a god."

"Lucky bitch." Shelly pouted as Lena winked at her.

JOSH DANIELS WAS HAVING a bad day.

He'd just come from his lawyer's office, and he was *not* happy. His last client was trying to skip out on making their final payment, stating that Josh's company had gone over by two days.

Stupid prick. If we hadn't gone over, they would've ended up with shit work. Knowing the slimy little weasel, he would've sued for that too.

He was definitely *not* having a good day.

Around six months ago, Josh had decided to move back to Chicago after he broke things off with Melissa. They'd moved to LA because she'd wanted to pursue an acting career. *Cue the curtains and the eye rolling.* Turned out, she saw the quickest way to get to the top was by being on top—of the casting agent.

Is it really so hard to find a nice, sweet woman who wants to settle down and marry? Apparently it was, because here he was back in cold-ass Chicago, which was currently rainy Chicago, making his way over to his friend's new restaurant—alone.

Mason Langley. He hadn't seen the guy for a little over two years.

Since Josh got back to town, he'd been so busy moving in and getting his business up and running in a new town that he didn't have the time to track him down. It wasn't until recently, when he'd caught a review on TV about Exquisite, that Josh had kicked himself into gear.

When they'd gone to school together, and even through their college years at different universities, they'd been trouble with a capital T. He remembered many parties involving lots of hot girls and even hotter nights. They'd spent those formative years, as they liked to call it, "networking."

Yeah, networking our way into girls' beds, cars, dorm rooms, and parents' holiday homes. Josh chuckled. If you could think of a place, they'd been there and done *that* there. *Yep, it's going to be good to meet up with my old friend.*

He'd heard talk around town about Exquisite, Mason and Rachel's restaurant, and after the TV piece, he was looking forward to checking it out for himself. After all, he couldn't remember how many times Mason had told him that one day, he'd be *so* famous that all the women he wanted would line up around the block for him. *Pretty-boy bastard probably achieved that goal too.*

Josh parked his white Ford F-250 in the tiny parking lot behind the address on his GPS. Walking to the back door, as he'd been told to do, he noticed a shiny red BMW convertible and rolled his eyes. It reminded him of a Barbie car. He chuckled at his own thought and then stopped at the door and knocked twice.

SHELLY AND LENA made their way over to the table that'd been set for eight and took a seat. Lena had refilled her margarita, and she had to admit Lena's Margarita was pretty damn delicious.

As Lena took a seat, she beamed at Shelly. "Look, before everyone gets here, can I ask you something?"

Shelly nodded and took a sip of her drink, noticing that Lena was keeping an eye on the kitchen doors. "Sure. Hit me with it."

Lena licked her lips then blurted, "Will you be my maid of honor?"

Shelly smiled so widely her face hurt. If anyone had asked her not even a year ago if Dr. Magdalena O'Donnell would ever look so happy, she would've said that they were out of their mind. After the death of her sister, Lena had closed down, determined not to let anyone in—until Mason. As Lena's eyes twinkled, Shelly was hit with such joy for her friend's happiness that she almost started to cry. Nodding quickly, she took Lena's hand and squeezed it gently.

"I'd love to be...but do I really need to be called *maid* of honor? It makes me sound so old and kind of stuffy." Shelly wrinkled her nose.

Lena smiled as she sat back, lifting her glass to her lips. "Fine. I'll call you that in secret meetings only."

Shelly winked at her over the rim of her glass. "Sounds like a plan. So when's the big day?"

"Oh, we haven't decided yet. But guess what? One of Mason's old school friends is back in town, and he's coming here tonight. It's so exciting. I've never met any of his school friends. They all moved away after graduation."

Shaking her head, Shelly felt the hair at the back of her neck rise as she slowly lowered her glass. "Please don't tell me you're—"

"He's going to be the best man—if he agrees. Wouldn't it be great if you two get along and—"

"Stop, stop," Shelly interrupted, sitting forward in her chair. Lowering her voice a little, she glared at Lena and shook her head. "No. No, no, no, Lena I'm-so-in-love O'Donnell. Do *not* try to fix me up. Ugh, I hate being fixed up."

Lena's brow rose. "Need I remind you that you were the one who told Mason to come stalk me at O'Malley's? Look at how that turned out."

Shelly rolled her eyes and picked up her drink. She was well on her way to feeling relaxed. "Yeah, but look at him. We knew, or let me say *I* knew, that he was smokin' hot and you should grab him and take a bite." Shelly licked the salt off her bottom lip. "This guy could be balding and fat for all we know. You do *not* get to set me up with anyone until I see him first."

Lena's eyes had moved, looking past Shelly's shoulder. They widened slightly, and Shelly thought she almost looked comical, as though her eyes would pop out of her head.

"Well, maybe you should turn around because, as far as I can tell, Josh isn't fat *or* anywhere close to balding," Mason said from behind Shelly.

Shutting her eyes on a groan, she shook her head at Lena, who was biting her lip and trying hard not to laugh. Putting her glass down, Shelly slowly turned, ready to face the music.

∽

SO BARBIE HAS a mouth on her. Big surprise. Josh watched the blonde's back stiffening. He knew from what Mason had told him that the woman currently facing him, trying to contain her laughter, was Lena. Her green eyes smiled at him, and her long brown hair spilled over her shoulders in a riot of curls.

Yep, Mason had described her right down to the smirk, so he knew she was the woman who'd won over his friend. That left the blonde to be Dr. Shelly Monroe. Josh looked back to the woman who was slowly placing her margarita glass on the table and turning toward them.

The first thing Josh had noticed about her was the hair. *Man, she has some perfect hair.* It landed just beneath her shoulders in a completely straight line. The color was almost platinum, but it had several darker shades of gold through it, which could've only been achieved at a high-end salon. He knew *that* courtesy of Melissa.

The second thing he noticed was her cherry-red skirt. Not only was it short enough to show off a good portion of her thigh, it was the same bright shade as, he was presuming, her Barbie convertible in the parking lot. When she finally faced them, she smoothed her black blouse and he noticed her eyes. They were such a startling deep cerulean that he could barely take his eyes away from them.

She flicked those eyes toward Mason. "Didn't anyone teach you it's not nice to sneak up on people?"

Mason crossed his arms, looking at the petite blonde. "Don't try to wiggle your way out of this, Shel." Mason turned toward him while Josh watched her red lips tip up. "Josh, this is Dr. Shelly Monroe, and that gorgeous woman over there is *my* doctor, Lena." Mason looked back to Shelly. "This is my *non*-balding friend, Josh Daniels."

Josh stayed focused on her as she looked him in the eye. Not only did she seem unembarrassed, but she also seemed to be challenging him to make it an issue.

"Yes, I can see that," she almost purred.

Josh felt her voice skate up along his spine. *Oh, holy shit, this is not good.*

He was not in the market for upper class and high maintenance. He wanted middle class and low maintenance. However, as Dr. Monroe ran her incredible eyes over his body, he felt all the blood in his brain disappearing quickly.

Trying to stop the blood from reaching his interested cock, he held out his hand to her. She looked down at it then gently slid her own against his. Her eyes moved up from their joined palms to meet his again as she bit her bottom lip slowly.

"Not an ounce of fat either," Shelly whispered seductively.

Mason cleared his throat with a small laugh and shook his head. "Okay, Shel, leave the poor man alone."

Letting go of his hand, she shrugged and turned back to her friend. She must've done something when she faced her because Lena let out a small giggle, and Mason sighed. Josh turned to find Mason shaking his head.

"Ignore them. Most of the time, they act like they're in high school instead of behaving like two of the smartest women I've ever met."

Josh nodded, still trying to work out what had just happened.

∼

SHELLY STOOD AND turned on her heel toward Lena, who was looking at her with a giant smirk. When Shelly arched a brow and mouthed, "No," it sent her friend into a fit of giggles. Rolling her eyes, Shelly sat down and reached for her drink.

Delicious. That'd been the first word that came to mind when she saw him. The second had been a very loud *no*. No way would she get involved with a man like *that.* He was everything she swore she'd never go back to.

Wearing worn jeans with a rip across the knee, he had broad shoulders that looked so strong and powerful, he could probably lift her above his head in a bench press. Add in all that amazing wavy brown hair that was just long enough to curl behind his ears, and she thought, *Crap, I'm screwed.*

Sipping her margarita, Shelly continued to discreetly watch him as he walked around the table with Mason. Even the way he walked was sexy. She closed her eyes, letting out a small groan.

"Something wrong, Shelly?"

Her eyes snapped open, and she glared at Lena, who was grinning with glee. Shelly decided right then that if she could've reached, she would have kicked Lena in the shin. She was about to respond when her phone buzzed. Looking down, she turned it over and noticed a text message from Lena.

Lena: You've seen him. So?

Shelly raised her eyes to see Lena had turned toward Mason and Josh, pretending to listen to their conversation. *Sneaky little shit.*

Hitting reply, Shelly lied. **Nope, not my type. You know me—suits and ties all the way.**

Shelly put the phone back on the table, and Lena looked down at hers when it buzzed. As Lena arched her brow and typed back, acting like they actually *were* the teenagers Mason had accused them of being, Shelly looked at the two men discussing what sounded like a job proposal.

Mason caught her eye and winked while Josh grabbed his glass. With an arched brow Mason cocked his head toward his friend in a so-what-do-you-think kind of way. Shelly rolled her eyes, shaking her head. Mason's gaze went right back to his friend as though he hadn't been doing anything mischievous. *Another sneaky little shit.*

He and Lena deserved one another.

Again, her phone buzzed. Looking at Lena, who was once again pretending to pay attention to the boring *man* conversation, Shelly picked up her phone. She'd just taken a sip of her drink when she read:

Lena: Corporate's not fixing the issue. Time to hire a handyman to flush out the plumbing.

Shelly sputtered on Lena's Margarita, almost choking.

"You okay over there?" Mason asked.

Glancing up, Shelly saw Lena grab her drink and take a sip. Looking back at Mason and Mr. Delicious, Shelly smiled slightly. "Yeah, just went down the wrong *pipe*."

Shelly was about to say something else when the double doors behind her whooshed open, and Rachel squealed. Looking over her shoulder, Shelly saw the currently purple-haired pastry chef zero in on Josh—a.k.a. Mr. Delicious Handyman.

"Joshua Daniels. Oh my God. You are even hotter now than you were back in high school."

Hot, he definitely is. Shelly turned to watch Josh stand, then he pulled out his biggest weapon—a smile so slow and so sexy, it could've dropped a woman's panties in five seconds flat. Hers in particular.

Rachel ran across the room, launching herself at him for a huge hug. Shelly watched those powerful arms wrap around Rachel, and for the second time that night, she thought, *I'm screwed.*

CHAPTER 2

TUESDAY MORNING ROLLED around, and Shelly was relieved when she noticed she was alone. Sometime during the night, she'd had a fantastic dream in which she'd cornered Delicious Daniels and dragged him home to her bed. She was thrilled to discover that was not, in fact, reality.

She'd made it through the rest of the dinner last night with what little dignity she could find after almost choking on her drink. Then she'd hightailed it out of there.

Today was her day off, and she planned to make the most of it. She was looking forward to getting her hair cut, her nails buffed, and her feet massaged—pretty much reveling in a full day of self-indulgence. She made sure to treat herself once a month. After all, why shouldn't she enjoy something when she worked so damn hard?

Grabbing the juice from the refrigerator, she poured herself a glass, thinking about her father. He was the kind of man who always went out of his way to make her feel as though anything remotely self-indulgent was a waste of money and a "female thing."

In her father's mind, she'd committed two major sins. First, she'd been born a girl. That had been a major disappointment to her father, and it was completely her fault of course—as if she'd actually had a say in the matter. Second, she'd chosen not to become a surgeon like him. Instead, she'd specialized in a less-demanding field in case there ever came a time when she wanted to maybe—and this was a huge maybe—start a family.

But those two sins were just the tip of the iceberg. Shelly sighed as she sipped her juice, wondering how he had the ability to aggravate the shit out of her even when he was hundreds of miles away.

Pushing thoughts of him aside, she focused on more pleasurable things—like Mason Langley's fine-looking friend. She didn't want to get involved with a man like him—meaning a man who moved from state to state for a contract job, essentially living with no stability. A man who could have her on her knees in ten seconds flat if he knew her weakness.

However, he was the exact man she was drawn to. For some reason, her screwed-up DNA had decided that her girly parts would only get tingly for a man dressed in ripped-across-the-ass jeans.

It wasn't fair, Shelly thought as she lifted the glass to her lips. All she wanted was a predictable man who went to a boring Monday-through-Friday job in a boring suit with a boring everyday personality. Instead, she was attracted to the kind of man who was likely to pound her into her bed, floor, or couch, then roll off, walk out the door, and leave the state. She knew from experience that relationships based solely on instant attraction never ended well.

After placing her glass in the sink, she made her way to the bathroom and stopped in front of the mirror to glare at herself.

She held her hair back from her face. *Maybe I should just chop it off? Be more serious—less girly.* She turned her head to the left then came back to face forward. *Nah, who am I kidding? The men love it.*

JOSH WOKE TO A WARM, wet tongue licking his cheek.

Cracking an eye, he saw his six-year-old German shepherd, Mutley, sitting next to the bed. His long snout was resting on the mattress, and his big brown eyes were focused on Josh's face.

"Need to go out, boy?" he asked as though the dog would actually answer.

Mutley whined and wagged his tail, making his big body twitch from side to side. Scratching the dog's head, Josh yawned and pulled back the covers. Swinging his legs over the side, he winced when his feet hit the cold hardwood. Cold-ass Chicago.

Josh unlatched and opened the sliding glass doors that led to the backyard, and Mutley dashed outside to relieve himself, probably cursing Josh for oversleeping. He looked out at the hot tub that was half-installed on the left side of the deck. Another project he'd decided would be a fun challenge, but it was still unfinished and untouched.

Last night had been interesting.

Meeting up with his old college friend had been great. He'd forgotten how much fun he'd had with Mason back in the day. He was so easygoing, and his family was awesome. Rachel was exactly as he remembered. Crazy, he thought with a chuckle, but he thought there was something else going on with the crazy—or maybe he was just imagining it.

He leaned a shoulder against the glass door as Mutley took the opportunity to sniff every plant in the yard.

Josh had been happy to see Rachel still sporting the colorful hair— so colorful that she almost looked like an Easter egg, not that he'd ever tell her that.

The Langley family had been through a rough year. He'd been upset to hear of Catherine's passing. Mason's father had died a few years back, and Josh had sent flowers when he couldn't make it to the funeral. But to learn that the gentle lady with the warm smile had passed—well, there just weren't any words. The world had lost a wonderful soul.

Mason's Lena was adorable and absolutely perfect for him. He couldn't have found a better woman if he'd gone around with a list of requirements and marked off each one. She was funny, stubborn, and quick as a whip, and his friend was completely and hopelessly in love. He hadn't known what to expect when Mason told him he was engaged. After all, she would have to be someone pretty special to get Mason to finally give up the bachelor life, but after being around the two of them for a few hours, he saw they were a perfect fit.

Then there was Shelly Monroe—who was another matter altogether. With her blond hair, huge blue eyes, and a body that wouldn't quit, he'd found it hard to keep his eyes off her. He'd made a conscious effort to have as little to do with her as possible, but that didn't mean he stopped trying to catch glances of her reflection in the mirrors behind the bar. The lady was a knockout. Not only was she stacked, but she oozed sex and was as smart as Lena. Combine those three ingredients, and you've got one dangerous package. The woman was a man-eater, and he had to admit he was finding it difficult to avoid offering himself up for a bite.

He reminded himself for the millionth time that she was not what he wanted. Melissa had been the same way—stunning, funny, and a spitfire in bed. In everyone's bed.

No, he needed someone gentle, sweet, and possibly cute. For that very reason, he was going to stay the hell away from Man-Eater Monroe.

LATER THAT EVENING, Shelly let herself into her apartment and dropped several shopping bags on the floor. She fished through her purse for her ringing cell phone, grabbed it, and saw Lena's name. "Hey, you. What's up?"

"Not much. Just sitting here, watching TV and waiting for Mason to get home."

Shelly moved around the couch and sat down, kicking off her purple heels before propping her feet up on the table. "So I'm your I'm-bored phone call?"

"No. You know that's not true."

Shelly laughed. "I know. I'm just giving you a hard time."

"Figures," Lena mumbled. "So...?"

"I knew it. I knew there was a reason why you called me. Spit it out, O'Donnell."

"I just wanted to know what you thought of Josh?"

"He seemed nice," Shelly replied, keeping it vague.

"That's not what I meant, and you know it."

Sighing, Shelly shook her head even though her friend couldn't see. "I don't know what you want me to tell you. He's not my type."

"You need to broaden your horizons. Did you ever think Mason would be my type?"

"Ahh, Lena?"

"Yeah?"

"No one was your type. You didn't date. I do," Shelly stressed.

Lena sighed then said softly, "Okay, so you're right, but obviously something isn't working. You're miserable. You always complained about Paul, and before that Steve, and before that—"

"Yeah, yeah, I get the picture. But that doesn't mean I want to date Josh the handyman."

"Well, actually—"

"No. There's no actually in this conversation. He's not for me. Now find me a cute banker, CEO, or lawyer."

"Paul was a lawyer," Lena pointed out.

"Okay, not a lawyer, but not a construction worker, or an inventor, or a salesman. Ugh."

There was silence, then Lena asked softly, "What's wrong with all those things? At least they're jobs."

Shelly thought about what she'd said and agreed it did sound obnoxious. "You're right. I'm being a jerk. They are jobs. I'm just not interested in Josh, okay?"

"Okay, okay, I get it. Mason and I just thought it would be nice."

Shelly laughed and replied good-naturedly, "You and Mason are two interfering busybodies. Go practice making babies."

"Hmm. Now there's a good idea," Mason's deep voice came over the phone.

"Lena. How many times have I told you to tell me when I'm on speakerphone? What if I'd been telling you about the latest penis I'd—"

"Stop. Stop. My ears—they're bleeding," Mason yelled, laughing.

"Well, it serves you right. Now go and keep your fiancée occupied so she leaves me alone."

Mason's voice sounded much closer when he answered, "With pleasure."

Then the connection died.

Looking at her silent phone, Shelly let out a deep breath and glanced around her empty house. God, when had it become so lonely here? About five minutes ago, when she'd heard from lovers' paradise, that's when. She stood and headed down to her bedroom. She needed to stop feeling sorry for herself.

Maybe she needed a pet. A dog, perhaps? Oh no. All that slobbering. Or she could get a cat. When she reached her room, she stopped and shook her head. No, not a cat either. The implications of an older single woman with a cat were horrifying.

She unzipped her skirt and stepped out of it when it fell to the floor, then she walked into the bathroom. She turned on the sink and grabbed the face scrub in her cabinet. Tying up her hair, she watched the basin fill, and suddenly, it hit her—the perfect pet.

Tomorrow, I'll go buy myself a fish.

JOSH HAD THOUGHT about Mason's renovation proposal for the last two days. He wasn't sure if it was good to mix business with friendship, but Mason had balked at the idea of Josh doing the work for free.

So here he was, walking through the dining room of Exquisite on Thursday morning, looking for the owner. He found Mason standing behind the bar with his head bent over, reading something.

When Josh walked over, Mason looked up. "Hey, Daniels. How you doing this morning?"

"Good, man, good. Yourself?"

"Can't complain," he said, grinning widely.

Josh nodded as he set a folder on the countertop.

"Is that the bid?" Mason asked.

Pushing it toward his friend, he replied, "Yeah, I think I got it all in there. You wanted an estimate for the wall to be knocked down and the space next door to be brought up to code for the restaurant to be expanded, right?"

"You got it," Mason answered, grabbing the folder. He opened it and flipped through the pages.

Josh turned and looked around the dining room, giving Mason a moment to look it over. Damn, the place was something else. The tables were perfectly arranged, and the fancy silverware and crystal glasses made the place look refined and elegant. The beautiful big bar also gave the restaurant a cozy feel. Josh could imagine Friday and Saturday nights here were insanely busy.

He was about to turn around when he heard Mason ask, "So, ahh... Josh, you single? Dating?"

Turning back toward Mason, he chuckled. "Why? You interested?"

"Sure, smartass, that's why I'm asking."

Josh shook his head. He was pretty sure he knew where this was going, and he wanted to can it before—

"Well, I was thinking it might be nice if you and Shelly got to know one another. You know, the good-looking blonde who was here the other night. She's single," Mason suggested with a devious grin.

Josh shook his head. "No way, man."

"What do you mean no way? Did you see her?"

Laughing, Josh pointed out, "I have eyes, don't I? Of course I saw her. She was pretty damn hard to miss."

"So what's the problem? Are you seeing someone?"

Crossing his arms, Josh narrowed his eyes. "No, I'm not, but I'm not going to start seeing her. I'm not going to do anything with her."

Mason tilted his head. "Why? What's wrong with you? She's exactly what you normally go for."

"Oh, really? And is Lena what you always went for?"

Mason's spine straightened, and he shrugged. "What do you mean?"

"People change. That's all I'm saying. You found a woman who is wonderful, and yeah, she's not what you used to go out with, but it works." Josh knew Mason thought he was going to say something about models and beauty queens, but that's not what he meant. "I'm looking for someone a little quieter than I think Man-Eater Monroe knows how to be."

Mason let out a booming laugh. "What'd you just call her?"

Shaking his head, Josh said quickly, "Nothing."

"Oh yeah, you did. Did you say 'Man-Eater Monroe'?"

Rolling his eyes, he nodded. "Yeah. Don't tell me you haven't noticed. The first thing she did when we met was size me up like her next meal."

That set his friend off again. Mason was laughing so hard, he was in tears. "Ah, man. Don't you remember when we were in high school? We would've killed for a girl to look at us like that, and now you're acting like a horrified virgin." Mason grinned. "Which I know you're not."

"Shut the hell up, Casanova."

Mason's mouth snapped shut, and he glared at him. "All right, who told you?" Shaking his head, Mason narrowed his eyes. "Forget it, I know. Rachel's a dead woman."

Josh pointed at the folder. "So? What do you think?"

Placing the folder on the counter, Mason asked, "When can your guys start?"

"How 'bout Monday?"

"Sounds good to me."

Josh shook Mason's hand. Mason was about to pull back when Josh gripped his hand tightly and said in the most menacing voice he could find, "If you tell Monroe I called her that, I'll kill you, and I don't even care that it'd make Lena cry."

As Josh let go of his hand, Mason grinned unrepentantly and placed his palm on his chest. "You're breaking my heart."

"Do I look like I care?"

"Cold, Daniels, cold."

Smiling at his old friend, Josh said, "You live in Chicago. Suck it up."

CHAPTER 3

*I*T WAS MONDAY evening when Shelly finally sat down after a grueling twelve-hour shift in the intensive care unit. She looked at the messages on her desk and picked up one.

MEMO: 4:25 p.m.
Dr. Lawrence Monroe called.
Please call him back.

YOU FOUND some time for me, did you, Father? Squeezing me in somewhere between the nurses or maybe an intern? Sorry but not right now.
Shelly stuffed it into her pocket and picked up the second one.

MEMO: 11:52 a.m.
Paul Worthington called.

OH, he did, did he? Shelly sat back in her leather chair. She hadn't heard from Paul for almost three months. *What on earth would he be calling about now?* She dismissed the memo as she heard a knock at her door.
Looking over, she saw Dr. Roger McKinney leaning against the

frame with one leg crossed over the other. He wore his glasses, and his hands were stuffed into his lab coat. Shelly gave him a stiff smile, hoping he wasn't here for round three of what Shelly liked to refer to as *Uncomfortable Moments*, starring Dr. Roger McKinney and Dr. Shelly Monroe.

He pushed away from the doorframe, walking into her office. At five foot six, he wasn't a tall man, and Shelly knew that in a good pair of heels, she was most definitely taller than her boss. As casually as he could, he sat in the chair opposite her desk. He crossed his legs and smiled at her, and Shelly noticed for the first time that his mustache was gone—an improvement but still by no means someone she envisioned herself dating.

Shelly sat silently, hoping whatever was about to come out of his mouth was work-related.

"Are you finished for the night?" he asked.

That doesn't sound promising. She turned to face him directly. Nodding, she forced a smile and held up a yellow memo. "Just going through my messages before heading out."

"Great, great," he said, placing his hands on his knees.

Please don't ask me, please don't—

"So I was wondering if you'd like to grab a drink with me tonight."

Shelly groaned internally. No matter how many times she said no, he kept coming back. It was getting to the point that she was running out of creative and polite ways to refuse a drink with the man. Wincing, she reached into her pocket and pulled out the note from her father. "I'm sorry. Dad called to tell me he's coming into town, so I really need to get home."

Liar, liar, pants on fire.

"Oh. Oh, okay." He stood and brushed his hands over some imaginary lint on his lab coat. He quickly put his hands back in his coat pockets and nodded. "Maybe some other time. Be sure to say hello to Dr. Monroe for me."

Shelly forced a grin, refusing to be mean or rude, and nodded once. "Will do."

Sitting in her chair and gripping the yellow piece of paper, she watched her boss leave. She hated the fact that her father had just inadvertently saved her.

Oh, my father would love Dr. Roger McKinney, hospital administrator.

Even though her father was forever telling her she made bad choices in her relationships, he'd think McKinney was the perfect man to settle down with.

Dr. Lawrence Monroe was convinced his daughter would end up with someone she would have to support for the rest of her life, and Shelly was determined to prove him wrong. That was why it was such a shame that McKinney was about as appealing as a root canal. It wasn't his fault he didn't flip her switch, but...well, he just didn't.

Sighing, Shelly bent to pick up her purse and looked at the other piece of yellow paper. Paul Worthington. Lawyer, self-made man, educated, smart—maybe he was worth another shot. *After all, what do I have to lose?*

~

ON TUESDAY MORNING, Josh pushed through the front doors of Exquisite with the blueprints for the building next door and a tray holding four coffees and a bag of donuts. As the front door closed behind him, he saw Lena look up. He smiled and made his way over to her table. She had some kind of account book with columns of numbers open in front of her.

Numbers—I hate crunching numbers. Lowering his knees a little, he dumped the bag on the table as she stood and grabbed the tray.

She whispered, "What's in the bag?"

Looking around the empty dining room, Josh answered in a conspiratorial whisper, "Donuts. Why?"

Lena shook her head. "Have you ever been around Rachel when she's seen store-bought donuts?"

With a huge smile he placed the rolled-up prints on the table behind him. After pulling a chair out, he sat down and shook his head. "Nope. But if it's anything like the time she was caught looking at Mason's porn magazine collection, I have a feeling I'm in trouble."

Lena's mouth fell open, and he wasn't sure if she was shocked at what Rachel had been caught doing or the fact that the magazines had belonged to Mason. She quickly regained her composure though, grinning at him in a way that let him know she was cooking up some way to use this new information. "Really?"

"Really. He hid them in his closet in a shoebox."

"How original."

Laughing, Josh nodded. "Better than under the bed."

"True. That's the first place Catherine would've looked." Crossing his arms, he tilted his head. "That's where all naughty boys hid them. Did you know her well?"

His question must have hit a nerve because she stiffened then nodded. "Yes, I did."

Okay, message received. No more questions about Catherine. Josh ran his fingers through his shaggy brown hair, wanting to get back to a more comfortable topic. "Yep. Rach had just turned sixteen, and Mason and I walked in and found her in his closet with magazines scattered all around her. She had them all opened, displaying various..." He searched for the right word then winked. "Positions."

Gasping and bringing her hand to her mouth, Lena burst into giggles, and Josh couldn't help but laugh with her.

He was about to continue when he heard Mason ask, "What are you two laughing about?"

Turning around in his chair, Josh saw Mason walking across the dining room, smiling at him and his fiancée. Josh glanced over to see Lena watching her man. *See, that right there. That look in her eyes—the one that shows that when Mason's in the room, no one else exists.* That was what he wanted. That was how he wanted a woman to look at him.

Then that sweet look turned mischievous, and in the most matter-of-fact tone Josh had ever heard, she said, "Josh was just telling me about your porn collection."

Wincing a little, he watched Mason stop in his tracks and look at him.

Then Mason turned back to Lena. "Oh? And what did he tell you?"

Lena stood, and with her eyes on Mason, she walked toward him. "That you had an extensive collection hidden in your closet."

Josh watched Mason's eyes flick in his direction, so he shrugged and shook his head. "I was actually telling her about catching Rachel. You were just part of the story."

Lena wrapped her arms around Mason's neck. "A big part of it. He told me about lots of different positions."

Mason's head turned toward Josh so fast that he stood quickly, knocking the chair back. "Ahh, she said that wrong."

Lena giggled and kissed Mason's cheek. "Relax, Casanova. He said you two caught Rachel with your magazines open to all different positions, and she went nuts."

Mason kissed her lips hard then pulled back. "I'm confused. How did you get on the topic of porn again?" Josh reached behind him and grabbed the bag, holding it up. "Donuts?"

"Donuts?" Mason repeated.

Lena grinned and let him go. "Yep, donuts..." She looked toward the front door. "I was checking to make sure he knew that he was risking the wrath of Rachel because of the store pastries, and he told me her reaction could be no worse than—"

"Us finding her with the pornos. I got it," Mason stated.

Lena grinned as she sat down, and Josh breathed a sigh of relief when his friend walked over and took a seat. It had been so long since he'd hung out with Mason that he wasn't sure if he was joking or not about the whole situation.

Mason grabbed a powder-covered pastry, bit into it, and said around a sugary smile, "I'm not scared of Rachel, and neither is Josh. We have way too much on her for her to threaten us. Ever. Isn't that right?"

Josh nodded, picking up his own donut as the lady in question walked in. Her blue eyes, the same color as her brother's, zoomed in on his hand holding a donut, then her gaze locked on to Josh's. "Put it down, Daniels."

"Aw, come on, Rach. Just one little bite?" he asked, winking at her as she moved closer.

"Don't try to charm me. You're too much like my own brother for it to work. So put down the donut," she enunciated slowly.

She made her way across the dining room with a hessian bag. With her purple hair braided into pigtails, she was dressed in tight black leather pants and had a bright red hoodie zipped to just between her breasts. Josh tried to look at her as a woman, someone he'd never met, just to see if he could. But no such luck. She was Rachel, his best friend's baby sister. She would always be the little brat he'd picked on. It was a shame really, because she was extremely attractive in an in-your-face, wild kind of way.

She stopped in front of him and held out her palm, looking down at him with twinkling eyes full of mischief. "Give me that horrible excuse for a donut."

Josh lifted it slowly and licked right across the top of the powdered sugar, winking at her. That was when she pushed it into his nose.

Coughing, he pulled it away as Mason and Lena laughed.

"Don't mess with her pastries," Lena said through a fit of giggles.

Rachel grinned and swiped his nose with her finger. "Powdered sugar doesn't look right on you. You aren't that sweet."

Josh frowned. "Aw, come on, Rach. Now you're just trying to hurt my feelings."

She moved around the table and took a seat, putting her feet up on the chair opposite her.

As she crossed her arms, Josh asked, "How can I make it up to you?"

She sat forward. "Do you still like to dance?"

Groaning, Josh shook his head and rolled his eyes. Back in the day, he, Rachel, and Mason used to frequent the clubs. "Yeah, I don't mind it. Got a place in mind?"

She nodded, putting her feet on the floor. "Friday night. We'll all go to Blue Moon."

Lena coughed a little, so Josh turned toward her. "You don't like Blue Moon?"

Mason took Lena's hand and said, "We've only been once." He turned to Lena and said softly, "Let's go and change that memory, huh?"

Lena nodded, and Josh could tell there was more going on than he knew about. He turned back to Rachel, who was now quiet, lost somewhere in her own thoughts as she stared out the window. Josh kept his eyes on her, wondering what was on her mind.

Instead of asking, he said, "Okay, count me in. Friday it is." He pulled another donut from the bag. "Now can I eat my donut in peace?"

Rachel turned back to him, plastering on a too-happy smile, and took the offensive donut before dropping it on the table. She opened her bag, pulled out a cling-wrapped plate with what looked like homemade beignets, and placed it on the table in front of him.

Josh pulled his eyes away from the plate to look at Rachel. He grinned. "You're an angel. Anyone tell you that?"

"Stop sucking up, Daniels. Just know that when this melts in your mouth, I saved you from polluting your taste buds."

He took a bite of one and groaned.

"You can say it now," she instructed him.

"Say what?" he asked around the second bite.

"That I'm right, *and* I'm a genius," Rachel pointed out smugly.

Grinning, Josh kissed her cheek. "You're right, and you're a crazy purple-haired genius." Sitting back, he watched the smirk creep back onto her face. He looked at Mason and Lena and winked as he said, "Who loves to look at her brother's porn."

He watched with delight as her eyes widened, and the other two burst into laughter.

"Oh, I hate you, Daniels."

Finishing off the beignet, he blew her a kiss. "Nah, you don't. I'm gonna take you dancing."

CHAPTER 4

SHELLY WAS STANDING in front of her mirror, inspecting her reflection, when she heard the intercom doorbell peal through her condo. She dashed over and hit the enter button.

Lena had called her the other night and asked if she wanted to go out dancing. At first, Shelly had hesitated, thinking it was a setup, until Lena had told her to bring a date.

Enter Paul Worthington, a man who would most certainly prove my father's theory on my dating skills wrong. Enter a successful, stable, reliable man.

Shelly had called him back when she'd gotten home on Monday and was surprised when he told her he wanted to get together and maybe even give things another try. Not having any other interesting offers available, she hadn't seen the harm in giving it one last shot, even though she had a rule about repeats. *Never repeat bad words you hear, never repeat bad dates you had, and never* ever *repeat a bad sexual experience.*

In all fairness, Paul hadn't been bad at anything. But when she pushed for a physical relationship, he'd told her over and over that he wanted to wait so it would be special.

Wait for what? Marriage? Before she talked herself out of the date, she slicked her lips with gloss, tugged down the hem of her black dress, and made her way to the front door. Pulling it open, she found Paul standing with his back facing her.

He was dressed in a dark-brown sports coat and cream-colored slacks. When he turned, his green eyes shined as he smiled and looked her over. She reciprocated, looking at the blue button-up shirt tucked neatly in at his waist. She finally pulled her gaze up to his.

"Paul, it's so nice to see you again."

He took her outstretched hands and squeezed her fingers. "You too, Shelly." She turned away to grab her bag and coat as he said softly, "You look fantastic."

Smiling over her shoulder at him, she took his hand again. "So do you. Ready to go dancing?"

He tensed a little, and Shelly got the impression that he was *not* looking forward to it at all. *Ahh, prayers answered—a boring suit, a nice man, and a personality I can predict. That's what I want, right?*

THE MUSIC WAS PUMPING through the club and bodies were gyrating when Rachel dragged Josh through the doors. The dim lighting was a welcome relief from the floodlights outside where they'd been waiting in line. He scanned the sea of people for Mason, but he was coming up empty. *Man, I could use a beer.*

They pushed through the crowd, and when they got to the bar, Rachel rested her back against it. "Man, I love this place."

"Really?" he queried, looking at her as she scanned the crowd.

Josh was starting to get the impression that Rachel's outlandish hair and outfits were all part of some bigger picture he and everybody else may be missing, and he wanted to see if she would confirm it.

She turned her head toward him and grinned. "Yeah, really." She looked back out at the dancing crowd with that same almost-sad look on her face from the other day. Then she brightened again and nodded as if confirming her first thought. "You can totally lose yourself here. I love it."

Now that statement is completely Rachel.

She was dressed in a tiny pink PVC tank top and leather pants. She looked like a tiny dominatrix who had been spray-painted with Pepto-Bismol.

The bartender came down and took their orders. Josh watched the crowd shifting and swaying to the throbbing of the music.

When the bartender came back, Rachel turned around and grabbed her drink. Josh was about to ask when Mason and Lena were supposed to meet them when Rachel waved her hand in the direction of the door. He turned around, and that was when he saw *her* walk in.

Even from where he was standing, he could see every curve of her spectacular body, but that probably had something to do with the skintight black dress she'd painted on herself. Her perfect blond hair was pulled up into a tight high ponytail. As she stepped through the crowd, he noticed her feet flaunting a wicked pair of heels that looked so sharp, they could be deadly.

Josh took a deep breath, letting his eyes follow her naked legs up to the long stretch of creamy white thigh that was then cut off by the black dress. It hugged her thighs, hips, and all the smooth lines between before tightly clinging to her spectacular breasts. The sexy little dress ended in a halter, held up by two strips of material tied around her neck.

The woman looks fucking amazing. No matter what his brain had told him the other night, he couldn't help but want her. *Want. Her.*

He was about to make the dumbest move possible and go over there when his sanity was restored by a man stepping inside the club behind her. He was dressed in what looked like a sports coat and a pair of slacks and looked like he belonged at a business barbecue, not at a nightclub and *certainly* not with her.

Josh shook his head. Turning back to the bar, he picked up his beer. *Thank God for men in sports coats, because that schmuck just saved my ass from being a total dipshit.*

∽

SHELLY LET HER eyes adjust to the dimly lit club. Looking around, she couldn't see Mason or Lena anywhere, but suddenly, she spotted Rachel by the bar, jumping up and down and waving erratically. Shelly grinned and grabbed Paul's arm.

"They're just over this way," she shouted, pulling him into the crowd.

Pushing past the bodies, she noticed a man standing with his back to them. *Must be Rachel's date.* As her eyes worked over his relaxed form, Shelly felt a stab of guilt for the jealous thoughts entering her mind. *Damn, Rachel's date has one fine ass.*

He was bent over and leaning on the bar, wearing jeans that clung to his thick thighs and the posterior she was currently admiring. Stretched snugly across his huge shoulders was a black leather jacket that Shelly wanted to stroke.

God, that's hot. She stopped in front of Mason's sister. *Stop looking at him and start paying attention to your friend,* Shelly chided herself, then tacked on, *and your own date.*

"Hey, Shelly. Mase and Lena aren't here yet," Rachel said with a grin.

Nodding, Shelly looked over her shoulder at the crowd, then back at Rachel and her mystery boyfriend. Shifting toward Paul, she figured introducing him would get Rachel to encourage Mr. Sexy to turn around. *Hey, if I can't date these guys, I can at least look and drool.*

"This is Paul," she said, gesturing to him.

Paul leaned toward Rachel, holding out his hand. Rachel gave him a confused frown before she grabbed his hand and pulled him into a huge hug. Shelly tried to stifle a laugh at Paul's stiff posture.

"Hi, Paul. I'm Rachel, and this here is Josh."

Turning to the guy beside her, Rachel whacked him on the back before he stood and turned to face them.

Shelly felt her stomach tighten as butterflies took flight in her belly. *Josh Daniels. Just my damn luck.* She let her eyes wander down his jeans then back up over the tight black T-shirt that molded to every muscle he had. *Delicious. There's that stupid annoying word again, but holy cow, he looks edible.*

His shaggy brown hair fell down around the collar of his leather jacket, and a few stray strands flopped into his eyes. Those sexy chocolate-brown eyes were currently making no secret that they were unmistakably devouring every inch of her. When they finally got to her face, he winked.

"Dr. Monroe," he said in a voice that licked all over her naughty bits. "So nice to see you again."

Gripping her purse in one hand and Paul in the other as though he was her lifeline, she answered, "You too. Still no bald patches, I see."

A wolfish grin appeared on his mouth. "Not since the last time I checked. Would you like a closer look?"

Returning his slow grin, she shook her head and squeezed Paul's arm, trying to reassure him that she was with *him* tonight. "No, I'll take your word for it." Looking over Josh's shoulder, she caught the bartender's eye. "One cosmo." She then turned to Paul, who was looking around as though he'd never set foot in a club. *Poor guy probably hasn't.* "Paul? What do you want?"

He turned toward her and smiled. "I'm driving, Shel. That means water."

Turning back to the bartender, she ordered his water and rolled her eyes as she heard Josh chuckle. Her eyes moved to his as he picked up his beer, toasting her with a mocking look.

"I just saw Mason and Lena walk in, Rach. I'm going to go get 'em," he said before he turned and walked away, leaving Shelly muttering under her breath.

∼

WHY ON EARTH would a woman like her be dating Paul the Bore?

Josh shook it off as he got to his friend. Mason had a proprietary arm wrapped around Lena, and Josh had to admit he could see why. Lena looked smoking hot. She'd left her hair out in a riot of curls and was dressed in a corset top and tiny skirt with tall boots.

"Hey," Mason said, reaching out to shake his hand.

It reminded him of Rachel a minute ago, and he grinned.

"What?" his friend asked.

Shaking his head, Josh laughed. "It's nothing. I was just thinking about something that happened a minute ago with Shelly's date."

Lena tried to look around him but obviously didn't succeed because she peered up at him instead. "Shelly ended up bringing a date?"

Josh nodded before lifting his beer to take a sip. Lowering it, he wiped the back of his hand across his mouth. "Yep. He's a real winner too. Paul, I think his name is."

"Oh God," Lena sighed, rolling her eyes.

"Oh, I see you've met Paul too." Josh laughed.

"Ah, well…technically, no, I haven't. I only saw him once as he was exiting her office after being 'kicked to the curb,' I think is what Shelly called it."

Josh took another swig of his beer as Mason tugged Lena in against his side and said, "Isn't that the guy who wouldn't put out?"

Coughing, Josh lowered the bottle, and he felt his eyes widen. *Seriously? The guy is holding out? On her?*

Lena nodded.

Mason chuckled. "Geez, she must be hard up then. She doesn't do repeats."

Lena whacked his chest. "That's not nice."

"Well, it's true. I mean, I tried to get Josh to take her out."

Raising his bottle, Josh interjected, "That woman is hotter than hell, but I'm not touching her. She'll burn me to a crisp."

Lena's eyes widened, then she smiled slowly.

Josh shook his head. "No."

"Oh, come on, just dance with her. That's all."

Rolling his eyes, Josh looked at Mason for help.

His friend shrugged. "Don't look at me. You're on your own."

Lena smiled with her bottom lip caught between her teeth, looking so adorable he knew he was about to cave.

"Do you ever win an argument, Mason?"

"Only when she's close by, and I can shut her up."

Whacking him again, Lena protested, "Hey."

Rubbing his chest, Mason grinned before whispering against her mouth, "With kisses."

"No other way with a hot woman," Josh replied before he turned and made his way back to the bar.

SHELLY WAS STARTING to think that reconnecting with Paul had been a terrible mistake.

He was sitting beside her, drinking water. *Water in a bar.* He was asking her how her day was when she really wanted to dance. She wanted to lose herself in the music and forget about her long day, not rehash it.

She felt slightly guilty, too, because she knew she was being overly judgmental with Paul. But in all fairness, she had dated him before, and on *those* dates, she'd given him the benefit of the doubt. Now she knew it didn't get better than this. *Why did I call him back? Because I'm a lonely and confused moron apparently.*

She turned to look at Paul, and that's when she saw Josh take the seat on the other side of her date. *And that right there is another reason why I called Paul.* She'd known that tonight was a not-so-subtle way for Lena to try to set her and Josh up. Really, the idea was extremely appealing to all of her *bad* decision-making neurons. The good decision-making neurons were trying in vain to push her toward Paul, who had turned and was asking Josh what he did for a living.

Not wanting to listen to "work" talk, she looked around for a distraction and saw Lena walking toward her, dressed as she had been many months ago, when she'd been trying to seduce Mason. Judging by the death stares he was shooting at everyone glancing in Lena's direction, he planned to put a big "do not touch" sign on her. And the grip he had on her said that later, he'd let her seduce the hell out of him.

Sighing, Shelly smiled and noticed Lena's eyes stray to the back of Paul's head.

Mason grinned like a bad schoolboy then asked loudly, "So, Shelly, who's your boyfriend?"

Glaring daggers at him, she grimaced as Paul turned, then she forced a smile. "Mason and Lena, this is Paul. A *friend* of mine." So she happened to stress *friend* a little more than she probably should have, but she wanted it to be clear.

Mason released his grip on Lena and held his hand out for Paul to take. Standing, Paul shook it as Mason shouted over the music, "Nice to meet you, man. I've heard a lot about you."

Paul turned to Shelly with a questioning look, and she grinned at him. He turned back and told Mason he hoped it was all good. She almost died when Mason replied.

"Oh, yes, Shelly told me you're *nothing* but respectful and treat her like she's very *special.*"

Shelly heard a chuckle from down the bar and turned to see Josh's eyes on her as he tried unsuccessfully to conceal his laughter. Raising a brow at him, she tipped up her chin as he lifted his beer to take a sip. His throat as he swallowed mesmerized her, and she felt her thighs twitch.

Stop looking at him, she ordered herself. Turning back to the three in front of her, she was about to ask Paul to dance when Rachel bounced out of the crowd and over to them.

"Come on, Paul. You look like you could use some fun. Come dance with me."

Paul looked over his shoulder at her, and Shelly nodded, trying not to laugh at his worried expression. "Go, you'll have fun. I'll be here when you're done."

Rachel grabbed his wrist and pulled him into the sea of people.

Mason moved closer to Shelly and asked her with a devious grin, "So has he put out yet, or is he still making you feel special by waiting?"

Shelly turned her head so her mouth was right over his ear. "I'm going to kill you if you don't shut it."

Standing up straight, he nudged her under her chin then grabbed Lena, who grinned at Shelly as she was tugged into the crowd.

That left her and—*oh, terrific*—Josh Daniels sitting at the bar.

WATCHING HER CLOSELY, Josh noticed the minute she realized she was stuck with him. He almost laughed out loud when she turned on the barstool to face him. Picking up his beer, he finished it before he stood and moved to sit on the stool vacated by Paul. He'd told himself over and over that he would *not* get involved with her. But as he slid onto the seat, their knees brushing against one another, he also convinced himself that sex didn't require involvement.

She picked up her drink and brought it to her shiny, wet lips for a sip.

Oh yeah, you don't need to be involved to hit the sheets.

She watched him over the glass, and her blue eyes lowered in a slow, sensual blink as she seemed to size him up. "What are you looking at?"

"There's only one thing in front of me," he said, deciding to forget about his brain and all of its flashing neon warning signals for a minute.

She put the glass on the bar then made a show of licking her bottom lip. He knew she was one hundred percent aware of her own sensuality and how to use it to draw his eyes to her mouth.

"And do you like what you see?"

Feeling a grin pull up on his mouth, he nodded. "You certainly aren't hard to look at."

Leaning an arm on the bar, she crossed her bare legs, flashing him more of her thigh. His eyes drifted down to look at them then came back up to meet her fiery gaze.

"So why aren't you dancing?" he asked teasingly.

Her eyes roamed all over him, and he felt them as if they were her hands stroking his suddenly aware body.

"There's no one to dance with," she said in that sexy voice of hers.

He tilted his head as she reached for her glass again. While she lifted it to her mouth, he noticed for the first time how perfect the skin on her neck was. It was a perfect shade of creamy white that he suddenly wanted to suck.

"And what am I?" he finally asked.

SHELLY LOOKED AT JOSH, with his legs spread and booted feet on the floor, facing her with one arm on the bar while the other rested on his knee. The man was pure temptation, and she was finding him hard to resist. So hard in fact that she was trying to think of a way to have him—at least for a night.

"*You* are not an option," she replied.

His eyes narrowed, and he carefully slid off the stool and stepped closer, still resting his palm on the bar. Not one to cave to a man, Shelly looked up at him with a questioning expression. To anyone looking, she knew it just looked as if he were asking her to dance, but that was *so* not the case.

"Why? I can tell you want me. Your eyes are all over me, and your breathing is just a little too hard for sitting at a bar. Come on, Shel, you can admit it. Just like I can *almost* guarantee you're getting all hot and bothered down between—"

"Okay," she interrupted before he voiced what she knew was true.

She had to admit that the man was sexier than anyone she'd ever met. He attracted her like a bee to honey, and as she locked gazes with him, she *knew* she was going to have him between her legs at some point in the near future. Not into self-delusion, Shelly always went after what she wanted—and want him she did.

"Okay what?" he asked as he stood still, barely making a move with each breath.

She raised her eyes to his, speaking loudly enough for him to hear, "You're right. I do want you." She watched that panty-dropping smile appear on his face. "I've wanted you since the moment I turned around in Mason's bar. Happy?"

∽

JOSH COULD'T BELIEVE the words coming out of the woman's mouth. He didn't understand why he was so surprised. He'd known from the get-go that she was sexy, confident, and the kind of woman to eat a man alive. But to hear her state so bluntly that she wanted him? Well, that sent all the blood left in his head straight to his cock.

Trying to remember what she'd just said, he leaned down until they were almost nose to nose, then he moved at the last second to her ear. To someone watching, he looked like he was trying to talk to her over the loud music, but the hot woman in front of him and his out-of-control body knew it was more like adding a spark to a stick of dynamite.

"I'm horny, not happy. You're so fucking sexy that all the blood in my body is in my cock. But you already know that because you keep aiming your eyes down there to check."

Leaning back, he looked at her as she smiled, which automatically made him think of her mouth and his cock. *Together. Right now.*

"That's true too." Blinking her big blue eyes at him, she asked, "So do you want to make a deal?"

"A deal?" he asked, a little confused, either from the lack of blood to his brain or the way the conversation was going.

"Yes, a deal. You know, an agreement forged between two individuals."

Shaking his head slowly, he muttered, "Smartass."

"So do you want to?"

Josh looked her over, sitting there with her legs crossed and her thighs so close that he wanted to touch them. He answered the only way he knew how. "Hell yeah. What's your deal, Shel?"

With a smile touching her lips, she looked at the dance floor. When she was sure they were in the clear, she replied, "This stays between us. I'm not looking for anything other than—"

"Sex?"

Raising a blond brow, she dipped her head once and quickly added, "Hot, sweaty, great sex. Which I'm assuming you can deliver."

Josh was completely amused and turned on. He found himself battling to keep his hands off her, and at the same time, he wanted to burst out laughing. "Oh? And why would you *assume* that?"

She let her eyes travel down his chest, then to his jeans, where he was sporting a major hard-on, before she brought them back up to his face. "I guess I'm not assuming. I'm hoping. Because if not, I think I may have to just go ahead and end my life." She sighed dramatically and looked at the dance floor. She turned back to him before she continued. "Let's put it this way. If I found out Paul wasn't a firecracker after dark, it wouldn't be such a surprise. If I found out you weren't, I'd want to find a short pier and hurl myself off it. You have a body that's made to pound a woman into her bed. So I'm really hoping you can live up to that."

Josh clenched his fist on the bar and gritted his teeth as he shifted his feet, painstakingly trying not to reach down and rearrange what was pushing hard against his zipper. "What's the deal you're offering, Monroe? Spell it out to me before I pick you up and haul you and your dirty mouth out of here."

Grinning as though she'd won some kind of battle, she uncrossed her legs and slipped off the stool, standing so close to him her breasts brushed against his chest. He continued to stand where he was, refusing to give in to her aggressive stance. Raising a hand, she traced a line around one of his nipples pressing hard against his shirt. She looked up at him from under her dark lashes, and her hot blue eyes locked on to his.

∼

SHELLY WAS ABOUT to explode as she stood close enough to Josh that she could smell his cologne mixed with his own scent. She raised her eyes to his and grinned at his hot, primal expression. He looked as though he wanted to attack her, and quite honestly, she wanted to be attacked.

"The deal is this. No one knows about us. This is sex. Hot sex, but *just* sex. I want a nice, sweet everyday man to settle down with. And honestly, you scream complicated and not-so-sweet. So the deal is you, me, and sex. No one knows. Not Lena and *definitely* not Mason."

His scorching eyes melted away all her resistance. When he finally moved, he lifted his hand from the bar and took hers, which was still tracing his chest. He brought it down from his body, almost as though he couldn't control himself while she was touching him, then he held his hand out to hers as if they would shake on it.

Oh no, Delicious Daniels. We're going to seal this my way. Smiling, she stood on her tiptoes and whispered, "We'll seal the deal tonight when we come all over each other."

He groaned softly as she stepped back and smoothed her hands down her dress. She'd gotten herself so worked up that she could feel her damp panties sliding against her aroused flesh. "So? Deal, Mr. Daniels?"

She could have sworn she felt his eyes as they tracked down her body then came up to rest on her face as he nodded.

"It's a deal, Miz Monroe."

Smirking at the way he said her name, she went to step around him to go find Paul, but she stopped when she was beside him, shoulder to shoulder. "My number's in Lena's phone. I'll let you work out how to get it." He turned his head to look down at her, and she raised a brow. "No strings, Josh. Not one. Unless, of course, it's to tie me up."

He nodded, and she winked before she walked away.

CHAPTER 5

JOSH WATCHED SHELLY strut away on those ice pick heels. *What the hell just happened?*

Shit, he knew what had happened. His brain had left the building, and he had decided to forget all of his convictions for the sake of having her. All because the Man-Eater had arrived and taken a huge bite out of his ass.

The woman was sex personified, and she had no problems using it. In fact, she used it so well that she'd made him forget his entire conversation with Mason about his adamant refusal to touch her. She was a witch, and she had cast a spell.

His eyes searched the crowd quickly for Lena as he tried to devise a plan to get that cell phone number. There wasn't a chance in hell he was missing out on that.

Josh leaned back against the bar, crossing one leg over the other as he tried to discreetly run a hand over the front of his jeans to alleviate some of the pressure. Once he realized there was no use, he gave up. The only relief would be to—*how had she put it?*—come all over each other.

He was trying to remember if a woman had ever spoken quite so boldly to him, and he was pretty sure that the answer was a big fat no.

When Josh had decided to hell with all of his plans about not touching her, he'd thought he would just be blunt and lay it all on the line for the sexy doctor. What he hadn't expected was for her to give it back to him—and twice as good.

The woman is trouble, and I'm going to have fun getting into it. Or should I say her?

Finally, he spotted Mason pulling a hazy-eyed Lena from the dance floor. She was stuck to his side like glue, and Josh could tell by her expression that by the end of the night, she would be even closer to her man.

They stopped in front of him, and Mason smiled before he asked, "What's up with Shelly? You piss her off?"

Josh shook his head, making sure to keep his face as neutral as possible. "Who knows? That woman's touchy. Probably upset I even thought about talking to her. From what I can tell, she goes for someone of a different caliber than me."

Lena rested her flushed cheek against Mason's side and smiled softly. She looked as though Mason had already taken care of her and she was basking in the glow of a fantastic orgasm. *Who knew? Maybe he had,* Josh thought with a smirk.

"That's not true," she said. "Shelly doesn't know what she wants. She dates all these boring, stuffed-shirt guys who never leave her satisfied. Why do you think she's still single?"

Josh shrugged as though it was of no concern to him. Deep down, he was thinking, *There is no way in hell she's going to leave unsatisfied tonight.* "Hey, Lena, do you mind if I borrow your cell phone? I need to call..." *Shit, who do I need to call? Hello, make someone up, moron. She doesn't know you.* "I need to call my neighbor. I forgot to let Mutley out before I left, and I don't want a mess in the house."

Nodding, she moved a little from Mason, and in Josh's frustrated state, he was almost brought to his knees when she bent over and unzipped the top of her boot before pulling out a phone.

When she stood and handed it to him, Mason asked, "Man, are you okay? You don't look so good."

You think? I'm dying over here. Dr. Barbie has me hard as a steel rod, and your woman is pulling a phone out of fuck-me boots. Instead of answering Mason, he nodded mutely before he grabbed the phone, making a mad dash for the exit.

SHELLY WAS STANDING at the sink in the crowded bathroom, slicking her lips with gloss. She'd pretty much licked it all off as she'd salivated over Josh Daniels. *So what? I've given in to my urge to pounce on him. He is very pounceable. Is that even a word? Probably not, but if it is, it was made for that man.*

Just thinking about him made her thighs twitch and her tummy do a somersault. He was sex on legs, and she wanted him to walk all over her. Looking at her reflection, she saw the subtle changes that hinted at how aroused she was. Her cheeks were slightly flushed, and her eyes were dilated. But the telltale sign was the moisture between her thighs.

Damn that man. She hadn't wanted to get involved with Josh Daniels, Mason's best man. Not to mention he was Mason and Rachel's childhood friend. *Way too complicated.*

But she wasn't going to get involved. She was going to have sex, fantastic sex that would leave her completely and utterly satisfied, then she'd leave. She'd done it before, and if this guy was for real, she'd do it again—*real* soon.

∽

JOSH WAS STANDING in the parking lot by his truck. He was scrolling through Lena's phone, searching for the sexy doctor's number. *Jackpot.*

Pulling out his own phone, Josh added her into his contacts under *Barbie*. *Well, she wants it to be a secret,* he thought with a smirk before dialing the number.

He waited. One ring, two rings, and on the third, he heard a click, and loud music pulsed through his phone. Smiling, he knew she'd answered it somewhere in the club.

"Hello?"

Mmm, there's that silky voice of hers. "Outside in the parking lot, now. I'm ready to seal the deal." Then he ended the call. *Now let's see what she does with that.*

∽

LOOKING AT HER phone in the dark corner she'd moved to, Shelly felt her hand shaking as she ended the call. *He wants to do this now? More to the point, am I really going to let him?*

Shelly felt some movement to her side and noticed Paul had come over to stand with her. He was kind of—and by "kind of" she meant he actually was—bopping to the music as she imagined an awkward kid would.

Shaking her head at her own stupidity for pulling him into a situation so totally foreign to him, she decided now was the time to slap herself for even contemplating reuniting with him.

She tapped his arm, and when he turned to face her, she turned on her sexy smile as she leaned in to whisper against his ear. "I'm going to step outside for some fresh air for a few minutes."

Paul nodded. "Want me to come with you?"

Shaking her head, Shelly thought, *Nope, I have a man in mind who's going to do that.* "No, it's fine. I'm just going to stand by the door with the bouncer."

Paul squeezed her hand, shouting over the music, "Okay, but make sure you do. Can't be too careful."

Shelly turned and walked toward the door. *Oh, I'm about to be anything but careful.*

JOSH SAW HER the minute she stepped out under the floodlights. They seemed to light up her blond hair, almost giving her a halo, but he knew she was no angel. She looked from left to right then spotted him leaning against his truck in the far back row of cars. He watched her tilt her head before moving toward him.

She walked in a way that made him want to stand and watch her for hours. Sure, it was just like everyone else, one foot in front of the other, but she made it a statement. With each step, her hips swayed and her ponytail swished behind her. Her shoulders were so straight and her chin was tilted up, making her look like a confident sex kitten about to devour him.

He heard the gravel crunching beneath her heels, but she never faltered. When she finally got to him, she stopped and ran her gaze over his body as he remained where he was. He knew she'd notice the hard-on pressing against his jeans, and he also knew the moment when she saw it, because her tongue came out again.

"You do that a lot, you know?"

Her eyes came back to his as she raised questioning brows at him. "What's that?"

"Look at my cock and lick your lips."

She stepped closer, and he had to uncross his legs or she would have bumped into them. Reaching past him, she tossed her little purse in the back of his truck, then she moved one step closer until she was positioned snugly between his thighs with her amazing breasts pressed against his chest. He watched as the lips in question tipped up in a sexy smile.

"That's because I want to lick it," she said in true man-eater style.

Josh clenched his teeth and his hands. As of right now, she still hadn't given him permission to touch her, and she hadn't touched him either. "You don't have a subtle bone in your body, do you, Shel?"

She looked at his mouth then let her eyes come back up to his.

SHELLY WAS BREATHING hard as she felt his inner thighs flex around the outside of hers. His hands were resting by his legs, and she decided it was time to touch. She ran a finger over the shoulder of his smooth and supple leather jacket.

"Why be subtle? We both know what we want, and we're both consenting adults."

He took a breath as his whole body shuddered, then he raised a hand to her hip. The minute he placed it on her, she could have sworn she felt electricity and heat sizzle all along her frustrated nerves. It had been so long since she'd had great sex, and she knew this would be fantastic. *Hell, the guy almost has me coming from touching my hip.*

"That's true, and the last thing I remember was us coming to an agreement."

Shelly nodded. "Well, yes, a verbal one." She leaned forward until her lips were by his ear, and she took a deep breath of his delicious cologne. "Now we need to *seal* it."

He groaned as his fingers flexed on her hip, tugging her forward. Placing her hands on his chest, she squeezed his tight pecs. *Damn, the man is built*. She couldn't wait to rip off his shirt and rub all over his hard naked chest.

He leaned his head down a little, and she could no longer resist flicking her tongue out to swipe at his lobe. His other hand came up and pulled her in so close that she could now feel his erection pushing into the apex of her thighs. He groaned and flexed his hips.

Shelly chuckled in his ear. "So we're going to do this out here?"

Although she was completely scandalized by the idea, Shelly had to admit that she was completely turned on. Another deciding factor was she wanted to know if he *could* actually do *that* out here.

"That's the plan. I want this set in stone before you strut away from me."

She moaned, rubbing her achingly covered mound against his hardness. *God, that feels incredible.* Running her hands down his chest to his stomach, she gripped his shirt and started bunching it up.

He rocked his hips against her then turned his head. "Give me your fucking mouth, woman."

Feeling herself clench and dampen, Shelly smiled before she laid her lips against his.

~

HIS HEAD WAS ABOUT to explode.
Both of them.
The woman was molten lava, and she was melting him with every touch. Her hot little hands were burrowing in under his shirt, and her glossy lips were parting beneath his. He groaned, and without any finesse or preliminaries, he thrust his tongue deep into her mouth. She moaned, gripping his shirt, as he yanked her up against his cock.

Goddamn, she is sweet. Sweet, hot, and wickedly sexy.

Just when he thought he was about to combust, she lifted her hands from under his shirt and wrapped them around his neck, tugging on the hair brushing his collar and ramping up his temperature all over again. He ran one hand over the curve of her sweet ass, then all the way up her spine, and when he reached the back of her neck, he gripped it and pulled her away from him.

Panting, she stopped as she looked at him. Her eyes were wide and dilated, her cheeks were rosy and flushed, and her wet mouth was parted as she squirmed against him.

Amazing, he thought as he tried to catch his breath. *She's absolutely fucking amazing.* "I believe we're supposed to do something very specific to seal this deal." He squeezed her hip and neck gently.

She swallowed then nodded as she reached between them to unbutton his jeans. Looking around the parking lot, he was starting to get a little nervous. *She's going to do this here—for real?* He'd just been teasing, but as he felt her pull down his zipper, he knew she was going for it.

Taking his hand from the back of her neck, he turned them so his back was to the club, and she was shielded from any eyes. It also gave her the opportunity to see if anyone was coming. *Well, anyone other than us.*

"Well then, now that you have me here and your hands are down my pants, what are you going to do with me?" he asked.

She brought her sex-clouded eyes to his as she grabbed the hand he had on her hip and brought it to her bare thigh. "I'm going to keep my hands down your pants, and you need to get *this* hand up my skirt."

Feeling a grin tug the corners of his mouth, Josh asked, "Is that right?"

Nodding, she bit her lip. "That's right."

Running his fingers up her naked skin, he smoothed them around her hot thigh, moving to the inside. When he slid his fingers up and in between, she panted and squirmed as her busy hands slid deeper into his jeans. Now inside his boxers, she wrapped her fingers around his aching cock.

He took a breath. "And when all is in hand?"

She smiled in a way that made him think she'd just devoured him. "Then we come all over each other."

HOLY SHIT. DID I really just say that? What is wrong with me? She'd always been a sexually confident person, but she'd never *ever* behaved this way before. It had to be him. A wolfish grin appeared on his mouth, and she shuddered when she finally felt his fingers trace her soaked panties.

"Fuck, you're wet."

She moaned, stroking his hot, hard flesh. "And you're so deliciously hard."

He didn't waste much time after that, and she figured if he felt anything like her, they were damn close to erupting like a volcano. Finding the edge of her lace panties, he pulled it aside, sneaking his fingers in to slide through her folds. She couldn't help the loud moan that tore out of her as she gripped his cock, stroking once, then twice, and again, keeping time with his teasing fingers.

She couldn't believe she was standing in a parking lot, mutually getting off some guy she'd sworn she wouldn't touch. But when his finger finally pushed into her, she panted and clenched her thighs around his hand, rocking onto him and thinking that all her good intentions could take a flying leap. He let out his own groan as his fingers pushed in deeper, and she dragged her hand up and down his throbbing flesh. She noticed he watched her face as he dragged his fingers in and out. While she continued to stroke him, they rocked their pelvises against one another's hands.

Then, in a voice so deep and low she almost didn't hear it, he said, "For fuck's sake, Monroe, come on me."

That did it. She felt her climax slam into her as she squeezed her thighs around his hand, screaming as she came all over his fingers. She gripped his cock tightly and milked him as he groaned. His hips pistoned in her palm—once, twice—then he buried his face in her neck as he came all over her hand.

Hmm, so damn messy and unrefined.

Oh, yes, Josh Daniels would deliver, and she couldn't wait.

JOSH WAS BREATHING hard as he stood on shaky legs with a hand burrowed beneath her skirt and his mouth pressed against that pretty neck. When he finally caught his breath and moved back an inch to look at her, he was satisfied to see her eyes were glassy and her lips were swollen.

Mission accomplished.

Other than those two differences though, she was still completely put together for someone who'd just moaned through an earth-shattering climax. Her hair looked perfect, and her dress wasn't even an inch out of place, except for the middle of the skirt that was riding high over his wrist. Slowly, he dragged his hand out from under her dress as she removed her hands from his jeans. He reached into the truck and pulled out an old rag he had back there. *Handy.*

After they'd wiped their hands, he buttoned up while she tugged down her skirt.

Then, as calmly as possible, she asked, "Can I have my purse?"

Raising a brow at her, Josh reached into the back of his truck again. When he found it, he pulled it out and handed it to her. She was about to walk away. He could feel it.

Sex. No involvement. That's the deal. I'd do well to remember that.

As she stepped around him, she stopped by his shoulder just as she had in the bar. Still facing the back of the parking lot, he turned to look at the perfectly put-together doctor.

"So? Do we have a deal?"

He grinned before nodding. "Signed and sealed, I believe."

She gave him one last look as she blew out a breath. "Oh, yes, it was, Daniels. Yes, it was."

With that, Man-Eater Monroe walked away with a piece of him between her teeth.

CHAPTER 6

ON SATURDAY MORNING, Josh was flat on his back in his office. It wasn't really his office. He'd converted the small space into a homemade gym with a treadmill and bench press. Currently, he was on his back, lifting weights. He had to admit that last night, he'd slept like a baby. It probably had something to do with the spectacular orgasm he'd had in the club parking lot. He was still mulling over the rest of the night though, trying to decide how he felt about it.

After Shelly had left him in the lot, he'd taken a moment to pull himself together before making his way back inside, past the gigantic bouncer with a huge smirk. Josh knew the asshole had heard Shelly's scream as she'd shattered all over his hand, and for some reason, that had completely pissed him off.

Shaking off the memory, he went back to thinking about what had happened once he got back into the club.

Shelly had been sitting next to Paul at the bar, and he'd had his hand resting on her bare knee. Rachel had pulled Josh straight out onto the dance floor. Knowing he'd owed Rachel, Josh had gone reluctantly, considering all he'd wanted to do was get close enough to Shelly to smell her. *Or to smell myself on her.*

However, no such luck. For the rest of the night, which had been three more excruciating hours, she'd managed to completely avoid him and spent the whole time *pretending* to be interested in Paul.

Just sex, he kept repeating to himself. *It's all about sex. Great sex, but just sex.*

He gripped the bar above his head and did five reps before placing it back.

I can do just sex, right? Granted, he'd never done it before, and honestly, he had never even thought of it as a possibility. *After all, how can two people be so close with one another yet remain uninvolved? And how does this work anyway? Am I supposed to just dial for a booty call? Or is she going to call me?* The hell if he knew.

Staring at the ceiling, he was about to grip the bar again when the phone rang beside him. He grabbed it, answering, "Daniels."

"Joshua, it's Cole," his lawyer and friend announced, even though his stern tone could never be mistaken for anyone else.

"Hey, man. How's it going?"

"Good. I have no reason to complain. I just wanted to touch base and let you know that the disgruntled—"

"Asshole?" Josh injected.

"Well, yes, I was going to say client, but asshole will work. He called and dropped the case. He's going to pay you the full amount."

Sighing a huge breath of relief, Josh asked, "How'd you get him to change his mind?"

"Threats and lies. All threats and lies," Cole told him in an almost sinister tone, which was only lightened by the dark chuckle he added.

"Ahh, just the kind of lawyer I want on my side."

"That's right. Now tell me, are we all still going to your brother's for poker?"

Josh sat up, grabbed the towel he'd slung over the end of the bench, and wiped his face. "Yep. Jeremy told everyone to come by at noon."

"Okay, I'll be there. Should I bring anything?"

"Maybe some beer? It is poker, *sooo* maybe some luck? Last time you played, we killed you."

Josh got the reaction he'd been expecting in the ever-so-serious tone he'd become accustomed to from Cole.

"Be careful, my friend. I read up on it and now know all the rules."

Laughing, Josh threw the towel into the dirty clothes basket. "Is that right? Could you sound any more like a nerd? Or a lawyer?"

"I'll have you know, Daniels, this *nerd* just saved you ten thousand dollars."

Conceding this round, Josh nodded. "You sure did, so I'll go easy on you."

"How accommodating of you." Cole laughed good-naturedly. "See you soon."

"Yep. I'll be the one taking all your money."

SHELLY WAS STANDING outside the door to Mason and Lena's home. It was strength training day, and every Saturday, they went down to the local gym to do an hour of weights. Shelly had been let into the building by Ed at the front door, and she had now knocked twice. Still, there was no answer. She moved closer and pressed her ear against the door.

She heard Lena giggle and say emphatically, "Mason, stop."

Shelly moved back as the handle twisted, and the big door was pulled opened by a flush-faced Lena.

"Getting in some early morning cardio?" Shelly asked with a raised brow.

Mason strolled forward in a white T-shirt and some low-riding sweats and placed a hand on Lena's shoulder. "I was trying, but she's conserving all her strength for you."

Poking her tongue out at him, Shelly strolled into the loft. "Lucky me." Stopping at the kitchen, she found the usual OJ was sitting on the counter. She picked it up and took a sip. "Oh, Mason. Forget Lena. Come live with me and squeeze my oranges."

Mason let out a loud laugh as Lena punched Shelly lightly on the arm.

"That did not sound right," Lena muttered. "He better not squeeze anything of anybody's, except mine."

Smiling, Shelly took another sip and shrugged. "Hey, it was worth a shot."

"Yeah, well, you can forget it. This chef, playboy, and charmer is all mine."

"Ahh, ladies? I'm still in the room. Although I have to tell you, being fought over is kind of hot. Can you maybe start pulling hair?

Ripping clothes?" Mason pretended to look around then opened the fridge. "I'm sure I can find some Jell-O for you to both roll in."

They all laughed.

"Perv," Shelly said before she finished the glass of OJ.

Mason moved around the kitchen, cooking them breakfast. This had become a ritual for them. She would come over to pick up Lena, and Mason would cook them a healthy and scrumptious breakfast then send them on their way. The man was a genius in the kitchen, so it certainly wasn't a hardship to eat his food. He also wasn't hard to watch.

Shelly bet he and Josh had broken hearts all through school. Two good-looking guys—one a complete charmer, all polished and smooth around the edges, and the other a little wild with sharp, jagged edges—who were the perfect good boy and bad boy. And they just happened to be best friends.

Hell, if her friend wasn't engaged to the pretty boy, Shelly may have found herself entertaining a hot ménage à trois scenario. However, Lena was in love with him, so that was an automatic no-go fantasy. So she settled for being friends with the sizzling hot chef currently wrapped around Lena and kissing the hell out of her.

Clearing her throat, Shelly watched with amusement as the two lovebirds pulled apart. They were so happy together; it was hard not to envy what they had. Shelly was woman enough to admit to feeling a small stab of jealousy.

"Hello? I'm still here. Wait until I leave to get naked, please," Shelly teased.

Lena moved away from Mason and leaned up against the counter. "So? Where'd you disappear to last night?"

Busted, Shelly thought with a wince. "Nowhere. What do you mean?"

Lena's mouth pulled up in a smug I-got-you smirk. "It means that while we were dancing—"

"And making out," Mason injected.

"Yes. Thanks, babe. While we were dancing and making out, we noticed you had disappeared. Did you have a fight with Paul?"

Shelly thought about it for all of two seconds before she latched on to that excuse. "Yeah, he was annoying me. Not even having one drink. And then, did you see the way he danced?"

"Yep," Mason said, looking over his shoulder at her. "Boy cannot move."

Shelly nodded, feeling bad for throwing Paul under the bus. When he'd dropped her off last night, they'd decided that theirs was a relationship better left in the past. *Way in the past.* "Yes. So anyway, I went to the little girls' room for a breather."

Lena picked up a slice of apple from a fruit platter in front of them and bit into it, nodding. "Huh, well, that's too bad. I was hoping it'd work out for you." She moved away from the counter to walk around a partition into their bedroom. "I'll be right back, just going to put on my shoes."

Shelly grunted an unintelligible answer as Mason plated the eggs he'd been scrambling. She stood, made her way to the stove, and took the plate he was offering. But when she gripped it, he held on to the edge, making her look at him.

"Funny thing. Josh was gone at the same time you were," he said with a curious expression on his too-handsome face.

Shelly felt every muscle in her body freeze. She tried to remain calm and not give herself away. As she stood there, her gaze locking with Casanova's, she felt as if maybe her poker face was crumbling. "Huh. Yeah, that is funny. I don't know where he was. Probably off in a dark corner somewhere."

Mason's eyes narrowed, and he nodded as he let go of the plate. Shelly felt as though he could read her mind as he stared at her. God, she hoped not, because it was currently screaming, *I'm lying. I'm lying.*

"Yeah, probably. Josh never had a problem getting a woman into a dark corner."

I bet, Shelly thought. He'd had no problem getting her into a dimly lit parking lot.

"Typical," she responded just to say something while she spun away from Mason's probing stare. When she was seated at the bench, she watched him move over to the counter with a towel, wiping his hands.

"What do you mean typical? He's a good guy, got a good job. Why not give him a chance?"

Shelly stabbed a fork into the eggs as if they were her mortal enemy then raised them to her lips, grinning. "Because I gave a guy like him a chance once, and he used it all up for every other guy like him."

Mason threw the towel on the counter as Lena came out from the bedroom.

"What do you mean 'guys like him'? That doesn't seem real fair, does it?" Mason watched her. "I didn't think you were such a snob."

Shelly let her fork drop onto the plate with a clang. "And I didn't think you were such a gossipy woman. Geez, Mason, let it go. Why do I need to be banging your friend?"

Lena stopped at the end of the counter, looking back and forth between Shelly and her fiancé.

Mason rarely got upset or annoyed at anything, but right now, he looked a little bit ruffled. "You don't, although it might help with the bitchy attitude."

Sighing, Shelly picked up her fork and looked at the man opposite her—a man who had surprisingly become a really good friend. "You're right about one thing. I need to get laid. But not with Josh, okay? It's too complicated and messy with us all knowing each other." If she were Pinocchio, her nose would have grown past Mason, through the kitchen wall, and out into the hall. "I had a bad experience with a man, and guys like Josh remind me of him. So I just try to steer clear."

Mason put a hand on hers. "Okay. I'll lay off." His killer smile and twin dimples appeared. "But for God's sake, go and find someone to jump. You're turning into an old frustrated broad."

Lena gasped, and Shelly giggled.

"Are you telling me to get laid, Langley?"

"Yes. Go find a willing man, which I know will be extremely easy for you, and ride him home."

Shelly looked at Lena, who was staring at Mason with a what-the-fuck-did-you-just-say expression. Then she turned back to Shelly and shrugged.

"Okay, okay. You've convinced me. I'll go find a man to—what did you say?—ride. So I no longer act like a bitch to my two closest and dearest friends." She lifted the fork and shoveled eggs into her mouth. "Damn, the things I do for you two."

With that, the three of them burst out laughing.

JOSH ARRIVED AT his brother's house a little after eleven in the morning. Parking near the side of Jeremy's place, Josh got out and made his way through the back door and into the kitchen. He found Jeremy at the counter, putting a bag of chips into a bowl.

"Hey, Martha Stewart," Josh said from the doorway.

Josh's younger brother turned and flipped him the finger. "Up yours. How you doing?"

After strolling into the kitchen, Josh grabbed a chip. He leaned up against the sink and shrugged. "Not bad. You?"

"Same," Jeremy answered as he turned to the fridge. Opening it, he searched around then came back with a jar of salsa. Jeremy was two years younger than Josh, had blond hair that was longer than most men's, and almost looked like a "surfer dude."

"So, who's coming today?" Josh asked, taking another chip.

"Vince and Cole."

Nodding, Josh picked up the two bowls and followed Jeremy through the house to the game room. Vince was Josh's crew manager and now friend. He'd hired him around two years ago, and he'd been running things in Chicago when Josh had been in LA. He was short, stocky, and as some of the other guys called him, scary as hell.

Jeremy had set up the usual poker table, and Josh put the chips and salsa on the side table where the cooler sat.

"I can't believe Cole agreed to come. Last time he was here, we cleaned the floor with him."

Josh laughed, moving to the stereo. "I know. I told him the same exact thing, but he has informed me that he 'read up on it and now knows all the rules.'"

Jeremy looked over at him, and they both laughed.

"God, that guy is something else. He's such a suit and yet so flippin' scary cool at the same time. I don't know how he pulls it off," Jeremy said, shaking his head.

Josh finally found what he was looking for—*ahh, classic Pink Floyd*—and put the vinyl on. "No one knows what makes that guy tick, and shit, I've known him for years. He never gives anything away either." Josh smiled as the doorbell sounded. "I'll go let them in."

"Okay, I'm just gonna get the rest of the food," Jeremy answered, walking back into the kitchen.

∼

TWO HOURS LATER and several beers in, Josh was down twenty bucks but was *almost* positive he was about to win fifty. Sitting across from a stoic Cole, Josh was starting to think the guy was up to something.

Cole had been kicking everyone's ass. He'd walked in dressed in a three-piece suit from an earlier meeting in the office—yes, on a Saturday—and acting as though he'd just read up on how to play last night. Then he'd sat down and proceeded to clean house.

The guy was playing them and playing them well, but Josh felt as though he had this one. After all, he had a straight flush. There he sat, staring at his five hearts, as Cole smirked at him like a cool, seasoned pro.

"You know that I'm-better-than-you smile makes you look real ugly, Madison."

Cole just smiled wider. "Does it? I thought it made me look…" He cocked his dirty-blond head to the side as the other two sat back, watching. "Rich?"

Josh shook his head and picked up his beer before taking a swig. "Nope, sorry, just ugly."

Cole nodded. "So what's eating you? Usually you're a much better loser when these other guys win. Is it because it's *me* kicking your sorry ass?"

Josh laughed a little and ran a hand through his hair, thinking about a certain blonde. "Nah. Not that I've *lost*. You going to show your cards or keep talking shit?"

Cole casually put down his five cards. Sitting up and leaning across the table, Josh and the other two men stared in complete shock at Cole's beautiful royal straight flush.

Josh shook his head, throwing his cards on the table. "How in the hell, Madison?"

Cole leaned over and picked up the cash. "I told you. I read up on how to play."

Jeremy chuckled, and Vince let out a loud bark of laughter.

"You read a fucking book, then just beat us all and took our money?" Vince questioned in disbelief.

Cole folded the cash and pulled out what appeared to be a money clip.

The guy has a money clip? Who even knew they still made those?

Clipping his money and tucking it away, Cole nodded. With that same annoying-as-shit grin, he said, "Yes, that's exactly right."

"Not cool, man. Not cool," Josh said, shaking his head.

"Sorry, just the way it goes."

They all sat back, shaking their heads.

Then Jeremy said, "You *have* been in a funk today, Josh. What gives? Woman trouble?"

Is that the reason I've been kind of pissy and irritable? Because I don't know what the deal is with Shelly? Josh scratched his head. *It doesn't matter anyway. It's supposed to be a secret. Well, it could still be a secret if they don't know her name.* "Well, yeah, actually. I met this woman."

All of a sudden, the guys sat up and moved slightly forward. It was like a bad scene from a movie. *Tell me more, tell me more. Anyone?*

Josh sighed and again found himself running his hand through his hair.

"So? What about her? Why's it bothering you?" his brother asked.

"Well, it's complicated." Relaxing back in the chair, Josh grabbed his beer as Jeremy, Cole, and Vince stared at him.

"Why? What's so difficult about the woman? And if it's such a fucking pain in the ass, kick her to the curb," Vince suggested.

Josh thought about that, rubbing his stomach, then blurted out, "She's fucking hot. I'm not kicking her to the curb. I kind of want to haul her to my bed." *And keep her there.*

Jeremy jumped in. "So what's the problem? She won't let you?"

Josh laughed, took a gulp of beer, and put the bottle down. "Oh no, she wants to, but that's *all* she wants."

The table went quiet. Cole, Vince, and Jeremy stared at him with bewildered looks.

"Forget it," he told them with a self-deprecating chuckle.

Jeremy's mouth was the first to fall open. "Ahh, I don't understand what the problem is here. Hot chick who just wants sex. What's your issue? You feeling degraded?"

Josh glared at his brother. "Shut the fuck up. She and I? Well, we know the same people, and she came up with this deal about sex and secrets. She's so insanely sexy, but she's trouble with a huge neon T. I don't know the rules for this kind of game—" Suddenly, Josh realized how much he'd said and shut up real quick.

Cole was the first to speak. "There are rules?"

Josh nodded. "There's one. It's a secret. That's the fucking rule."

Cole blew out a breath, scratching his head. "She's hot, you say?"

"Fuck yeah."

"She worth the trouble?" Vince asked with a raised brow.

Josh shrugged. "I have no idea."

The room fell silent before Jeremy asked, "Can you do that? You're not real good at just walking away. Look at Melissa. Five months later."

Josh glared at his brother. "Sure. If she can do it, so can I. After all, she doesn't want feelings. She just wants sex." *And that is what I'll give her.*

CHAPTER 7

DD: So…how does this work?

It was Monday, and Shelly was standing in line at the hospital cafeteria. She'd been staring at her phone for the last twenty minutes, trying to understand exactly what he meant. As she stared at the contact name she'd filed him under—DD, a.k.a. Delicious Daniels—she smiled and thought about how delicious he'd been in that parking lot. *Oh yeah. Those hands, so big and talented, and that mouth, so sinful. The man is positively scrumptious.*

How does what work? Shelly thought as she swiped her employee badge. *I was pretty clear, wasn't I? Sex. No strings. Secret. What more needed to be said?*

"Dr. Monroe?"

Like a schoolgirl getting caught passing notes in class, Shelly shoved her phone in her pocket and turned to see Dr. McKinney behind her. *Great, just what I needed.*

"Sir," she said, tipping her head slightly.

"How's your day going so far?"

Shelly shuffled along the line, picking up a bottle of water and an apple. Moving down farther, she looked at her boss. "Busy. People always need to breathe."

He smiled at her lame joke. "That would be true." He then asked quietly, "Hey, listen, are you ever going to say yes to an invitation from me? Or is this a hopeless case?"

Shelly glanced around as discreetly as she could, hoping no one had heard. Then she turned back to him and smiled. *Really, what harm could there be in going for a drink with the man? Maybe he really is fun and interesting outside of work.*

She was about to answer when she felt her pocket vibrate. Plus, she had Josh as an outlet for those other things. So yes, maybe now *was* the time to take Roger up on his invite, considering she didn't need him to flip her switch. It was already being flipped—in a big way.

"How about tonight?" Shelly asked.

Roger's mouth fell open a little. "Really?"

Shelly smiled. "Sure. I usually go to Lena's fiancé's restaurant for dinner on Mondays."

"Oh, yes, Exquisite."

Nodding, Shelly picked up a pre-wrapped chicken salad sandwich. "Yeah, that's the one. Would you like to come with me?"

The usually calm and professional McKinney stumbled around a little. He nodded with a slight flush. "Yes, I'd love to."

Shelly grinned and winked at him. "Great. So we can go from here tonight if you like. Say seven? I'll come to your office."

"Okay then. Yes, that sounds wonderful."

Turning, she waved at him as she made her way out of the cafeteria. "See you then."

"See you," he replied, waving back.

Shelly almost missed his good-bye because she was too busy digging in her pocket for her phone.

DD: So? How does it work? Do I just tell you I'm hard, and you come running?

Sucking in a deep breath, Shelly moved to the side of the busy hospital corridor and quickly typed. **I assume you mean our deal?**

Shelly hit Send and started back down the hall. Not two seconds later, it buzzed, and she glanced down.

DD: Of course, Shelly. Why else would I contact you?

Well, that kind of stung. Shelly winced, but he was right. That was the deal in place. Stopping in front of the elevator bank, Shelly leaned in and pushed the up button. Taking a step back, she typed. **It can**

work 1 of 2 ways. You can either text me or call to request the time. If I'm available, I'll tell you.

After she hit Send and the doors pinged open, Shelly got inside and stood at the back. *Geez, this all seems so impersonal and almost business-like. Why not just ask for a fee, Monroe?* She mentally kicked herself. *Why on earth did I decide to do this?*

DD: Okay. I'm hard, horny, and want YOUR lips around my cock at 2p.m. Can you make that happen?

That was why she did this. Shelly felt her thighs clench and her stomach flip upside down. The damn man was nowhere in sight, and she was already twitchy. Shelly glanced at her watch. It was just going on one thirty, and she knew she had her schedule blocked out until three.

Hmm, all the possibilities... But if she was going to be the one on her knees, he should have to make an effort too. Smiling, Shelly squeezed her thighs together, trying to ease the ache that had started to throb, and typed.

If you can work out where my office is by 2 p.m., I'll make that happen.

Then she hit Send.

The elevator came to a stop at her floor, and she got out and walked down toward her office. She was almost there when she heard her name being called. Turning, she saw Lena coming down the hall, dressed in scrubs and a lab coat today.

"Hey there. I'm glad I caught you. Are you coming tonight?"

Pushing aside her little phone-tag game, Shelly tried to focus. "Ah, yes, actually. I hope you don't mind me bringing someone."

Lena smiled. "No, not at all. Who are you bringing?"

Shelly knew this wouldn't go over well. "Roger McKinney."

It was almost—*almost*—comical the way Lena's mouth fell open. "Please tell me you're joking?"

Shelly shrugged and shook her head. "Nope."

Lena rubbed her forehead. "Why would you want to date McKinney?"

Shelly laughed and moved past Lena to her office. Lena pivoted on her heel and jogged to catch up.

"I'm serious, Shelly. The guy is a hard-ass who's balding." She said triumphantly, "You told me you didn't want to date a balding man."

Shelly shook her head slowly. "I told you I didn't want to go on a *blind date* with a balding man. I know McKinney." Shelly sighed. "Plus, the man's been asking me out for months. It was the easiest thing to do. And who knows—maybe he's fun outside of work?"

Lena stood at the doorway of Shelly's office. "Have you lost your mind? Mason and I said go and get a guy to bang, not date, least of all McKinney." She pretended to shudder. "Are you going to sleep with him?"

Shelly sat in her chair and removed her phone, looking at it then placing it down on the desk. *Still nothing, huh?* Maybe he'd changed his mind when he realized she wouldn't be the only one making an effort. "No. I'm bringing him to dinner to get him off my back...and also to see if there's even a remote possibility he's relationship material."

Lena threw her hands in the air. "You've gone mad." She rolled her eyes and shook her head. "No sex is making you mad."

"Who said I'm not having sex?"

Lena froze then stepped forward, placing her palms on the back of the empty chair facing Shelly. "You had sex? With who?"

Shelly arched a brow and crossed her legs. "Who I have sex with is not yours or Mason's concern, and no, I haven't had sex, but I had a really good orgasm."

Lena stood back up, placing her hands on her hips. "By yourself doesn't count."

Licking her lips slowly, Shelly grinned. "It wasn't by myself. Now go. Leave. I need to finish up so I can go to dinner with you and McKinney."

Shelly walked around the desk just as her phone vibrated on top of the stack of folders. Both women stared at it, but luckily, Shelly had turned off the screen notifications, so the screen was blank.

"Was that him?" Lena whispered.

Shelly finally started to push Lena out the door. "Was that who?"

Lena dug in her stubborn heels. "Mr. Orgasm?"

Shelly burst out laughing and shook her head. "I have no idea."

Geez, when did I become such a liar? When I started this ludicrous deal with Josh, that's when.

Now at Shelly's office door, Lena turned on her. "Fine, don't tell me. Just answer one question for me."

Shelly put her hands on her hips. "What?"

"Was it worthy of a repeat?"

Shelly felt a smile so wicked and smug spread across her face, she almost wished it hadn't been caused by a man she could never keep.

"Oh yeah."

Lena returned the smiled then turned. "About time," she muttered as she walked away.

Racing over to the desk, Shelly grabbed the phone and unlocked it to see a message that made her breath catch.

DD: University Hospital. 8th floor. See you at 2.

While her whole body shivered and her thighs clenched, all Shelly could think was, *Two o'clock can't come quick enough. Pun intended.*

JOSH FIGURED HE'D pretty much broken every single traffic law to get his car parked at the University Hospital parking lot by one fifty. He glanced at his watch as he raced through the lobby to the directory board.

All through Sunday, he'd mulled over the decision to call Shelly. He'd gone back and forth on the pros and cons of having this kind of a fling.

Sure, he'd heard all the time of people who had friends with benefits. *But are we even really friends?* As far as Josh could tell, he and Shelly had friends in common, but as far as the two individuals went, they hardly knew anything about one another.

One thing he was certain about was the fact that he'd told Mason a huge "hell no" to dating her, which worked perfectly since she had made it clear she wanted to keep things a secret.

So of course, it all made perfect sense that he was now standing in the lobby of her place of employment, searching for her name, so he could go upstairs and get his sex on.

Finally, he spotted "Dr. Shelly Monroe, Pulmonologist, Level 8." *Good, the website was right.*

He made his way over to the elevators and stood with five other people. One lady turned and looked him over quickly. When her eyes met his, she gave him a shy smile. Josh winked and watched a blush spread across her cheeks. He grinned as the elevator pinged and they got in with the others. They were both at the back of the crowd, and she kept sneaking glances at him. Each time he caught her, he smiled and she blushed.

She was cute in a soft way. Her dark-brown hair was held back by a black headband. Josh noticed she was fiddling with the strap of her purse as she looked at him, and he figured it was some kind of nervous gesture. *See, this is the kind of woman you're supposed to want, not the dirty-talking man-eater upstairs.*

However, when the elevator stopped at Level 7 and the young lady beside him moved to get out, Josh watched her go with only one thought. *I'll never be able to do what I'm about to with a woman like that. Wouldn't that be a damn shame?* After all, he had a feeling what was about to happen was going to blow his mind—literally.

SHELLY GLANCED AT her desk clock as it flicked to 2:03 p.m. He hadn't shown. She hadn't expected to feel so disappointed. It wasn't as though they were an item—or ever going to be.

Sighing, she sat back in her chair, rocking it as she tapped her pen against the desk. She was in such a funk about it that she was about to call McKinney and tell him she needed to cancel their date tonight. Then her office phone buzzed.

Sitting up straight, she dropped the pen and answered over the speaker. "Yes, Amy?"

"Dr. Monroe, there's a Joshua Daniels here to see you."

Shelly sucked in a breath and looked at the clock. It read 2:05 p.m. He was late, but there was no way in hell she was turning him away. She wanted this, and she wanted it *now*. Clearing her throat, Shelly buzzed her assistant. "Send him in, Amy."

Letting go of the intercom button, Shelly sat back in her chair with her legs crossed and her eyes on the door, waiting for him to enter.

She knew she had the advantage, and she planned to use it. Feeling her heart hammer, she waited in dead silence, straining to hear the moment he was close. Then there was a soft but firm rap against the wood. Choosing to stay silent, she watched as the handle turned, the door opened, and then—*holy hell, there he is.*

The man was the definition of sex. His hair looked as though he'd run his hands through it, and several long brown strands fell forward into his face. He was dressed in jeans today—worn, torn jeans that were faded and well-loved by the look of the washed denim. His long-sleeved navy flannel shirt was unbuttoned and hanging open over a white tee that molded over every delicious muscle of his chest. On his feet were workman boots, and for some reason, this hardworking handyman look was *really* pushing all of Shelly's buttons in exactly the right way.

He stepped into the office and shut the door, waiting silently for some sort of cue from her.

Finally, when she'd looked him over thoroughly, she stated, "You're late."

He brought his arm up and looked at his watch, then he dropped it back down by his side and sauntered into the room. "Not by my watch." He moved around the chair that faced her and leaned across the desk. "Want to check, doctor?"

She grabbed his thick wrist, tugging him farther over the desk. He placed his other hand flat on the glossy surface to brace himself as she looked at his watch. It did in fact show two on the dot. Raising her eyes to his, she saw him quirk up an eyebrow.

"What was my punishment going to be?" he asked as she sat back in her chair, then he straightened and took a seat in the free chair.

Shelly looked at him sitting across from her, his legs spread and his hands resting on his jean-clad thighs. "I was going to send you away."

He seemed to think that over then nodded once. "*Sure*, you were."

Shelly cocked her head to the side then stood. She watched his eyes track her as she rounded the desk and came to stand in front of it. Leaning back, she rested her butt against the edge, looking down at him.

"You don't think I would've?" She let her eyes fall to those spread legs and the expanding bulge between them. "My time is very valuable, especially around here."

He tilted his head, those deep-brown eyes sliding down her scrubs before they came back up to rest on her face. "Oh, I believe it. You're a doctor, and this is a hospital. Of course you're valuable. Makes me wonder though if you brought me down here to tease or to deliver?"

Shelly had to hold back a smile. *So he thinks I'm a tease, does he? Well, he's in for a rude awakening then.* Keeping her eyes on him, she leaned over and pressed a hot pink-manicured nail on the intercom button.

"Yes, Dr. Monroe?"

Smiling the sexiest smile she had in her arsenal, Shelly let her eyes fall to his crotch. "Why don't you go and have lunch now?" she said to Amy.

His thighs tensed, and she raised her eyes to meet his hot ones.

"Are you sure?" Amy asked.

Without taking her gaze from his, Shelly pushed the button again. "Yes. It's slow, and I won't be going back up to the units until around three."

There was silence as they sat in her office, the air crackling with tension, then the intercom buzzed.

"Okay, I'll be back by three."

Standing up and stepping away from the desk, Shelly answered, "Very good." Then she stepped forward until she was beside Josh's chair. "Don't *you* move a muscle."

∼

JOSH SAT GLUED to the seat.

He couldn't have moved if the building was on fire, and he had a feeling in about two minutes, it very well could go up in flames. He knew one thing for certain. *He* was on fire, and the reason for that was currently walking to her office door to—*click*—lock it.

Taking a deep breath, Josh closed his eyes and tried counting backward from thirty to calm down. He'd known the minute he stepped in and saw her, sitting behind her big wooden desk in her sky-blue scrubs and lab coat, he was screwed. The woman was so unbelievably gorgeous, it almost hurt to look at her. She literally looked like a Barbie doll and was absolutely flawless, except for all of her stupid notions about rules and secrets.

Today, she had pulled her hair half up and tied it at the back of her head, leaving the rest to fall to her shoulders in a straight line. Those amazing blue eyes popped even more with the scrubs she was wearing, and her curvy little body tested the boundaries of the flimsy fabric, somehow managing to make even *them* look unbelievably hot. *A diamond in the rough.* The lady was a diamond, and as he sat there trying not to explode before she even touched him, he thought he was most definitely the rough.

He felt her walk back toward him. As she moved by his chair, she dragged a perfectly manicured nail across his shoulder. She walked in front of him and stopped between his thighs.

Looking down, she asked softly, "Aren't you going to undo your pants?"

Josh swallowed. *Shit, this is really going to happen. She's really going to get on her knees and give me a blow job in her office at two o'clock in the afternoon. Hell, maybe there is a plus side to this sex-with-no-strings deal.*

Nodding, Josh moved to stand, and she stepped back. He wasn't an overly tall man, but at six feet, he topped her by a few inches. She watched his face as he undid his belt.

"So this is it? I'm going to undo my belt, drop my pants, and then you'll—"

"Get on my knees"—she stepped up close to him—"take you in my hand, then *suck* you into my mouth."

Josh looked at the face only a couple of inches from his and breathed in deeply. *The woman smells fantastic, like*—he sniffed again —*apples.*

"No small talk?" he asked with a raised brow as he finally undid his jeans.

She looked down between their bodies then gripped the open denim and spread it apart. She ran a finger up and down the hair leading to his now painfully hard erection. "What is there to say? The deal is what it is. You called. I answered. You're here, and I'm willing."

With that, she lowered herself to her knees, looking up at him with her beautiful, perfect face an inch from his aching cock.

SHELLY WAS SO TURNED ON, she could barely talk. Josh had her so hot and bothered that she was surprised she hadn't melted through her scrubs. He was standing in front of her with his feet spread apart and his jeans wide open, and she was dipping her hands inside his pants to lift him free. He groaned softly when her fingers wrapped around his naked flesh. Looking up at him, she blew a light breath across the tip of his throbbing erection.

"Fuck," he cursed as his legs shuddered.

She felt his whole body tremble. Lowering her lashes, she bent over him and flicked her tongue across the swollen head. His hands flexed by his sides and she thought he might try to grab her hair, but he didn't. He just clenched his fists against his legs. Grinning against his pounding sex, she gripped the base firmly and stroked her tightly wrapped fingers around his hard length.

He let out a strangled groan. "The request was for you to *suck* it, I believe."

Nodding, Shelly whispered against his vulnerable flesh, "I believe you are correct."

Then she opened her lips and took him deep inside her mouth.

THE WOMAN IS a fucking sex goddess. Josh had decided she was from some other planet where sexy women were created to torture helpless men. As she knelt at his feet, sucking his cock deep down her throat, all he could think about was possessing her—*forever*.

He really needed to stop thinking like that, but damn, it was hard when she was sucking him like a pro and moaning as though she loved it. He refused to mess up her hair, out of fear she'd never let him touch her again, so he kept his hands clenched by his sides.

He'd let his head fall back and was thrusting his hips toward her to get his cock as deep as she could take it. Josh groaned when he heard her whimper. He wondered why some sick part of him was totally getting off on the fact that this woman—this beautiful, smart, highly educated professional woman—was currently on her knees and sucking his cock. *Fuck if that doesn't turn me on.*

Finally past his breaking point, he let go and gripped the side of her head, not caring anymore what happened after this immediate moment in time. She moaned around him, and the vibrations reverberated up his stiff shaft, sending shockwaves of pleasure up his spine, which made him thrust harder.

She raised a hand and cupped his balls, squeezing gently, and that was all it took. Josh groaned loudly and thrust deep, spilling himself into her mouth. Then he watched as the sexy siren swallowed every last drop.

SHELLY SAT BACK on her heels on her office floor and stared at the disheveled man above her. *What the hell is going on? This man makes me lose my ever-loving mind.*

She was so worked up that she wanted to strip out of her scrubs and beg him to take her. His breathing was labored as he looked down at her. With his jeans open and his erection right there, barely deflated at all, Shelly thought he was the sexiest man she'd ever seen.

"Wow, Shel," he said with a smug smile. He rearranged himself and pulled his jeans back together before zipping up.

Shelly blinked and tried to gather her wits about her.

"That sure was something else." He ran his hands through his sexy hair, then he looked at her, still sitting at his feet on the floor.

He held out a hand, and Shelly gripped it, letting him pull her to her feet. Once she was there, she was about to tell him *no problem* and send him on his way, but he nodded once and turned, walking to the door. She watched as he unlatched it and reached for the handle.

Before he walked out, he turned toward her, sitting with her butt against the desk to hold herself up, and winked. "Thanks again, doc. Now I feel great."

With that, he left before Shelly could say one damn thing.

CHAPTER 8

SEVEN O'CLOCK ROLLED around, and Shelly found herself outside of Roger McKinney's office. She knocked twice and waited until he called her inside. Entering, she noticed he was wearing a black buttoned-up shirt and some black slacks. While it was obvious he wasn't in the same category as Josh and Mason, she found herself taking a second look at the older doctor.

She supposed for a well-educated man, Roger McKinney was exactly the way he should be. He was extremely smart, slightly stuffy, and according to Lena, arrogant and obnoxious. All of those qualities were what made him an excellent doctor and director and a man her father would be impressed to call his son-in-law.

The only problem with that scenario was Joshua Daniels, who kept flashing through her mind with his unzipped jeans and his sexy, satisfied grin.

"Shelly. You ready to get going?"

Smiling at the man currently moving around his desk, she looped her arm through his when he offered. "I sure am." She looked him over and said, "You scrub up pretty good, McKinney."

He shot her a slightly embarrassed grin, which was in direct contrast to his usual cocky attitude. "Thanks. You look absolutely stunning as usual."

Smiling, Shelly squeezed his arm tight against her side. "Come on. Let's go eat."

∽

JOSH HEARD HER the minute she walked in. He hadn't meant to be at the restaurant when she arrived. He knew Monday nights were reserved for the Langley family dinner, and he'd been working like a dog all afternoon to get the heck out of there before *she* turned up. However, luck was not with him, and maybe it was his own fault. After all, he had taken two hours off this afternoon for *extracurricular* activities. Now it was coming back to bite him in the ass.

Standing in the building adjoining Exquisite, he listened carefully as she seemed to make her way through the restaurant. He couldn't see her, but he could hear her talking, and occasionally, that laugh of hers echoed through the air. Josh swore he felt it stroke right down his arm, making the hair at the back of his neck stand up.

He was about to call it a day and leave without going next door when he heard a deeper voice fill the silent space. Moving closer to the connecting walls, Josh crept past the sawhorse and stood still as a statue.

"Dr. McKinney. It's so good to see you again," Mason said.

Listening carefully, Josh heard who he assumed was Dr. McKinney.

"Thanks, Mason. You too. I was thrilled when Shelly told me we were coming here tonight."

Now *that* got Josh's attention. Standing straight up and inching backward, he accidentally stepped into the wooden sawhorse, sending it falling with a loud crash. *Shit.* Looking around for a quick exit, Josh made a beeline for the door. He almost made it.

"Josh?"

Shit, shit, shit. Turning slowly, he saw Lena standing in the door.

"Yep. Hi, Lena. Sorry about the noise. I was just leaving."

Please leave it at that and let me leave. Josh inched toward the main door. He did *not* want to spend the next two hours sitting across from a woman who had been on her knees in front of him several hours ago and who was now entertaining her rich, smart Dr. Date.

But no, luck was definitely not on his side.

Mason chose that moment to stick his head through the door. "Josh. Come eat with us, man."

Josh groaned, seeing no other way out, and made his way over to his friends. *Shit.*

∽

SHELLY WATCHED IN horror as Josh Daniels stepped through the door where Lena and Mason were now standing. He was dressed as he had been earlier, but now he had a tool belt—*oh God*—wrapped around those amazing hips.

Lena must have noticed it too.

Let's face it. Who wouldn't look at his crotch when that damn belt was designed to display it?

"You were leaving with your tool belt on?" Lena pointed out with a small laugh.

Josh glanced at her quickly, then he looked at Roger with an assessing gaze before returning to Lena. "Ah, yeah. I was on my way out and was going to put it in the back of my truck."

Mason clapped him on the shoulder. "What'd you do? Trip in the dark?"

Josh glared at his friend then nodded slightly. "Shut the hell up."

Laughing, Mason moved to go back into the kitchen. Shelly kept her eyes on Josh as he stepped around Lena. He started to unbuckle his tool belt as he and Lena walked over to a table across the room.

Shelly felt Roger nudge her arm. When she moved her eyes to his, he asked, "Who's Bob the Builder?"

Shelly almost winced at Roger's condescending question. *Am I just like that?* Dismayed with herself and feeling almost protective of Josh for some inexplicable reason, she answered softly but firmly, "That's Josh Daniels. He's one of Mason's longest friends and his best man. He's renovating next door."

Roger nodded. "Ahh, I see. I've never really understood the need to build things. Don't really have the patience for it."

Or the muscle, popped into Shelly's head. She smiled. "Yes, it seems like hard work."

Turning in the direction Josh had gone, Shelly saw Lena chatting with him. Shelly found herself making excuses and moving away from Roger, headed toward her friend and DD.

DOES THIS WOMAN ever look anything but perfectly put together? Josh thought as Shelly walked toward them.

The minute he'd come through the door, he'd felt her eyes land on him. He'd made a conscious effort not to look in her direction until it was absolutely necessary, and even then, he'd made sure to keep his cool and not give anything away.

However, at this moment, while Lena was facing Shelly, Josh let his eyes roam all over her. She must've changed at work, because she was wearing a navy dress with white polka dots all over it. The sleeves hit her arm just above the elbow, and the pencil skirt of the dress landed an inch or so under her knee. The modest outfit hid her body in the most sophisticated way, but to Josh, the fact that he couldn't see anything made it that much sexier. *Damn, damn, damn.*

Finally, she stopped in front of them and her eyes latched on to his as she asked, "Playing with your tool so late at night, Josh?"

Feeling his mouth curve into a wicked grin, he was about to reply, but Lena snapped at her. "Shelly."

Lena faced him quickly with apologetic eyes, and he saw Shelly giving him a thorough once-over.

The woman is insane. How am I supposed to just stand here, letting her drive me crazy, and keep everything a secret? Hell, who knows, maybe she gets off on the thrill of being caught.

"Don't worry, Lena. It's okay," Josh said. Looking back at Shelly, he returned her smug smile. "I was cleaning up for the evening actually. I played with my tool a little earlier today."

Lena shook her head. "You two are idiots. Can we go eat? Or are we going to start talking about secret gardens next like we don't know that we're alluding to a..." She apparently wasn't brave enough to say it.

Shelly asked sweetly, "Alluding to what, Lena? I don't have a garden. Mine's just a nice bare patch. What about you? Does Mason prune your garden?"

Josh choked on a strangled groan as Shelly looked at him with an evil smile full of mischief. That was when Lena threw up her hands and groaned, turning to stomp away. Josh looked at the sassy woman who glanced behind her to see that Mason had come out and was talking to Dr. Date.

"Did you do that on purpose?" he asked.

Shelly's eyes strayed down to his mouth then came back up to meet his own. "Do what? Embarrass Lena? She'll be fine."

"No. Run her away?"

She bit her bottom lip, and it brought to mind other activities her mouth had been involved in earlier.

"Now why would I do that?" she asked a little too innocently.

Leaning a little closer so he could smell her—*mmm, apples again*—he said in a low voice, "So you could be alone with me."

Turning her head an inch, the corners of her mouth tilted up. "And why would I want to do that?"

Josh stood back slowly and said in a whisper, "Because I owe you." He watched with complete satisfaction as her eyes clouded over.

She grabbed the back of a chair. "Do you?"

He moved around the table and was about to brush past her when she stepped in front of him. Looking down, he noticed her head tilted back, her eyes locking on his. *What kind of game is she playing with me?*

She had a date here, and now she was looking at him as though she wanted to take him out back and show him what was underneath her skirt.

Suddenly, Josh realized he didn't like this deal anymore.

Leaning down slightly, he whispered, "New rule to our deal. You'll get what I owe you, but first, you have to tell me something about yourself."

Her mouth fell open a little, then she whispered, "That causes strings. I said no strings."

He shrugged. "Then I say I don't owe you a thing."

And for the second time that day, he walked away from her.

SHELLY HAD JUST TAKEN her seat next to Roger when Mason came in, carrying a huge bowl of pasta and a basket of garlic bread. He handed it to Lena, who dished out her own, then he sat at the head of the table and passed the food around. The meal smelled absolutely amazing. The only problem, as far as Shelly could tell, was the immediate company.

To her left sat Roger, who was chatting with Wendy and her husband, who'd arrived around fifteen minutes ago. Directly across from Shelly was Lena, who was seated beside Josh, who was currently watching every single move Shelly made.

Oh, he's being subtle. But she felt his eyes tracking her like a predator tracking its prey. *He needs to back off, or he's going to get a punch in the gut —from me.*

"Hey, everyone. Sorry I got held up," Rachel said as she moved in behind Lena and Josh, taking the vacant seat beside him.

Shelly smiled at her. "Hot date?"

Rachel pulled her chair in, laughing. "Ah, no. Not unless you call a flat tire a hot date?"

Shelly pretended to think about it, picking up her glass of wine. "Depends on who fixed it for you. Was it some hot, sexy mechanic in overalls?"

Lena snorted. "Is this another one of your warped sexual fantasies?"

Mason decided to add his two cents. "Better watch out, huh, Roger?"

Shelly almost spat her wine everywhere as Roger chuckled and nudged her arm.

"I'm game. I may have to buy some overalls though."

Shooting a glare at Mason, Shelly couldn't help but notice Lena trying extremely hard not to laugh.

Shelly was about to say something quick and witty, she was sure, when a cool, familiar voice asked, "Are there any other warped sexual fantasies you'd care to share?"

Shelly let her eyes lock with Josh's, and she arched a brow. "Not with you, Daniels. I've heard all about you."

Rachel took that opportunity to jab Josh in the side, letting out her own laugh. "Hell yeah. Man, he and Mason used to clean shop back in the day."

Lena sat forward to peer down the table at Rachel. "Do tell."

Happy the discussion was off of her, Shelly looked at Roger and found he was laughing and smiling right along with everyone else. It appeared McKinney could still surprise her.

"Rachel," Mason warned with a low voice.

"Oh, come on. Are you trying to tell us Lena doesn't know all the dirty details of your past yet?" Wendy asked as she cuddled into her husband's side.

They both smiled at Lena, and Shelly watched as her best friend looked at her frowning fiancé.

"Worried?" Lena asked Mason.

Mason shook his head. "Not overly. Josh was worse than I was, but I know how you like to get jealous."

Lena grinned. "Do not."

"Do too."

"Ah, guys?" Shelly interrupted. "If you don't mind, *I* want to know."

Silence fell around the table as everyone turned to face Rachel, who was looking at Josh with a huge grin. Josh shook his head and raised a hand to run it through his hair.

"You're a pain in the ass, Rach," he muttered.

"Why? It's true. You and Mason had girls lining up to date you. Every weekend they had a different girl." She laughed. "They were all morons."

When Roger passed her the bowl of pasta, Shelly scooped some out then handed it back to Mason. She looked at Josh, who was sitting silently and shaking his head.

"Is that what turns you on in a woman, Josh?" she asked.

His eyes snapped up and locked on hers. "Not lately."

The whole table went silent, and Shelly felt her stomach tighten. She was about to speak to break the awkward moment, wanting to ask about what had changed, when Mason broke the tension instead.

"Nope. Josh told me he's looking for a girl who's sweet and kind. A proper little angel."

Shelly arched a brow. *Really? Now* that *is interesting.*

Josh flipped off Mason. "Screw you, man. Is nothing sacred?"

"Not around here." Mason shoveled food in his mouth with his mischievous eyes now on Shelly.

Roger asked seriously, "Sweet is kind of boring, don't you think?"

Everyone paused as seven pairs of eyes, including Shelly's, landed on him.

"Wow. I think I was just insulted and complimented at the same time," Shelly said with mock amusement.

Roger laughed and shook his head, putting his hand over hers. Looking down at it, Shelly had to physically force herself *not* to remove her hand. She glanced across the table, catching Lena and Josh looking at their joined hands. They seemed to be equally appalled for completely different reasons.

"No, not at all. You're amazing. I mean, look at you," Roger explained.

Shelly heard a cough and noticed it had come from Josh. Looking at him with a pointed glare, she raised her eyebrow. *You got something to add?*

"You're gorgeous, sexy, *and* smart. That's rare these days." Roger stood. "I'd take *that* in bed over sweet and kind any day."

Shelly swallowed and couldn't help herself from looking straight into a pair of hot chocolate eyes that belonged to Josh Daniels.

∽

JOSH WAS TRYING REALLY, *really* hard to behave himself, but it was getting damn difficult. This stuffed shirt was pretty much insinuating in front of all of them that he was going to take Shelly to bed.

Judging by the look on her face, however, McKinney was in for a massive disappointment, and *that* was the only reason Josh stayed in his seat, biting his tongue.

Roger stood and excused himself, and the minute he was out of earshot, Lena placed her hands on the table.

"Are you out of your mind?" Lena asked Shelly.

Josh remained silent, waiting to hear what was about to go down. He'd noticed Shelly's eyes shift to his several times over the last hour, and he knew she was making sure he kept his mouth shut and didn't give them away. *No problem, Barbie. Things are getting interesting without my help.*

"No. Shut it," Shelly warned Lena through clenched teeth.

"Shut it? Our boss, Dr. Roger McKinney, just basically told the whole table he wants to bang you."

Josh chuckled.

Shelly's eyes gave him what would've most definitely been a lethal stare. "Got something to add?"

Holding up his hands, he shook his head. "Not at all."

Rachel was munching on some bread and piped up, "Seriously, Shel, what's your deal? Always going for these stuffed shirts."

Shelly rolled her eyes. "He's not a stuffed shirt, he's—"

"Balding," Josh threw in with a shit-eating grin.

Mason chuckled. "You did seem very specific about that just a little while back."

Josh fully laughed, completely enjoying himself. He was sure Shelly was about to deliver a scathing reply when a phone rang. Shelly reached into her bag, pulled it out, and glanced at the number. Sighing, she clicked it off and set it on the table. *Interesting,* Josh thought as she looked at Mason again.

"Yeah, well, that was the other day. Maybe I changed my mind," Shelly told him.

"Please do *not* tell me that he's Mr. O," Lena hissed.

Josh looked from Lena to Shelly, who, for once in her life, had gone slightly pale and completely silent. She seemed to be glaring at Lena, trying to get some kind of message across to her.

"If *he* is who you told me about this afternoon, I think I'll die," Lena continued.

"Mr. O?" Rachel asked as Mason and Wendy laughed. "Would someone please answer the number-one question floating around the table? For all of us either ill-informed or stupid people, who or what is Mr. O?"

Shelly seemed to straighten her spine as though she was about to do battle, then her eyes met his in what he could only describe as a direct challenge.

That was when Lena stated plainly, "Some guy who gave her the big O."

Everyone at the table laughed as though this was a normal conversation, but Shelly's eyes were glued to his, her eyebrow rising in challenge.

"Got something worth saying, Daniels?" Shelly asked.

Josh pushed his tongue into his cheek and shook his head. "Nope. But for someone who got the big O, you seem awfully grouchy. Maybe he wasn't very good?"

He could see she was about to probably agree and try to make him feel like shit, but Lena ruined it for her.

"Oh, yes, he was," Lena said in a singsong voice.

He watched with complete satisfaction as Shelly appeared to kick her friend under the table.

"Shut up," she hissed at Lena.

"Geez. It doesn't matter. They all know and love you. We're family."

Shelly looked back at him, and Josh had to admit that he was wearing the most arrogant grin he'd ever sported in his entire life.

∽

WELL, SHIT, SHELLY thought as she conceded defeat. Lena had completely and utterly outed her, giving Josh Daniels ammo for life. *Hang on a minute. Life? Where did that come from?*

Not only was she stuck here with everyone grinning at her as though she was the evening's entertainment, the phone call she had ignored had been her parents calling. She heard it beep, which meant she had a message.

Standing, she smoothed her hands on her skirt and held up her phone. "Thank you for completely humiliating me, Lena. I need to go and check this message. Can you let Roger know I'll be back in a second?"

Lena nodded with a smile.

Mason chuckled. "Don't be mad, Shel."

"Shut it, Casanova. I'll be as mad as I want." Then looking at Lena and her fiancé, she smiled. "Traitors."

She turned to walk out into the back kitchen. When she got there, she turned on her phone and listened to the message.

"Shelly, love, it's your momma. Your father and I would love it if you'd come on home for the weekend sometime soon. I promise to make your favorite dinner, chicken-fried steak, as long as you're sweet to your father. You know I don't like y'all fightin'. Give me a call, and we can set it up. Love you, dear."

Shelly sighed, leaning a shoulder against the wall, and closed her eyes. She really didn't want to go home right now. Whenever she got there, she ended up fighting with her dad, then she came back from her "vacation" more stressed than when she'd left.

"Everything okay?"

She spun around to see Josh standing just inside the frosted doors to the kitchen. Nodding, she slipped her phone back into her purse. "Yes. Did you need something?"

He didn't move. He stood there watching her with a serious expression. "I need a lot of things. But let's start with, why guys like Dr. Douchebag?"

"Dr. Douchebag?"

Tilting his head, he spoke so softly she had to strain to hear him. "Try not to be a smartass for once and answer. Why guys like him? It's obvious you don't want him. So why date him?"

Shelly put her bag on a counter and took three steps forward. She raised her hand and laid her palm flat against his chest. She kept walking, pushing him out of view from the doors, until his back hit the wall. She knew he let her push him, and when he came to a standstill, she placed herself directly in front of him.

"Who should I go out with? Guys like you?" she asked.

He seemed to contemplate that then shrugged. "Sure. Why not? You seem to like doing *other* things with me. Would eating a meal really be that big a step up?"

Shaking her head, she whispered, "That's the problem. I'd like it too much and would want it all the time. And you know what? That clouds judgment. I don't *want* to want a guy like you."

JOSH LEANED DOWN until they were an inch apart. He wasn't fazed at all as he whispered across her lips, "Yes, you do."

Her eyes were clouding over, and as she stood on her tiptoes to kiss him, he raised his head and shook it. Her blue eyes blinked open and focused on him.

"No. Not until you tell me something about you."

She licked her lips. "Didn't I just do that?"

Josh shook his head, feeling his heart pound and his erection throb as he looked at the most kissable lips he'd ever seen. "No. I want to know something about *you* that has nothing to do with *this*."

She dropped her hand and took a deep breath, and Josh had to admit that he thought she was about to back away.

Looking over her shoulder before turning back to face him, she asked, "What do I get if I do?"

Josh felt his grin appear, and he replied in a low voice, "Satisfaction."

Looking him over, she ran her eyes down his jeans and back up to his face. Then she shook her head as though she was fighting with herself. "Okay. I'm originally from Georgia, and while I love a lot of things about that place, I took speech lessons during med school to disguise my accent. A lot of people these days will—how should I say this? Judge you just because of a slight inflection in your voice."

Josh couldn't have been more stunned if she'd admitted she had a third eye. "Be serious."

She grinned, then she completely floored him with her Southern lilt. "Why, I am being serious, sugar. It ain't my fault I do such a good job of hidin' my accent."

His eyes widened, and he felt a genuine smile spread over his face. She was adorable, and with that accent, she was absolutely lethal.

"Wow," was all he could manage.

She spun on her heel to move away, but he snagged her arm and pulled her back against him.

Josh pressed his chest and body against her back and breathed against her ear. "I didn't think you could get any sexier. God, was I wrong."

Josh felt her take a deep breath, and he let go of her arm. But she remained right where she was, leaning against him.

"So do you always cover it?"

Turning to look at him over her shoulder, she whispered, "That's two questions. You said only one."

Josh conceded, knowing this was a bigger step than what she had wanted. He found himself nibbling her ear. "Come on. Give us a chance?"

He was pretty sure he wouldn't get an answer.

What he hadn't counted on was Mason walking through the kitchen doors.

"THIS IS NOT WHAT YOU THINK," Shelly said as she stepped away from Josh.

Mason looked from her to his friend, then back at her with a smug grin. Shelly almost gave in to the urge to punch him.

"Oh?"

Shelly marched over to Mason, looking into his laughing blue eyes. Mason was tall, well over six feet. He probably stood around six foot three, but that didn't stop Shelly from glaring at him.

"Then what is it, Shel?" he asked, grinning like a loon.

Shelly jammed her fists on her hips, furious that she'd been stupid enough to cave for one lousy minute. Narrowing her eyes, she snapped, "None of your business."

Laughing, Mason looked over her shoulder at the silent man standing just behind her. "Should I start addressing you as Mr. O from now on?"

"Mason, shut up," Shelly warned through clenched teeth.

Looking back at her, Mason shook his head. "Sorry, this is too good to let go."

He stepped around her, and she turned, watching him move toward his friend. Josh had his eyes on her while she was trying to somehow melt into the floor. Finally, he dragged his gaze away to look at Mason.

"What happened to 'hell no'? And what was the other one? Oh yeah, 'she'd burn me to a crisp'?" Mason asked Josh.

Shelly asked, "Burn you to a crisp?" Suddenly, *this* was a much more important issue than getting Mason to shut the hell up.

Josh looked at her with a crooked smile, then he had the audacity to wink. "Yeah, because you're so damn hot."

Mason let out a loud laugh as Shelly fumed. *Damn him.* He'd just confirmed everything with that single sentence. Even though some kind of relationship between them had been a fairly reasonable assumption, up until that moment, they could have played it off. *Right?*

"Ha. You just couldn't help yourself, could you, Daniels? I knew it. She's totally your type," Mason said.

"Ah, hello. *She* is still here, you morons." Sighing as though she was extremely put out, Shelly turned on her heel, stalking to the door, when she heard Josh call her name. Turning, she looked at him standing next to the grinning idiot otherwise known as Mason.

"The deal?" Josh asked.

Lifting her chin, she shook her head. "Is done."

Leaving it at that, she stormed out of the kitchen and went back to her date.

∼

JOSH STOOD THERE watching the doors swing slowly until they stopped.

"Holy shit. When did this all happen?" Mason asked with a devilish smile.

Josh rolled his shoulders and shook his head. "Nothing happened. We just got together a couple of times. We had a deal."

Mason moved around him to the fridge and grabbed a couple of beers. He passed one to Josh, who took a long sip.

"What kind of deal?" Mason asked.

"A fucked-up one." Josh ran his hand through his hair.

"I didn't think you two really talked. Although Lena and I did start to get vibes. Do you even know her full name? That burned my ass once—big time," Mason explained around a grin.

"Just barely. God, what a mess. That night at the club—"

"I knew it," Mason shouted, interrupting Josh's train of thought.

"Huh?"

"I asked her about that night, and the little brat lied right to my face."

Taking another sip, Josh nodded. "Doesn't surprise me. She wanted to keep it our dirty little secret."

"Hmm, I don't understand." Mason leaned back against the counter.

Josh shook his head and pointed his beer toward the door. "The deal she's talking about—that night at the club, we came to an arrangement of sorts."

Mason slowly grinned. "Oh, this just gets better and better."

"Are you gonna shut the hell up so I can tell you? Or keep interrupting me?"

Holding his beer up, Mason nodded. "My apologies. Please go on."

Rolling his eyes, Josh continued. "We agreed that we liked what we saw and wanted to explore it, but she told me it needed to stay a secret and it was just going to be sex." He stopped, waiting for Mason to comment. When he stayed silent, Josh asked, "Do you really have nothing to say to *that*?"

"Oh no, I have plenty. I was just waiting for permission to talk, sir."

"When did you turn into such an asshole?" Josh asked with a smirk.

"Hey, man, I was always this way. You're just feeling sensitive right now because Sexy Shelly closed the lid of the cookie jar."

Josh shook his head and placed the now empty bottle on the counter. "I never got into the cookie jar." *Well, maybe I dipped my fingers in a little—okay, bad pun—but nothing else.*

"So why the secret? And *why* is she here tonight with her boss if you two are—well, you know, heating up the sheets?"

"Because we're not. We fooled around in the parking lot and today at her office, but that's it."

Mason's mouth fell open. "At her office? In the hospital?"

Josh felt a smug grin spread across his lips and nodded. "Yep. She made sure she gave me a very thorough physical."

"Ha. I really didn't think you'd touch her since you dubbed her the Man-Eater."

"Yeah, me either."

Mason finished his beer and pushed off the counter, walking toward the door. "You never told me why she doesn't want to date you."

Josh shrugged, following him. "She didn't make any sense, but she said something about losing focus and ending up wanting too much."

Mason stopped. "Well, surely that isn't a bad thing."

"Apparently it is when you're Shelly Monroe."

CHAPTER 9

THE DINNER WRAPPED up fairly quickly after the disaster in the kitchen. Shelly had barely glanced at Mason or Josh the whole way through dessert, and once that was gone, she stood, grabbed Roger's arm, and pulled him out the door. Lena had watched her carefully but kept quiet, and Shelly had to wonder how long it would take Mason to share his juicy gossip.

As Roger walked her to the lobby door of her condo, she was preoccupied with thoughts about Josh and how she'd been looking forward to finally getting into bed with him. Now that the opportunity was gone, she totally missed the cue that Roger McKinney was leaning in for a good night kiss. Completely blindsided, Shelly froze and clamped her mouth shut.

Feeling her tension, Roger stepped back, giving her a regretful look. "This"—he motioned between them—"isn't going to happen, is it?"

Shelly sighed and shook her head with an apologetic look. "I'm sorry, Roger."

He smiled and stuffed his hands in his pockets. "Nah, don't be. It's okay...you and Bob the Builder—there something going on there?"

"No," she answered a little too quickly.

Roger nodded and stroked her cheek. "Well, maybe there should be."

Shelly felt her mouth open then shut without saying anything.

What can I say? She didn't want to date a man who was unreliable, especially in this economy. *Been there, done that.* "Not going to happen."

"Hmm. Well, I'm going to leave you to it." He started to walk down the path back to his car. Then he stopped and turned to her. "Shelly?"

She smiled. "Yeah?"

"Thanks for taking me tonight. I had a good time."

Shelly nodded, wishing there was something there. "You're welcome. Drive safe."

He waved, walking backward to his car. "Sure will. Have a good night."

JOSH WALKED THROUGH the door to an excited ninety-pound Mutley, who was jumping up on his hind legs and placing his huge paws on Josh's chest. Scratching his dog's head, he smiled as Mutley ran a huge tongue up his cheek.

"Hey, boy. How you doing?"

Mutley's tail wagged as his mouth fell open, letting the same wet tongue loll as though he was grinning.

After pushing him down, Josh watched the dog circle him, then he made his way through the hall down to the kitchen. "Want some dinner, buddy?"

Sitting by his bowl patiently, Mutley looked at him as if to say, *Well, yeah, genius.*

Moving to the pantry, Josh pulled out the dog food then went over to grab Mutley's bowl.

He was still thinking about the evening and Shelly's quick departure after the scene in the kitchen. He didn't understand why she was so upset about Mason knowing they were *involved*. No, not involved. That implied they knew one another, which they certainly didn't. Fooling around—those were the words he was looking for.

For some reason, she wanted to give the impression that she was interested in men who were, as far as Josh could tell, so boring they could put her to sleep.

Why? That was what he wanted to know. *What did she mean she didn't want to get involved with someone like me because she'd get too distracted?*

The woman baffled him. She was such a firecracker, yet she wanted to settle down with someone like Paul the Bore or Dr. Douchebag.

After feeding Mutley, Josh walked over to the sliding door leading to his back porch. Opening it, he walked outside and looked at the stars. It was so beautifully clear tonight, the perfect evening to take a walk with a hot woman. However, the woman he wanted to walk with had walked out the door with another man.

He was such an idiot to still be thinking about her. *That's it*, he thought as he pulled out his cell, intending to delete Barbie the Man-Eater from his phone and life. But when he got to her number, he found himself dialing it instead.

SHELLY'S PHONE BUZZED as she climbed into bed. Looking at the cell, she saw DD displayed on the front. She shook her head, telling herself she shouldn't answer. *Like that ever worked.*

She put it to her ear. "What do you want, Josh? I told you tonight. The deal is done."

"Well, hello to you too, Shel."

Closing her eyes, Shelly slid down, laying her head on the pillow, and allowed herself a minute to fantasize that the deep sexy voice was coming from beside her on the bed instead of through the earpiece.

"I want to keep the deal," the voice told her.

Shaking her head and keeping her eyes closed, Shelly relaxed. "You broke it. The deal was sex, no strings, and *definitely* no Mason. You broke all *three* rules."

He sighed, and if she had to guess, she figured he was running his hand through his hair. "I want a new deal."

Shelly laughed. "A new deal? Just like that? What else can there be? I told you that I don't want to get involved."

"With me," he said.

"Huh?"

"You don't want to get involved with *me*. You're quite happy to parade around a string of completely wrong choices, yet you won't even give me a five-minute date." He paused, and Shelly knew what would be the next word out of his mouth. "Why?"

She opened her eyes and looked at the ceiling. She started to count the little boxes that were painted in checkered black and white across it, which she loved. "Because you're not my type."

"Excuse me if I don't believe you. You fall apart all over me."

She let out a frustrated sound. "Not sexually. It's pretty obvious that part works. It's everything else."

After a pause, he asked, "Like what? I'm not in the health industry? Because that's ridiculous."

"No. Geez, why do you care? You told Mason you didn't even want to date me. I believe 'hell no' was the answer he said you gave him." Sitting up, Shelly leaned back against her pink headboard. "Look, I think it would be better to forget all of this. Nothing really happened—"

"I beg to disagree. Something most definitely happened. You're just being stubborn. Give me a new deal."

Shelly heard a bark in the background. "Do you have a dog?"

"Huh?"

"A dog? I heard a bark. I asked if you own a dog."

"Yeah. His name's Mutley. Stop changing the subject."

"I'm not a fan of dogs. They're too slobbery."

Shelly could almost hear his eyes roll. "Of course you're not. Are you always so perfectly put together?"

With a grin, she lowered her voice. "Do you always look like you just got out of a woman's bed?"

The phone went quiet, and the silence was so thick that it was hard to hear his words as they slid through the phone and into her ear. "Is that how I look?"

Groaning softly, Shelly let her eyes close, thinking about how sexy Josh Daniels was. Everything about him appealed to her, and right now, she wished he was in her bed on top of her. *A new deal? Do I really want to do this?*

"Shelly?" he asked in a voice designed to seduce.

"Yes, that's how you look. You always look like you just rolled out of some woman's bed—as if her hands tunneled through your long hair, hanging on for dear life. And to answer your question, no, I'm not always perfectly put together. I'm not right now."

JOSH KNEW THERE had never been a better opening for phone sex—*ever*. That, however, was not what he wanted.

Knowing exactly what he wanted, he said, "A new deal. Stop trying to distract me. Give me one."

He moved to sit in the reclining chaise lounge on his deck, waiting patiently for her answer. Mutley lay down beside him, resting his big head on his paws as he watched Josh with a raised eyebrow. He swore his dog understood everything he was saying.

"Okay, I have one," she announced.

Josh had to remind his cock it was *not* coming out to play tonight. "I'm waiting."

She took a breath as though she was unsure, then she asked, "What are you doing next weekend?"

Josh hadn't seen that question coming. He thought about the barbecue he was supposed to have with his brother then shrugged. *It isn't like I have to go to that.* "Nothing. Why?"

There was complete silence.

Then, as though she'd change her mind if she didn't get it out, she asked quickly, "Want to go on a road trip? Can you ask your boss for some time off? I was thinking I could leave Friday morning and make it home by Monday night."

"Hey, doc?"

"Yeah?"

"Where are we going?"

There was another stretch of silence, and then she said, "You'll come with me?"

Josh chuckled, wondering what the hell he was doing. But deep down, he knew. He was getting involved. He was just hoping she'd take it easy on him.

"I'd like to say I already have." He heard her take a deep breath. "But that's a different conversation. Yes, I'll come. Are you going to tell me where?"

Josh looked at Mutley, who had raised his head with his ears perked.

Yep, you're coming, too, bud. Josh grinned, knowing Shelly would freak out.

∼

SHELLY WAS BITING HER LIP, gripping the cell phone tight. *What the hell am I thinking, inviting him home with me?*

In all honesty, her plan was genius. Her father would have a fit when she walked through the door with Josh, but on the other hand, the idea of having him with her was more and more appealing for other reasons.

"Savannah, Georgia."

"As in your hometown?" he asked quietly.

Shelly thought about what she was doing for one second more before she blurted, "Yeah. My mom wants me to come home, and I told her I'd come this weekend." She stopped, having a rare moment of nerves.

"You want me to meet your parents, but you didn't want Mason and Lena to know about us? I don't get it, doc."

She didn't get it either. All she could come up with was she didn't want to disappoint or hurt Mason and Lena. Whereas her father was already disappointed with her. And her mother? Well, she pretty much thought as he did. *So what the hell?* "Look, you're either in or out. My new deal is you come home with me for four days—"

"In what capacity?"

"What? Man, what is it with you interrupting me?" Shelly chuckled, feigning exasperation.

"Well, I'm trying to nail down the facts because last time we made a deal, you blindsided me by using all that sex magic you have."

Shelly couldn't help it. She burst out laughing. "Sex magic?"

"Yeah. You get around me, and I lose my mind. So you must be casting spells."

"No secret spells here, Mr. Daniels." She paused then said, "I want you to come home with me as my friend. However, when we're alone together, I don't see why we can't have added benefits."

"Such as?"

"You know what I mean."

"I know, but I love it when you talk dirty."

Closing her eyes, she had to bite back a moan. "Benefits such as hot, sweaty, back-scratching sex."

"Hmm. We haven't done that yet," he pointed out in a voice smooth as whiskey.

"No, we haven't."

"But we will. Won't we, Shel?"

She took a deep breath. "I really hope so."

There was another quiet moment, then he asked in a scandalized tone, "In your parents' house?"

Laughing, she replied in the most Southern accent she could dig up. "Oh, you naughty man, Joshu-ah Daniels. Well, I did always want to be ravished in my old bedroom. Think you could manage that, big boy?"

"You keep talking like that, Man-Eater, and you can count on it."

"What did you just call me?" she asked, still chuckling.

"Man-Eater. Damn, you're sexy as hell. You know that, right?"

Choosing to ignore him, she asked, "Will your boss give you the time off?"

~

JOSH WAS ABOUT to explain that he *was* the boss. Then it occurred to him that she thought he was a construction crew worker. *Ha, imagine that.* In all fairness, he *was* a construction worker. He happened to also own Creative Construction and Remolding Co., but he decided he wasn't going to let her in on that just yet.

It was nice actually—not to be looked at as though he was a bank and would always foot the bill. Melissa had treated him like that, but he wanted Shelly to be with him for *him*.

"Sure, he will. It's this weekend, so that should be enough time for me to finish my work for the week. How long does it take to get there?"

"Usually I fly, but this year, I felt like a road trip. I looked it up, and it said eleven and a half hours."

Josh nodded, patting Mutley on the head. "Okay, so you want to leave early Friday morning then?"

She let out a breathy sigh. "Uh, yes. I was thinking early—around four o'clock."

"Damn, doc, that is early."

"It's a long trip."

"It sure is. Are there any rules to this deal I should know about?"

There was silence, then he heard a whisper so quiet he almost missed it. "Don't make me want to keep you."

Josh felt a huge grin spread across his face. "Well then, don't make me want to be kept."

He was about to wish her a good night when she said, "Josh?"

"Yeah?"

"I'm breaking all my rules for you."

"Are you? How's that working so far?"

"I don't know yet. I'll let you know."

He closed his eyes, imagining her beautiful blue ones. "Get some sleep, Man-Eater."

He swore he could see her smile when she answered in a breathy voice, "Will do, *Delicious Daniels*."

Before he could comment on *that* nickname, she'd hung up.

CHAPTER 10

March

SHELLY SAW HER the minute she stepped into the cafeteria.

Lena was seated at their usual table in the far back to the left. Shelly went through the line, grabbing a bottle of water and a ham sandwich, then made her way over to her friend. With a smug smile, Lena watched her approach, and instantly, Shelly knew Mason had spilled the beans.

Pulling out the empty chair, Shelly sat and raised a brow at her friend. "Okay. Go ahead."

Lena nodded. "So I guess you *used* the plumber after all?"

Rolling her eyes, Shelly asked, "How long did it take you to come up with that?"

"Not long. Around ten minutes."

"You're so original, I can barely stand it," Shelly told her with a smirk.

"Oh, don't even try with the snarky attitude. That's my department. Plus, you had to know Mason would tell me."

Shelly twisted the lid off the bottle. "And what exactly did your gossipy old man tell you?"

Lena grinned and took a bite of her sandwich. "That you and Josh had a deal."

"Man. Did Josh tell him everything?"

"Well, they are best friends. You tell *me* everything...well, you used to."

"Stop trying to make me feel guilty. It won't work."

Lena sat forward and whispered, "And why not? You made me tell *you* all the details. So come on, tell me. How amazing does he look naked?"

Shelly felt her eyes widen as she stared at her friend, who was waiting patiently with her reading glasses perched on the end of her nose, her lab coat falling open. Laughing, Shelly shook her head. "Mason's right about one thing."

"Oh, and what's that?"

Opening her sandwich, Shelly pulled it out and took a bite. "You and I act like we're in high school."

Sitting back, Lena crossed her legs. "Well, if that's true, then tell me about the boy you were kissing in the parking lot." She ended that mature comment by poking out her tongue.

Shelly grinned, ready to play the game. "Well, he's really cute."

"Josh? Cute? I don't think that's the right adjective," Lena interrupted.

"Yeah, you're right. He's really, *really* sexy. Oh boy," Shelly sighed, fanning herself. "He took me to heaven in less than seven minutes in that parking lot."

Lena's mouth fell open. "He did not." After looking around to make sure they weren't overheard, she leaned in closer to Shelly. "You did *not* have sex with him in the parking lot."

"Geez, Lena, what version of that game were *you* playing in high school?" Shelly asked, pretending to be scandalized.

Lena arched a brow, shaking her head. "You're hilarious. Don't try to distract me. Answer the question."

"What was the question again?"

Lena pouted. "I said"—she sighed with frustration—"you did *not* have sex with him in the parking lot."

"So is that a statement or a question?" Shelly asked, raising a brow.

"It was a question. Answer it please."

Finishing off one side of her sandwich, Shelly nodded. "No, I didn't have sex in a parking lot, but he sure did make me happy. In fact, I'm going to go out on a limb and say that he gave me the best orgasm I've ever had—*and* it was in a parking lot."

Lena blinked once, twice, then let out a deep breath as she sat back in her chair with an annoying grin. "You are so screwed."

"Why?"

"Because I've never seen that look on your face."

Shelly thought about her conversation with Josh last night then nodded. "Yeah, you're probably right."

Lena continued to smile like a cat that had gotten into the cream. "I told you so."

"Yeah? Well, you have either made me the happiest person in the world, or I may still kill you for it. I'll let you know after this weekend," Shelly told her with a small smile.

"Why? What's this weekend? Is he taking you on a date?"

Shelly stood, picking up the other half of her sandwich and her bottle of water. She pushed her chair in and shook her head. "Nope, I'm taking him home to visit Mom and Dad. We're going on a road trip."

Lena looked at her with a frown.

"What?" Shelly asked.

"I'm trying to keep up. It was only two weeks ago you told me you would never date him. Why the sudden change?"

Shelly thought about it for a minute. *Why am I suddenly having a change of heart?* She was throwing all of her rules out the window for this man. Maybe it was because he was a friend of Mason's, so she figured he would be a good guy. She had no idea. All she knew was that she was giving Joshua a chance. *What can it hurt? It's just a weekend. Right?*

Looking at Lena, Shelly shrugged. "I'm not sure. I guess somewhere between *my* orgasm in the parking lot and *his* orgasm in my office, he convinced me to give it a shot. Have a good afternoon, Dr. O'Donnell."

With a smug grin and a perky wave, Shelly turned and walked away, leaving a shocked but silent Lena staring after her.

∼

JOSH ARRIVED AT the worksite and let himself in when his

phone rang. Pulling out the phone, he saw Cole's name on the screen. "Daniels here."

"Hello, Joshua. How are you this morning?"

Stepping over a toolbox, he moved toward the makeshift table he'd put up. "Good, man, good. What's up?"

"Well, Harris called this morning. He said he's going to come in and sign the papers on Friday. Will that work? Can you be here?"

Wincing, Josh stopped and ran a hand through his hair. *Of course it had to be Friday.* "I can't do Friday. I'm going out of town. Won't be back until Monday morning."

He heard some rustling on the other end of the phone.

"Hang on, I'm checking my calendar," Cole told him.

Josh waved to Vince as he walked in for the morning. Three other guys—Alex, Gary, and Chris—followed, looking at Josh and nodding. Acknowledging them, he smiled then turned his attention back to the phone.

"How about Tuesday then?" Cole asked.

"Yep, I can do that. Time?"

"Ten thirty looks good. If it changes, I'll let you know." Cole paused then asked, "Where are you going this weekend?"

Josh smiled, thinking about the road trip ahead. "Savannah, Georgia."

Cole chuckled. "Business or pleasure?"

Oh, definitely pleasure. "Pleasure. I'm going with that woman we were talking about the other night."

"Really?" Cole asked. "So you worked things out with her?"

Josh laughed then shook his head, even though Cole couldn't see him. "Not really. We kind of got caught before things got started. Then she was going to nix the whole idea, but in the end, we decided to go on a road trip. That's a good way to get to know each other, right? Eleven hours in a car with a dog?"

Cole laughed. "Either that, or you'll kill each other. Why Georgia?"

Josh leaned against the table. "She's going home to see family."

"And you're going with her?" Cole asked in a tone that implied Josh was out of his mind. "I thought you two were just starting, and it wasn't even a dating thing."

Sighing, Josh ran a hand through his hair. "Yeah, well, the deal changed. I think I'm going as a buffer, but she wants me to go with her, so I thought why the hell not."

"Hmm, the deal changed how?" Cole asked in that cool, serious tone he usually reserved for business.

Josh thought of the sexy doctor. "The deal changed in the fact that she asked, and there was no way in hell I was going to say no."

"Oh shit," Cole muttered.

"Oh shit indeed. I'll see you Tuesday at ten thirty. If the time needs to be changed, let me know."

"Will do, Josh. Have fun down south."

Chuckling, Josh asked, "Was that a sex joke? From you?"

Josh could have sworn he could see the lawyer's eyes rolling.

"I'll have you know I can tell a sex joke just like the next guy."

"Sure, you can, man. You just choose to be mysterious. Is that it?" Josh laughed.

"That's exactly it. See you Tuesday, Joshua."

"See you Tuesday," he replied before he ended the call.

THURSDAY NIGHT TURNED up much more quickly than Shelly had anticipated. She was in the process of packing her bag when her phone beeped. Leaning over, she saw DD on the display and opened the message.

DD: Don't pack much.

Smiling, Shelly texted back. **Why?**

Throwing the phone on the bed, she moved to the closet and pulled out her cowgirl boots, grinning. She had a good feeling about this trip. Maybe not so much about the eleven-hour car ride, but she was looking forward to spending time with Josh. She found she was a lot more excited than she had thought she would be. Walking back to the bed, she placed the boots in her suitcase and looked at the phone.

DD: You only need enough clothes for meals with your parents. Around me — nothing.

Shelly turned, resting her butt against the bed. She closed her eyes for a moment, picturing Josh. *Hot damn. The guy pushes my buttons.* She couldn't wait to get her hands on his naked body.

Licking her lips, she wrote back. **We're staying at my parents' house. You plan to have me naked under my father's roof?**

There, take that. She grinned wickedly.

Moving to her chest of drawers, she opened it and looked at her panties. *Hmm...* Picking out the sexiest items she owned, she threw them in the bag. The phone vibrated.

DD: I plan to have you naked under me. If that happens to be in your father's house, then so be it.

Giggling, Shelly called Josh's number.

He answered immediately. "I mean it, Shelly."

"Is that right? But then you'd miss seeing all the pretty panties I just packed." She took great delight in the soft groan she heard from the other end.

"What color are they?"

"My panties?"

"Yes, Shelly, your panties that you just packed. What color are they?"

Looking into the bag, she answered, "Black, white, hot pink."

"Bikini or thong?"

"Why?" she asked, picking up the black lace thong that had a pearl in the middle of the waistband.

"Because I'm picturing the color disappearing between your perfect pale ass cheeks, and if they're bikinis, I need to change the fantasy."

Holding back her moan, Shelly dropped the panties. "How do you know my behind is pale? You haven't seen it. And don't change your fantasy. You're spot-on."

When he groaned louder this time, she could have sworn she felt it rumble through the phone.

"I'm picturing it in HD as we speak—your deliciously round ass with a sexy strip of lace running down the middle."

Shelly laughed. "Oh yeah? And what am I doing? Just standing with my back to you?"

"No, you're turned away from me, and my finger is pulling that little strip of lace out of the way as you ride my cock like a cowgirl in reverse, Georgia."

Georgia? Shelly smirked. Now *that* was a new nickname. She closed her eyes and bit her lip. *God, he was so damn sexy.*

The man had her thighs clenching and her palms sweating. "Is that right, cowboy?"

"Oh fuck yeah. Shelly?"

She was breathing a little faster than usual when she answered. "Yes?"

"I'm loving this new deal, and I can't wait to get inside you. Now, text me your address. We have an early start tomorrow." With that, he hung up.

Shelly stared at her phone and shook her head. She had a feeling that this man-eater had met her match in Joshua Daniels.

∽

ON FRIDAY MORNING, Josh pulled up at the valet of Shelly's apartment at 3:55 a.m. It was dark, and the air was cool. As he sat in the cab of his truck, he found he didn't care that it was so early because he couldn't wait to see the doctor. He texted her to let her know he was there then waited. He watched the lobby for her and grinned as the doors opened.

Shelly came out wearing a tight white T-shirt with a loose-fitting black cardigan and jeans. As she made her way down the path with a bag, he had to admit that the woman was stunning. Her blond hair was down and spilling over her shoulders. Although she wasn't wearing anything flashy, he found this version of her much more appealing on so many levels.

As she reached the curb, Mutley sat up behind him, putting his big head out the window. Josh watched as Shelly froze, looking at the dog with eyes so big, Josh thought they might pop out of her head.

"What is *that*?" she asked from where she had stopped.

Josh had to smile. Her adorable nose, which was usually tipped in the air, was scrunched in a look of disgust. "Mutley, my dog."

Her eyes went from him to the window behind him, where Mutley still sat panting. "I am *not* getting in the car with *that*."

Josh laughed and climbed out of the truck before stopping just inches away from her. "Yes, you are."

Shaking her head, she looked around his shoulder then turned her eyes back to him. "No, I'm not. He's huge."

Josh grinned and reached out, giving in to the urge to touch her hair. He picked up the ends of it, running his fingers through it. "He's harmless."

She narrowed her eyes at him. "Like his owner?"

Josh shook his head and lowered it until his lips were brushing against hers. "Oh, no, he's harmless. *I'm* not."

With that, he kissed her.

SHELLY FORGOT ALL about the gigantic dog in the back of Josh's truck as he pressed his hot lips to hers. Not even thinking twice, she opened her lips and felt his tongue slide deep inside to rub against her own. She moaned as she gripped his leather jacket, feeling his muscular arms underneath. She heard him grunt softly, then he wrapped his arms around her waist, pulling her flush against his jeans.

Oh yeah, Shelly thought as his lips shifted and the kiss took a deeper dive toward hot, steamy sex. She felt his tongue trace over her teeth and come back to slide over her lips. He moved his head back, and she moaned at the loss of his mouth as he looked down at her.

"Where's your suitcase?"

Shelly looked into his deep-brown eyes. "Huh?"

He chuckled and brought one of his hands up to cup under her chin. "Your suitcase, Shelly. Where is it? If we don't hit the road, we'll never get there."

That shook her out of her lust-clouded haze. "I'm not getting in there with him."

Josh moved around her and walked toward the lobby, yelling over his shoulder, "Yes, you are."

"No, I'm not," she called back, staring at the huge animal that was looking at her intently.

"You got your keys and purse?" Josh asked.

Shelly nodded and patted the bag on her arm. She heard him moving closer, then he rolled the suitcase past her. She took her eyes off the beast for a minute to watch Josh as he moved to the back of his truck.

Shelly watched Josh's biceps bunch and flex as he picked up the suitcase and threw it into the bed of the truck. *Okay, so the suits I usually date don't have the muscle and brawn to—oh my.* Sheer animal magnetism and sexy-as-hell muscles *definitely* weren't things a suit usually had. Shelly wanted to lick him.

"Come on," he told her as he walked around the truck, opening the passenger door.

Shaking her head again, she could see him looking at her through both windows as he leaned his arms on the frame, the truck now separating them. Her eyes drifted back to the huge dog that was now eyeing her with a raised brow.

Oh, so the dog has attitude too? Forget that. Shelly crossed her arms.

"Get in the truck, Shelly."

"No."

Grinning at her, Josh warned, "*Georgia*, get in the truck."

She felt a grin tug on her lips, deciding she *really* liked that nickname on his lips. "I'm not getting in the car with *that*." She pointed at the dog that had now placed his head down so it was resting on the open window.

"Mutley's harmless. You're hurting his feelings."

Ha. The beast wants to eat me. Okay, so maybe not eat me, but definitely slobber on me.

"One more chance, Georgia."

Shelly crossed her arms. "And then what happens? You leave?"

He straightened up on the other side of the truck, then he walked back around the front, making his way over to her. His face was dead serious, not a smile in sight.

Oh shit, maybe this isn't such a good idea. She'd never seen him upset.

When he reached her, he didn't stop walking. He just hauled her up and over his shoulder in a fireman's carry as though she didn't weigh a thing.

~

JOSH GRINNED WHEN he heard Shelly shriek as he tossed her over his shoulder. Pivoting, he carried her down the path as she pummeled his back.

"Are you insane? Put me down right now, Joshua Daniels."

He chuckled and continued around the truck. When he got to the passenger side, he slowly lowered her and stepped in close, giving her no option other than to step back with her butt against the passenger seat.

"Now, get in the car, before I strip off your clothes and take you in the front seat of my truck in front of all your nosy neighbors."

She closed her mouth then looked around as though to make sure no one was outside. "Maybe I'd like that."

Josh grinned at her and leaned in, resting his arms on the roof of the truck. Trapping her between the seat and his body, he rubbed himself up nice and close against her. "Oh, Georgia, I'd make sure you loved it. But do you really want Mutley to watch? His poor sensibilities might get hurt. Plus, we need to get going."

Josh watched her look over her shoulder, and Mutley gave her a goofy doggy smile and whined.

"Oh, fine. But he better not come near me," she said, giving up as she climbed into the truck.

Josh closed the door with a huge smile. *Yes, ma'am.*

He sure did like this Southern girl he'd met this morning, and he wanted to get to know her a *whole* lot better.

CHAPTER 11

*A*ROUND FIVE HOURS into the trip, Shelly was getting antsy. She started to understand why people took planes or, more importantly, why *she* took planes.

This trip was just too damn long. If you included the fact that a ninety-pound hairball was sitting behind her and giving her the evil eye, then you not only had a long trip, you had a long trip from hell.

The whole way out of Chicago, Shelly had bitched about the hairy dog in the truck until Josh told her that if she mentioned the dog once more, he'd move him into the front seat. *That* had shut her up real quick.

They'd stopped for coffee and a quick breakfast at a fast food joint and had been driving straight through with no breaks since.

On the plus side, she'd had plenty of time to study Delicious Daniels.

He'd put on a pair of black aviator glasses after the sun had made an appearance. His arm rested by the window as they drove while his other hand lightly gripped the top of the steering wheel, giving her a lovely view of those strong, thick biceps of his.

He'd removed his jacket once they had gotten in the truck, and his black shirt molded like a second skin to all of his bulging muscles. As she ran her eyes down to the jeans he seemed to live in, she had to catch herself from licking her lips. They cupped him like a lover's hand, then wrapped tightly around his thighs.

Unconsciously letting out a small groan, Shelly was mortified when he turned and caught her staring. She quickly brought her gaze up to his. Deciding *what the heck*, she gave him a flirty smile and a raised eyebrow. "Keep your eyes on the road, Josh."

He gave her a smug grin then turned back, facing the long stretch of road ahead of them.

So far, they had discussed everything from how he'd met Mason—which was in grade school—to when she had met Lena—which, of course, had been when they had started working at University Hospital.

She now knew he had one brother, Jeremy, who lived in Chicago, and their parents had retired to Florida. He now knew that she'd grown up in Savannah, Georgia, and was an only child.

When they had exhausted all the getting-to-know-each-other talk, he'd told her to relax and maybe try to sleep, but she had known that would be impossible with the dog slobbering on her. Instead, she had rested against the window, watching the scenery pass by. But now she was getting antsy and needed a pick-me-up.

Reaching into her bag, she pulled out her iPod and the car jack and moved to plug it in.

Josh looked at her. "And what do you think you're doing, Georgia?"

"We need some music," Shelly told him, getting it hooked up.

"We had music," he pointed out as his huge dog decided to take that opportunity to move forward and rest his head against Josh's seat.

He's eyeing me, Shelly thought with a shudder. He definitely wanted to eat her, and she knew it.

"What?" she asked the dog as though he would actually answer her.

"He just wants to know what you're about to force us to listen to."

Rolling her eyes, Shelly gave him a mischievous grin, and he shook his head.

"I don't like that look."

"What look?" she asked innocently.

"*That* one. The one that says you're about to subject me to something I'm not going to like."

Shelly laughed, making sure she had the volume up good and loud, then hit Play. As the music blared through the speakers, she took great delight in Josh's pained expression.

He whipped his head around to face her. "No."

"Yes," Shelly told him over the loud beat of the music.

"No way, Georgia," he told her, trying to grab the iPod. She pulled it out of his reach and hit Pause. The music stopped. "You need to concentrate on the road."

Rolling his eyes, he asked, "How am I supposed to concentrate with that noise playing?"

Shelly laughed again. "I told you *no* about *that*." She pointed at the beast, who took that moment to cock his head and raise an eyebrow. "Oh, don't act sweet and innocent with me," she said to the hairball.

"Are you talking to my dog? You do know he can't understand you, right?"

Shelly harrumphed. "Well, it was worth a shot." She grinned. "Now, shhh. I'm enjoying—"

"I'm not listening to Shania Twain, Georgia."

Shelly leaned her head back against the seat, singing to him with a sexy smile. "But, Josh, I feel like a woman."

∽

JOSH SHOOK HIS head at the woman beside him, singing loudly the ode to all females. He couldn't believe he was actually sitting here, listening to this song, and smiling.

Shelly had rolled up her jeans to mid-calf and slipped off her shoes, resting her sock-covered feet on the dashboard. She was tapping her foot and smiling as she sang about wearing men's shirts and short skirts.

Looking at her, he thought, *This is honestly the first time those lyrics have ever been appealing.*

Her face was lit up with pure joy, and every time she hit that ridiculous chorus, she sang the lyrics at the top of her lungs.

The woman is insane. And he liked her—a lot. All she needed was a cowgirl hat, a pair of boots, and some Daisy Dukes, and she would be one of his sexiest fantasies come to life.

She continued singing about the best parts of being a woman, and Josh found himself smiling and—*holy shit*—tapping his hand on the steering wheel.

When she got to the main line of the song, she looked him over and winked. "Damn, Josh, you make *me* feel like a woman."

Oh shit. He wanted to kiss her. He wanted to grab her, pull her over his lap, and kiss that sassy smile right off her smirking lips—but he was on a damn highway and needed to concentrate.

The song ended, and he was relieved when it changed to The Who singing the anthem to Woodstock and stoned teenagers. *"Baba O'Riley"—classic.*

"When we stop, I want you to play that song again," he said.

"I thought you didn't like that song."

He looked her over, letting out a deep breath. "Suddenly, I've had a change of heart."

"Is that right?"

"Yeah, it is. I want it to be playing while I have my hands all over you."

Shelly laughed. "So you can make me feel like a woman?"

"Hmm," he answered, watching the road.

Before he knew it, she was right up beside him, sliding her hand along his thigh. He whipped his head around, and their eyes met.

"Careful, I need to concentrate."

"So concentrate. I just need to touch you for a minute," she told him while continuing to stroke his thigh.

Josh let out a ragged groan, moving his arm away from the window to grip the steering wheel with both hands.

"You don't even need to touch me to make me feel like a woman. I'm finding if I just sit and think about you—or even better, if I sit here and look at you—I have absolutely no problem feeling like a woman." She slid that hot little hand over his leg toward the inseam of his jeans, stopping mid-thigh.

He sucked in a deep breath.

"I can't wait to get you naked. Hot, naked, and mine. Mmm, I can't wait," she whispered.

Josh took a chance and looked sideways at her. She was so close that he could see her pupils had dilated, and he knew she was as aroused as he was. His cock was so hard that he was surprised it hadn't busted through his jeans. She hadn't even touched him *there*, and he was ready to go off like a rocket.

"Move your hand," he managed, trying to keep his attention on the road despite her torture.

Her eyes sparked with mischief, and she moved her hand up his leg toward his throbbing hardness.

"Not there," he told her through clenched teeth. "Move your hand away from me, or we're going to have an accident."

She grinned and squeezed his thigh while she leaned up to put her mouth next to his ear. "Find a motel."

Josh felt every muscle in his body clench, but he looked at her and shook his head.

She pouted, squeezing his thigh again. "Why not?"

Josh licked his lips. "If we stop, we won't ever leave. Have mercy, Georgia. Take your hand off of me before I explode, and move back to your side of the truck before I go insane."

Josh groaned as she kissed his cheek and brushed her palm against his erection. Then she moved back to her side of the truck. He looked over at where she was sitting, staring at him with hot eyes and a strained smile.

"I hate that you're right," she said.

He replied softly, "Believe me, so do I."

∾

SHELLY WAS SO FRUSTRATED.

She was so hot and bothered that she was tempted to undo her jeans and stick her hands inside to take care of her own ache. But as she looked at the beautifully tense and stiff man navigating the truck's steering wheel, she knew that waiting would bring its own reward.

She couldn't believe how turned on he had gotten her, yet he hadn't done anything but drive and say a few words. The man was potent and so hot that he set her on fire by just looking at her. *Forget that. He set me on fire by just breathing.*

His dog was now lying down across the back seat, and Shelly took a chance by looking at him. He raised his head, and his mouth fell open. She could have sworn he was smiling at her. She felt her heart squeeze a little, and she couldn't help but smile back.

"Stop flirting with my dog."

Shelly's eyes moved to Josh. "I'm not flirting with your dog. I don't even like him."

She could have sworn the dog understood because he whined, and she immediately felt guilty.

Josh took that moment to look in his rearview mirror. "Don't worry. She said that about me too."

Rolling her eyes, she slumped down in the seat. "Do you want me to drive for a little bit?"

"My truck?"

"No, your Lamborghini. Of course the truck."

Josh shook his head. "Ahh, no, it's fine. I'm going to pull over for lunch in a few minutes, then we'll go the rest of the way."

Shelly nodded and watched out the window until she saw a motel. She glanced at Josh longingly.

He shook his head. "No."

Sighing, Shelly capitulated. "Fine. Food it is."

She was no less frustrated when he laughed and pulled off the highway to get some food.

~

SIX LONG HOURS LATER, Josh was navigating through downtown Savannah, admiring how beautiful it was. It was just going on six thirty, and there was a light breeze in the air. They'd made good time. As they rolled down the main street, Josh couldn't help the smile that was stretching across his face.

Shelly had told him that she wanted to take him down through the Savannah Squares. At first, he didn't have any idea what she had been talking about, but as they turned onto Charlton Street, it became obvious.

Every couple of streets, he noticed a park was located in the center of them. The first one they passed was Pulaski Square, then they drove by Madison Square. As they were approaching the third park, Lafayette Square, Shelly pointed and told him to pull over.

He parked the truck and watched her get out, stretching her hands above her head. She looked around with a soft smile as the wind whipped through her blond hair. He found himself mesmerized not by her sexiness that usually took aim at him like a fully loaded weapon, but by her simple beauty as she stood on the outskirts of the park with the wind blowing around her.

Josh opened the truck door and stepped down, letting Mutley out. He grabbed a leash, hooked it to his dog's collar, and came around to stand beside the woman who seemed to have morphed into a stranger. She had transformed into a different version of herself, and he had to admit that he liked this version.

"These parks are amazing," Josh said, stopping beside her.

Shelly turned and smiled at him. The sudden tightening in his chest from her radiant look shocked him.

"I know. This is one part of my hometown that I absolutely adore." She looked at Mutley, who sat beside him, and raised a brow. "The mutt has to come?"

Josh chuckled, shaking his head. "Well, yeah, he's been cooped up as well, and this is a park. Kind of his thing." He winked.

"Fine," she sighed. Then she shocked him by holding out her hand.

Josh took it, feeling her warm palm slip into his. She squeezed his fingers, and they made their way down the path into the lush green park.

~

SHELLY FELT RELAXED as she walked with Josh and the beast through her favorite square.

As of 2012, twenty-two squares were littered throughout Savannah. As a young girl, her father had often taken her to Lafayette Square, where they had walked for hours, sometimes taking a break to eat ice cream. On each occasion, he had brought her to this fountain and they had thrown in pennies, making wishes together.

Shelly stopped by the large water feature and looked at Josh, who was looking around as the sun started to set. The lights in the fountain and on the path started to blink on, and suddenly, the moment turned romantic. That wasn't something Shelly had anticipated.

Josh looked at her with a gentle and warm expression. She'd never seen that look on him before.

"Who *are* you?" he asked as he stepped closer, letting the leash go slack as his dog lay down on the ground.

Shelly fidgeted with her hands, feeling nervous, which was *very* unlike her. "I don't understand. What do you mean?"

He stopped when he was a breath away from her before running a finger down her cheek. "Back in Chicago, you're this sex goddess, incredibly hot but intimidating as hell—"

"I didn't intimidate you."

"Oh, yes, you did. Man-Eater Monroe—the kind of woman who would eat you up in one bite. I wasn't going to touch you because I knew you'd burn me or rip me apart."

Shelly licked her lips, hypnotized by this man and his words. All of a sudden, Shelly didn't give two hoots what he did or didn't do for a living. She wanted Joshua Daniels. The biggest shock, however, was that she wanted to keep him. For how long, she wasn't sure, but she wasn't ready to let him go.

"And here in Savannah?" Shelly asked, wanting to know what he was getting at.

"Here"—he took that final step to close the distance between them—"here, you're different. You're relaxed and casual, still incredibly sexy but in a much more approachable way. This Shelly—*Georgia Shelly*—she's the girl next door wrapped up in subtle sex. *Man-Eater Monroe's* the ball-busting doctor who oozes blatant, sizzling hot sex." He leaned down to whisper across her lips. "So, who are you, Shelly?"

Shelly blinked and locked eyes with him. "Both."

His lips moved against hers into a smile before he nipped her bottom lip. "I was hoping you'd say that."

Then he gave her the sweetest, hottest kiss she had ever received.

JOSH WASN'T SURE when or how it had happened, but as he stood in possibly the most romantic place he'd ever been, he felt his heart beat faster as he gave himself permission to care.

This complex woman, now standing glued to his front as her lips molded to his, was creeping inside him.

Nowhere in sight was the Shelly he'd first met back at Exquisite. The woman he'd exploded with in the parking lot—not to mention the hot-as-hell doctor who had given him a thorough once-over in her office—had been replaced by this sweet, wholesome woman who was kissing him as if they were on a high school date.

Josh changed the angle of his head and wrapped his free hand around her waist, pulling her in a little bit closer. He felt her soft moan and slid his tongue inside her mouth to rub against her own. Her hands came up, grasping behind his neck, and he felt her fingers spread out, pushing up into his hair. She gripped it and tugged gently until he raised his head, his eyes locking with her beautiful blue ones.

"I like your hair like this," she told him as she lightly dragged her fingers through it again.

"Long? I forget to get it cut, so it just keeps growing."

She smiled, still running her fingers through it. "I like it. Very badboyish."

Josh couldn't help but snort and chuckle at that. "Bad boy? Is that how you see me?"

She moved her eyes to his mouth then back up to meet his gaze, pulling again at the end of his hair. "I was kind of hoping."

"Oh yeah?"

She let out a breath across his mouth, and he smelled that intoxicating apple scent on her. Leaning in, he put his nose to her hair. *Ahh, it's her shampoo.*

"Apples," he whispered.

"Huh?" she asked in a daze.

"You smell like apples."

She grinned. "It's my shampoo."

Josh nodded then backtracked their conversation. "Why do you think I'm bad?"

Her fingers traced down his neck before coming around so her palms were flat on his chest. She squeezed a little then raised an eyebrow at him. "You gave me an orgasm in a parking lot. You think a good boy would do that?"

A smirk tugged at the corner of his mouth as he traced her arched brow with his fingertip. "Well, you gave me a spectacular orgasm in your office. Do you think a good girl would do that?"

That familiar sexy smile appeared on her lips. Her eyelids lowered so she was looking up at him from beneath her lashes. "I never said I was good."

"Neither did I," he replied, tracing her lips with the same finger that had just been against her brow. "I asked you why you think I'm bad."

She let out a deep breath then whispered, "Because no one good could make me want to be so very bad."

Josh felt his whole body stiffen, and he removed his finger from her face. Stepping back, he reminded himself that he needed to watch it. Man-Eater Monroe was still there, lurking beneath the surface. He needed to keep his wits about him and not get fooled by *Georgia*.

She was a lethal combination.

"Touché, *Georgia*. Now we better hurry if we want to make it to your parents' house by seven, like we told them."

She blinked then nod, seemingly shaking herself out of a daze, then she turned to walk away. Before she got too far, he called her name. She stopped and turned around.

"Why this park and not the others?" he asked.

She looked at the huge church behind them, then she turned back to him. "My father used to bring me here when I was a little girl. We'd always end up at the fountain. He chose this park because I was baptized in that church over there, St. John the Baptist. We would always come here and make a wish before tossing in a penny." She took a deep breath. "I just wanted to remind myself of that before I see him tonight. When you meet him, you'll understand why." Then she turned, walking back through the park.

Mutley stood and looked at him while Josh pulled a penny out of his pocket.

Staring at the huge cathedral that was lit up and peeking out above the trees, Josh was pretty sure he'd never seen anything so spectacular. He thought about what Shelly had told him and wondered what he was going to witness this weekend. Before he turned away, he brought the penny to his mouth, closed his eyes, and made a wish. Then he kissed the penny and tossed it into the fountain.

CHAPTER 12

AS JOSH TURNED the truck onto a small pebbled lane, all he saw was darkness. "Are you sure you haven't forgotten how to get there?"

"Funny. It's just up here around the bend."

The truck crawled along, bumping and swaying over a couple of potholes. As it made the final bend in the road, Josh's mouth dropped open.

Right in front of him, like something out of *Gone with the Wind*, was a driveway lined by huge oak trees draped in Spanish moss. They were stunning all on their own, but with the six light posts on both sides of the driveway illuminating them, they were absolutely spectacular. As Josh turned into the drive, he saw a huge white plantation-style mansion at the end of the road.

He abruptly stopped the truck and turned to the woman beside him. "This is your house?"

She gave him a lopsided grin and nodded. "Yep. This is home."

Josh turned back to the opulence in front of him, suddenly extremely intimidated. "That is not a home, Georgia. That's a damn mansion."

She chuckled. "Try not to be too impressed when we get there. My father loves to gloat."

Josh could understand why. He looked down at his thirteen-hour-worn shirt and jeans, then back at Shelly. "Maybe we should go somewhere and change."

She looked him over quickly and raised her eyebrows. "If we go somewhere and you take your clothes off, I'm not going to leave until you've been inside me."

Josh felt himself harden, and his eyes widened. "We are right outside your family's house. I don't think now is the time to be acting that way."

She laughed—hard.

"What?" he demanded, knowing her laughter was at his expense.

"You." She giggled. "You're so proper all of a sudden. It's just a house."

"Georgia, that is not a house. My place back in Chicago is *just* a house."

She bit her lip, probably to keep from laughing. "Well, I wouldn't know. I haven't seen your house."

He grunted. "Well, maybe you can visit when we get back."

She moved across the truck, putting her hands on the middle seat to lean up to him. Josh looked down at her.

She whispered, "I have another deal for you."

Josh shook his head and felt as if this woman was weaving her hot Southern magic around him again. "Oh yeah? And what's that?" he asked like the stupid, lust-hazed fool he was.

"I don't have to go back to work until Wednesday. So when we get back in town, if you show me your house on Tuesday morning, I promise not to put on a stitch of clothing until I need to head home on Tuesday night at ten."

Josh looked at the woman seducing him with her words, instantly deciding he could call Cole and postpone their meeting. "You're trouble."

She flicked her tongue across his bottom lip. "And you love it." Sitting back up, she said, "Let's get this show on the road. I suddenly want it to be Tuesday."

∽

SHELLY TOOK A deep breath as the truck made its way up the

long driveway. Josh was right. This place was a *mansion*, and she knew it was extremely impressive whenever people saw it for the first time.

She had loved growing up here.

It was a cool night, but nowhere near cold when compared to Chicago. A lovely breeze was blowing through the majestic trees draped with moss. The leaves and branches danced with the wind, giving off an almost eerie but beautiful quality. The main house was a throwback to the days of the plantations. It was massive and had four white columns at the front, supporting a balcony on the second level and a huge roof.

It was remarkable and enormous. That was what mattered to her father. *Other* people were impressed.

Sighing as Josh pulled the truck to a stop, Shelly flipped down the visor and looked in the mirror. She was a mess, but there was nothing she could do about that. Running a hand through her hair, she opened the passenger door.

Her mother appeared on the porch. "Well, I'll be damned. You made it here on time."

Shelly smiled and moved up the stairs to hug her tightly. "Of course, Ma, we told you seven."

"Oh, I know, I know. I just thought the traffic might hold y'all up a bit." Her mother's charming Southern accent wrapped around Shelly like a warm embrace.

Her mother made a move, looking at the man and dog behind Shelly. Shelly turned to stand beside her so she could also look at the pair. They looked disheveled and tired, but all in all, Shelly thought they made a fine team—even though one was a hairy beast.

"And who do we have here?" her mother asked, walking down the stairs.

Shelly had always thought of her mother as a tiny powerhouse. The only problem was that she had never been strong enough against the steel force that resided in this house—her father.

"Ma, I'd like you to meet Josh Daniels and his dog, Mutley."

Josh raised an eyebrow when she finally referred to the dog as a dog. He stepped forward and took her mother's hand. "Please excuse me, ma'am. We've been traveling for nearly thirteen hours now, and I'm not as clean as I'd like to be."

"Oh, please. Don't you worry yourself 'bout that. You look mighty fine to me."

"Ma."

"Well, it's true. Fine young man you have here, Shel."

Shelly groaned, moving down the stairs to the grinning Josh. "Yes, well, this fine young man is going to grab his suitcase, and I'll grab mine. We'll be inside in a minute."

Her mother turned and walked back up the stairs. "I don't know why you insist on talking like you ain't from the South."

Josh chuckled, and she turned to glare at him before giving up and grinning.

She asked in the sweetest, most Southern accent she could muster up, "Hey, Ma? Where's Father tonight? I thought for sure he'd be out here to greet us at the door."

Josh sucked in a deep breath, and she knew he was reacting to her accent. *Sucker.*

"He'll be here, sweetheart. Don't you worry yourself. He wouldn't miss y'all for the world," she replied before walking inside.

Shelly turned and leaned up against the truck. "Well?"

"Well what?" Josh asked as he lifted out the first bag.

"I know you're dying to say something to me, cowboy," Shelly said, still putting on the thick country accent.

"Hmm. All I'm going to say to you is the next time we're all alone and you're wrapped around me... I want you to talk just like that."

"Why?" she teased in her Southern twang as she sidled up closer and wrapped her arms around his waist. Tipping her head back, she bumped her hips against his. "Oh, I see. You like the way I talk all country. Is that right, *Joshuahh?*"

He took her face between his hands. "Yeah, I like this country girl."

"Well, good, cowboy, 'cause she likes you too."

She went up on her tiptoes and was about to kiss him when another truck drove up the driveway. Letting go of him, Shelly stepped back, glancing at Josh with a tight smile.

She dropped the accent altogether and straightened her spine. "Good thing you didn't have your lips on me. My father would have shot you on sight."

With that comment, she walked around the truck to greet her father.

∼

AS SHELLY MADE her way over to the truck that had pulled up, he leaned against the side of his own truck with his arms crossed, watching the man getting out of the Ford F-150. He was tall and blond, instantly reminding Josh of Robert Redford. The guy was good-looking, and Josh could see where Shelly had inherited her fair skin and blue eyes.

When the man kissed her cheek, Shelly was still and stiff, losing that relaxed air she'd had only five minutes earlier.

Mutley took the opportunity to run around the truck, heading over to the stranger. Shelly's father bent down, his hand reaching out to ruffle over the dog's head. Mutley, of course, licked his hand and wagged his tail. With a smile, Josh noticed Shelly discreetly step away from the dog, still not quite comfortable with him.

Josh found himself grinning until her father stood and turned to look at him. As their eyes locked, Josh felt the other man assess him straight away. Shrewd eyes took in the truck first, then they moved back to him, looking over the T-shirt and jeans, then he turned back to the dog and his daughter.

Josh was left wondering if he had passed or failed. *Well, I'm about to find out.* With a pinched expression, the man made his way over to Josh, the dog trotting along one side and Shelly on the other.

Stopping when they reached Josh, her father held out his hand. "Hello. I'm Dr. Lawrence Monroe."

Oh shit. Josh looked at Shelly. *Her father is a doctor too?* He wondered if that had anything to do with the cool relationship between the two of them.

Josh took his hand in a firm clasp and shook it. He had to look up at the man and found himself caught in a kind of stare down.

Josh had promised himself he wouldn't be intimidated. After all, he was successful and owned his own company, not that Shelly knew that. Overall, he was a good guy. *A good guy who wants to sleep with this man's daughter. So?*

"Nice to meet you, sir. I'm Joshua Daniels."

Since when did I start calling people sir and ma'am? When I entered the South? Who knows?

"Yes, so my daughter was just tellin' me." He turned to look at Shelly, effectively dismissing him. "Dinner will be served at seven thirty."

Shelly nodded. "We'll be there."

He looked his daughter over again then turned back to Josh, looking him over too. "Cleaned up, I presume?"

"Of course," Shelly muttered.

Josh watched as her father walked up the stairs and into the house.

Shelly turned to face him, giving him a smile so painfully false, it almost looked as though it hurt her face. "And *that* is my father."

WITH JOSH'S HELP, Shelly had managed to get her things inside and upstairs to her bedroom. Then she'd directed him to the room across from hers. She had just finished washing up and was slipping into some cutoff jean shorts when there was a knock on the door. She tied her blue-and-white gingham shirt at the waist and opened the door to see a fresh-faced, cleaned-up Josh leaning against the frame.

He looked her up and down then moved back out into the corridor, glancing both ways. After pushing her into her room and following her, he shut the door and leaned back against it, pinning her with fiery eyes. She had finished tying her hair into a high but messy ponytail and hadn't put on any shoes yet.

"Whatcha doin', Josh?"

He reached down between his legs with one of his big hands and adjusted the hard-on that had obviously formed behind the faded denim. *And doesn't that just send a shiver of desire straight down between my thighs.*

"Just looking at you. I had this exact fantasy earlier today."

She licked her lips and moved closer to him. "Oh yeah? And what was the fantasy?"

He let his eyes travel down her legs, then they came back up to rest on her face. "You in a cowgirl hat, some Daisy Dukes, and cowboy boots."

Shelly laughed, placing a hand on his chest. "Well, one out of three ain't bad, sugah."

"When you talk like that, the other two don't even need to exist."

"Hmm," Shelly hummed in the back of her throat. "We've still got thirty or so before dinner."

"We do, don't we?" He pushed himself off the door, walking forward. He grasped the knot that rested over her navel.

With each step he took forward, Shelly took a step back. "And just what do you think we should do in those thirty or so minutes?"

"Well," he drawled, his eyes watching his fingers untying the knot. "I think we should start with this." He gripped the material and pulled it apart, the buttons popping from the shirt.

Shelly gasped, then a smile touched her lips as Josh gave her the most deliciously wicked grin she had ever seen. She was now standing in front of him in her ripped shirt, her breasts barely covered by a black demi-cup bra, and cutoff jean shorts. "And then what?"

"Then"—he stroked a fingertip down her chest, dipped it into her navel, and stopped at the top of her shorts—"I'll undo these."

Her heart starting to beat rapidly, Shelly gripped his hand.

His eyes came up to meet hers, and he asked, "No?"

Chuckling, Shelly shook her head and whispered, "I don't have a lock on my door."

He blinked, then what she was telling him seemed to sink in. He looked over his shoulder at the unlocked door then back to her. "You don't?"

Biting her bottom lip, Shelly gave him an impish grin and, with a fingertip, traced his shoulder. In the country voice she knew melted him, she drawled, "Nu-uh, sugah. Ma didn't trust me to have a lock on the door."

∼

JOSH FELT HIS mouth fall open after that comment. *Fuck, she is sexy.*

As she stood there with her ripped shirt and her sly little grin, Josh almost fell to his knees. He was debating if it was worth the risk to do what he wanted, knowing that the door was unlocked, when she took the choice out of his hands.

"I've always wanted a boy to kiss me in my bedroom."

Josh licked his lips, knowing he was up, *literally*, for that challenge. "No boy ever came up here?"

Shelly shook her head, and for some reason, that answer greatly pleased Josh. *How stupid is that?*

"Georgia, if *this* boy kisses you in your room, he's not going to stop," he warned her, touching her sexy lips with his finger.

True to form—well, true to the man-eater he knew—Shelly nipped his finger, once again shocking him to his boots. "I'd be disappointed if he did."

Groaning low, Josh made up his mind.

Slipping his fingers into her shorts, he unsnapped the buttons and parted the material. As her bare skin appeared, Josh sent up a prayer of thanks that he was the one standing here, about to lie down with Shelly Monroe.

He slid his hand into her jean shorts and panties, turning it so his palm was cupping her, and watched as her mouth parted on a sigh.

Her eyes were on his, and he couldn't help but smile as he whispered, "Shh, got to be quiet up here. Don't want anyone to come in and ruin the moment."

SHELLY WIDENED her legs a little to get Josh's hand deeper inside her Daisy Dukes. Closing her eyes, she wiggled closer and tried to slow her breathing as she felt his clever fingers slip between her wet lips.

"So tell me, Georgia, you think you can keep it down?"

Opening her eyes, Shelly looked into his sparkling ones. "I don't know. Willing to risk it?"

"Fuck yeah." With his free hand, he hauled her in close. He kept his other hand down her shorts while his mouth crashed down on hers, his tongue spearing into her mouth.

Shelly squirmed against his fingers as she wrapped her arms around his neck. Tilting her head, she moaned as he deepened the angle of the kiss, his tongue rubbing and stroking against her own.

"Josh," she begged. Then his hand left her pants. "No."

He chuckled as he put that hand under her ass, hitching her up into his arms. Shelly immediately wrapped her legs around his waist as he walked to the bed she had slept in her whole adolescent life. When he placed her on the edge of it, Shelly scooted across the comforter before lying back with her legs hanging off the side.

"So you really *are* going to have me under you—under my father's roof?"

Josh shook his head, reaching out to grip her shorts and panties. Biting his lip, he concentrated on tugging them off of her. "Let's not discuss that right now."

"Why not?" Shelly asked. After her shorts and panties were removed, she raised a foot to the edge of the bed, giving him an unobstructed view of how excited she was. "Do you feel guilty?"

∽

JOSH SURE AS shit did *not* feel guilty.

He felt horny, hungry, and ready to fucking explode.

She was lying across her bed with her shirt ripped apart, her sexy bra still in place, and nothing on from the waist down. As if that wasn't enough, she had raised her foot to rest on the edge of the mattress, and he could see her plump lips glistening for him.

"I don't feel guilty at all. I just don't want to talk about your father right now," he told her as he unsnapped his own jeans at a record pace.

"Well, I can understand that," she told him as though she wasn't lying there naked and open to him. "But you need to understand something."

Josh stepped out of his jeans and boxers then pulled his shirt over his head. He stopped, completely naked, and raised a brow. "What? What is it I need to understand, Georgia?"

∽

SHELLY COULDN'T REMEMBER.

She had been about to tell him something. But after he had lost the pants and stood back up, her eyes latched on to that amazing hard-on and all thoughts left her head.

She licked her lips then raised her eyes to his. "Huh?"

A sensual smile spread across his lips as he moved to the edge of the bed. He slid a long finger slowly through her wetness. Sucking in a deep breath, Shelly let her bent leg fall open.

"You don't have a shy bone in your sexy-as-sin body, do you, Shel?"

Keeping her eyes on his, she asked, "No. Should I?"

"No, you sure as hell shouldn't." He gripped the ankle of her bent leg. Tugging her down until her ass was at the edge of the bed, he kept hold of her ankle, pushing her leg back toward her body.

Holy fuck, the way he's looking over me—it's making me so goddamn hot. I'm surprised I haven't set the mattress on fire.

"Do I need to get something?" he asked, his eyes battling for where they should look.

His voice, so low and deep, felt as if it had vibrated right through her. Shelly tried to comprehend what he was asking, but she was coming up blank. She wanted him, and she wanted him *now*.

"Shel?" he asked with a little more force, tightening the grip on her ankle. "Do I need protection?"

"Oh," she sighed, shaking her head. She lowered her eyes and raised her hips. "I'm on birth control. So unless you think—"

"I'm not thinking much about anything but getting inside you. I'm safe. It's been months. You?"

"I'm good too." She sighed, her eyes moving down to his pulsating cock that was so close yet still so damn far away from her.

"Well, in that case—"

"In that case, discussion is over," she almost whined. A feral grin met those sexy lips of his, and she batted her eyelashes. "Please?"

He looked to the side and grabbed a pillow. Shelly felt even more moisture pool between her thighs, knowing exactly what he had planned.

"Lift up," he told her in a deep, gruff voice.

Raising her naked hips, she watched as Josh placed the pillow beneath her, making her the perfect height for his own. Reaching down his own body, he gripped that fantastically hard cock, and Shelly thought she might come from that alone.

He lifted his burning gaze from her aching body and moved closer, dragging his hot tip through her folds. "Now, Georgia?"

"Yes?" Shelly panted, feeling her body contract with each slow, delicious slide of him against her throbbing clit.

"Do you need something to scream into?"

Her eyebrows rose. "Scream, huh?"

Josh nodded, gripping her hips tightly as he thrust his cock so deep and hard inside her that she had a hard time keeping a scream from leaving her mouth. Instead, she bit her lip with so much force that she thought she might draw blood.

When he was buried to the hilt in her warmth, he stilled and looked down at her, trying to get a hold of his breathing. "So? Do you need something, Georgia?"

Feeling her breath coming fast and her body contracting from the thick intrusion of his body, Shelly lifted her legs to his hips and wrapped them around his ass. She then brought the end of her shirt to her mouth. "Do your best, rock star." And she clamped her teeth around the material.

∽

JOSH GRIPPED HER naked hips and hauled her tighter to his body, if that was possible. He felt as though his cock was encased in a warm fist. Although she was dripping wet, she was so tight that Josh thought he might have hurt her at first. But no, it was clear that Shelly was ready to enjoy the ride.

Rocking his hips a little, Josh closed his eyes and groaned.

"Do *you* need something to keep *you* quiet?" she asked.

Opening his eyes, he noticed Shelly had removed her shirt from her mouth and now had her hands busy, squeezing her bra-covered breasts.

"Pull it down," he instructed.

She immediately obeyed. He flexed his hips, and she moaned softly as she pinched her tight nipples.

"Make me scream, Josh."

Never one to disappoint a lady, Josh gripped her hips and ass and slowly pulled out of her snug body. Her eyes latched on to his, and her hips chased his as he thrust home.

"Fuck, Georgia," he said, starting to move his hips at a fast and steady clip.

He couldn't slow down. The climax was barreling down his spine, urging him toward completion. There wasn't a damn thing he could do about it.

Looking at the sexy woman below him, he watched one of her hands trail down her body to where his cock was sliding in and out, then she touched him. Her flirty little fingers stroked his wet cock with each pull and every thrust back in until his climax gripped him hard, and he gritted his teeth. Her body gripped his cock tightly while he heard her muffled scream, and he flew over the edge of sanity with her.

∽

LATER THAT NIGHT, as they sat around the dining room table, Josh wondered how he could have gone from feeling such bliss only an hour or so earlier to such extreme awkwardness.

Dinner was painful. He sat opposite Shelly while her mother and father sat on each end. At least, the food—roast beef and vegetables—was absolutely delicious. As the meal was winding down, Josh sensed a shift in the air. Now that the small talk was over, it seemed the real stuff was about to happen.

He just wasn't sure what the "real stuff" involved.

Josh had been right in his first opinion of Dr. Lawrence Monroe. He did look like the actor Robert Redford. He had sandy-blond hair that was a little longer than a classic clean cut, and his eyes were a piercing blue that seemed to slice right into you without a second thought. *Did I mention the man is tall?*

By the looks of him, he was strong, not at all fitting Josh's picture of a doctor. Usually doctors were wiry, lean, and intellectual. Not this guy—he looked like a tough quarterback.

"So, Joshua, what is it that you do?"

"Here we go," Shelly muttered as she picked up her glass of red wine.

"What? I'm just askin' the boy what he does for a livin'," her father told her matter-of-factly.

"He's not a boy, Father, and you weren't just asking. You're judging when you have no room to."

"Shel, please," her mother whispered.

Josh decided that now was a good time to answer. "I'm in construction."

Shelly stiffened in her seat, then he noticed her father arch his eyebrow the same damn way she did.

"You work in a construction crew?"

Josh thought about it and wondered if it were a trick question. He looked at Shelly, who was taking another sip of her wine. Then she did something he wouldn't have expected. She gave him a smug look and turned toward her father.

Suddenly, it all fell together as he sat there in the firing line. *He was the target.* For some reason, she had brought him all the way across the country to deflect her father's bullets onto an unsuspecting bystander—*him*. While he didn't overly care about the man's opinion, Shelly's behavior pissed him off. So she *did* care that he was in construction, and she had decided to use that as ammunition against her father.

Nice, Man-Eater, real nice.

"Yes, I work with a construction crew—as in building things such as restaurants, offices, and hospitals, in case you weren't sure."

Josh didn't like to be rude. When he heard Mrs. Monroe suck in a breath, he felt a slight twinge of guilt—until Shelly's father spoke.

"And that satisfies you? Is it really the kind of job that's stable enough these days to provide for a family?"

Josh felt a headache forming and clenched his teeth. He was about to answer when Shelly decided to pipe up.

"Father, Josh doesn't have a wife. Otherwise, I hardly think he'd be here, trying to get to know *me* better."

Josh blinked at her.

"Shelly, why do you feel the need to be so blunt and distasteful about these things?" her father asked.

Josh sat dumbfounded as the sweet Southern girl disappeared and the Man-Eater appeared.

"Why shouldn't I? I took lessons from the best. If I'm attracted to someone, I should just tell them or *show* them, and I am most *definitely* attracted to Josh." She took another sip of her wine before she turned her smoldering blue eyes on him.

Josh felt that hot stare all the way down to his toes, but he was livid with her. He wasn't sure if he wanted to nail her or strangle her.

"I mean, look at him," she added.

"Shelly Monroe. That's quite enough," her mother snapped, her accent sharper, like a whip cracking.

Shelly turned to face the small woman at the other end of the table. "Is that right, Mother? When will what *he* does be enough for you?"

"Shelly," her father boomed.

She stood. "What, *Father?*" Her tone added an ugly twist to the word. "You're quite happy to sit in lofty judgment of everyone else in this world, but when it comes to you—shhh, we can't talk about that." She moved to leave the room. When she reached the door, she turned back to look at her mother. "I'm sorry, Ma, but what he does, it just isn't right. Not for me and *certainly* not for you."

With that, she left with her wine glass in hand. Josh sat completely still in the aftermath of a storm he didn't quite understand.

Then her mother's soft accent floated across the quiet space. "I'm sure she went to the barn, Josh, if you'd like to go after her. It's down the back of the property."

Josh nodded, placing his utensils on his plate. "Thank you for dinner," he said as politely as he could before he left the now cold and silent room.

CHAPTER 13

SHELLY WAS PISSED. She was pacing in the barn from one side to the other. Her father was such a damn hypocrite that he drove her nuts. For years, the man had paraded his affairs right under his mother's nose, but her mother had stuck around.

Not to mention that when Shelly had been interning at the same hospital as him, she had seen him chase nurse after nurse—or pretty much any kind of woman that walked through the hospital. The sad part was he usually succeeded.

Well, I'll be damned if I end up like my mother. Used by different men over and over in the past, she was determined to find a man who respected her. She wasn't going to be stuck in a dead-end relationship with a man who took everything from her, only to watch him walk away when he was done.

She heard her name being called from the front of the barn. She'd known Josh would follow her, but she didn't want to talk to him either. Wiping her tears away, she stayed silent.

"If you don't come out, Georgia, when I find you, it won't be pretty," he warned in a pissed-off voice.

Shelly took a deep breath and moved out from the shadows to see him standing at the end of the barn.

He marched forward with his hands on his hips and stopped when he was a foot away from her. "You want to explain what that was all about in there?"

Shelly shook her head. "Not really."

He took another step, making her retreat. "You used me tonight."

She nodded. "Yes, I did."

"Well, at least you're honest about it."

Shrugging, Shelly asked, "What do you care? This was just a detour for you, so you could get laid."

"Excuse me? Screw you, Shel." He inched closer with each menacing step until her back was against the barn wall. "I do *not* like being used."

Shelly was breathing a little harder now that he was all up in her space. She forgot about her father and dismissed all the pain her mother had suffered. "Then use me, and we'll be even."

JOSH STEPPED BACK and looked at her leaning against the wall, breathing hard. Her bare legs were slightly parted, and her palms were flat against the wooden wall. All the lights in the barn were off, and she was illuminated by only the moonlight. She looked magnificent, and she was offering herself up on a platter.

"I don't *want* to use you. That's the problem *and* the difference."

She closed her eyes. "Why don't we use each other?"

He wasn't feeling kind though, and she needed to know that. "I'm not very happy with you right now, Georgia, so if you prefer to wait—"

"No," she replied quickly. "No. I don't want to wait."

Josh looked her over one more time then looked back toward the house. "Will they come out here?"

She shook her head once.

"Are you sure?"

"Not one hundred percent, but doesn't that make it better?" She let her eyes wander down to his jeans. Then she pointed out, "The idea seems to be flipping your switch."

He gave her a smug look and said in a deep, throaty whisper, "If we do this, it's by my rules. You humiliated me in there tonight. This is *my* reward." He watched her breasts rise and fall under the new blouse she had put on before dinner. "Got it?"

"Yes. I understand."

He let his eyes wander over her body. "Good. Now unsnap your shorts."

~

SHELLY WAS DAMN glad she had the barn wall behind her because she would have otherwise crumpled to the ground. The man standing in front of her was so intense, she could feel the waves of sexual energy rolling off him.

Holy shit. She was about to get it, and she couldn't wait. As quickly as she could, she unsnapped her jean shorts. She went to push them down, but he halted her.

"No. Leave them like that. Now unbutton your shirt."

Shelly wasn't shy *at all*, and as she untied the shirt, she almost laughed, thinking of the one he had ripped apart earlier. As she started on the buttons, she let her eyes roam all over the hot, tense man in front of her. His jean-clad legs were spread wide, showing off an impressive hard-on, and his arms were crossed, making all his muscles bulge. Shelly wanted to see them.

She got to the top button of her shirt and raised her eyes to his. What she saw was scorching heat, and it flickered over her, making her insides melt and her thighs clench as moisture pooled between her legs.

"Spread the shirt apart. I want to see your breasts this time."

Licking her top lip, Shelly spread the shirt and left it hanging at her sides. Then she slowly peeled down her lace bra cups, baring her breasts to him. He sucked in a harsh breath, and she watched with anticipation as he peeled off his own shirt before throwing it on the floor.

Mother of all that is holy. He had an intricate design tattooed around one of his huge biceps. Shelly felt her knees shake, and her panties went from damp to soaked. The guy was her every burning hot sexual fantasy wrapped into one big muscular package, and right now, all she wanted was for him to pound her into the barn wall. *Please?*

~

JOSH MOVED FORWARD, watching her lust-filled eyes trail

across his chest and zero in on the tattoo around his arm. He could tell she liked his eighteen-year-old mistake because a shiver ran through her, and her mouth fell open a little.

He looked at the beautiful breasts she had put on display for him, and his mouth just about watered. She stood, her back pressed to the barn wall, with her shorts unsnapped and her shirt wide open. She looked so fucking sexy that his heart almost ached as much as his cock —*almost*.

He took the final step toward her, closing the distance between them. With a soft growl, he told her, "Don't move."

Then he dropped to his knees in front of her.

SHELLY LOOKED DOWN TO see Josh kneeling in front of her open shorts, and she sent up every prayer she knew, hoping he was about to do what she thought.

He raised his big hands and parted the denim, then he leaned up on his knees to place a hot, wet kiss just below her navel. She hissed out a breath and brought her hands around to grip his hair lightly.

Looking up at her from beneath those long dark lashes, his eyes were so hot they just about singed her skin. Giving her a smug smile that melted her insides, he raised his hands, tugging the denim down her legs.

He didn't take them all the way down. He stopped mid-thigh and ran his hands up her legs to her panties. Josh gripped the edge, pulling the panties down out of his way, then leaned in with no hesitation to kiss her bare, aching mound.

Shelly gasped and thrust her hips toward him, gripping his hair a little tighter. She wanted to widen her legs, but she couldn't with where the shorts were. He dragged his tongue over her bare flesh and up to her abdomen, nipping and licking it until she was so hot and wet that she gripped his hair and tugged his head back.

"Hmm, you smell so good—like you *and* me," he said, reminding her of what they had done earlier. "Want something, Georgia?" he asked as though he'd been waiting for her to say something.

She smiled at him and replied the way she knew he wanted—*dirty*. "Yeah. I want your tongue between my thighs, *tasting* you and me."

∽

JOSH HAD BEEN WAITING for the sex goddess to show up. And there she was—her fingers gripping his hair, a siren's smile saying "I know you want to," and her legs straining to widen for more pleasure.

He knew once the shorts were gone, all bets were off. He was giving her a chance to change her mind. Granted, it wasn't much of a chance because he was about a second away from snapping. *God, she smells amazing.*

Josh looked up at her. "Is that right?"

She panted and thrust her hips again. "Oh yeah. I want your mouth, your tongue, and maybe your fingers, but I definitely want your cock." She smiled innocently at him and sweetly asked, "In that order. Please."

This woman was going to kill him slowly and pleasurably. He was going to enjoy it, but she was killing him just the same. He shook his head and gripped her shorts and panties. He pulled them all the way off and threw them somewhere behind them.

He looked back up at her and grasped her left thigh. He hitched it up and over his shoulder, bringing her hips in line with his mouth. She took a deep breath, watching him with sizzling hot eyes, then she licked her lips, pushing her hips toward him.

Keeping his eyes on hers and feeling her fingers tighten in his hair, he leaned forward and flicked out his tongue, licking across her throbbing clit.

∽

"JOSH," SHELLY MOANED as his wicked tongue flicked back and forth across her hot, wet skin.

The man had his eyes glued to hers as he teased her relentlessly with his tongue. Sliding it between her slick folds, then sucking each side individually. With blazing eyes, he watched every move she made. When she gripped his hair, he took her throbbing nub between his lips and sucked hard, making Shelly scream and climax way too quickly all over his tongue.

She was limp against the wall, but she knew this was nowhere near finished. She felt him slide her leg gently off his shoulder, then he moved away from her. She opened her eyes and saw him picking up his shirt and sliding it over his head.

"What are you doing?" she asked as he walked back to her.

"I'm going inside to get some sleep. It's been a long day. Plus, I need to check on Mutley."

Shelly blinked and shook her head. "Huh? What the hell?"

He cocked his head to the side. "Is there a problem?"

Gripping her shirt, Shelly pulled the sides together. "Yes, there's a problem. You said—"

Josh moved back to her and brushed her hands aside. He started to button her shirt for her. He didn't even seem to realize she was without her shorts. "I said this was *my* reward—what I wanted. You agreed."

"But—"

"No buts. I took what I wanted, and now we're even. You used me, and I used you. Quite well too, I must add." He leaned down and kissed her nose.

Shelly narrowed her eyes, almost going cross-eyed. "That was *not* the deal, Daniels."

"I don't care what you think this was about. I'm telling you. I will not be used like that *ever* again. If you have issues and want to talk to me, then fine, we'll talk. But don't ever use me to fight your battles without at least telling me what I'm getting into."

Shelly stood silent, shocked that he was so angry about what had happened. *After all, why does he care? We hardly know one another.* "I thought we were going to—"

He let out a deep breath, and it slid over her mouth and tickled her nose. "I know what you thought, Georgia, but I will not have sex with a woman who is angry, hurt, and who just finished humiliating me. This lowly construction worker has higher standards than that."

With that, he turned on his heel, leaving her standing in the barn with her shirt, no shorts, and what little dignity she thought she had broken in pieces.

CHAPTER 14

IT WAS FIVE thirty in the morning, and Shelly hadn't gotten any sleep at all.

After she had gone back to the house, all the lights had been turned off and it had been so quiet, you could have heard a pin drop. She had made her way upstairs and come precariously close to knocking on Josh's door. But after her performance at dinner, she didn't think he would have welcomed her.

Instead, she had gone into her empty bedroom and climbed into a cold bed.

What the hell was I thinking, bringing him home with me? He didn't know me, my problems, and more to the point, my family. Maybe that had been the whole point. She was finally realizing that she wanted him to know all of it.

A little happier with that conclusion, Shelly climbed out of bed and got ready to face the day. She needed to remind Josh that he wanted her, then she would show him why he should like her.

Putting on a different pair of Daisy Dukes that were faded at the pockets, she paired it with a flowy white shirt that had long loose sleeves. After tucking in the shirt at her small waist, she framed it with a brown leather belt. Leaving her blond hair down, she pulled on her cowgirl boots and made her way downstairs.

When she reached the kitchen, she heard movement and made her way toward it. Shelly stopped quietly at the door and watched her mother stand in front of the large bay windows that overlooked the back lot, scrubbing the big pots she must have used last night. Her mother was humming softly as she worked with the sudsy water.

Shelly walked over toward her, and as her boots hit the tile, her mother turned to look over her shoulder. Stopping mid-stride, Shelly locked eyes with the woman she loved more than anyone else, even though the woman had always managed to let her down in some fundamental way.

"Good mornin', Shelly," her mother said softly as she turned back to the sink. Gone was the use of "Shel," which meant she was in trouble.

Sidling up beside her mother, she took the hand towel hanging over the rail and started to dry the dishes. "Morning, Ma."

The silence was awful. It stretched and tightened with each breath Shelly took.

Finally, when the air was pretty much suffocating her, Shelly asked, "So where's Father?"

Without looking her way, Shelly's mother answered, "Your father got called into the hospital. He'll be gone most of the day."

Before she thought better of it, Shelly muttered, "Typical."

A pot clanged down, hitting the bottom of the stainless steel sink, as her mother whipped her head around to face her. "What on earth has gotten into you, Shelly Monroe?" She took a deep breath before shaking her head. Softly, in a tone that almost sounded defeated, she said, "I don't remember raising such a rude and cruel young lady."

Shelly couldn't bring herself to look at her mother, so she continued staring out the window at nothing in particular.

"What did you hope to achieve with your lil' performance last night?" her mother asked quietly. Her country accent was still present, but it wasn't as obvious when her emotions were tense, her tone clipped and curt.

Swallowing, Shelly turned to look at the small lady beside her. She shrugged slowly, not wanting to speak.

"Not only did you embarrass yourself, but you humiliated that lovely young man you brought here to meet us." She picked up the pot out of the sink and rinsed the suds from it before placing it in the drainer.

Finally, Shelly decided to say something. "I just can't stand the way he treats you."

"That is none of *your* business," her mother stressed, looking at Shelly with annoyed eyes. She blinked slowly and shook her head. Once again, her annoyance and disappointment were evident on her face. "Your opinion on *my* marriage does not count. Do ya hear me? And it certainly did not need to be announced across the dinner table in front of a guest. For all your father has done to me, he's *never* humiliated me on purpose like you did last night. He is discreet and—"

"And cheats," Shelly yelled. "He cheats on you, Ma. Over and over again. How can you let him keep coming back?"

After throwing the sponge into the sink, her mother wiped her hands and turned to face her daughter full-on. Shelly straightened her spine, preparing for whatever was about to come. For years, she had watched this woman let her husband emotionally destroy her. Shelly couldn't comprehend why her mother let him get away with it.

"I will say this once, and then you're to never speak of it with me again. Do I make myself clear?"

Shelly nodded sharply and waited.

"Your father and I met when I was sixteen years old. *Sixteen*, Shelly. We dated and fell in love. It was wonderful, full of flowers an' rainbows. That's the way you think it should be, am I right?" Her shoulders slumped a little. Stepping closer to Shelly, she ran a finger down her daughter's cheek. "You look so much like him."

"Don't," Shelly muttered, pulling her face away from the touch. "I wish I looked nothing like him."

Her mother shook her head. "I don't. I look at you, and I see all the goodness that he was. When we fell in love, life was easy. We were young and had the rest of our lives ahead of us. But then we grew up, and life changed. He went into a grueling medical program, and I got pregnant."

"I'm so sorry," Shelly snapped.

"Stop it," her mother told her firmly, the strong Southern woman making an appearance. "Stop being so angry at him. I chose this life. *Me*—not him. He has told me on numerous occasions that he'd look after me if I wanted to move on, but I don't want to. This is my life.

It's where you grew up not wanting or needing anything, and he's my friend."

Shaking her head, Shelly stood there looking at her mother, but all she saw was a stranger. Suddenly, everything crumbled down around Shelly's shoulders. All the anger she had held for her father, thinking that he was the one destroying her mother's dignity and her good name, now seemed misplaced. It had been her mother's choice to stay? Shelly's heart seemed to be splitting. She felt pure betrayal from the woman who had loved and raised her, teaching her to respect herself at all costs. *How can someone voluntarily stay with a man who doesn't want her?*

"A friend?" Shelly sputtered. "He's your husband. He's supposed to love you and look after you and—"

"He does all of that," she replied, stepping closer. She took Shelly's face between her small palms. "Your father fell out of love with me a long time ago. I know that because he told me. The problem is that I will always love him, so I'll take any part of him I can. Friendship and companionship are what he offered—not to mention stability for you."

Shelly blinked once and felt her eyes welling up. "That's no way to live, Ma. Everyone else gets to be happy except *you*? Don't you want someone who loves you completely?"

Her mother's eyes became glassy, and a tear slipped free, running down her cheek. "Of course I did, you silly girl, and I had it. Do you really think anyone is lucky enough to find that twice? So I took what I had and stored it away. Shelly, when I lie down at night and think about the man in the room next door to mine, I am still so happy I get to see him every day."

Shelly felt tears streaming down her cheeks as her mother stood in front of her, calmly explaining her loveless marriage. *How does someone survive that? How does someone not die from being so incredibly lonely? And how on earth can I not hate my father for not freeing my mother from all this pain and heartache? Why didn't he push her to move on? Like he obviously did.*

"Ma, don't you think you would be happier to go and—"

"No," she said firmly. "I've looked at this from all angles, my dear, for years, believe me. I know what people say about me. I know they whisper about how your father runs around, but he ain't doing anything I don't know about." She turned to face outside. She put her hands on the sink and leaned into it as though she needed it to help hold her up. "At first, I figured I would be better if he left. He did for a couple of weeks, but it was so much worse. So I invited him back into our lives and told him what I wanted and expected of him. And, Shel, he agreed and has done everything he said he would. How can I fault him for that?"

Finally, her mother looked back at her. "I'm gonna go out to the yard for a while, but think about what I told you. You need to forgive him. He hasn't done anything to you, and he certainly hasn't done anything to me that I am unaware of. He loves you very much and is so proud of you. He just hasn't done what you wanted." She stopped, the last tear falling over her cheek. "He fell out of love, and that is not a crime."

∽

JOSH STOOD AT the bottom of the staircase, just outside of the kitchen, as the back door slapped shut. He had come downstairs around ten minutes ago and heard two voices. He had turned to make his way toward them until he heard Shelly crying.

Holy shit, Josh thought as he ran a hand through his hair. *How on earth does a daughter comprehend what her mother just told her?*

Mutley, of course, took that moment to bark.

Josh looked down at his dog and shook his head. "Thanks, buddy."

He walked through the kitchen door to see Shelly facing him with tears on her cheeks and a lopsided smile. She stared at the dog by his side.

"Did he just out you?" she asked, gesturing to Mutley with her chin.

Josh gave a half-smile as he walked toward her. "Pretty much." He stopped in front of her and traced her wet cheek with his index finger. "You okay?"

She shook her head, then she leaned her face into his palm. He cupped the cool cheek nuzzling his hand while her wet blue eyes looked at him with more tears shimmering and threatening to spill over.

"Not really. How much did you hear?"

Josh grimaced. "Enough. I'm really sorry, Shelly."

She shrugged. "Not much I can do about it, right? It's her choice."

Josh dropped his hand, stroking it down her arm, and entwined their fingers together before squeezing gently. "Yes, it's her choice, but it couldn't have been easy hearing all of that. Does it make you feel any different toward your father?"

She took a deep breath, looked at their fingers, then back up to him. "I'm not sure. I wish I could ask him what happened, you know? Why did he stop loving her? What changed for him?"

Josh took a step closer, so she had to stand up straight. With his free hand, he cupped her chin. Tipping her face up toward his, he gently kissed her lips. "Maybe he wouldn't have an answer for you, but you won't know unless you ask. Then maybe you can start to forgive him."

She shook her head and asked softly, "How would I even begin to ask that? I'm so disappointed and sad right now."

Josh sighed, dropping the hand at her chin to grip her other fingers as well. "Disappointed in whom? Your mother?"

"Both of them. I'm angry and disappointed in both of them," she fumed as Josh held her hands. "How dare they do that to their daughter. I never knew any of that. I never knew about this cozy understanding they shared while I was working with the women he was having his *freedom* with. Ma got to stay at home and avoid those awkward moments. I had to work with those women. I *still* cannot forgive him for that."

Josh tugged her toward him and wrapped his arms around her shoulders.

"You wouldn't do something like that," she whispered into his chest.

"No, I wouldn't." He kissed the top of her head.

"You wouldn't even have sex with me when I asked you to."

Josh choked out a rumbling laugh. "Oh, I wanted to, Georgia."

"Yeah?"

Josh ran one hand down her hair. "Oh yeah. I dreamed about how good you tasted all night."

∼

SHELLY LEANED BACK, looking up at him. "I'm sorry I used you last night."

He looked down at her with understanding eyes. "I know you are."

Shelly snuggled back into his chest and took a deep breath. "You're making it so easy to fall for you."

His arms tightened around her as he replied softly, "Is that such a bad thing, Georgia?"

Shelly placed a palm on his chest and felt his heart beating strong. "I'm not sure yet."

He placed his lips against her head, giving her a gentle kiss. "Take a chance, Shel. I'm not going to hurt you, use you, or take any part of you for granted." He ran a hand down her hair and lightly squeezed her neck. As he stepped back, he said, "Look at me, Georgia."

Shelly raised her eyes to his and almost felt her heart explode from the pure raw emotion in Josh's gaze. She shook her head, unbelieving. "How can this be happening?"

"What do you mean?" he asked with a crooked grin.

"You and me? This is all so fast. Maybe bringing you here was a mistake. It's clouding—"

"It's clouding nothing," he told her, cupping her face again. He lowered his mouth to hers. "It's stripping you bare, and I'm falling for you so hard that I can feel the scrapes on my knees. I understand you're scared, because I'm absolutely terrified, but I'm not going to hurt you or kick you when you're down."

Shelly couldn't believe everything he was saying. It was every single thing she had ever wanted to hear, and suddenly, she found it hard to breathe. She needed space. She needed a distraction. "Will you come somewhere with me?"

He blinked at the sudden change of subject. "Avoidance?"

Shelly nodded as he grinned at her.

"I'll only let you avoid me for so long, you know," he pointed out.

"That's fine," Shelly squeaked.

"Okay, where do you want to take me?"

Shelly was close to saying, *Anywhere as long as it's with me*, but she decided to keep that to herself. "It's a place I loved going to when I was younger."

A smile spread over his mouth, and she couldn't help but stand on her tiptoes to kiss him.

"Okay then, let's go," he whispered against her lips. He stepped back, looking her over. "By the way, you look beautiful this morning."

"Thank you." She paused then remembered something. "Oh, wait here a second," she said as she ran out of the kitchen.

∾

JOSH WATCHED HER run off and took a moment to compose himself. *What the hell am I doing? Oh, that's right. I'm falling head over heels for Dr. Monroe, a.k.a. Georgia, a.k.a. Man-Eater. Am I insane? Yeah, probably.*

Every second he was with the woman, she sneaked in a little deeper. He knew there would be more obstacles for him to climb over after what had happened between her and her mother. But as he watched her practically skip back into the kitchen in her cowgirl boots, clutching a cowgirl hat, he felt himself fall further in love.

Hang on—love? Oh shit, I'm screwed. First Melissa and now Shelly? Why can't I ever learn from my gigantic mistakes?

However, Shelly had these moments of complete vulnerability that made him want to wrap his arms around her and never let go. He had never gotten that from Melissa—not once.

Georgia, on the other hand, was one surprise after another.

"You okay?" Shelly asked as she stopped in front of him.

Josh looked her over and nodded. "Yep. Mutley and I were just wondering where you were taking us."

"I suppose he can come, but it's a surprise."

Josh kissed her on the nose. "I'm starting to find I love surprises."

SHELLY SAT IN the front seat of Josh's truck, pointing left and right, as he followed her directions without complaint. She had to admit that when they talked about their feelings, she had freaked out. She wasn't supposed to be falling for Joshua Daniels. She was supposed to be having fun with the added bonus of no-strings sex. *Scratch that. Great sex.*

So what had she done? She'd had such great sex that she had almost confessed she was falling for him.

What on earth do I think I'm doing? I have no clue. That's for sure.

Instead of being brave like him, she had freaked out and told him she wanted to take him somewhere. And where was she taking him? To the place she treasured most. It was a place she had labeled the "dreaming tree."

As he pulled off the main street and started down a little dirt road, the huge oak tree came into view. Its twisted and gnarled branches spread out in all directions, including several that reached across a small river that ran behind an old abandoned property.

Josh brought the truck to a stop, and Shelly jumped out before running over to the edge of the river. She turned back to see him standing at the front of his truck, leaning his butt up against it. Shelly shielded her eyes against the bright morning sun, looking from the man to the loyal dog that sat beside his master.

What a pair they are—both silent and solid in their stillness. Was there ever a question I would fall for this man? Not really.

It had only been a matter of time, and suddenly, it felt as though time had run out. In a few short weeks and only a handful of days, she had fallen hard for Josh Daniels. That scared the hell out of her.

"What is this place, Georgia?" he asked, moving toward her.

Shelly turned back to the river and took a deep breath, trying to decide how she was supposed to function now. She had given her heart permission to be vulnerable, risking the potential of it being broken into a million pieces.

Hang on, this is Josh. He told me he wouldn't hurt or use me, right? Surely she was safe to step forward and give her heart to him.

When he stopped beside her, Shelly turned, seeing his profile as his hair blew in the slight breeze, and she couldn't help but smile.

"I'm finding it really hard to fight wanting you," she whispered.

He turned his big muscular body toward her, reaching out to cup her face. "Well, that's nice to hear, Georgia, because I stopped fighting a while ago."

Shelly blinked, shaking her head as best she could with two strong hands holding her face. "This doesn't make sense."

"What doesn't?" he whispered, moving in closer.

"This. Us. How I feel," she whispered back.

"And how do you feel?"

Shelly felt her heart pound while she considered what she wanted to reveal. "I feel like I've fallen so far down the rabbit hole that I can't get out."

She held her breath as he leaned in and pressed a soft, gentle kiss to her mouth. Shelly sighed, pulling back from all the emotion.

"This isn't a dream, I promise you," he assured.

Shelly blinked, confessing, "I'm so scared."

He stroked her cheek with his fingers. "Of me?"

Shelly shook her head. "Of us."

~

JOSH STEPPED BACK, looking over to where Mutley had stretched out beneath the shade of the tree. "Why did you bring me here, Georgia?"

Shelly turned back to face the river. Closing her eyes, she took a deep breath and seemed to let go of the anxiety she was holding on to. "I would come down here when my parents argued—or when someone told me they saw my dad kissing some woman on the corner of their street." She turned to face him. "That actually happened more often than you would think. I called this my dreaming tree. I would come down here and dream of where I wanted to escape to and who I wanted to meet."

Josh smiled at her, watching her blond hair whip around her shoulders under the cowgirl hat. Then he thought of something and hoped he had what he wanted in the truck. "Can you wait here for one second?"

She nodded and stayed by the riverbank while he jogged back to his truck. He held his breath as he opened the toolbox in the bed of the Ford F-250, and inside, he found an old blanket. He grabbed it, smiling, and walked back over to the woman he was about to make love to.

~

SHELLY TURNED WHEN she heard him coming toward her. Her heart thundered as she watched him stride down to the riverbank with a blanket beneath his arm. He was dressed in a white T-shirt and the usual jeans and boots. She looked him up and down and smiled.

"It's too early for a picnic, isn't it?"

Josh stopped in front of her and held out a hand. "That's not what I had in mind."

"No? Then what?"

He tugged her forward and kissed a little harder than the previous two kisses they had shared this morning. "Tell me what else you would dream about under your dreaming tree."

Shelly looked up at him, dazed and caught under his spell. "I would lie under the tree and dream about the man I'd end up with—who he would be and what he would look like."

A grin appeared on his face—that panty-dropping smile from the first time she had ever seen him. "Oh yeah?"

Nodding, Shelly stepped forward, placing her hands on his chest. "Oh yeah."

"And?"

Shelly moved to step around him toward the tree. She looked over her shoulder and winked. As he groaned, letting his head fall back, she felt a shiver run all the way down to her toes.

"And he turned out much better than anything I could have imagined."

CHAPTER 15

WHEN HE REACHED a spot under the tree, Josh spread out the blanket as Shelly leaned against the thick trunk, watching him. After he had arranged it the way he wanted, he moved around the edge to where she stood. A sexy smile appeared on her lips.

"What are you thinking about, Georgia?" Keeping a little space between them, he watched as she removed her hat and tossed it on the ground beside her.

"I was just thinking about how right this feels, even though it's so sudden."

Letting his eyes wander over her, he nodded, holding out a hand. She slid her small palm against his. He tugged her forward, away from the tree, until she was close enough for him to hold.

Tilting her head just a little, she whispered, "I was determined not to fall for you, and somehow, I don't think I ever had a chance of resisting."

Josh stroked his free hand down her blond hair. "Sometimes things just happen."

"Like fate?"

"Fate, or in my case, good goddamn luck." He chuckled a little then sobered. "I looked at you and instantly wanted you, but my past was telling me not to touch."

She tilted her head to the side. "Why? Am I allowed to ask what happened?"

He nodded. "Of course. It was nothing out of the ordinary. I was involved with a beautiful woman who used her beauty to get where she wanted to go, and she used me as a bankroll."

Shelly's face tightened, and she stiffened in his arms. He let go of their joined hands and reached around to rub a soothing hand up her spine.

"I've had boyfriends who were all about my money too," she confessed.

Suddenly, things started to fall into place for Josh. She dated rich, successful men because she'd been burned just as badly as he had. However, he had steered clear of the beauties, and she had steered clear of the men who looked at her profession as a cash advance.

Leaning down by her ear, Josh clarified, "I don't want a single penny from you, Shelly Monroe. I want your mind, your heart, and your sexy-as-hell body, but not your money."

Josh felt her take a deep breath and let it out with a whoosh. He placed a gentle kiss against her neck just below her ear, smiling against her soft skin as she tilted her head to give him better access. He made his way back to her earlobe and sucked it gently, then he felt her hands come up and grip his chest.

She let out a soft moan as his whole body shuddered in response. Lifting his head, he looked down at her, noticing her eyes had clouded over and her plump lips had parted.

"I want to take off all your clothes, lay you down here in the morning sun, and love you from your head to your toes. Would that be okay with you?"

~

HELL YEAH, IT'S *okay with me,* she wanted to scream to the heavens.

However, all of a sudden, Shelly found it hard to form any kind of coherent sentence. When Josh had started kissing her neck, she had felt goose bumps rise all over her skin, but when he had sucked her earlobe into his hot mouth, her thighs had clenched and her stomach had taken a flying leap off of a huge building.

She was sunk. This man had sneaked up and worked his way quickly and efficiently into her heart, as though it were some kind of stealth operations mission. She hadn't even seen him coming, and now, he was seducing her mind right along with her willing body.

Removing his hands from her, he slowly undid the buckle of her brown leather belt. "Did I tell you how much I like your outfit today? You're wearing every single item on my fantasy list."

Shelly found herself breathing harder than usual, so she nodded instead of speaking. She watched as one side of his mouth quirked up.

"Have I rendered you speechless, Georgia? Because I have to say, I didn't think that was possible."

He paused as the belt finally gave, then he gripped an end in each hand, tugging her forward with a little more force than she was expecting. She ended up flush against him, her hands reaching up to grip his biceps for balance.

"Well, maybe Georgia would be speechless," he continued as he lowered his head. His lips whispered across hers in a quick kiss. "But Man-Eater Monroe, who eats men for dinner, definitely would not be."

With that, he kissed her with so much heat, she thought she would go up in flames.

Shelly felt his tongue swipe across her bottom lip, and she didn't hesitate for one second before opening her mouth to him. He groaned softly as his tongue dipped inside to rub against hers. He still had a firm grip on her belt and tugged her even closer, rubbing his straining zipper against hers.

Tilting her head a little, she moaned as he deepened the kiss by sucking on her tongue when she dipped it into his mouth. Shelly felt herself becoming more and more aroused with every dip of his tongue and every suck from his wonderful mouth. When he finally pulled his head back, it took everything she had not to whimper from the loss of it.

Shelly stood still as her heart raced. Josh's breathing was coming a little too fast as well, and Shelly felt a smile slide across her mouth. *She* had caused that.

∼

JOSH TOOK A small step back, still gripping her belt in both hands. That kiss had just about fried his brain cells, and as Shelly smiled up at him in the morning sun, he knew he was about to give his heart away.

His breathing felt labored as he looked over the beautiful woman in front of him. Her amazingly blue eyes were focused on him with such sexual intent that he thought if they just touched fingers, they would explode. Then she smiled and licked her lips, and Josh knew he wanted to touch her everywhere and be consumed by her.

Yeah, so I can't do sex without feelings. So what?

Dropping one end of the belt, Josh gripped the buckle and slid it deftly through the loopholes of her Daisy Dukes. It made her hips jiggle a little, and that, in turn, made her breasts sway under that breezy top.

Holy hell, this woman is something else.

A laugh bubbled up out of her, and he raised his eyes to meet hers.

"Am I amusing you?" he asked with an arched brow.

Shelly bit her bottom lip, shaking her head. "No, you just seem hypnotized by my breasts."

Josh couldn't help but laugh. There she was, Georgia mixed in with the Man-Eater, blunt as always.

Keeping the belt dangling in his hand, he told her, "Well, maybe you should take your top off and see what you can make me do—once I'm under hypnosis and all."

Josh knew Shelly wasn't shy, and as her mouth turned up in an okay-mister-you-asked-for-it smile, he stood still and waited for the unveiling.

There in the shade of the beautiful old oak, the Shelly who had morphed somewhere between Chicago and Savannah tugged her shirt from her jean shorts and took it off before throwing it on the ground beside her. In true man-eater style, she reached behind her and undid her bra, throwing it to the ground as well.

Josh gripped the belt tightly as her breasts were bared to him. The morning sun streaming down seemed to kiss them all over. Shelly tilted her head and cocked her hip out, resting her hands on her waist, which jutted those perky rose-colored nipples even closer to him.

"What do you plan to do with that belt?" she asked.

Josh looked down at the hand still holding the belt, then he let his eyes come back up to the half-naked woman in front of him. He grinned, tossing it aside. "Not a damn thing."

Shelly chuckled as she stepped toward him. "Good, because I have to tell you, that is so not my scene."

Josh let his eyes run all over her when she stopped so close her nipples were brushing his white shirt.

"Oh no? Then what is?" he asked.

SHELLY GRINNED AT Josh as he waited for her to do something.

It was almost comical to Shelly that she felt more comfortable, more like her old self, since Josh had suggested she take off her shirt. She knew how to be this person—a sexy siren who could seduce a man. Shelly understood her.

She didn't understand or have any idea how to handle the vulnerable, smitten, and lovesick Shelly.

Shelly let her hands wander under the bottom of his shirt to his jeans, releasing the snap and unzipping them. Josh stepped back from her. He quickly pushed his jeans down and kicked them aside with his shoes, leaving him standing in his white shirt and navy boxer shorts.

Shelly let her eyes roam all over his body, and she had to admit that his muscle tone was amazing. She had always liked a little bulk on her men, but Josh was ridiculously buff.

Instead of moving toward him, Shelly watched him closely as she kicked off her boots then unsnapped her own shorts. She slid them, along with her tiny excuse for panties, right off her excited body. Josh sucked in a deep breath as she kicked aside her final pieces of clothing, then she moved to lie down on the blanket under her dreaming tree.

"Are you coming?" she asked.

He stood in the sunlight, watching her in silence. Finally, he seemed to regain motor function and moved so he was standing at her feet. He shook his head. "Not yet, but I'm really close."

Shelly winked and stretched her hands out behind her. Completely unashamed of her body, she arched her back and had a good stretch in the sunlight.

"Holy shit," Josh muttered, shaking his head.

Shelly saw his erection as it strained against his boxers, and she licked her lips. "Are you going to get down here on this blanket? Or stand there all day, staring?"

∼

JOSH RAN A shaky hand through his hair, looking at the sex goddess stretched out buck-ass naked on his old blanket. "The view is pretty amazing from up here."

Shelly propped herself up on her elbows. "Take off your clothes. I want to feel you naked, rubbing all over me."

Now who can argue with that? Certainly, not me. Josh whipped off his shirt then pushed his boxers down and stepped away from them. He watched as Shelly's eyes zoomed in on his hard-on, but he wasn't ashamed and he sure as hell wasn't going to hide it. If the way her eyes lit up then came back to his was any indication, she didn't want him to hide either.

Josh dropped to his knees at her feet and made his way up her sun-warmed body. When he was finally mouth to mouth, chest to chest, and—*thank God*—hip to hip with her, he winked at her.

"Now what did you want, Georgia? Me rubbing myself all over you?"

∼

BETWEEN JOSH'S BODY finally touching hers in all the right spots, his sexy voice, and his wink, Shelly was about to come with absolutely no physical stimulation.

However, when he lowered his hips and rocked his hard cock against her bare mound, she closed her eyes, letting out a small moan of delight. Shelly gripped his arms as they flexed while he held himself above her, still rubbing himself against her slowly.

"Shelly, look at me," he demanded softly.

Shelly found herself obeying without question, letting her eyes open and focus on his.

"You feel absolutely amazing underneath me."

A grin crept across her lips as she raised one leg, placing her foot flat on the blanket, and lifted her hips to push against his. "Well, you feel pretty amazing on top of me."

When he groaned and lowered his mouth to hers, Shelly knew this was different. The emotions behind the actions had changed, and she felt them slowly wrapping around her heart as they bound them together. His tempestuous kiss stripped her mind of anything other than having every part of him deep inside her.

She let a hand roam up and slide into his hair before gripping it tightly. She held his mouth close to hers so she could devour him as much as he was consuming her. She sucked on his bottom lip and gave it a little nip, producing his rumbling groan and a flex of his hips.

He moved back, inched down her body to her breasts, and finally —*thank God*—took one of her hard nipples between his lips. He sucked on it while his other hand traced down her naked side to her hip. Sliding his hand under her ass, he lifted her, grinding her against his body, as he continued his sensuous assault on her sensitive nipples. Suddenly, Shelly felt a little bite and her back arched as she gripped his hair. His eyes came up to meet hers in question, and when Shelly nodded and widened her legs a little more, he got his answer.

JOSH HAD HIS mouth on one of her rosy little nipples and his other hand under her ass, pulling her up hard against his body while he ground his aching cock against her. *Fuck, she's on fire, and I want to be burned by her.*

He moved his attention to her other nipple, licking and biting it before ending the delicious torment with a strong suck that had her arching and begging for more.

Smiling against her skin, he came back up her body and kissed her with everything he had. He slid his tongue between her parted lips, mimicking the act he so desperately wanted. As he changed the angle of his head for a deeper kiss, he felt her hands slide down his back to grip his ass, pulling him hard against herself. Both of her legs were bent now, cradling his hips between her thighs. As she thrust her pelvis up, finally sliding his cock against her hot mound, he knew it was time.

Raising himself up above her, he looked at her lying beneath him and the sun, and he rocked his hips so the head of his erection slid between her wet folds. As her mouth parted and her eyes fluttered shut, he pushed his hips forward and slowly sank into her. He kept his eyes on her face as she let out a moan and her eyes opened, latching on to his. He pushed forward, letting more of himself slide deeper inside her wet heat.

When he finally bottomed out, he lowered himself down slowly. "I'm so lost in you, Georgia. I don't even know where you end and I begin. You feel so fucking amazing. I want to stay here forever."

∼

SHELLY BLINKED AS she raised her hands to grip Josh's ass and pulled him in deeper, if that was possible. She was trying to comprehend what he had just told her, but instead of letting the full impact of his emotional confession sink in, she chose to make light of it and deal with their feelings later.

As he braced himself above her on arms she wanted to bite and lick, she couldn't help but roll her hips and reply, "Well, that might make it difficult for me to walk."

Josh pushed his hips down toward her. His face was serious. He clearly knew exactly what she was doing, but he chose to once again let her get away with it. "Let's see if I can make it difficult for you to walk tomorrow anyway."

Shelly groaned and felt him pull slowly out before thrusting back in. She held on to his ass as it flexed and bunched with each strong slide. He kissed her beneath her ear—then did something she hadn't expected. He rolled them over, and Shelly was now sitting on top of a hot, tense wall of male muscle.

Oh, hell yeah.

Looking down at Josh, Shelly placed her hands on his chest and slowly rolled her hips. She watched his eyes as they traveled all over her, then she spotted her hat behind his head. Biting her lip and grinning, she stopped and leaned over him, which made him slip from her body.

"Shelly, what's wro—" Then he saw her move back to sit on his thighs with her hat in her hand.

Smiling at him, she placed her cowgirl hat on her head before she gripped his cock at the base. Lining it up with herself, she rose up on her knees and sank down onto his waiting hardness. She heard his groan and watched as his eyes opened, focusing on her.

"Jesus, Georgia, you're my every fucking fantasy right now come to life."

Shelly grinned, licked her lips, then brought her hands up to play with her breasts as she worked herself on his cock. He bucked his hips up as his big, strong hands gripped her thighs, and she rode him like he had told her he wanted.

As the tempo changed and Josh breathed harder, Shelly leaned down and braced her palms against his chest. Rolling her hips up and down as he thrust along with her rhythm, she arched her back and clamped her legs hard around his waist. His mouth opened on a loud groan, and Shelly came right along with Delicious Daniels.

WITH THE SUN streaming down on him through the oak leaves, Josh was stretched out on his back as the naked woman on top of him pressed her ear to his chest, tapping her small fingers along to the sound of his heart.

"You have a solid heartbeat. It's steady and strong," she told him.

Josh felt a smile form, then he chuckled. "Oh, for a minute there, I thought you were going to tell me I had something else that was nice and solid."

Shelly looked up at him, grinning. "Well, that too. But, no, I was listening to your heart."

Josh ran his hands up and down her smooth skin and ended by cupping her sweet ass, pulling her farther up his body so her mouth was within kissing distance. He leaned his head up and pressed his lips to hers. "That was pretty amazing, cowgirl."

She grinned against his lips. In her Southern voice, she said, "Well, you know how that lil' ol' saying goes, sugah. Save a horse and ride a cowboy."

Josh groaned, rolling his eyes. "Please, not the accent."

She squirmed around on top of him. "What do ya mean, sugah? I thought you liked my lil' bit of country."

Josh laughed as he hugged her, kissing her right smack on the lips.

"That's the problem. I'm tired, and I like it too much."

She giggled before she said, in the best country twang she could, "Well, what good are ya to me then? I need me a cowboy who can ride all night. Not one who's done after one lil' ol' session."

Josh gripped her ass, rolling her over onto her back as she squealed with laughter. "Okay, Georgia, but remember, you asked for it."

"Oh, I nevah forget a challenge, cowboy. Now giddy up."

Josh groaned as she winked at him with a sassy smile and smacked him on the ass. *Oh yes, Shelly Monroe is trouble with a capital T, and I love it.*

CHAPTER 16

AROUND TWO HOURS later, Josh was driving them back to the house. As he turned onto her parents' drive, Shelly was sitting on the far side of the truck, facing him, and Mutley was lying down on the back seat.

Josh looked over at her and winked, and Shelly felt a delicious thrill all the way to her toes. They had spent most of the morning down by the river, laughing, making love, and in Shelly's mind, falling further down the rabbit hole.

When they got closer to the house, she saw her father's truck parked off to the side. As her eyes moved to the front porch, she saw him sitting on the top step, watching their approach. All of a sudden, last night's dinner and her morning conversation with her mother came hurtling back with full force and clarity.

"Shel?" Josh's voice broke into her thoughts.

Turning her eyes to his, she noticed a worried look on his face.

He took her hand. "You don't have to talk to him right now."

Shelly nodded and squeezed his hand, grimacing a little. "Yes, I do. He knows."

"You don't know that, Georgia."

"Yes, I do." She took a deep breath. "He always sits there when he wants to talk."

Josh looked over to where her father was waiting, then he turned back to her. "Do you want me to come with you?"

Shelly shook her head and removed her hand from his. "No. This is something I need to do by myself." She unlocked the truck door before pushing it open. "It's been a long time coming."

Josh nodded. "I'll be inside with your mother if you need me, okay?"

Shelly jumped down out of the truck and nodded once. Then she closed the door and moved around the front, walking toward her father, who was now standing on the top step of the house.

Shelly walked right past the stairs, making her way down the side of the house, and she heard her father follow. She'd be damned if they did this where her mother could walk outside. She'd been through enough already this morning.

~

WHEN SHELLY REACHED THE BARN, she turned around and saw her father come to a stop at the door. He leaned against it and waited. She didn't really know where she wanted to start, so she figured she'd just begin with the question that had been nagging her all morning.

"How could you have let her stay all these years?"

The illustrious Dr. Lawrence Monroe took one hand out of his pocket to rub his chin, then he asked in his sophisticated Southern drawl, "I'm trying to decide, Shelly, what right you think you have to question me and my motives."

Shelly looked at him as though he had gone slightly insane. "Gee, I don't know? Maybe the same reason why you think you have the right to question *my* choices."

"Well, you're my daughter. I want to make sure you're makin' the *right* choices."

Her mouth dropped open at his sheer arrogance. "Could you possibly be more condescending? You know, as my father, you were supposed to set a good example of the right choices. Wow, what an epic failure on your behalf, wouldn't you say?"

He pushed off the door, stepping toward her. "What d'ya want from me, princess?" His smooth charm faltered as his accent got stronger.

Shelly spun away from him, shaking her head. "I don't know, Dr. Monroe, maybe a tear?" She turned back to him. "Maybe then I'd know you care. I keep waiting to feel that you understand how much pain and embarrassment you have put me through. Not to mention what you must have put her through over the years."

Shelly turned away from him again, pacing across the barn. She was so angry at him. *Can't he see? Can't he understand how his actions have totally destroyed any faith I could ever have in a man? Does he not realize that he is the example I have used and applied to every single man who walked into my life? How am I supposed to trust one word out of the mouth of the opposite sex when I can't even trust my own father?*

"Shelly." When she didn't respond, he said her name again. "Shelly Monroe, stop pacin' and look at me."

Shelly stopped on the opposite side of the walkway, tilting her head to look up at the man she strongly resembled. She wouldn't give in to him, and she would *not* let him see her cry.

"I never meant to hurt you—" he started, moving to walk toward her.

"Don't come over here," she snapped.

"Shelly, your ma and I have had an understandin' for years. I just don't think we realized how much it affected you."

"Wow, do you think?" Shelly asked with so much bitterness, she almost choked on it.

"Princess," he said softly.

Shelly shook her head as angry tears formed. "Don't be sweet to me. Not now, not here. I deserve answers. You owe me that." She wiped away a tear that had escaped.

"What, Shel? What do you need from me? An apology? Okay, I'm sorry you were so affected—"

"But not sorry for your actions? Don't pity me, *Father*." Shelly tipped up her chin and swallowed. "I'm not doing so badly." She took a deep breath and finally told her father everything she had ever wanted to get off her chest. "You know who you should feel sorry for? The little girl who saw all your fights and was teased constantly because her father kept getting caught sneaking out of their neighbor's house...or maybe the young woman who interned beside you and looked up to you, who tried to do everything she could to make you proud, even when the nurses laughed because they had slept with her father." Shelly stepped forward and pointed at him. "Yeah, you're damn right to feel sorry for her. You let her down big time. You completely failed her at every turn. And now, now, you want to judge *my* choices? You want to stand there and tell me someone like Josh isn't a good enough man for me?"

He arched a brow, but he stood silent, letting her finish.

"Well, that's where you are dead wrong. He's an amazing man. Yes, he may be a construction worker, which doesn't fit your lofty ideals, but you know what? I don't give a shit anymore. You did this to each other. I am over trying to do what you want and over trying to save myself from being used the way Ma is."

Before he could say a word, Shelly marched past him and stopped at the door. She looked at him over her shoulder. "The sad part is you also did this to me. I may forgive you eventually. But how on earth do I ever forget what I now know?"

With that, Shelly stormed back toward the house.

JOSH HEARD HER the minute she stormed through the back door. Shelly's mother looked at him, grimacing as she stood.

Josh stood as well, saying softly, "Why don't you let me go?"

Shelly's mother gave him a strained smile. "Okay. That's probably for the best."

Josh made a move to walk past her, but she reached out and touched his arm. Turning, he looked down at two sad eyes.

"Look after her for me?" she whispered.

Josh placed a hand over hers where it lay on his arm and squeezed gently. "I will. I promise."

She took her hand back, nodding. "I believe you, Joshua Daniels."

Walking to the door, Josh glanced once more at the small woman in the large sitting room, and he felt his heart break a little from the loneliness in this house.

As he moved into the foyer, he saw Shelly disappearing up the stairs. He took them two at a time, and when he got to her door, he rapped on it then waited. When there was no answer, he turned the knob, pushed the door open, and walked inside.

Facing the large window, Shelly was sitting on her bed with her legs crossed and her head in her hands, sobbing. Her back shook with each shuddering breath.

As Josh moved toward her, he felt completely helpless. "Shelly?"

He came around the bed, and when he stood in front of her, he put his fingers beneath her chin. Tilting her face up, she blinked wet eyes and gave him a tremulous smile.

"What's all this?" he asked softly.

She gave him the saddest smile he had ever seen. She pointed at her face. "This is my brave face."

Josh gave her chin a gentle squeeze. "I hate to tell you, but it's not very good. We may have to work on it."

That made her chuckle and sniffle. "Yeah?"

"Yeah. It's kinda pathetic." He gave her a crooked grin then tacked on, "But cute."

Shelly laughed halfheartedly. "Can we go home early?"

Josh arched a brow. "Like tonight? We just got here. Are you sure you want to leave?"

Shelly nodded and wiped her eyes. "I think I need to. Plus, I can't imagine this has been wonderful for you." She looked up at him with pleading eyes. "I think they need me to go, and I think I want to be gone."

Josh knew at that moment there wasn't one thing he wouldn't do for her.

Nodding, he wiped her cheek with his thumb. "Okay, then let's pack and hit the road. Maybe this time we can stop at a motel and split up the trip."

That got a full-blown smile from her, and she nodded as she stood. She wrapped her arms around Josh's neck, and he kissed her softly.

"Come on, Georgia, let's go home so I can have you naked in my bed until Tuesday night."

"That was the deal, wasn't it?"

"Ahh, yes, the famous deals. I believe the deal was I would show you my house if you stayed naked for at least ten hours of the tour," Josh told her with a grin.

"Then what are we waiting for?"

"Absolutely nothing. Let's get packing."

Josh let her go and moved toward the door. When he got there, he looked over his shoulder at her. She was standing exactly where he had left her, looking at him with a ghost of a smile.

"We'll talk in the car," he told her.

She nodded, and he turned to go pack.

⁓

THEY ENDED UP driving straight home. Josh had told her the sooner they got home, the longer they would have together. He had put pedal to the metal, and they were currently driving into the outskirts of Chicago. It was strange to be coming home after only two days away. It felt as though they had been gone for weeks.

They had come such a long way in the short time they had been together, and as they rolled through the dark streets right before dawn, Shelly was settling into the idea of them as a couple. On the trip home, he had asked her how things had gone with her father, and Shelly had calmly told him everything she'd finally been able to get off her shoulders.

Being able to talk to a man and know he wouldn't judge her was freeing. Josh just listened. Every now and then, he would say something, but generally, he just sat steady and listened to whatever she was telling him.

As they exited the main highway and rolled down the streets toward what looked like the suburbs, Shelly faced the man behind the wheel. He had shrugged on his leather jacket over his familiar white T-shirt and jeans. The man looked sexy and relaxed, and as she watched him silently, he turned to her and smiled.

"What are you thinking about?" he asked.

Shelly gave him a half-smile as she yawned. "I'm thinking about how you're going to strip me down and have your bad old way with me."

He laughed and nodded. "You got that right. I've been thinking of nothing else for the last..." He looked at his watch. "Ten and a half hours."

"Is that right?" Shelly probed.

"That's right, Miz Monroe."

Laughing, Shelly asked, "So now that we're back in the city, I'm Miz Monroe?"

Josh's mouth quirked on the side as he nodded. "Yeah. The city seems to bring out the Man-Eater." He told her in a deep voice, "But I kind of like her now that I know Georgia is in there too."

Shelly raised her eyebrows at him then licked her lips as she looked pointedly at his denim-covered crotch. "Well, I have to tell you, I am really looking forward to living up to my name."

Josh groaned and shook his head. "Thank God we are nearly there."

Shelly laughed and settled in for the remainder of the drive.

JOSH LOOKED ACROSS the truck at Shelly as she lay with her eyes closed, her head leaning back against the seat. Mutley was lying down on the back seat, and Josh had to smile at the fact that Shelly now seemed okay with his dog. They had talked all the way home about her mother and father, and Josh had gotten a much better understanding of the way Dr. Shelly Monroe's mind worked.

He was happy she had been able to confront her father and maybe set some demons to rest. He also hoped, somewhat selfishly, that it had opened the possibility in her mind that they could have a real shot at this. Everything had happened so suddenly between them, but for Josh, it felt so incredibly real. He couldn't explain why, but he knew this was meant to be. He knew he had to come clean and tell her he owned the construction company. She would probably be pissed at him, but it was nothing they couldn't get past. He was sure of it.

As they rounded the final street, Josh couldn't help but feel completely excited about the next day and a half. Shelly had agreed to spend that time at his house and in his bed. *Hell yeah. Can anything be better than that?*

He pulled the truck to a stop at the curb, got out, and walked around to Shelly's side where she was now sleeping. The sun was just starting to come up, and it was going on seven o'clock. Josh had plans, and they involved carrying the sleeping doctor inside, cuddling with her, and waking in a few hours to make love to her.

SHELLY HEARD HER DOOR UNLOCK, and she opened her eyes, noticing the truck had come to a stop. She turned her head and saw Josh outside her door, smiling at her through the window. Sitting up, she let him open the door.

He placed his hands on the roof and leaned in to kiss her. "We're here."

Josh moved back, allowing Shelly to get out. Once she was free, she stretched her arms over her head, yawning, then stood on her tiptoes to wrap her arms around his neck.

"I believe we have specific plans for the next couple of days," she told him before planting a sweet kiss on his lips.

He grinned and hugged her tightly before humming against her mouth. "Hmm, I believe you may be right. You and me naked in my bed sounds familiar."

That was when Shelly looked over Josh's shoulder at the house behind them. It was a nice house that looked as if he had bought it with restoration in mind, knowing his background. As her eyes moved to the driveway, they stopped on a blue Ford Fusion and a tall brunette leaning against the driver's side, staring at them.

"Josh?" Shelly pulled away from him.

He looked down at her. "Yeah, Miz Monroe?"

But Shelly had left the sexy thought process behind. Suddenly, she had a new one.

Who the hell is that woman?

∾

JOSH NOTICED SHELLY HAD STIFFENED, and he moved a step back, wondering what was going on. He was about to ask when he heard a familiar voice.

"Joshua."

Now it was Josh's turn to stiffen. Shelly's eyes narrowed and her shoulders straightened. He wanted to explain something, anything, but he was interrupted when he heard his name being called again by that annoying high-pitched voice. He pivoted on his heel and saw the last person on earth he wanted to see.

"Melissa," he replied in a tone so defeated he didn't even know where it had come from.

He just knew Shelly was thinking the worst, and at this moment, he didn't blame her. *But she needs to let me explain. She has to, right?*

As he watched his ex-girlfriend strut down the driveway toward them, he felt Shelly retreat farther as he turned to look at her. Her eyes were so glacial, they pretty much froze him on the spot.

"I can explain," he told her quietly.

"Why would you need to?" Shelly asked coolly.

Josh wanted to scream. *Because you are jumping to the wrong conclusion.* He looked at Shelly then at the woman fast approaching. *What the hell is she doing here?*

"Melissa is her name, huh? The woman who did a number on you?" Shelly queried, regaining his attention as she climbed back into his truck.

"What are you doing?" he asked without answering her question.

"I'm going to wait in your truck until you do whatever you do to get rid of a woman, then you are going to drive me home because I don't have a car."

"Shelly..." Josh tried again.

"I don't want to hear it." She slammed the truck door shut between them.

Josh was staring at the side of her perfect, angry face when Melissa stopped in front of him.

"Where have you been? I have been coming by since Friday," she said.

Josh shook his head, not quite believing how shitty this morning was turning out.

"Who's that?" Melissa asked, gesturing to the truck. "You looked nice and friendly."

"What are you doing here?" he asked her through a stiff jaw and clenched teeth.

She flashed the smile he used to adore and do anything for. "Isn't it obvious?"

Josh shook his head and kept glancing at the truck door. All he continued to see was Shelly's profile. When he finally looked back at Melissa, he was beyond pissed. "What? Why are you here?"

She grinned and shrugged. "Because I made a mistake. I want you back."

CHAPTER 17

*S*HIT, SHIT, SHIT. So it wasn't the most eloquent moment of her life, but as she sat in the passenger seat of Josh's truck, that was all Shelly could come up with. Out of the corner of her eye, she saw Josh standing by the window, talking to the leggy brunette, Melissa.

Over and over, Shelly chastised herself and her quick fall into la-la love land. *Did I really think for one moment that it would be that easy? When did I become so naive?* Fairy tales didn't happen overnight. Heck, they rarely happened at all. She just had to look at her parents for that wonderful reality check.

Pulling out her phone, Shelly texted Lena. **Need to talk… NOW.**

Almost immediately, she received a response.

Lena: Are you okay?

Shelly shook her head then noticed, out of the corner of her eye, Josh walking around the truck. Looking at her phone, Shelly texted back quickly. **Will call in thirty minutes to talk.**

The driver's door was pulled opened, and Josh climbed inside the truck. Mutley whined and sat up on the back seat.

"Shelly…" Josh said hesitantly.

Turning to face him, Shelly plastered on the most painfully fake smile she had ever given. "Josh…"

He sighed, shaking his head. "Are you going to talk to me about this?"

"Nope." She stared out the window, avoiding his gaze.

That was when she noticed the leggy brunette leaning up against the little Ford again, glaring at them. So Shelly gave in to a sudden impulse and offered her a perky little wave that screamed, *I'm in the car with your man, biotch.*

"She doesn't mean anything," Josh told her as he started the truck.

Shelly rolled her head along the headrest so she was facing him. "Really? To me either," she said, her voice dripping with saccharine sweetness.

"Why are you being like this?" Josh questioned, pulling away from the curb.

Shelly looked back out the window. "I'm not being like anything."

JOSH LOOKED AT the silent woman beside him. Gone was the soft, country Georgia he had been with all weekend, and in her place was Man-Eater Monroe. She wouldn't look at him, she wouldn't talk to him, and he had to believe that as she sat there staring at nothing in particular, she sure as hell wouldn't let him touch her either.

How could this morning have gone so wrong? He had been five minutes away from having a naked Shelly beneath him, over him, all around him, and then Melissa had happened. As if this weekend hadn't been stressful enough, the arrival of his ex had to top it off.

There was no way Shelly was going to let this go, especially after her parents' confessions on the delicate subject of cheating. The real kicker, however, was that even though she knew Melissa was his ex, being confronted by another woman wasn't what she was ready to deal with now.

Josh turned to look at her again. She was beautiful in her silence. Hell, she was beautiful all the time, including the moment she'd confessed her feelings to him down by the river.

"Are you really going to sit there and pretend I don't exist?" he asked, no longer able to bear the silence. How had this woman slipped under his skin so damn quickly?

"I'm not pretending you don't exist. In fact, I am very aware you are right there. I am pointedly ignoring you," she told him while she continued to stare at nothing.

"Is that right?" Josh asked, starting to get annoyed.

"Yes, it is. I don't understand what you expect me to say." She finally turned to face him. "Is she leaving?"

Josh knew his answer wouldn't be what she wanted to hear, but he wasn't going to lie. "No, she wants to talk to me."

She rolled her eyes.

"What?" he asked.

"Nothing."

Josh stopped at a red light and looked at Shelly. "Tell me."

"That's what all women say when they want to get a guy back."

Josh sighed, moving the car forward when the light turned green. "Well, I don't want her back. I left her, remember?"

As he waited for her response, he thought this was probably a good time to confess about owning the construction business too. After all, she was already pissed. Probably best to get it out and just let her get over all the bad at once. *Then we can focus on the good, right?*

"Look, I don't want Melissa. She has some stupid idea that she wants to discuss things with me. But, Shelly, she cheated on me. Why would I go back?"

"But you're going to go and talk to her?" she asked as if driving home a point.

"Yes. I told her I would."

"Fine," she responded and went back to silently looking out the window.

He drove them the rest of the way without saying a word. When he pulled up at the parking zone in front of her building, he parked the truck and watched as she unlatched the door. She seemed ready to get out without saying a word to him.

Josh felt it was crucial to stop her. For some reason, it seemed imperative that he make her talk to him before he drove away. He didn't know why, but he felt as though something was slipping away from him. "Wait."

She stopped her movements and asked coolly, "What, Josh?"

Josh swallowed. *What the hell? I'm already in her bad books. Might as well lay it all on the table. Here goes nothing...* "If this weekend meant anything to you, anything at all, then please let me take care of this, and then come and get you."

SHELLY PUSHED OPEN the truck door and climbed out without answering him. Her chest felt tight, and she wanted to scream, *It meant everything.* However, as her feet hit the pavement and she walked to the end of the truck, all she could think of was her mother's sad face as she told her how she loved a man who didn't love her. As she banished that thought, she was swamped with visuals of her father calmly telling her that it was an arrangement between them, as if it was some damn contract.

Now, here she was, standing on the curb in front of her building, with a man who had to leave her to go appease another woman. No, thank you. That was not what she had in mind for herself—not ever.

Josh pulled her bag out of the truck and put it down in front of her, extending the handle. Shelly gripped it, and suddenly, he put his hand on hers. His anxious eyes gazed down at her, but Shelly steeled herself against them.

"Don't end us like this," he said softly.

Standing tall, Shelly swallowed. "End what? Nothing began. We had a fling."

He stood back. Removing his hand from hers, he ran it through his hair. "Wow. Just like that, huh?" He bent down to get nose to nose with her. "You sure don't have any trouble writing off people as you judge them, do you?"

Shelly raised a brow. "Excuse me?"

"I was worried you'd be pissed when I told you about my job. But I didn't even need to do that because you're pissed for no reason at all, aren't you?" he asked in angry disbelief.

Shelly straightened her spine and tilted her head. "What about your job? You don't work in construction?"

He shook his head. "What do you care? You're done with me, isn't that right?"

Shelly felt her heart clench. *Am I really done with him?*

However, before she could even answer herself, he continued. "Fine, go ahead and keep lying to yourself. Go and date Dr. Drab and the most boring men you can find because I tell you what—any man worth his weight would not stand here and be judged for something he didn't do." He went to move around her, to walk away, but he stopped beside her. "I own the construction business Mason hired, and this weekend meant everything to me. Have a nice life, Shelly Monroe, and do me a favor—lose my number."

Shelly watched him march over to his truck's door, haul it open, and get in. Just as he pulled away from the curb, that stupid mutt poked his goofy head out the window. Shelly tried to remind herself that this was all Josh's fault, but as they drove away, she found it harder and harder to convince herself.

She was perilously close to feeling sorry for herself when her phone rang. Pulling it out, she hit Accept where she stood on the sidewalk.

"Okay, what happened?" Lena asked without any kind of preamble.

Shelly sighed, trying to push Josh's parting words and the thought of him going back to Melissa from her head. "I need to get drunk."

"Tell me what happened."

"Josh Daniels happened, and I need alcohol to recover."

There was silence, then Lena said, "Rachel has been bugging me about this place she goes to. She says it's off-the-chain wild."

See, this is what I need—a night with the girls. "If it's Rachel, I'm sure it will be. Count me in. What's this place called?"

Lena laughed, and Shelly groaned, knowing it was going to be some crazy place no one had ever heard of.

"I believe she said it's called Whipped."

What the hell? It could be fun. "Okay, call me with details."

"Will do. Hey, Shelly?"

"Yeah?"

"Are you going to be okay?"

"Sure," she said in a soft voice. "Just don't ever fix me up again. You suck at it."

With that, she hung up, wheeled her bag to the lobby door, and went inside to try to sleep the horrible morning away.

JOSH WAS FUMING as he made his way back to his house. He couldn't believe Shelly had reduced their weekend to a fling.

A fling.

The woman was so pig-headed and stubborn that she couldn't

even see what was in front of her—which, of course, was him. Well, not anymore. He wasn't going to be one of those guys who waited around for a woman saying no, thanks and wiping her hands clean. He wanted a partner—someone to share his life with.

The problem was he also wanted Shelly.

Turning into his street, he saw the blue car still parked in his driveway. He had been hoping that maybe, just maybe, Melissa would have left. He parked the truck in the spare space beside his home and got out, opening the door for Mutley. Melissa smiled at him as she got out of her little car.

Josh walked over to her. "Okay, what do you want?"

She smiled, reaching out to touch his arm. It was almost strange how much he wanted to pull away. "I told you. I want to try again."

Josh looked at the sky and closed his eyes. He took a deep breath then looked back to Melissa, focusing on her. "I don't understand. It's been months. Why now?"

He watched as she stepped closer, and he waited, not moving.

"Can't we go inside?"

Clenching his jaw, Josh shook his head once. "No, we can't go inside. You can tell me why you've turned up here. Did you run out of money?"

Her brown eyes widened in feigned shock, and he couldn't help but compare them to a startling blue pair he had come to adore. Melissa's were suddenly lacking.

"No. What a horrible thing to say to me."

Josh ran a hand through his hair. "Look, I'm tired, annoyed, and just want to go inside and get some sleep. Stop jerking me around and tell me what you want." He added in an annoyed tone, "Or leave."

She looked around, then finally her eyes came back to his. "Fine. A friend of ours saw you the other day with the blonde."

Josh blinked once, trying to comprehend what she was telling him, then he shook his head again. "Are you serious? You came all the way here because someone told you I was out with another woman?" Beyond incredulous, Josh demanded, "Where did they even see me? No, wait a minute. Who cares? Tell me you didn't come back here because of that."

She bit her bottom lip in a gesture that had once worked every time, but suddenly, all Josh could think of was a certain man-eater.

What the fuck is wrong with me? He internally berated himself and his poor choices in women. He was obviously delirious from lack of sleep.

"Well, I've been thinking about it for a while—how much I missed you—"

"That must have been when Dave was at home with his wife, right?" Josh asked coolly.

"Being an asshole doesn't suit you, Joshua."

"Well, I didn't think being a cheater would suit you, but you made it work," he told her, watching as she registered his words. Then he said what he had wanted to say for years. "I wanted a life with you. I wanted to make it work. Hell, I moved across the country to try to make it work." Shaking his head, he looked over his shoulder and whistled at Mutley. His dog's ears pricked up, and he trotted over and sat by Josh's legs. "It was you who chose otherwise. So please don't come back here, pretending to care because you heard I might be moving on. Get in your car, drive away, and please don't ever look back."

"But—"

"No. There's nothing else to say except good-bye." He spun on his heel and made his way to his door.

When he got there, he turned and watched as Melissa, the first woman he thought he had loved, reversed down the driveway. As she pulled away from the curb, he realized he felt nothing. He wondered if that had anything to do with the fact that he'd left his broken heart at a certain blonde's feet not even an hour earlier.

IT HAD JUST TURNED ten when Shelly's intercom sounded.

After buzzing the girls up, she applied one last coat of gloss to her lips, then headed to the door to unlock it. Several minutes later, the door opened and in walked Lena and Rachel. Shelly tried to smile at them both.

With her hair flowing over her shoulders, Lena was dressed in a tight black dress and bright red shoes. It was her go-to dress, as Lena liked to joke. Hey, it worked, and she looked gorgeous.

Rachel moved from behind Lena and shook her head as she looked over Shelly. "No."

"No?" Shelly questioned, looking down at her black strappy top and flirty pink skirt. "What's wrong with it?"

Rachel rolled her eyes, shaking her head. She was dressed in a black backless halter top and skintight black leather pants. Her dark hair was pulled up in a tight, high ponytail, and the purple tips were brushing the nape of her neck.

As Rachel walked around her, Shelly noticed, for the first time, a wicked-looking tattoo running vertically along the length of Rachel's spine and disappearing beneath her leather pants. Shelly looked at Lena, mouth hanging open, and her friend shook her head.

"I didn't know she had it either." Lena chuckled. "She has a whole bunch. She was showing me on the way over here."

Shelly turned back to look at Rachel, who was still frowning at her. "What's wrong with my outfit?"

"You look like you're going to a high school dance," Rachel told her with a smirk.

Shelly tried not to be offended. She decided if Rachel was going to turn up looking like the sexiest version of a goth dominatrix, then Shelly needed a drink to deal with the fashion advice.

Most of the time, Shelly was the one handing out opinions. Tonight, apparently, it appeared she was totally out of her depth.

After moving to the kitchen, Shelly poured them all a lemon drop martini. She turned, handed the drinks to the girls, and looked at Goth Barbie in the corner. "Well, I'm sorry I don't know how to dress appropriately for a place called Whip Me."

Lena laughed as Rachel raised a brow.

"It's Whipped, Monroe, and don't be so quick to judge. I hear your nickname is Man-Eater," Rachel said with a grin.

Shelly's mouth dropped, then she shut it, shooting a quick glare at Lena. "I'm killing Mason. Next time I see him, he's dead."

Lena gave her a pretend pout as Shelly turned back to face this morphed version of Rachel. Gone was the fun-loving pastry chef, and in her place seemed someone slightly detached and cool.

Almost as though she was removed from the entire discussion, Rachel looked over Shelly. "You want to bring sex."

Shelly raised a brow and put a hand on her hip. "Excuse me? This isn't sexy?"

Rachel nodded. "It is. But it's not the right tone. You want dirty sex."

After narrowing her eyes at Rachel, Shelly turned to Lena, who was grinning like a fool.

"Does Mason know where we're going tonight?" Shelly asked Lena.

"Um...he knows we're going clubbing," Lena said with a smile. "Rachel doesn't want him in her business."

Shelly turned back to Rachel. "What is this place? You're freaking me out, Rach."

Rachel took a sip of her martini. "Just a place I go to escape. It's nothing illegal or bad. I just don't want my big brother there. Is that cool?"

Shelly shrugged but sensed there was more to this than she knew. The three of them had been out before and had even gone out with Mason. Heck, they had all been to the Blue Moon that night with Josh.

Yes, that amazing night in the parking lot with—no. She was not going to think about him tonight.

Instead, she focused on Rachel. Usually, she was relaxed, happy, and fun. Tonight, she seemed edgy and wired, almost as though she was going to explode if her fuse was lit.

Shelly raised her glass, toasting them. "Tonight is a girls' night out. No men allowed."

They clinked their glasses and gulped down the rest of their drinks.

Shelly turned to Rachel and tried for a real smile this time. "Okay, come and find me a dress that screams dirty sex."

JOSH WAS CLIMBING into bed at around ten thirty when the phone rang. He picked it up, almost hoping it was Shelly. "Daniels."

"Hello, Joshua," Cole's voice greeted him.

"Hey, man. What's up?"

"I was just looking over my work schedule and called to remind you about our ten thirty meeting."

Josh sighed then yawned. "It's ten thirty at night. And you're working?"

Cole chuckled. "I'm always working, Daniels. That's why you hired me."

"No. I hired you because you're mean, ruthless, and scare the shit out of me."

"Oh good. My image is intact. Have a good night. I'll see you tomorrow."

"Night, man." Josh hung up, wondering what Shelly was doing at that very moment.

CHAPTER 18

*W*HIPPED WAS DEFINITELY not what Shelly had been expecting.

As the cab pulled up to the curb, Rachel got out first.

Shelly turned to Lena and whispered, "Do you know anything about this place?"

Lena shrugged. "I think it may be a little S&M."

"What?" Shelly squeaked.

They got out, clutching their coats around them to fight off the chill of the late March air.

When they were all standing on the pavement, Shelly said, "All right, look, before I walk in the door..." She stopped and looked over Rachel's shoulder. "Ah, where's the door?" Shelly giggled and moved closer to Rachel. "Or is it like a dungeon?"

Rachel raised her eyebrow and shook her head, her sleek ponytail swishing from side to side. "You, my friend, are an idiot. The door is around the side of the building. No dungeons and no cages."

Shelly frowned then asked seriously, "Um, Rach? What should we be expecting?"

Rachel smirked before walking past her toward the corner of the building where a crowd was loitering. "Just drinks and dancing."

Shelly turned to Lena. "I don't believe her."

Lena slipped her arm through Shelly's and grinned. "Neither do I, but you did say you wanted drinks to forget Jos—"

"Don't say his name," Shelly said as they finally reached where Rachel had taken a place in line.

"Okay, I won't say his name, but it is a shame. I thought things would work out."

Rolling her eyes, Shelly sighed. "Just because you're happy and boning Langley every night—"

"Eww," Rachel chimed in. "That's my brother you're talking about."

Shelly grinned unashamedly. "*Okay*, Miss Dirty Sex." Then she continued speaking to Lena. "Not everyone is as lucky as you and Mase."

Lena nodded. "I wish you could have been."

Shelly turned to face the front of the line. "For a moment, I was."

The line moved fairly quickly, and they were inside before they knew it.

The lights in the entryway were dim, and Shelly wondered why it mattered that she had changed. It was so dark that it would be impossible to see the blue skintight tube dress Rachel had picked out for her. Rachel had also insisted on tying a black ribbon resembling a choker necklace around Shelly's throat. After Shelly had been dressed like a human-sized Barbie doll, Rachel had handed her a pair of spiked stilettos and declared Shelly ready for dirty sex.

Now, where is Josh when I need him?

Like it mattered. She had nipped that in the bud, and he had told her to lose his number. Now she could go back to looking for someone suitable who didn't have an ex-girlfriend popping up to be a match contender.

Once they were finally allowed into the main area, Shelly felt her eyes widen as she gaped. By the similar expression on Lena's face, her somewhat more prudish friend also felt a little out of her depth—or more like *a lot*.

Rachel, however, strutted through the crowd, which actually moved for her, and made her way over to the bar. Not knowing what else to do, Shelly and Lena followed, looking around.

This place sure was something. The low lighting continued through the center of the club, and red velvet booths with black tables lined the far wall of the establishment. In the center of the space was a medium-sized dance floor, and on the other side of the club was the bar that ran along the wall.

However, it wasn't the décor that was slightly shocking. It was the people that had Shelly gobsmacked. Following Rachel, Shelly noted men and women of all different shapes and sizes dressed in anything from leather to PVC to—*Is that spandex? Wow.*

Clearly, some of the people rocked the look. Like Rachel Langley, who had now reached the bar and was leaning on it, talking to the bartender with a sexy smile.

Lena gripped Shelly's arm as they made it through the throng of people dancing *and* heavily kissing until they reached Rachel.

Over the loud music, Rachel yelled, "What do you two want to drink?"

Shelly was so busy staring at the way people were moving and acting in all their different outfits that she didn't answer.

"Shel?" Rachel asked her again.

Shelly turned to look at her. "I need a tequila shot please."

Lena yelled, "Me too."

Rachel spun back around to the bartender and leaned her palms up on the counter, effectively moving her body halfway across the bar. The younger-looking man, probably in his early twenties, stepped forward immediately.

"Did you hear that, Riley?"

The bartender nodded, his eyes only on Rachel. Then he said something that almost made Shelly fall flat on her face.

"Yes, Miss Rachel."

"Good boy. Now come here," *Miss* Rachel told the young man.

Lena gripped her arm and squeezed. "What the hell is she doing?"

Rachel stretched across the bar's counter.

"I think she's sealing a deal or proving a..." Shelly was utterly bewildered and looked at Lena. "I have no goddamn idea. Did you know all about this? No wonder she doesn't want Mason to know. He'd flip his lid."

Lena's eyes were huge as she looked at her soon-to-be sister-in-law. "I'm worried about her."

"Because of this?" Shelly asked, looking back to see the bartender was licking Rachel's neck slowly with his hands behind his back.

Mesmerized by the odd nature of what was going on before her,

Shelly stood frozen, unable to look away. Once the bartender had completed his...*task, goal? Shit.* Shelly had no clue what to call it. He stepped back and waited patiently for his next order. Aha. *That's the word—order.*

Rachel moved from the bar and shook her hands by her sides, as though coming out of a trance, before facing them both with a smile. Shelly imagined that she and Lena looked as if they could have caught flies as they stared slack-jawed at the usually bubbly and fun-loving pastry chef. *Oh yeah, Mason would have a shit fit if he knew where his baby sister was spending her nights.*

"Riley is going to bring us tequila for the rest of the night. It would be rude not to drink it," Rachel informed.

Shelly raised a brow at the forceful tone of Rachel's statement. *What the hell? You only live once.* Looking at Lena, Shelly grinned. "I wanted to forget Josh Daniels. I can't think of a better place to do that than here. You game?"

Lena looked at her fiancé's sister, who was staring at them with those serious blue eyes again. Shelly followed her friend's gaze and also zoomed in on the stranger formerly known as Rachel. *Who is this woman?*

"You promise I'll get home safely?" Lena asked.

Rachel finally smiled in a somewhat familiar way, and Shelly had to admit the power she was throwing their way was kind of cool.

How does she do that? Super Domme powers? Ha ha, Super Domme. Shelly giggled, giving the words a low, deep "movie announcer" voice in her head. *Put on leather pants, and BAM, you're an instant hypnotist?*

Either way, Shelly wished she had been wearing a pair when she saw Melissa this afternoon. She would have advised her to take a long walk off of a short pier.

"I would never let anything happen to either of you, Lena. You have my word," Rachel said.

Shelly had to admit that this version of Rachel could tell her it was safe to go into a dark padded room, and she'd probably believe her.

Turning toward Lena, Shelly smiled and nodded before looking back at Rachel. "Well? Where's the tequila, my friend?"

Rachel looked over the bar at the statue of Riley and said nothing. She just gave a slight nod, but he must have understood because he scurried off.

As he walked away to presumably get the shots, Shelly couldn't help but liken him to a certain ninety-pound hairball.

ONE-AND-A-HALF SWEATY HOURS later and four tequila shots each, the three of them moved off the dance floor toward the bar. When they reached it, Lena leaned her back against it. Shelly stood next to her, and beside her was Rachel, who turned to face the ever-present Riley. Once again awaiting orders.

Shelly had to admit that, as far as she could tell, Rachel had a good system going. *Hey, more power to her. No man would ever tell Super Domme in the leather pants what to do.* Her vision of Rachel started to blur a little. Giggling, she watched as Rachel turned toward her.

"Having fun?" Rachel asked.

Shelly nodded then turned her head back slowly so she could focus on Lena. "Yep, we're drunk," Shelly slurred as she leaned into her closest friend and colleague. "The room is spinning a little."

Lena nodded before looking out at the sea of black leather, silver-studded collars, and PVC booty shorts. She giggled. "You know these people all look *ahh-ma-zing.*"

Looking at the dance floor, Shelly had to admit that the club had lost quite a few patrons as the time had ticked by—probably since it was a Monday night. Then she noticed that the remaining people were from a different kind of crowd. This crowd looked fitter, younger, better-looking. It was almost as if the young ones came out to play later at night.

As Shelly leaned back on the bar, the three of them all watched the dancers.

"He's sexy," Rachel pointed out.

Shelly looked over to where she was pointing. He was an auburn-haired man dressed in a white T-shirt and jeans, bobbing his head to the music. *Yeah, he's attractive*—but his hair was the wrong color and it was too short. He wasn't muscular enough either, and when he turned to look at them, his green eyes weren't chocolate brown.

Damn Josh Daniels. Even drunk in a place called Whipped, he was still in her freakin' head.

Lena took that moment to peer around Shelly at Rachel. "Would ya fuck him?"

Shelly looked at her fellow doctor in shock. "Oh hello, nosy?" Shelly singsonged with a giggle. Then she turned to Rachel and asked, "So would you?"

Just as Rachel was about to answer, a low voice interrupted. "She would, but she shouldn't."

Lena, then a more controlled Rachel, turned to peer down to the very end of the bar where a man sat with his back against the wall. He was out of the light, so in their inebriated state, they really couldn't see much. Shelly noticed he seemed to be twirling a lowball scotch in his hand.

"And why shouldn't I?" Rachel asked, acting much bolder than Shelly had expected.

"Because he's not your type," the guy said in that same smooth I-know-I'm-right voice.

Rachel rolled her eyes as she turned away to look back out at the crowd.

Lena took that opportunity to walk over and stand in front of Rachel. "Do you know that guy?"

Rachel shook her head. "No. I've never seen him before." She seemed thoughtful for a moment. "But guys like him—they're all the same."

That interested a drunken Shelly immensely. Moving to stand beside Lena, she stumbled over her own shoe but caught herself in the nick of time. Straightening with an amused giggled, Shelly faced Rachel, looking at her as though she held the answers to the universe.

"What d'ya mean?" Shelly asked conspiratorially.

Just then, Riley came over with three shots, three lemons, and a salt shaker.

Rachel opened her mouth to answer before her eyes lifted above their shoulders and zoomed in on the person now standing behind them. Shelly and Lena turned to see a tall man, at least six foot two, maybe three, with short dirty-blond hair. Shelly knew that all three of them were staring.

He wasn't dressed in anything ridiculous, like a studded collar or leather shorts. He was dressed in a pristine white dress shirt buttoned and tucked perfectly into charcoal pin-striped pants that narrowed at his waist. Draped around the open collar of his shirt was a crimson tie. However, the outfit didn't end there. Resting over his arm was a jacket being held in place by his hands resting in his pants pockets.

Wearing what appeared to be his work suit, he looked so out of place in this club that his outfit was almost more comical than the men and women in the leather and studs.

"Ladies," he greeted with the same tone the man at the end of the bar had used.

Shelly muddled through that with her inebriated mind. *Ahh, same man.*

"I hope you don't mind. I'd like to dance with your friend."

Shelly turned to peer at Rachel.

Wouldn't you know it, cool-as-a-cucumber Rachel looked Mr. Incredible over, shaking her head. "No, thank you. You aren't my type."

Lena squeaked and looked at Shelly, mouthing, *Seriously?* This guy was every woman's type. Well, every woman but Rachel apparently.

"Is that right?" His voice was so smooth and cultured that Shelly knew this guy was educated in some way. Or maybe he'd just had a few less drinks than they had.

Rachel dipped her head slightly and elegantly for someone who had to be feeling more than a little tipsy. "That's right. *Nice suit.*" She almost made it sound like some sort of challenge.

Shelly and Lena were looking back and forth between the two like a tennis match—only this was better. This was Super Domme and...*well, heck, what does that make him?* Shelly was almost afraid to know.

"*Nice hair*," he threw back. "Are you sure you won't take me up on my offer?"

Rachel sharply shook her head once. "I told you. *You* are not my type."

The man moved in closer to Rachel. Shelly was ready to tackle him if need be, and by the looks of it, Lena was also ready to jump up on his back and start hitting and kicking if backup was required.

However, it wasn't needed. He merely leaned past Rachel, freeing his hand from his pocket to take the salt shaker. Bending his head, he licked the skin of his hand between his thumb and index finger, then he tapped some salt onto it. He moved the lemon, placing it close by, and picked up the shot glass filled with tequila, gesturing to her.

"Oh fine. If you insist. Hold your hand up where I can lick it," Rachel instructed, eyes blazing, chin held high.

Fascinated, Shelly watched as he lifted his salt-covered hand to Rachel, daring her.

"Lick," his deep voice instructed. It seemed *he* was now giving the orders. He lifted his other hand and raised the shot to her. "Sip. Suck." He nodded at the lemon.

Apparently not one to back down from anything, Rachel leaned forward, eyes locked on the stranger's. She licked his hand, took the shot he offered, then picked up the lemon on the bar and sucked.

Lena gasped, and Shelly wondered if her friend was also feeling the crazy sexual tension hissing and crackling around them like a roaring inferno.

Then he spoke. "See? I too can follow orders. Sometimes."

Rachel glared at him with narrowed eyes.

Shelly was shocked at this whole other side of Rachel. In fact, Shelly was starting to think that maybe she was hallucinating her very own superhero and *Super Domme* was what she had come up with.

Rachel stepped forward and tilted her chin up toward the man, further investigating their battle of wills. "Once again—no, thank you."

Suddenly, it felt as if the man heard some underlying message in Rachel's response.

Lena gripped Shelly's arm tightly as if they were watching a great movie, then they both froze as he dipped his head in retreat.

"Very well." He turned as though to walk away. But before he took a step, he looked over his shoulder. "By the way, I think I am *exactly* your type."

With that, he walked through the crowd and out of the club.

RACHEL BLINKED TWICE, then she seemed to pull herself out of some kind of moment.

Well, hell, Shelly thought, *that's how I felt when Josh was all up in my space*. Mesmerized, intoxicated, hot, and bothered.

But Rachel had said *no* and clearly shown that she was not interested. As Shelly looked across the club at the auburn-haired man, she had to wonder what was so appealing about *that* guy over Mr. Incredible.

Lena took that opportunity to grab their shots. After she handed one to Shelly, they both passed on the licking and sucking and went straight to downing the fiery liquid. As it burned a hot liquid trail down her throat into her tummy, Shelly felt a giddy buzz come over her.

"One more dance?" she asked Lena and Rachel.

Lena had a pinched expression on her face from the shot, and Rachel was laughing.

"Sure, one more dance, then in a cab to head home," Rachel told them both.

Shelly followed them out onto the floor, thinking with a giggle, *Yes, Miss Rachel.*

JOSH WOKE TO a loud knock on the front door.

Rolling over, he looked at the clock and saw it had just turned 1:43 a.m. He was going to ignore it until the knock came again, and this time Mutley sat up, barking.

Great. Now I have to get it.

Getting out of bed, he grabbed a T-shirt and walked toward the obnoxious knocking. When he got there, he opened the door and found Shelly on his doorstep in a skintight electric-blue tube dress. A jacket dangled from her fingers, her hair was a mess, and she smelled like a bottle of tequila.

"What are you doing here?"

She wobbled a little, so Josh grasped her shoulder to steady her. She smiled at him, her face lighting up, but her bleary, bloodshot, sad eyes detracted from it.

"I can't get you out of my head," she slurred. "I lost your number... the...the way you told me to, but I re-rem-remembered how to get to your house."

Fantastic, Josh thought as she swayed again. "Where were you tonight?"

She moved a step closer and looked up at him. "You were so easy to fall for."

Josh shook his head. *Shit. Not like this.* Of course he wanted to hear this, but not now, not when she was drunk. He was about to say something when she swayed in the opposite direction.

"I be okay, Josh. Josh?"

"Yes, Shelly?" he asked patiently.

"Can I come inside?"

This was *so* not what he wanted right now and definitely not how he had wanted to show her his place.

"I'm going to drive you home," he told her.

"Why?" she whined, frowning.

"Because you and I are over, remember? We just had a fling?"

"Fling schming," she said with a goofy grin. "You're sexy."

That's it. Josh reached back, grabbing his wallet and keys off of the small side table. He shoved his bare feet into some sneakers by the entrance then moved toward her before shutting the door. Swinging her up into his arms, he carried her to the truck and opened the passenger side door. He slid her inside and closed it with a firm hand. Walking around to his side, he saw her looking out the window at him with a sappy look.

Boy, is she toasted. She's going to hate herself in the morning. Getting in the truck, he started it and made his way to her place.

She took that opportunity to talk. "I wished you were with me tonight."

Josh took a deep breath. "Where were you?"

"Whipped."

"Huh?" he asked, thinking he had misheard.

"At Whipped. With Super Domme."

Josh was beyond confused and suddenly worried some guy had been harassing her—or maybe she had been harassing some guy. *In that outfit, any guy would welcome it.*

"Josh?"

He turned to look at her. She was leaning against the truck's seat with her head back and her face turned toward him, her eyes focusing on him.

"I really did fall for you under my tree."

Josh grimaced and felt his heart crack. "Oh yeah?"

She nodded. "Yeah."

Josh swallowed and licked his lips. "Then what happened?"

She took a deep breath and smiled sadly. "Reality."

Then she promptly passed out.

WHEN THEY ARRIVED at Shelly's condo, Josh woke her with a gentle nudge and helped her inside.

Waiting by the elevator with Shelly clinging to his side, Josh asked, "Which floor are you on, Georgia?"

She tilted up her face, giving him a lopsided smile. *Even drunk, the woman is gorgeous.*

"Three," she told him, holding up her fingers. "One. Two. Three. Yep, three."

Josh shook his head and tapped his foot impatiently. He wished the doors would hurry up and open so he could get her inside her condo then go home. Finally there was a loud ping, and the doors swooshed open.

Securing his grip around Shelly's waist, he moved forward, making sure she came with him. He wasn't quite sure what the security guard would think of him standing there in his T-shirt and boxers. Not to mention Shelly looked like she had been sexed up really good. Her hair was a royal mess, her shoes were now in his hands, and she was clinging to him as though they hadn't had a huge ugly fight earlier in the day.

As the doors shut and the elevator moved, she slipped a hand under his shirt.

"What are you doing?" he asked.

"Hmm..." she cooed. "I'm playing with you."

"No shit." Halting her hand, he asked, "In more ways than one?"

Removing her palm, she pouted, and those full pink lips called to him. He was still so mad at her, yet he couldn't help the way his cock twitched and his heart ached just from looking at her.

She had kicked him out of her life less than twenty-four hours ago. Without even waiting for an explanation, she had decided they were done and over with. And now, she was looking like the man-eater he had first met—batting those eyelashes, pursing those sexy-as-sin lips, and inviting him to do all kinds of wicked things to her.

"Fine then," she told him when the doors opened.

She removed herself from his grip and sauntered forward with as much grace as she could manage, which wasn't much considering she stumbled a couple of times.

"If you don't want me, maybe you should go back to Melanie."

Josh rolled his eyes and made his way over to where she was struggling to insert her key into the door. Taking it from her, he unlocked the door and pushed it open. "Her name is Melissa. And don't you think if I wanted her, I would be in my bed now, wrapped around her, instead of standing out here in your hallway in my shirt and boxer shorts at"—he glanced at his watch—"three a.m.?"

∼

SHELLY HAD TO admit that she may have drunk more than she thought she had.

As she stood just inside her doorway, Josh was starting to sway, and she didn't think it had anything to do with him wanting to slow dance.

"Well, maybe you left her in your bed so she'd be there when you got back home." Before she could stop her stupid runaway mouth, she added, "Just like you left me to go to her this afternoon."

Obviously that had *not* been the right thing to say. Before she could blink, Josh was through her door, gripping her arms as he pushed her back against the wall.

"Do you even know what you did to me this morning?" he growled as he lowered his head to look her in the eye.

Shelly tried to focus, but she was finding it hard, so she closed her eyes and licked her lips.

"It was *you* I wanted in my bed tonight, Georgia—not fucking Melissa."

Shelly's eyes flashed open, and she arched her hips toward him. He was so close, and she wanted to touch him.

"But you decided what kind of person I was, and then you left." Lifting his hands off of her, he stepped away.

She watched as he turned on his heel. She knew he was about to walk out her door, and there was nothing she could do about it.

Or maybe there was.

"You don't have to leave," she whispered seductively, moving away from the wall. The room spun a little, so she steadied herself. "You can stay."

He looked her over. "Why would I stay, Georgia?"

Shelly looked him right in the eye this time. She thought she saw something, almost like defeat. She knew she had caused that, but she wasn't in the right frame of mind to deal with it. Instead, she reverted to what she knew.

Gripping the top of the electric-blue tube dress, she slowly peeled it down, revealing a blue strapless bra. Now she had his attention. "Well, maybe you could stay for this."

Keeping her eyes on him, she continued to push the dress down, wiggling it past her hips until it fell to the floor. Stepping out of the fabric, she turned on the balls of her feet and made her way down the hall. Just before she disappeared into her bedroom, she looked over her shoulder at him.

"Either lock the door on your way out, or lock it and come to bed."

∽

JOSH WATCHED IN quiet disbelief as Shelly walked into what he presumed was her bedroom.

The woman is driving me in-fucking-sane. Had she really just stood there and stripped down to the sexiest blue lingerie he'd ever seen in his life then invited him to bed? *What the fuck is going on?* Just this afternoon, she had told him to get lost.

Turning, he made his way to the door, determined to walk right through it and leave, but apparently his hard-on and his goddamn heart had different ideas.

Locking the door, he rested his forehead against it and took a deep breath. He could do this. *Just go in there, keep my heart out of it, tear up the sheets with her, and walk away.*

Yes, he could do this.

Determined to prove himself right, he turned and made his way down to her bedroom.

However, what he saw when he got there almost blew his mind. She had turned on a side lamp and made her way onto her large plush bed. Somewhere along the way, she had stripped off the last two remaining pieces of lace, leaving them haphazardly on the floor. Looking at him from beneath her wickedly long eyelashes, she was centered on a crazy-looking comforter, lounging back against the pillows.

She is too fucking enticing.

"Good decision. You just going to stand there?"

Josh finally kicked his ass in gear and made his way into the room.

Her décor was insane—pink, white, and black everywhere—but he didn't give a shit about that at the moment. He walked toward the end of the bed, staring at her in her perfect naked glory.

"If we do this, you keep quiet, and we do this my way," he told her.

One side of her mouth tilted up while her eyes dilated. He couldn't be sure if that was a result of alcohol or desire, but if he had to guess, he'd say it was a bit of both.

"Ohhhh. Want to gag and blindfold me too?"

Trying not to laugh, Josh stripped off his boxers, which were doing nothing but constricting him, then he whipped off his shirt over his head. He took an inordinate amount of pleasure in the way her eyes zeroed in on his cock as her mouth parted. She lifted her right hand and moved it down between her thighs, pressing it firmly against her bare mound.

Oh no, none of that tonight. Josh moved up and over her like a panther on the prowl. "Move your hand, Georgia. It's not needed down there tonight." He watched as she slowly removed her hand. When he was finally settled above her, he lowered his mouth to her lips. "Open your legs."

Her eyes slid closed, and he felt her shift, those beautiful legs parting at his command. Settling his weight between them, he rubbed his rock-hard erection up against her wet lips.

He groaned as he bit her lip. "You were so ready to throw this all away, weren't you, Georgia?"

Her eyes snapped open. When he saw she was going to say something, he decided that he didn't want to hear it.

So Josh took her mouth in a tempestuous kiss.

∼

SHELLY THOUGHT SHE must have died and gone to heaven.

After she had climbed into bed, she was sure she heard her door open, shut, then lock. But now, here was Josh lying above her, settling between her thighs, and pressing all those rock-hard muscles against her.

Wrapping her arms around his neck, she arched her breasts up to rub against his chest. She heard a rumble in his throat as he lifted his mouth from hers, bringing a hand up to stroke her face.

His eyes were locked on hers, and she knew she must have been dreaming when he whispered against her mouth, "How can you not see how perfect this is?"

Shelly closed her eyes, hanging on to the moment like a perfect memory, then her lips parted as the dream took an erotic turn. A delicious pressure pushed between her thighs, then suddenly she felt full —fuller than ever before.

Clinging to shards of reality, she arched her hips and sighed as he thrust home, her whole body thrumming with sensation. Her eyes slowly opened, and there he was, deep chocolate eyes looking at her with so much desire and such raw emotion that Shelly thought her heart would burst out of her chest.

Then her dream opened his mouth and spoke, telling her everything she wanted to hear. "You feel so good, Shel. You're so tight. So warm."

She felt kisses along her neck and a hardness pulsating deep between her thighs.

"How can you not see how good we'd be together and how much I would love you?"

His final words hurled her over the blissful edge of pleasure then lulled her into a peaceful sleep.

CHAPTER 19

Two months later

May

SHELLY HAD BEEN on her feet for the past eight hours, and she saw no end in sight. She was currently bedside in the ICU, preparing to perform a bronchoscopy procedure.

She was tired—*exhausted* actually.

Over the past couple of months, she had been working extra shifts and doing everything she could to avoid examining her recent life choices.

Her mother had been calling her every weekend to see how she was doing and when she would be coming back to *talk*.

Honestly, all Shelly wanted to do was forget that they had ever talked in the first place. However, she knew the time would come when she would have to see them both, and she felt it would be better if she did it sooner rather than later.

Then there was *him*—the man who had somehow imprinted himself on her mind and body after such a short amount of time.

How is it that Josh is still always on her mind? It had been months since she last saw him, and that had been so emotionally gut-wrenching that Shelly didn't think she would ever recover. *So what do I do?*

She had worked herself into the ground to avoid dinners at Exquisite, skipped late nights out with Mason and Lena, and evaded working out with her friend. She had essentially disappeared. After all, that was what Josh had accused her of wanting to do. So why not live up to it?

∽

SHELLY WOKE TO *the sun streaming through her window and across her pillow. It was hitting her right in the eyes. As she blinked, she raised her hand to her face, trying to block the intruding rays. She groaned, "Oh God."*

"Head hurts, huh?" *a voice asked from the corner of her room.*

Squinting at the comfy reading chair she had placed under her window, she saw Josh sitting in his—wait, T-shirt and boxer shorts?

Looking down at herself, she noticed she was in bed with the sheet over her. Turning away from him, she slowly lifted the sheet and peeked under. Naked except for panties. *She knew she must look like a total mess, which didn't help her disposition—not to mention, her throbbing head.*

Just as she was about to speak, Josh beat her to it. "Before you even start, you wanted it too."

Shelly bit her lip and ran a hand over her, apparently, bird nest of hair. She frowned and cleared her throat. "I wasn't going to say anything."

Because honestly, she couldn't remember. Images kept flickering through her mind of him above her, inside her, but she was too embarrassed to clarify if it had been real—or worse, if it had been a fantasy.

Josh quietly accused, "Now that seems more like you."

"What's that supposed to mean?" *Shelly snapped as dignified as she could while hungover.*

Josh stood and walked to the end of the bed. He looked around at the outlandish décor then back at her. He placed his palms on the comforter on each side of her covered legs, then he made his way up and over her.

"It means you never say what you actually mean," *he told her as he hovered above her.*

Shelly clamped her mouth shut, not wanting him anywhere near her after the things she had drunk the night before.

He didn't smile. He merely held himself up as he looked over her face. "I think you're the most amazing woman I have ever met."

Shelly clutched the sheet tighter to her, gnawing hard on her lip.

"And that completely terrifies you for some reason. It makes you want to just disappear from the moment," he said, his eyes locking with her own. Lowering himself down, he lay next to her before gently stroking her hair. "You got upset last night when you came to see me."

Finally, Shelly had to say something. "What did I say?"

Josh leaned in, and she tried not to even breathe as he laid a gentle kiss on her cheek. He whispered in her ear, "Nothing I didn't already know."

Then he rolled across the bed and got up.

"What does that mean?" Shelly demanded, sitting up fast.

She clutched her head, wincing, then remembered the sheet, which had now fallen down in her lap. She used her other hand to slowly pull it up—although why she bothered, she didn't know. When she finally looked back at him, he gave her a sad smile.

"You're not ready for me, Georgia," he told her softly. "And that's a real shame."

Then he turned and walked out of her life.

SHE FINALLY MADE it into her office as the phone was ringing.

Pushing aside memories that continued to haunt her, she picked up the phone and was not surprised to hear Lena on the other end.

"Okay. I don't care what excuse you think you have or can look for or what the hell else you do whenever I've asked you out lately. You are coming to Mason's tonight, and we are all going to go down and watch the fireworks."

Shelly groaned and sat back in her chair.

She was definitely in a funk. She hadn't even started her new dating campaign. Maybe Lena was right. She just needed a night out with friends.

"Will Josh be going?" she asked hesitantly. She reminded herself yet again that this was why she had avoided getting involved with him in the first place.

"Mason asked him to go. I don't know if he'll show."

Shelly shook her head against the chair and shut her eyes. *Am I really going to do this to myself?* "Okay, I'll be there." *I can do this and be an adult.* "What time?"

"We're meeting at seven for drinks. Shelly, we've missed you."

"I know. I'll be there," she promised then hung up.

∼

JOSH WAS ON his way home to get ready for tonight.

When Mason had first asked him to come along, he had been unsure. He hadn't seen Shelly for nearly two months, and now that it was the start of all the holiday festivities, he knew it was more than likely that they would start running into one another.

Chicago had a hidden secret—well, not that hidden to the natives. Every Saturday between Memorial Day and Labor Day, the city let off fireworks from Navy Pier.

Tonight was the first night. They were all going to meet at Mason's for drinks then go across the park to watch.

Josh had kept himself busy over the past weeks, working on the restaurant expansion for Mason and changing a few minor details on his house to make it more buyer-friendly. Around a month ago, he had decided to put his house on the market. It had been one night after a few too many beers when an idea had come to him of what his next project should be, and it sure as hell didn't involve restoring the house he was currently living in.

Mutley looked at him, and Josh nodded. *That's right, buddy. Once things are tidied up at the restaurant, I have a new project and some direction for my life to go in.*

First though, he had to get through tonight. Since Shelly never went anywhere alone—*and God only knows who her "exciting" date will be tonight*—Josh was going to ask Jenny. She was a nice girl he had met recently and had a few coffees with. A nice, sweet girl who had no baggage and seemed to want something permanent. Unfortunately though, nothing seemed to erase those big blue eyes and perfect blond hair from his mind.

∼

SEVEN O'CLOCK ROLLED AROUND, and Shelly was standing in the lobby of Mason's building, waiting for the elevator. She had pushed the button and was tapping her foot when she heard a pair of heels clicking behind her. When they stopped, she glanced over her shoulder and felt her heart skid to an abrupt halt.

Standing behind her, looking as gorgeous as she remembered, was Josh—and beside him was a small woman in a yellow sundress and strappy white heels. The lady had honey-brown hair, and as she smiled at Shelly, all she could focus on was Josh's hand on the woman's back. Lifting her eyes to his, she thought she detected a moment of discomfort before he made himself smile.

"Shelly. It's been a while."

Shelly was trying to remember how to talk. *Open mouth. Project sound. Nope, it's not working.*

Luckily, the elevator pinged and the doors swooshed open. Shelly almost ran in and pressed herself into the back corner.

The little woman next to Josh looked at him and smiled, probably at Shelly's odd behavior, then she stepped in and stood on the other side of the elevator. Josh moved inside, pushed the button, then leaned back between the two of them.

As the car lurched and started to rise, he turned toward Shelly. "This is Jenny."

Shelly looked at him and knew her eyes must have been screaming something—maybe, *What the hell are you trying to do to me?* But really, she had no recourse. This was what she had done to him.

Telling herself to act like an adult, Shelly looked past him and smiled at the lady holding his hand. "Hi, I'm Shelly. I work with Lena."

Jenny's face lit up as she nodded. "Oh, yes, I've heard Lena and Mason talk about you. I'm so happy to finally meet you."

What the hell? Shelly thought as the car came to a jolty stop. *They've been double-dating with Lena and Mason? Oh God.* She felt ill. All of a sudden, she wanted to throw up.

When the doors opened, Jenny got out first, and Josh turned to look at Shelly where she was plastered up against the wall.

"It's good to see you, Georgia. You look great," he told her.

Then he walked over to Mason's front door, leaving Shelly and her emotions shot to shit.

～

WHEN MASON OPENED THE DOOR, Josh could tell he was shocked to see all three of them waiting in the hall. Josh knew his face must have looked strained. He was trying really hard not to let it show because he didn't want Jenny to be uncomfortable, but standing so close to Shelly had him all kinds of wound tight.

"Hi, guys," Mason exclaimed with a big grin, letting them all in. As Josh moved past him, Mason whispered, "What the hell, man?"

"Don't ask," Josh mumbled and moved forward, following his date.

Mason said softly, "It's so good to see you, Shelly. You look beautiful."

Oh, and she does. Josh walked into the kitchen to grab a beer.

His eyes found Shelly's as she moved over to Lena. Tonight, Shelly looked absolutely stunning, wearing a white gauzy dress that seemed to float over her body as she moved. The halter dipped into a low V-shape between those beautiful breasts, and the waist was cinched by a taupe satin ribbon.

However, the kicker was the back of the dress, or should he say, the lack of one. The whole creamy expanse of her back was on display, and the material started up again at her waist, extending to the flowy skirt.

She had a frown though, and he noticed her eyes kept darting over to Jenny.

Great. Josh had really thought she would bring somebody. *What a fucking mess.*

That wasn't the biggest part of this mess though. The biggest part was he wanted to touch her.

∼

SHELLY STOOD IN front of Lena and thought it was pretty spectacular of her to have even walked into the condo.

"You didn't tell me he was dating someone," Shelly accused softly.

"Well, you never asked," Lena said gently. "You've hardly talked to me for me to tell you."

Well, she has a point. Shelly silently hated her for it. "I hate that you're right." *Okay, maybe not so silent.*

Lena told her quietly, "Would it help if I told you that you look beautiful and he hasn't taken his eyes off you?"

Shelly looked over and locked eyes with the man she had said she wouldn't and *couldn't* love. She tried desperately to think of what her reasons for that had been again.

He was dressed casually in a white button-up shirt and jeans, and he looked sexier than she thought he ever had. He didn't look away and didn't hide the raw emotion that filled his eyes as he ran his gaze over her. As Shelly felt her body respond, she pointedly looked away from him to his date, the lovely Jenny. When she looked back, he had moved over to chat with Mason.

Turning back to Lena, Shelly said, "No, that doesn't help, and I need a very stiff drink."

Lena nodded and moved away to get it.

∽

SO JENNY WAS NICE, which made Shelly even more miserable.

She was an elementary school teacher and was so sweet.

Shelly was feeling ill. *What is the matter with me?* She was the one who had ended things with him after his ex turned up that morning months ago. *She* had panicked and sent him away.

Shelly knew it had been for the best because she had been *and still was* way too raw over the whole mess with her parents to even think about getting into a relationship. However, whenever she looked at him or heard him talk or laugh, her heart clenched and her body throbbed.

She had never been a believer in instant connections, but that weekend in March, whether it was because she had been raw with emotions or because he was the right man at the right time, she thought she had really fallen for him. Maybe she had for a day, before reality came back to slap her across the face. But now, she had to stand here with this kind, sweet woman and watch as *she* discovered that he was very possibly the perfect man.

∽

SEVERAL HOURS LATER, after all the fireworks had gone off, they walked back through the park to catch a cab home. Lena and Mason were at the front of the group, holding hands and laughing, and Josh found himself beside Jenny, wondering about the woman a couple of paces away.

He was listening to Jenny answering correctly, but his eyes and mind were on the naked back of the woman walking ahead of him. She had been so subdued tonight, not the usual man-eater he was accustomed to *or* the sweet Georgia. She was just quiet. Almost sad.

He knew she had to still be dealing with her parents' revelations, and he figured that him showing up with Jenny probably hadn't helped. It pained him to see her that way. She was usually full of life. Tonight though, she just looked so tired.

When they reached the road, Mason hailed a cab for his guests, and Jenny was the first one in because she lived across town. She kissed Josh gently when he wished her a good night. She really was a good girl, but he was pretty certain she knew that they weren't a forever match.

As the cab pulled away, Mason cleared his throat. "I'll let you get Shelly a cab. We're going to call it a night."

Shelly rolled her eyes and shook her head as their friends crossed the street.

From the other side, Lena yelled, "I'll call you tomorrow with the time for the dress fittings, okay?"

Shelly nodded as Lena turned, taking Mason's hand as they walked into the lobby.

Josh had to envy them. They had found each other and loved one another so much that it made him smile just to look at them. Turning, he saw that Shelly had taken a seat on a bench that edged the park. Josh put his hands in his pockets and moved over to stand in front of her.

"Jenny seems nice," she said, finally looking up at him.

He nodded. "She is nice." He watched Shelly look down at her lap and pick at her skirt. This wasn't the woman he had met a few months back. He took a seat beside her. "What's going on, Shel? Talk to me. Is it your parents?"

She turned her head, and her blond hair spilled over her shoulder. He pushed it behind her ear, and she sucked in a breath and bit her lip.

"Why do you think I'm such an idiot?" she asked.

Josh felt the side of his mouth quirk up. "Idiot? You? Now that's not something I would ever accuse you of being." He raised an eyebrow. "Stubborn maybe, but not an idiot. Why would you even think that?"

She looked away, and Josh felt his heart clench. He didn't want to feel like this for her, a woman who didn't want him. But as she sat there looking like a lost girl, he couldn't help but stroke the back of his finger down her cheek to her chin. He tipped her face toward him, and as her blue eyes blurred with tears, he let his emotions show as well.

∽

HIS EYES ROAMED all over her face as though he was memorizing every little feature. She couldn't help the tear that had slipped from her eye, falling down her cheek.

"Talk to me," he said.

Shelly wanted to. She wanted to tell him everything she was thinking. How much it had hurt to watch him with Jenny. How much she had wished it was her. How every time he had touched his date, Shelly had pretended he was touching her instead.

But as he looked at her so intently, she knew she couldn't do that to him. He had moved on. He was dating a wonderful woman who really was the sweetest woman Shelly had ever met.

So instead of telling him everything in her heart, she whispered, "Mason was right, huh? Blondes really are your type."

Josh dropped his hand and took a deep breath before standing. Shelly stood beside him as he raised a hand for a cab. When one pulled up, he opened the door for her. Shelly took a step and was about to get in the cab when he gripped her arm gently.

She turned as he said, "*She* is the imitation of what I want. Unfortunately, the original is not available."

With that, he let go and stepped back onto the sidewalk.

Shelly looked him over, feeling another tear slide down her cheek, then she slid into the cab's back seat. As it pulled away from the curb, she turned around and watched as Josh faded away into the night.

CHAPTER 20

June

TWO WEEKS LATER, Shelly was standing in front of a full-length mirror, looking at the dress Lena had picked out for her. She had to admit the dress was gorgeous. It was pastel blue, strapless, and flowed gently over her curves, ending an inch or so above the knee. The dress complemented her and Rachel perfectly. With her eyes on the mirror, Shelly looked at the two women standing behind her.

"So? What do you think?" she asked, raising a brow.

"Are you serious? It looks fantastic," Lena exclaimed, stepping forward to run a hand down the material covering Shelly's hip. "It's seriously unfair how you sometimes resemble a Barbie."

Rachel laughed. "I don't know if that's a compliment or an insult."

Lena looked over at Rachel, who wore a long purple, blue, and pink tie-dyed shirt and cutoff denim shorts that were frayed around the thigh. *The girl sure does have an eclectic choice of clothes.*

"It *was* a compliment. Didn't every little girl want to be Barbie when they grew up?" Lena responded.

"Not if she wanted to get laid. Ken always had his tighty-whiteys on," Rachel said with a wicked smirk.

Shelly chuckled, and Lena burst out laughing.

"Okay, okay. Forget the Barbie reference. We all definitely like sex," Lena said.

"Although it's been a while for some of us," Shelly mumbled.

All of a sudden, she had two pairs of eyes on her.

"How long?" Lena asked quietly.

Shelly looked at Rachel, who seemed interested in her answer as well. *Oh, what the hell?*

"Since Josh." Her friends' eyes widened, and Shelly shrugged. "Don't read anything into it. I just haven't wanted to date after that whole thing."

Rachel stepped up, still keeping their gazes locked. For a minute, Shelly thought Super Domme was making an appearance, but then Rachel's eyes softened. "What happened with you two? He won't tell me shit, and that's not like him."

Shelly looked at Lena, who was the only person who knew the whole story. Then her eyes moved back to Rachel. "He wanted more. I didn't. So we ended it."

The room was silent for a moment. Shelly took the opportunity to step down from the small round platform and move toward the dressing room.

"Are you high? Why wouldn't you want something more with Josh? He's one of the most amazing men I know," Rachel asked.

Shelly felt her temperature rise. Instead of answering Rachel, she went on the defensive. *Always a great move among friends. Not.* "Why don't you date him then, if he's so wonderful? Or maybe you're afraid he won't follow orders?"

Rachel's eyes narrowed as Lena moved to stand between them.

"All right, kitty cats, sheathe your claws," Lena said.

Rachel was the first to speak. "I don't understand. He's attractive, successful, and kind, and you're going to just let him move away?" She stopped, shaking her head. "For a doctor, I thought you'd be smarter than that."

Shelly blinked as Rachel continued pointing out all of her faults, but Shelly had blocked out the sound. All she kept hearing was, *You're just going to let him move away.* Those words repeated over and over in her head. Finally, she snapped, "He's moving away?"

Lena and Rachel nodded.

"He told us last night at dinner," Lena confirmed.

Shelly walked into the dressing room like a zombie. *He's moving. He's leaving.* She would never have to see him again. She would never have to worry that he would be at Lena and Mason's or down at Exquisite.

She should have been thrilled, but as she stood in the dressing room, she felt as though her heart was finally completely broken.

JOSH WAS SITTING on his couch with a beer, watching the Cubs. His afternoon couldn't have gotten much better. He had finally taken the plunge the other day and gone down to the bank to apply for a loan. When Cole had called to tell him he had been approved, he'd felt elated.

Finally. Finally something was going the way he had planned. He had worked things out with his crew, currently working on Mason's renovation, and arranged things so he only had to be present once a month.

Ahh, the beauty of owning your own business. If you want to work on other projects, you can. You have no one to answer to, except your employees and the person who hired you. As long as you can deliver your services and pay your staff, then the sky's the limit.

However, Josh didn't want to go to the sky. No, he had somewhere more specific in mind.

As he took another sip of his beer, there was a sharp knock at his door. Looking out the window, he tried to see who was there, but whoever it was was standing too close to the door. He placed his beer on the coffee table and went to answer the door. When he pulled it open, he was surprised to see Shelly, but in the back of his mind, he had known, or suspected, that she would eventually show up.

She stood on his porch, wearing a bright yellow T-shirt, a pair of cutoff jeans, and white flip-flops. She had her hair pulled to the side in a messy-looking braid. She looked cute, refreshed, and so utterly appealing that he almost felt like nixing his whole plan.

But no, in the long run, what he was doing was for the best, and it would eventually work out for him. *Right?*

"Shelly? This is a surprise," he said.

SHELLY LOOKED JOSH over as he stood there holding the door open. She didn't know him as well as she wanted to. And that was her fault. As she stood there taking him in, she thought it was highly unfair that she was just now realizing the enormity of her own stupid mistake.

"Is it true?" Shelly asked with no greeting whatsoever.

He stepped aside, and Shelly walked past him. Taking a deep breath, she closed her eyes for a moment before continuing into his front hall. When he shut the door, she turned and saw him watching her.

"Is what true?" he asked slowly.

He had to know what she was referring to, but he wanted confirmation. So, dropping her bulky leather bag on the floor, she gave it to him. "Are you really leaving Chicago?"

He nodded, but he stayed where he was, not making any move toward her. "Yes, it's true. I'll be leaving in a couple of days."

Shelly sucked in a deep breath, not realizing until that moment how much his admission would affect her. She felt as if he had punched her in the gut. Stepping toward him, she was a little shocked when he stepped back.

"What are you doing here, Georgia?" His face was serious and devoid of all emotions.

Swallowing deeply, Shelly turned away and looked around the living room. "Where's Mutley?"

He laughed. "Really? You want to know where my dog is?"

Shelly turned back to face him, shaking her head. "No."

"Then what?"

Trying to find her courage but not locating it anywhere, Shelly opted for evasive maneuvers. "Well, I wanted to say good-bye." Shelly rolled her eyes at herself then shook her head. "I'm doing a terrible job of lying, aren't I?"

Finally, he moved.

He stepped forward until they were only inches apart.

Shelly looked into his warm chocolate eyes and whispered, "I've been working on my brave face."

JOSH CUPPED HER face with both hands. "It's still pathetic." He stroked her cheeks with his thumbs. "What do you need to be brave about?"

She bit her lip, blinking those beautiful eyes at him. "I wasn't like this before you."

Josh tilted his head. "Like what?"

"Vulnerable. You've made me a walking bag of emotions."

Leaning down, Josh laid his lips against hers in a gentle kiss. Lifting his head, he said softly, "But we were just a fling."

She tried to shake her head, but with him holding her face, she could move it only slightly. "You were never just a fling."

"Then, what was I, Shelly Monroe?"

She licked her lips and locked eyes with him. "You were a game changer."

SHELLY COULDN'T BELIEVE she had just said that to him. *What on earth am I doing?* Laying her heart on the ground was what she was doing. Laying it down and saying, *Here you go, please tread carefully*.

Sadness flickered into his eyes before quickly disappearing. "And what game are we playing, Georgia? Yours?"

Well, that didn't sound good. Shelly pulled back. *What did I expect?* Well, she had expected...

"I thought you wanted this?" She pointed at him then herself. "Us?"

He turned away, shaking his head. "I don't trust you."

That hit hard. It actually physically hurt. "I don't understand. I've never cheated on you or betrayed you."

"Haven't you?" He ran his hand through his hair, spinning back to her as he dropped his hand by his side. "Didn't you betray me and yourself when you reduced everything we did that weekend to a fling?"

Shelly stepped back until she bumped into the wall. "I was confused. I didn't believe it could happen that quickly."

"Well, that's convenient—*for you*. But me? I'm just thrown aside. Not trusted because an ex showed up?" he asked, moving toward her.

"I'm left feeling like shit because you freaked out. And now that I'm leaving, now that I have my shit together and know what I want, you want to tell me how you feel? Jesus." With a loud sigh, he pushed past her, storming into the kitchen.

Shelly stood with her back pressed to the wall, breathing hard. *Is that what I'm doing? It probably is, but screw that.* She was fighting for what she wanted. She was going to push all the sweet Jennys out of his mind and remind him who he met first—and that was Man-Eater Monroe. Delicious Daniels liked *her*. He couldn't resist her.

Maybe she just needed to reintroduce them.

∼

JOSH STOOD IN THE KITCHEN, staring out the back window. Mutley was outside running around, and he was in his house on this perfect afternoon with Shelly confessing her feelings for him.

Of course, that was what he had wanted all along, but somehow, her showing up just because he was leaving pissed him off. He'd wanted her to turn up because she'd realized every day would be better if they were together. Not because she was afraid that he was walking away forever. *Shit, her timing is horrible.*

"Josh?"

Turning, he saw Shelly standing at the door to his kitchen. She had let her hair out of the ponytail holder and had kicked off her flip-flops, and suddenly, Josh was thrown back to months ago when he had first met this firecracker.

"What, Georgia?" he asked as she looked him over. *What the hell is the woman trying to do to me?*

"Why are you angry at me? I just wanted to tell you how I felt before you left. You always tell me I never say what I'm thinking."

He shook his head as she pushed off the doorjamb, moving toward him. "That's the problem, Shel. You're telling me *because* I'm leaving—or because of Jenny."

She stopped and tilted her head. "Are you and her serious?"

Josh almost lied. He almost said *yes*, just so he wouldn't get pulled into her spell and be caught for the rest of his life. As he stood there with his ass leaning against the sink, Georgia walking toward him with those big eyes and her sexy hair spilling over her shoulders, he thought, *Fuck it. Sometimes a man has to know when to give in.*

∼

SHELLY WAITED IN the middle of his kitchen as he looked her over from head to toe.

He said quietly, "Jenny and I only went on three dates."

Something heavy lifted off of Shelly's chest, and suddenly, she felt confident. She stopped in front of him to trace a finger down his white T-shirt.

That was another thing she liked about Josh. He was such a simple guy when it came to the everyday things, but then again, he could afford to be. The man filled out a T-shirt and a pair of jeans like nobody's business.

"Shelly?" he seemed to warn her.

Looking at him with a raised eyebrow, she smiled wickedly, teasing a finger under his shirt to the top snap of his jeans. She was thrilled when he uncrossed his arms and braced his hands behind him on the sink.

"Josh?" she asked in turn.

His muscular chest expanded with a deep breath. "If we do this, you need to understand that I'm still leaving."

That was *not* what she was expecting, but at this stage, she was willing to take what she could. "Okay. Would you be open to email?"

She was pleased when surprise crossed his face.

"I don't understand what you mean," he said.

She continued to swirl a nail around the bare skin between his navel and the top of his jeans. "Will you email me—stay in contact with me?" She bit her bottom lip. "Or are you leaving and never coming back?"

∼

JOSH LOOKED DOWN AT HER, feeling every emotion he had tried to squash rush back in. "I'm undecided at the moment, but yes, I'll email you if you want me to."

Her eyes clouded, but she quickly blinked and nodded. "I'd like that." She rose up on her tiptoes, placing her palms on his chest as she laid her lips against his. "You know what else I'd like?"

Josh's breathing was getting more and more labored with every word she spoke. He finally gripped her upper arms. "No. Why don't you tell me?"

"I'd like to feel you inside me again."

Groaning, Josh nodded as he straightened up from the sink. Reaching into her hair, he pulled her face forward, pressing his lips to hers. She parted her mouth straight away, and he slipped his tongue into the warm interior. He heard her moan and felt her hands move around behind his waist, landing on his ass.

Oh yeah, it's been too long since I've kissed this woman.

As she pressed closer to him, he walked her backward until her back hit his stainless steel fridge. Her eyes opened and focused on his as he tugged the hem of her shirt up and off her head. Tossing the shirt behind them, he looked down at her beautiful breasts encased in a lacy yellow bra.

I've never liked that color so much. With both hands, he gently cupped and plumped them forward before lowering his head, biting at one straining nipple through the bra. A moan reverberated through her as her hands came up and dragged through his hair before gripping it tightly.

Rubbing his tongue against the lace-covered tip, he'd finally had enough. He wanted her flesh. He slipped his fingers in the cup, moving the lace out of the way. Once the nipple popped free, he latched on to it, sucking the hard tip into his mouth. The scream that left her throat was deep, and as she flexed her hips toward him, he knew that she wanted this as much as he did.

"What, Georgia? Tell me what you want."

SHELLY TUGGED ON JOSH'S hair until he moved away from her sensitive nipple. She was standing in his kitchen in only her shorts and her bra, which was now pulled down, and all she wanted was to be completely naked. *Right now.*

She panted. "I want you."

"Well, that's good because I want you too."

Shaking her head against the fridge, she told him, "I want you in me, over me, all around me. *Now.*"

He smiled and reached down to pull off his white shirt. Shelly felt her mouth part as her eyes traced every wonderful defined muscle of his chest. She wanted to lick and bite *all of them.*

He unsnapped his jeans and pushed them down his hips. All of a sudden, Josh—a.k.a. Mr. Delicious—was standing buck-ass naked in his kitchen in the middle of the afternoon. Shelly licked her lips, tugging on her own nipple as he proudly displayed his obvious attraction to her.

Holy shit. The man is hard. His cock looked like an arrow pointing right at her. As she played with her nipples, he groaned, and she lifted her eyes from his hard-on to his face and smirked.

"You don't even need me," he told her as he stood a few inches away, watching her.

Shelly pushed her hips out as her back leaned against the fridge, and she moaned while she tugged a little harder on the sensitive tip. "Hmm, yes, I do."

"Oh yeah?" he asked, stepping closer. "What for?"

Shelly let her eyes flutter closed, but when she felt his big hands on the button of her shorts, they flew right back open.

"I need you to put that"—she pointed at his cock—"in here." Then she palmed herself through her shorts, thrusting her hips forward.

AS SHELLY PLAYED with her nipples while pressing her hand between her thighs, his control snapped. He grabbed the hand between her legs and tugged her forward. Caught off guard, she squeaked when she almost fell, but he was there to catch her.

He turned her around before pushing her toward the fridge. Her breasts were pressed up against the cool stainless steel, and his hot naked body was pressed firmly against her back. He moaned, rubbing his aching shaft against the denim covering her ass. He burrowed his nose under her ear, taking a deep breath. *Ahh, apples.* Reaching around her tiny waist, he slid his big hand down her shorts and into her panties. She groaned loudly as his fingers brushed past her hard little clit.

"Oh God," she moaned, pressing her cheek to the fridge. "Just do it."

Grinding himself against her, he asked, "Do what, Georgia?"

She squirmed, pushing her ass back against him. "Put your damn fingers in me."

Josh chuckled, loving this side of Shelly. She was so demanding and confident. She was never one to shy away, and she always asked for what she wanted.

"Not yet," he said.

Removing his hand, he unzipped her shorts then pulled them and her flimsy yellow thong off of her. If he hadn't been so desperate to get point A—his cock—into point B—her wet, tight slice of heaven—he might have stopped for a minute to appreciate the little thong. As it was, all his blood was between his legs, and it wanted to start pounding something *now*.

As he looked at her creamy white ass now on display, he dipped his knees and stroked his erection up between her ass cheeks. Smirking, he heard her curse as he did it over and over while he gripped her hips.

"*Josh*," she groaned.

"Yes, Georgia?"

She looked over her shoulder at him with her eyes clouded and dilated, her lips parting. She looked like someone who had been thoroughly fucked—or was about to be. "Sometime this year, please?" She pushed her hips back on him. "I never knew you were such a tease."

∽

SHELLY WAS OVERHEATING. She was burning up from the inside out, and Josh kept sliding his hard cock over her ass as if he was going to start a fire from rubbing wood—literally.

She was about to tell him to hurry up and get inside her when he pulled back and gripped her waist, tugging her over to the kitchen counter. Bending her forward so she was half lying on the cool granite, his large, hard body molded to hers from behind.

"Now, Georgia, you might want to reach across and hang on."

Feeling her juices dripping down her thighs, Shelly knew she was more than ready for a good pounding. It had been weeks—no, months—since she'd had good hot sex, and it had been with this man. As she felt his throbbing tip brush where she was aching, Shelly reached across the counter and held on tight.

∽

JOSH GRIPPED SHELLY'S HIPS, lining himself up, then he thrust deep inside where she was hot, tight, and oh so wet. She felt like every fantasy he had ever had, and as she moaned, she also sounded like it.

Bending over her so his chest was touching her back, he gripped her small hips and flexed his own, burrowing his cock deeper inside her. He felt possessive all of a sudden, like he wanted to mark her, imprint himself on her, *in her*, wherever he could.

As he pistoned his hips back and forth, he whispered, "God, Shel, how could you think this is anything other than fucking perfect?"

She cried out, pushing her hips back to him, as a deep chuckle left his throat from the sheer animalistic nature of the act. He had never been so rough or so forceful with a woman, but as she pushed herself up with her hands, arching that beautiful back toward him, Josh couldn't help but lean down and bite her shoulder.

∽

OH FUCK, SHELLY thought when she felt his teeth in her skin. He was fucking biting her, and she loved it. She lifted herself, using her hands to brace herself as she slammed back against him and felt his cock drive deeper inside her.

"Fuck, Shel," he moaned.

He wrapped one arm around her waist and really started to move. His hips bumped up against her ass with every forward stroke. As he leaned down, he growled in her ear. "Nothing ever feels as good as being buried deep inside you while your hot little pussy squeezes me every time something excites you."

Shelly clenched, and Josh cursed.

"You like it when I talk dirty, hmm?" he murmured in her ear. "Hold on tight, Georgia. I need to get deeper."

Shelly almost came right then. *Good God, the man has a dirty mouth on him.* She had to admit that she didn't mind it one bit. Usually she was the one who had to hold back, but when Josh pushed gently on the small of her back and she found her cheek against the cool granite counter, she knew he was her exact match.

"Now, Josh. Oh God," she groaned, needing completion.

He flexed his hips, his hands gripping hers on the counter. After three strong thrusts, he leaned down and kissed her ear gently.

He whispered, "I knew from the very first moment that you would change me."

He sucked her lobe and continued to move faster inside her. As her breathing quickened, she turned her head, and his mouth found hers. He kissed her hard, thrusting his tongue deep inside. As she felt him tense, flexing once more, she fell apart, body and soul, on his kitchen counter.

CHAPTER 21

July

HOME WAS ALWAYS hard to go back to. However, this time around, it was excruciating. Shelly had opted to take a plane back for the Fourth of July, and as she sat by the window looking out at the runway, she couldn't help but think about her last email from Josh.

He was being really mysterious about where he was. She had even tried getting it out of Mason, but he'd merely shrugged and told her he had no idea. Honestly, Shelly didn't believe him for one moment.

Why would Josh just vanish? Well, he had his reason, but she didn't buy that either.

SHELLY,

Please stop sending me naked pictures of you during the day. I lose focus on everything around me. At least if you send them at night, I can open them in private and enjoy them one-on-one. ;)

For the millionth time, no amount of skin that you send me is going to make me tell you where I am. I told you that I'm happy being alone for the time being. Plus, if I tell you where I am, I know you'll turn up, and quite honestly, Georgia, I'm not there yet. That's not to say I won't ever be—just not yet.

As always,

Josh

HE WASN'T THERE YET. *Well, aren't I stupid?* When he'd been ready, she had run away as quick as her legs could carry her, clinging to the insane notion that his ex-girlfriend was a threat.

Shelly had known all along there was no threat there. She had seen it in his eyes and heard it in his voice when he waited to make sure she was okay the morning after her late night out. Every single move Josh had made proved that he cared and his feelings were real.

And what did I do? Reduced them all to one ugly word—*fling*.

So really, this hopeless, unrequited infatuation she had with him was her own damn fault because now he didn't trust her.

As the plane taxied down the runway to wait in the holding line for takeoff, she recalled her own email with her anxious questions.

Maybe it was time to leave the man alone. Perhaps he did need his space, as he had said. Maybe he didn't want her to keep emailing him naughty snapshots. However, as the cabin rattled and the jet engines kicked in, Shelly couldn't help but think that if that were the case, then he would tell her to stop emailing altogether. *Wouldn't he?*

~

JOSH SAT DOWN with his laptop and a beer. He'd spent the morning at the worksite, eager to get home to open the most recent email from Man-Eater.

Yep, she had most definitely reclaimed that name. The woman was intent on giving him a hard-on in the middle of the day. On more than a few occasions, he'd been working at the site and checked his phone after he heard it chime. Then, right there in his inbox, snapshots of the stunningly sexy doctor had appeared.

At one point, he'd asked her why she sent them through email instead of a text message, and he had to laugh at her response.

If I text it, it's instant. If I email, you anticipate opening it. Plus, if it goes to the wrong person, then at least I have a chance of recovery. Imagine that going to Mason? Instantly?

Oh, hell no, had been Josh's reaction. There was no way he wanted

Mason's eyes on that, and he was pretty sure Lena wouldn't want it either. Shelly was breathtaking.

As he sat on his apartment's shabby couch, he opened the laptop and switched it on. There on his screen was the most beautiful face he had ever seen.

Her eyes were almond-shaped, and the blue was so stunning in its vibrancy that it almost looked unreal. In this picture, she was looking over her naked shoulder, her hair disheveled around her face. She had her phone in one hand, pointing it at the mirror. Her lips were parted, and her eyes were screaming *come and get me*.

Damn, she's beautiful. He had known leaving her would be hard, and honestly, Josh hadn't known what to expect after that desperate moment of passion in his kitchen. Letting her walk away had been the most difficult decision he'd ever made, especially knowing he was still going to leave. Nothing was going to sway him from giving them both the time they needed. If it was meant to be, they would find their way back to each other.

If not? Well, if not, I'm screwed.

AS THE PLANE touched down in Georgia, Shelly took a deep breath and looked at the rain drizzling down the plane's window.

What a miserable day. She wondered if it was an omen about what to expect on her visit. She wasn't looking forward to spending one-on-one time with her parents, and she was pretty sure her father wasn't either after her last spectacular visit.

When Shelly finally entered the waiting area by the arrival terminal, she saw her father standing toward the baggage claim area, leaning up against a big white column. Shelly noticed that most women walking by stopped to look at him. Shelly could see that he was an attractive man. She looked just like him, or so everyone told her, and for years, she had taken that as a bad thing.

When his eyes found hers and he smiled, she had to rethink her expectations. *Maybe he is looking forward to seeing me.* The man looking at her with a warm and friendly disposition was not the man she was accustomed to. This man looked relaxed and carefree, nothing like the stressed out, rigid man she knew as her father.

Walking toward him, Shelly hefted her carry-on bag over her shoulder. When he held out a hand for her bag, she slid it off of her shoulder and gave it to him.

"Hey, princess."

Shelly usually resented that name from him. He'd given her the nickname as a child, and when her opinion of him had started to change, she hadn't wanted him to call her anything special because it had hurt too much. So as he stood there holding her bright pink bag over his broad shoulder, she found herself shocked as she relented—*a little bit.*

"Hey."

"How was the trip?" Turning on his heel, he led the way out to the parking garage.

"Not bad. Considering the weather, it was fairly smooth."

When they got to his truck, he pulled back the bed cover to put her bag in the back, and she had an instant flash of Josh lifting her bags into his truck. That man was determined to stay in the forefront of her mind.

"So you decided to fly this time, I see," her father pointed out as they got into the truck. The engine rumbled, turning over.

Shelly nodded. "Yes, eleven hours in a car is only good once a year."

"I agree. It's a long way to drive." He tacked on, "By yourself."

As they pulled onto the road, the rain, accompanied by a strong wind, hit the windshield, making a swooshing sound. *It's a really miserable night.*

"I thought you might have brought that fellow with ya," her father said. "Josh, was it?"

Shelly winced a little, not wanting to talk about it. She had a sneaking suspicion they might get into an argument if they did. "Yes, that's his name, but we aren't together anymore. He moved."

The silence in the dark cab of the truck stretched painfully.

Then her father cleared his throat. "Look, can we talk 'bout what happened the last time you were here?"

Shelly looked at him and tried to see the man she had idolized as a little girl—before all the teasing had begun, before the relentless rumors had followed her everywhere, and before her perfect image of him had been shattered. She nodded. "Sure."

He glanced at her, and she found herself staring at her own blue eyes. They crinkled at the sides as he gave her a tight smile, then he looked back at the wet road. "I want to apologize to you."

Shelly stared at his profile, unable to say anything.

When he realized nothing was going to come out of *her* mouth, he continued. "For years, your mother and I had an understanding."

"God, that is such a horrible word to use for a marriage," Shelly said boldly.

He nodded before pointing out, "So is using the Lord's name in vain, but you just did. However, you're right. What we had wasn't ideal, especially for a young girl growing up."

Shelly couldn't look at him anymore. She stared out the window as the rain slid down the pane. Her heart started to ache, and as her father's deep voice continued, it ached a little more with each word.

"I don't know where ya ever got the notion that I wasn't proud of you. Your mother told me that. Truly, Shel, how could you ever think that I'm not proud of you?" He paused as though waiting for an answer.

She had nothing to give him except snarky comments like, *Maybe because you never told me.* Or perhaps, *Because you cared more about chasing ass?* Instead, she sat silent, letting him continue.

"Nothing made me prouder than when you decided to go into medicine. I remember thinking you were just like me."

She turned to look at him. "I'm nothing like you."

He frowned. "I know that now, but I figured that some of me had to rub off. And, Shel, honey? Maybe it was the good part?" He took a deep breath and raised a hand to run his fingers through his hair. "Maybe you're all the goodness I had in me." As he shook his head, a baffled expression came over his face. "I was never cut out to be a husband or a father. I'm a surgeon—a man who sets aside his emotions and goes into an OR to stop someone from dying. Not a man who can walk around a park and buy ice cream with a little girl in pigtails. That was never me."

Shelly tried to blink back her tears but knew she was failing, so instead of facing him, she continued to stare out the window and listen.

"For years, I tried to be what your mother and you needed and wanted, but that *wasn't* me."

"So why not leave?" Shelly asked, looking at him. "Why not pack your bags and leave us?"

He took a deep breath and reached across the truck to take her hand. Shelly found herself perilously close to yanking hers away, but at the last minute, she made herself keep it there.

He squeezed it. "Because I loved you both, just not the way you needed me to."

It was Shelly's turn to shake her head. "I don't understand what you're saying."

He took a deep breath and let it out on a long sigh. He let go of her hand and grasped the steering wheel. "I love your mother as a friend, a best friend, but not as a wife. When she got pregnant, she was so happy. I was terrified. I had just enrolled in medical school, and adding a baby to the mix wasn't going to be ideal in any scenario."

Shelly swallowed. "So you stayed because of me? Gee, that makes it so much better."

There was silence before he told her, "No, I stayed for me. I couldn't bear to leave you. Your mother kicked me out, rightfully so, when she had heard about my indiscretions. Those weeks were the longest of my life—the ones away from you and, in a sense, her too. In the end, I begged her to let me see you, and she did with one condition."

Shelly narrowed her eyes. "And the condition was that you didn't break up the family?"

He nodded. "Yes, that I raise you in a good, respectable Southern way by providing you with a mother and father living happily under the same roof."

Shelly barked out an odd sound, and she assumed it was some kind of sarcastic laugh. "Yeah, look how well *that* turned out."

He was facing the road, then he turned toward her. Shelly was shocked to see tears blurring his eyes.

"It turned out horribly wrong. Instead of raising a happy, proud, and beautiful daughter, we raised a scared, smart, stubborn, and incredibly beautiful young lady who's been embarrassed her whole life and made to feel ashamed of her family. For that, your mother and I are truly sorry, and we hope that someday you can forgive us."

Shelly wiped away tears. "I just don't understand where the man who took me to the park disappeared to. When did he become so quick to judge my life instead of supporting me?"

Her father grimaced and shook his head. "I don't know where he went. I can only say that I probably judged you harshly in your life because I was afraid you would make the same mistakes I made in my own."

"Meaning me? And Mother? We're your mistakes?" Shelly demanded.

"No, meaning the hurt I caused you and your mother. My own selfishness and stupidity hurt two women I respect and admire. The man who bought you ice cream by the fountain is not who I am, but he *is* the man who taught me how to love you, and he *is* the man you should try to love. Try to think about him, and maybe eventually you'll forgive me." They pulled up outside the house, and her father turned to her. "I love you, and your mother and I are so very proud of you. Don't let what we did to each other, and inadvertently you, destroy your life."

Shelly bit her bottom lip as she turned to push open the door.

"Shelly?"

She turned back to see her father give her a lopsided smirk.

"Your brave face is still horrible."

JOSH WAS WATCHING a baseball game when his laptop chimed, indicating he had a message. Looking at the toolbar, he saw it was from Georgia. He picked up the computer and put it on his lap, grabbed his beer, took a swig, and read.

Georgia: Can't sleep. You awake?

Josh settled on the couch and typed back. **Yeah, I'm awake, Georgia. How goes it?**

Georgia: Ugh. I'm down visiting my parents this weekend...need I say more?

Josh took a deep breath and let it out. *Wow, that must be rough on her.* He put the beer on the coffee table, and sitting back, he typed. **Horrible?**

Georgia: Pretty much. Drove back from the airport with my father.

Oh boy. Josh wasn't sure what she wanted at this stage, so he decided to keep it light and easy, letting her make the decision to either open up or move on. **How'd that go?**

Josh waited a good five minutes before he got her response.

Georgia: It was really sad. How is it that in the space of several months, I've had my heart broken twice?

Josh leaned his head back against the chair and reread that message twice. *Why is she determined to bring me to my knees?* He wasn't ready. His brain and his body were ready, but his heart was still telling him to tread gently. This woman had the ability, as he already knew, to break *and* burn him. **I broke your heart?**

Josh felt like an idiot. This conversation could only move him further toward aching for her when he was trying to work out what to even *do* about her.

Georgia: It breaks every time I think of you.

Josh's heart wasn't broken right now. It was thundering. He wanted so badly to call her and hear her voice telling him all the words she was writing. Instead, he wrote back. **Mine has never quite healed.**

There was a long pause as he wondered what she would write next. He was shocked when she changed the subject.

Georgia: It's raining here tonight. I'm sitting by my bedroom window with my laptop, watching the lightning.

Josh settled in, crossing his legs on the coffee table while he turned on some music. **Yeah? It's raining here too.**

Georgia: Where's here?

None of your business. He chuckled and added a smiley face poking out its tongue.

Georgia: Damn, I thought for sure I could get you that time.

Josh: Nice try, Georgia, but I'm on to you.

Georgia: Pretty sure you're not, or I'd be much happier right now.

She ended that flirty comment with a wink. Josh grinned, typing back.

Happier, huh? You're happy when I'm on top of you? *Oh yeah, sexy I can do. Heartfelt, I'm not ready for.*

Georgia: Happy is probably the wrong word. Hot? Horny? Wet?

Josh groaned then shook his head. *Crazy, sexy woman.* **What are you wearing?**

Georgia: A smile.

Laughing, Josh wrote back. **And...?**

Georgia: A bigger smile?

Josh smiled over her antics. **I want to kiss that smile soon.**

Georgia: If you told me where you are, I'd come see you.

Josh sighed as he always did when she asked.

I know. That's why I haven't told anyone. I'll be back for the wedding.

Georgia: That's in a month. That's a long time to wait for a kiss.

Josh sat up before writing. **Trust me, it'll be worth it. I gotta go sleep now. You okay?**

He waited, wanting to make sure she was feeling all right.

Georgia: Yeah, I'm fine. Josh?

Josh felt his heart hammer again. **Yes?**

Georgia: Thank you for being there. I wish you were here to hold me tonight.

Josh read the words and was just about to send, *I want to be there every night*, when he noticed she was already gone.

CHAPTER 22

August

JOSH WAS PACKING up his truck and getting ready to drive back to Chicago. He had a wedding to attend.

He opened the passenger side door for Mutley, and his dog took a bounding leap, landing in the passenger seat before turning back to look at him.

Yeah, you aren't as pretty as my last road trip partner, Josh thought before ruffling his dog's head.

Mutley whined then lay down.

As Josh walked around the front of his truck, he looked at the clear sky and took a deep breath of fresh air. He had been on his way to hitting the highway, but before he got on a long stretch of road, he wanted Mutley to stretch his legs a little. And he had some things he wanted to think over.

So he'd driven by a small place he had found recently and pulled the truck over. As he'd sat on the tailgate while Mutley sniffed, Josh thought about his future. He knew what he wanted, and she was living in Chicago. He wondered if she was happy there. *Is that where she sees herself growing old?* Shelly was such a contradiction of personalities, sometimes he wondered who it was he was talking to.

He knew it was time to lay out some options for her. He had to admit that in the months he had been gone, she had been extremely persistent. He didn't know if the saying *absence makes the heart grow fonder* applied to her, but she sure did keep in daily contact, and she made his evenings that much sweeter.

Taking one last look at the serenity in front of him, he stretched his hands above his head with a smile. *Now is the time, Shelly Monroe. Now is the time to let me know what you want from me and when you want it.*

He climbed into the truck and started the ignition. As the vehicle hitched and bumped over the gravel road, he smiled at his dog and rubbed his head. *Let's go see Georgia, Mutley.*

SHELLY WAS A mass of nerves.

It was ridiculous really. It should have been Lena who was nervous. After all, tomorrow was her wedding day, not Shelly's. However, as she stood in front of her full-length mirror, all Shelly could think about was her last email to Josh and the sexy but vague response she had received.

The man was utterly frustrating. He blocked her at every turn, never giving an inch. She wasn't sure if he still had real feelings for her or if she was fighting a losing battle.

Shelly was done fighting people. After the weekend with her parents, she had come home feeling freer than ever. Even though everything her father, and then her mother, had said to her wasn't ideal, the fact that they had apologized at all was a miracle.

After that weekend, she'd also started to reflect on her decisions in life.

Exiting was the Shelly who thought she needed to date a man based on his success, and entering was a Shelly who wanted a man she couldn't seem to get out of her head. And that man happened to be coming to the rehearsal dinner tonight.

TONIGHT, JOSH HAD opted to take a cab from his hotel. The dinner was being held at Exquisite, and Josh had to admit he was excited to see everyone. Hanging out with the Langley crew was like living with a family again.

He was also looking forward to seeing a certain blonde.

Oh yes. He hadn't seen her since the end of June in his kitchen, and that had been such a hot and desperate parting that he had trouble remembering anything about that day except for taking her over the countertop.

When the taxi pulled up in front of the valet stand, Josh got out and made his way to the front door with the sign that read, "Closed tonight due to a private party." As Josh pushed open the doors and made his way inside, he had to admit that he was more than ready to see Shelly.

He looked around the dining room and saw Rachel and Lena at a large table off to the left. They were chatting and hadn't seen him walk in yet. From the door, he saw a serious expression on Rachel's face as she shook her head. Then Mason's fiancée touched Rachel's shoulder and nodded.

Okay, something is definitely up there. It's none of my business though, so I'm not getting involved.

He was about to move forward when the door behind him whooshed open. He turned around to see who had walked in, and there, standing a few feet away from him, was Dr. Monroe. Tonight, every inch of her looked like the man-eater.

SHELLY OPENED THE door and was treated to a fine view of Josh's ass. She had forgotten how much she liked that part of the male anatomy.

When he heard the door close, he turned, and they locked eyes for the first time in over a month and a half.

"Well, hello, Josh," she purred as she stepped closer in her red high heels.

"Evening, Shel," he greeted, turning around fully to look her over.

She'd opted for a blue blouse tucked in at the waist of a simple black pencil skirt that ended an inch above her knee. She had secured her hair into a waterfall braid around the crown of her head. "You sure are a sight for sore eyes, Josh."

He stepped toward her and asked in a voice as smooth as whiskey, "Did you miss me?"

Shelly knew he was testing her, checking to see if she would hesitate or avoid the direct question that would make her reveal her true feelings. "Very much so."

∾

JOSH HADN'T BEEN EXPECTING a simple and honest answer, and as he was about to tell her that, Lena shouted her name. With the moment gone, he watched her smile at him with those sexy lips, then she brushed by his arm to make her way toward her friend. *Mmm, she even smells amazing.*

As he turned around, he saw Mason standing at the bar with a huge grin. Josh shrugged and walked over.

"Hey, man. What's up?" Josh asked as he settled on a barstool.

"Not much. The business is great, the weather is supposed to be amazing, and tomorrow, I'm marrying the woman I love."

Josh chuckled. "Could you be any more smug?"

Mason poured him a Goose Island Beer and shook his head. "Nope. Well, maybe. I could add to my list my prediction that you and Dr. Monroe would hit it off, but that would just be obnoxious or annoying, right?"

Josh lifted the glass to his mouth and took a sip. As he placed the glass back on the counter, he nodded. "Or just annoyingly obnoxious."

Mason laughed. "How are things going between the two of you?"

Josh thought about that for a moment. "Good. We've kept in contact while I've been away. I think things are going well."

Mason acknowledged that silently, then looked at the table of women. Josh turned around just in time to see Shelly let out a loud laugh that made Lena chuckle and Rachel frown.

All of a sudden, Josh found that he too wanted in on the joke.

∾

"*SUPER DOMME?* THAT'S my new nickname?" Rachel asked incredulously.

"Well, only in private, like in my head," Shelly said with a laugh.

Rachel did not look impressed. Lena was chuckling, and Shelly thought it was downright hilarious.

"Oh, come on, Rach, you took us completely off guard. Who knew you had that in you?" Shelly asked with a smile.

Rachel arched her brow. "Was I supposed to announce it?"

Shelly thought about that then lowered her voice. "Well, no, but hell, I didn't even know you had any tattoos until that night."

Rachel rolled her eyes. "I just like to keep that part of my life private. Is that such an issue?" She looked toward where Mason and Josh were now staring at them. Then she turned back to Shelly. "Kind of like you and Josh Daniels."

Shelly thought about that as she turned and gave Josh a flirty wink before looking back to the girls. "No secret there. I am head over heels for that man."

Lena's face split into a huge grin, and Rachel's mouth fell wide open.

"Does he know?" Lena whispered.

Shelly shrugged. "I'm pretty sure he has an idea since I've cyberstalked him every night since I don't know where the hell he's staying. But no, I haven't straight out said it."

∽

"SAID WHAT?" JOSH asked as he stopped beside the sexy doctor. She looked at him and smiled in a way that made every part of his body tense and achy. "None of your business." She gave him a smug smirk that he wanted to kiss.

Josh looked at the other two women sitting in front of him, and suddenly, he felt as if he had been a large part of their conversation.

"If I had wanted to tell you, handsome, I would have. I'll tell you when I'm ready," she said as she tapped his nose playfully.

He grabbed that sassy finger and squeezed it tightly as he brought her hand down from his face. "Watch where you're pointing that."

Her eyes narrowed as she stood and stepped closer to him.

Suddenly, everyone seemed to vanish from the room except for him and Shelly.

"Or else?" she inquired.

Josh felt his cock stir. Every single emailed word, innuendo, and thought that had crossed his mind over the last couple of months flashed before his eyes, and he was a millisecond away from dragging her somewhere, *anywhere*, to act them all out.

That was when Mason came up behind him and clapped him on the shoulder. "Okay, guys, let's eat."

∼

AN HOUR LATER, Shelly was still seated opposite Josh, and she had to admit that he looked sexy as hell. He was dressed in black slacks, something she had *never* seen him in, and a white button-up shirt that had been left loose and unbuttoned at the neck. As she licked her lips in anticipation of finally nibbling that spot, he looked up and locked gazes with her.

Shelly pulled out her dirtiest smile as she relaxed into her chair, taking a sip of her wine. The man was making her crazy with all of the stolen glances promising hot, sweaty, back-scratching sex. It was amazing she had even made it through dinner with the sexual tension he was throwing her way.

She wanted him, and she wanted him now.

"So, Shelly, are you ready for tomorrow?"

Lena's voice cut through her sensual haze, and she turned to look at her friend. "Yep, I sure am. All I have to do is walk down the aisle then stand off to your side, right?"

Lena grinned, nodding. "Yeah, that's it. Nothing special and nothing complicated. Just a simple, smooth wedding that will give me full legal rights to claim him." She grinned at Mason.

Mason took that opportunity to kiss her gently.

As he did, Shelly looked at Rachel, who was watching them with an odd expression. She almost looked sad. Shelly didn't know what that was about, but when Rachel looked her way, she plastered on a grin. Shelly returned it, not wanting to make her uncomfortable.

Then Shelly looked back across the table at the man she had been missing for the last month or so. He was finally here. She could actually touch him and tell him what she had been thinking about and what she had decided. She could finally ask him how he felt.

Her face must have given something away because all of a sudden, he stood and made an announcement. "Shelly and I need to leave."

Shelly looked around the table at the shocked faces now looking at her. "We do?"

Josh nodded then moved away from his chair and pushed it in. He gripped the back of it, and Shelly noticed his knuckles were going white.

"Yeah, we do," he said in a voice that warranted no questions and no explanations.

Shelly looked at his clenched jaw, then her eyes dropped to his slacks, and—*damn it, his shirt is covering his crotch.* Standing slowly, Shelly noticed Lena and Mason grinning like idiots, then she turned to see Rachel looking at Josh as if he had three heads.

Huh, apparently, this side of Delicious Daniels isn't often exposed. Quite honestly, Shelly wasn't sure she recognized him either. She moved around the table and made her way toward Josh.

When she got to him, she whispered, "In a rush?"

Josh grabbed her wrist and tugged her toward the front door. When they were out of view from the table, he made a quick detour and pulled her into the coatroom. The small space was dark, and when he tugged her inside and shut the door, they were thrown into pitch blackness.

∼

JOSH WAS GOING INSANE.

He had tried to be civil, play it nice, laugh, socialize, and all of that good stuff, but what it boiled down to was he wanted his hands and mouth on this woman. He planned to achieve that—right this second.

As he clicked the lock on the door, he moved forward and backed her up to the wall. She stumbled a little due to his haste, and when she was finally flush against it, she dropped her bag. He stood directly in front of her, his hands by each side of her head on the wall.

"Did you hear anything during that dinner?" he asked.

It was dark in the little room, and he couldn't see her well. All he could do was wait and listen. He heard her breathing kick up a notch.

Then she whispered close to his mouth, "Not a damn thing."

"Me neither."

He pressed his lips to hers in a crushing kiss. He dipped his tongue deep inside her mouth and felt his eyes almost roll back when she sucked on it. She moaned as her hands crept around his waist to land on his ass. Moving his body in against hers, he rubbed against the length of her as she molded her front to his. When he lifted his head, he heard her panting, and she clutched him close.

"God, I've wanted to touch you for weeks," she confessed.

He brought his hands down from the wall to trace along her body until they reached her hips, and he pulled her even closer. He nuzzled his face into the side of her neck, nibbling it, then he dragged his tongue up to flick her earlobe.

"I've wanted to be touched, Georgia. You've been making me crazy," he told her.

Her nails dug into his ass, then her fingers moved up his body and under his shirt, where they stroked his bare flesh.

Pulling his mouth away from her neck, he groaned in her ear. "I want inside you so badly."

∼

IF IT WAS POSSIBLE, Shelly could have sworn she just got wetter. It was hard to believe that the man held such power over her.

As they stood in complete darkness in the tiny room only a few feet away from their close friends, all Shelly could think about was how quickly she could remove her panties and hike up her skirt. Apparently, that was all Josh could think of too, because suddenly he disappeared from in front of her. She heard a soft thud and realized the man had gone down to his knees.

Yes, yes, yes, Shelly thought when his big rough hands cupped her ankles, made their way up her naked calves, then moved over her knees until he reached the hem of her black skirt. He paused there, and Shelly stood still, her harsh breathing the only sound thundering through her ears.

"Any reason I should stop?" he asked.

Shelly knew that he was trying to give her an out if things were getting a little too real for her, but as she stood with her back to the wall and darkness surrounding them, Shelly couldn't think of one reason for him to stop.

"Not if you don't want me to die," she said, trying to inject some lightness into the situation.

His hands squeezed her legs, slipping a little ways under the hem of her skirt. "I don't want anything bad to happen to you *ever*," he said much more seriously than she had anticipated.

Shelly heard a rustling, then his hands slid farther up her thighs, her skirt bunching up at his wrists and forearms. Then she realized the rustling had been him rising up higher on his knees.

As he kneeled in front of her in the dark with her skirt bunched up around her waist, he said, "I promised that the next time I saw you, I'd kiss you."

Shelly took a deep breath as he ripped her tiny black thong away. She couldn't have moved if the fire alarms had gone off and Mason had been pounding on the door. Her desire was so tangible that she was surprised her trembling legs were holding her upright. She supposed, somewhere in the back of her mind, that the wall was helping with that issue.

The fact that they were surrounded by darkness only added to her heightened sense of awareness. When she felt a rough finger slide back and forth between her wet folds, she couldn't help the guttural moan that was wrenched from her.

"Oh yeah," Josh groaned. "Goddamn, Shel, you're so fucking wet."

She whimpered loudly. "Now, Josh. *Please*. Do it now."

JOSH CHUCKLED AS Shelly leaned back against the wall for support, trembling in her heels with her skirt up around her waist. Since he had shredded her panties, she was naked from the waist down. As he took a deep breath, dragging his finger back and forth through her juices, he licked his lips in anticipation.

When she begged, Josh flicked his tongue out to play with her throbbing clit. It was so hard and wet from her excitement that it took everything Josh had to slow down and not devour her.

With his fingers, he spread her flushed lips a little farther apart, then he ran his tongue back and forth against her juicy flesh. When she cried out in pleasure and gripped his head, Josh grinned wickedly as he devoured the man-eater. *What irony*, he thought as she melted all over his tongue. He pleasured her until her moaning and panting was almost a sob, then he felt her grip his hair tightly.

"I need it now. Can't wait. Need to feel you inside me," she begged as she tugged on his hair, trying to get him to move.

Not one to turn down such a plea, Josh stood, unzipped his slacks, and pushed them down his hips. He heard her moan, then he moved forward. She wrapped her arms around his neck as he gripped her right leg behind the knee. Hitching it up to his hip, he held it there and rubbed his aching flesh against her, waiting for her next move.

∾

SHELLY WAS GOING to die if he didn't put his cock inside her *right now*.

As he played between her thighs, she gripped his hair at the back of his neck, tugging him forward in the dark, and kissed him roughly. She heard him groan, so she pulled back and bit his bottom lip.

"Please...inside me, Josh. I need to feel you stretching me, filling me up—"

He grunted against her mouth as he lined up the thick head of his shaft, then he thrust home. Shelly screamed, biting his shoulder, as he entered her forcefully, banging her solidly against the wall. While he continued to pound away at her, one of her legs hitched up over his naked hip, Shelly couldn't remember a man ever having such power over her. As she gave herself over to the powerful climax, screaming his name and shattering all around him, she also knew there would never be another man who would.

∾

STANDING IN THE cocoon of the coatroom, breathing hard, Josh felt a bead of sweat slide down his temple. He was still lodged deep inside her, and her arms were still wound tightly around his neck. Their reunion had been nothing short of spectacular.

As her breathing calmed, she whispered, "Josh, I—"

"Shh," he murmured against her neck. "Shh." He wasn't quite ready to hear that yet.

She tensed a little. "Why won't you let me tell you how I feel? I don't understand why you're making this so hard."

Josh kissed her lips. "I'm not trying to make it hard."

She sighed. "Then what are you trying to do?"

"I'm trying to make it right."

CHAPTER 23

THE NEXT MORNING, Shelly woke up early. As she lay in bed, she couldn't help but think about last night with Josh. It seemed that no matter how much she'd tried to open up to him, he was the one pulling back. *Or is he? It's all so confusing.* Shelly sighed.

One moment, she could swear he wanted nothing more than to touch her or hold her. In the next moment, when she tried to tell him her feelings, he stopped her.

Maybe he was right to make them wait. He kept saying he wanted things to be right. But how could they be when he was living somewhere else?

As the alarm sounded beside her, Shelly rolled over and looked at the time. Eight o'clock. Rubbing her eyes, she decided that now was not the time to try to work out the enigma that was Josh. Instead, it was time to focus on one important thing—a wedding at Promontory Point.

SEVERAL HOURS LATER, Shelly arrived at Lena's old condo.

She was actually surprised she remembered how to get there. Lena had put her place up for sale long ago, after she moved in with Mason, but in this economy, it still sat empty. That made it the perfect location to get ready and keep the bride away from the wandering eyes and hands of her impatient groom.

When she was buzzed in and let up to Lena's floor, Shelly had to admit that she was starting to feel nervous for her friend.

Today was a huge day in Mason's and Lena's lives. In front of family and friends, they were about to commit to one another, promising to love one another forever.

Forever.

That's such a long time. Shelly waited for Lena to open the door. As it unlatched, Josh flashed into her mind, but she quickly pushed him aside when Lena appeared, beaming.

"And how is the lovely bride on this beautiful morning?" Shelly asked as she stepped forward.

Lena moved aside to let her in. "Ahh, the bride is nervous, and the groom has already called five times."

Shelly had to laugh. It sounded just like Mason to be worried about his doctor today. The two of them had been through a lot to get to where they finally were. He was probably having a minor case of paranoia, believing it wasn't actually going to happen.

"Well, the groom is out of his mind. There's no way I'm going to be slacking on my duties, even if I have to pick you up and carry you to the wedding myself."

Lena laughed as she closed the door, and Shelly took that moment to lay her garment bag across Lena's couch.

"You don't have to worry about that. There's no other place I want to be this evening than standing at the altar with Mason," Lena told her with a smile.

Shelly returned it, reaching out to hug her friend. She felt herself getting somewhat emotional from hearing her friend was so sure of her path and direction, not to mention the person she intended to share it with.

"You're lucky you know," Shelly said.

"Oh, I know I'm lucky. But why do you think I am?" Lena asked with a laugh.

She stepped around Shelly and made her way into the kitchen. Shelly followed and took a seat on one of Lena's breakfast bar stools.

"Because you know exactly what you want," Shelly said with conviction.

Lena turned and arched a brow, holding a chilled bottle of wine.

"Wine? This early?" Shelly asked with a raised brow and a smirk.

"Just one—to calm the nerves a little and to celebrate. I do *not* want to be tipsy tonight."

Shelly let out a small chuckle. "I will not let you be tipsy for your own wedding."

Lena grinned, taking two glasses from the cupboard overhead. After she had poured them each a glass of wine, she turned to face Shelly.

"What do you mean I know what I want? In life? In general? Or with Mason?" she asked as she passed a half-filled glass in Shelly's direction.

Shelly took the wine and raised it. They tapped the glasses in a soft clink.

"All of the above, my friend. You have it all worked out, and that makes you a *very* lucky woman." Raising her wine glass, Shelly saluted Lena. "Cheers to you on your wonderful wedding day."

"Cheers," Lena returned before they each took a sip of their wine.

A LITTLE DISTANCE away from the girls, Josh sat on his friend's couch, looking out of Mason's huge living room windows.

Wow, what a view. Josh was waiting patiently for Mason to come back from making yet *another* anxious call to Lena.

Josh had to smile. Mason was nervous that Lena would disappear and not show, so every hour on the hour, he was calling his soon-to-be bride to ease his worried mind. Josh wondered what Mason would do if she was stuck under a hair dryer or something and wasn't able to answer the phone. He'd probably go a little insane.

Ahh, isn't love grand?

As he waited, his mind slipped back to the night before with Shelly.

He knew she had been close to telling him exactly what he had been waiting to hear, but it hadn't been how or where he wanted it. He knew he couldn't control when she was going to say it. That wasn't the point at all. The point was he wanted her to say it *and* feel it no matter what time of the day it was—not because she'd missed him and *certainly* not because he had just blown her mind in a coat closet.

As Josh slipped deeper into those thoughts, he was saved by Mason reappearing from the bedroom.

"So?" Josh asked.

"She's good. She and Shelly are in the process of getting their hair done."

Josh chuckled. "Fancy that."

Mason shook his head and sat down on the couch. "I'm going crazy, right?"

Josh smirked. "No, you're in love. You're about to get married, and you're just a little nervous, I'd say."

Mason took a deep breath then let it out on a sigh. "Yeah, I'm a little nervous, but not because I'm getting married." He looked at Josh with the most serious expression Josh had ever seen on his friend. "Have you ever looked at someone and just thought, 'Yes. I know you. You're meant to be mine.'"

Josh raised a brow, thinking about that for a minute. *How did it happen with Georgia?* Well, it had been more like a sledgehammer across his head.

Before he could say that, Mason continued. "Lena couldn't stand me when we first met, and I remember thinking she was so prickly and rude. But when she walked into the restaurant that same night, it just fell into place. I *knew* I needed to know her." Mason laughed at himself. "Listen to me, I sound like a total fool."

Josh shook his head. "No, you don't. You sound like a man who went after the woman he loves and got exactly what he wanted." Josh decided to let his friend in on his own secret. "I'm familiar with that, man."

Mason looked at him, cocking his head to the side. "You and Shelly?"

Josh nodded, letting out a deep breath. "But it's complicated."

"It always is. Look at Lena and me. We had a rocky moment at every turn. But if she's what you want, don't wait to tell her. Women like Lena and Shelly don't come along every day. Smart *and* beautiful—that's hitting the goddamned jackpot, man."

Josh laughed. "I won't wait too much longer, but she'd already pulled a fast one and run away once. I want to be sure she won't do that again."

Mason raised a brow. "And how do you plan to do that?"

Josh sighed. "I actually have no idea, but I've been working on it."

"So will you be sticking around after the wedding?"

Shaking his head, Josh stood and moved to the window. "No. I need to get back to work."

"Are you ever going to tell me where you're staying?"

Josh looked over his shoulder and shook his head. "Hell no, you'd squeal to Shelly in two seconds."

"Hey. I resent that."

Josh let out a loud laugh. "Hey. I don't give a damn." Looking at his watch, he noticed it had just turned four. "Well, you ready to head over?"

His friend stood and walked into the adjoining room. When he came out, he was carrying a garment bag that held his tux. "Yep. I'm ready. Let's go and get me married."

With that, they headed down to the valet, where Josh's truck was being brought around.

∼

IT WAS 5:50 P.M., and the time had rolled around quicker than Shelly had expected. As she stood inside the Field House at Promontory Point, she glanced out the window to see all of Lena's and Mason's family and friends seated under a lovely white tent that covered the lakefront patio.

The main aisle had been set up between two sections of white chairs. Each section held four seats across and twelve down, and every aisle seat had a small cluster of blue Singapore orchids and white roses attached to it to complement the bouquets and boutonnieres. Rachel had assured Lena that the flowers would look both elegant and classy, and Shelly had to admit that Rachel had developed a keen eye since she started working afternoons down at Precious Petals. Lena had chosen a color scheme that included crisp white and a lovely, vibrant shade of blue.

The wedding wasn't a huge event in terms of size, but for the city of Chicago and all of its single women, it meant one of the most eligible bachelors was going off the market in approximately—Shelly looked at the clock on the wall—eight minutes.

Turning, she found Lena standing with Rachel, who was fussing with the back of the bride's dress. Shelly made her way over to them, noticing Lena's father had also arrived.

She is so beautiful. Lena was wearing one of the most stunning wedding dresses Shelly had ever seen. It was made up of miles of white lace and had sleeves only a few inches wide. It sat perfectly on her elegant shoulders before sweeping down in a soft dip across her breasts. That, of course, was what Shelly saw before Lena turned around. The dress intricately covered her shoulders in a peek-a-boo fashion of lace and skin, ending in a V-shape at the small of her back. The fabric molded to every line of her body until it reached her mid-thigh, where it gently flowed out into a spectacular pool of lace and loveliness.

Simply put, Lena looked like a princess.

Under Lena's bust was a beautiful silver-and-diamond broach that Lena's mother had given her to wear. Lena had had two hair clips made to match and given them to Shelly and Rachel.

When Lena finally raised her eyes to meet Shelly's, Shelly smiled and nodded. Lena looked at the clock on the wall.

Six o'clock. It was time.

JOSH STOOD BY MASON at the front of the crowd and waited expectantly for the music to start, signaling Lena's appearance. He looked at his friend and noticed he looked a little tense.

Josh leaned in and asked, "You doing okay, man?"

Mason nodded. "Yep. I just want to see her."

As he said that, the music began. Instead of the usual wedding march, Josh grinned as the familiar chords of "Crash into Me" by Dave Matthews Band filtered through the speakers.

Several seconds later, Rachel appeared. Wearing a sweeping dress in a light shade of blue, she made her way down the aisle. Her dark hair was curled and clipped on one side, leaving the length of it to fall down over her back. She held a small bouquet of blue Singapore orchids and white roses, matching the orchid pinned to Josh's lapel.

Rachel's eyes met her brother's, and Josh noticed tears in them as she got closer to where they were standing. Josh wondered what exactly was going through Rach's head as she moved to stand on the left side of the aisle.

Her eyes finally met his, and Josh smiled, trying to assure her everything would be okay. He felt as though she needed it and wasn't quite sure why, but before he could think on it too long, the crowd was oohing and aahing over the next person.

Josh turned and found it hard not to do the same.

Making her way down the aisle in a much shorter version of Rachel's dress was Shelly Monroe. *Georgia.*

Her hair was pulled half up and back from her beautiful face, and the rest was left in a halo of soft curls around her shoulders. Josh assumed the clip holding it back was the same silver-and-diamond one that Rachel was wearing.

However, that wasn't what kept him entranced. Her eyes as she made her way up to the front were locked on his. She had glanced at Mason once, but then she had looked at Josh and had not faltered since.

He felt his heart thundering, almost feeling as if this was his own damn wedding. When Shelly reached the front and went to stand beside Rachel, he turned to look at her as she winked at him. Josh smiled and felt as though he was back on even ground. *Ahh, there's the Man-Eater.*

He needed to let her know tonight how he felt. He needed her to be aware that he wasn't aiming to make her anything other than a permanent part of his life. The thought that she wouldn't want to hear it terrified him.

All of a sudden, everyone stood, and the music continued as Magdalena O'Donnell and her father made their grand entrance.

As he watched her move down the aisle toward Mason, who was watching his bride with a look of complete and utter adoration, Josh had to admit that he could one hundred percent appreciate the reasons for getting married.

The woman walking toward her groom wasn't the Lena they all knew and loved. This was a woman radiating so much happiness and love that it was as though they were all seeing her for the first time.

Her gaze never left Mason's, and the unfettered love in her eyes was absolutely mesmerizing.

When she finally reached Mason, Josh's usually smooth-talking friend just stood and stared at her. Her father let go of her hand, and Lena smiled at her fiancé, greeting him softly.

"Hi."

Josh chuckled, and so did the rest of the crowd.

Mason shook his head then blinked once. "Hi."

The pastor made a little coughing sound. "If everyone could please be seated, we'll begin."

Josh heard all the chairs shuffle as everyone took their seats. He turned toward Rachel and Shelly and smiled. Shelly gave him a radiant one in response, and Rachel smiled, but it felt strained.

Josh turned back to face the bride and groom standing before the pastor. Just behind the pastor, a small table held a beautiful spray of tulips and an equally impressive vase of sunflowers, each representing the people in their lives who couldn't be here.

"Dearly beloved, we are gathered here in the presence of God and this company so that Magdalena O'Donnell and Mason Langley may be united in holy matrimony," the pastor began.

Lena looked at Mason and gave him a shy smile. His friend must have winked or done something equally smooth because she ducked her head bashfully and blushed a little.

Yep, Mason has his groove back now that he has Lena in his sights.

"Who here gives this woman to this man?"

Lena's father said, "Her mother and I do with our deepest blessing."

Mason turned and looked at his new father-in-law. "Thank you. I'll take care of her."

"We know, son," he said then sat down.

The pastor announced, "The bride and groom have opted to say their own vows over the traditional ones we all know. So when you're ready, Mason."

Mason took Lena's hands. Lena wasn't wearing a veil, and her hair had been pulled back into a sweeping side bun that was elegantly pinned at her neck. As she looked at her husband-to-be, Josh thought she was probably one of the most beautiful women he had ever seen—not including, of course, the woman just beyond her right shoulder.

"When I first sat down to write these vows, I had no idea how I was going to explain how much I love you, Lena. Life isn't easy, and anyone who tells you it is—well, they're lying. Life is hard. It gives you good times, and it gives you extremely bad times. You and I have had our share of both. We've struggled through pain and loss individually, and just last year, we struggled again—together. To me, *that* is what life is all about. It's about finding someone—you, Lena—to help me when I need it the most. To guide me out of my darkest moments and to bask with me in the lightest ones."

A tear slid down Lena's cheek.

"My mother loved you very much, and I know that she's sitting up there front and center, watching this wedding with the biggest smile on her face."

Josh heard several quiet sniffles in the background. Behind Shelly, who was gently wiping a tear from her cheek, Rachel stood clutching her flowers with tears falling down her face. She seemed immobilized.

Mason continued. "You walked into my life, and now, I never want to walk alone again. Magdalena O'Donnell, will you marry me and make me the happiest man on the planet?"

A dropped pin could have reverberated noise throughout the room. It was that quiet.

Then Lena began.

∼

SHELLY WATCHED THROUGH blurred eyes as her friend gripped Mason's hands and started her own vows. Although how she could manage after Mason's was a miracle. Shelly didn't think there was a dry eye in the place.

"I would marry you every single hour of every single day for the rest of my life. Before you, I didn't know how to live. I went through the motions of having a life, but it was all for show. I was broken in here." Lena raised one of Mason's large palms to her heart.

She held on to one of his hands and kept the other one pressed to her chest. She took a step closer and looked up at him. "You have given me so much, I can't even begin to express how deeply my love runs for you. Your strength and sensitivity, your complete love of your family, and your absolute perseverance and stubbornness are just some of the many things I love and adore about you, Langley. You taught me how to accept things I never could have without you, how to forgive myself, and how to give permission to my heart to open up and love again. Your happiness and joy is so strong that it left me no option but to let you in to warm up my soul, which had been cold for so long." Lena firmly and loudly said, "I would be honored to marry you, Mason Langley. Will you please marry me?"

Mason tugged Lena forward, and Shelly was pretty sure only those standing close to them heard him whisper, "Just try to stop me."

Then he laid the sweetest, most passionate kiss Shelly had ever witnessed on his bride.

~

THREE AND A half hours later, the reception was in full swing. There had been photos upon photos and so much food that Josh felt as if he was going to explode. He'd hardly had one moment to himself all night, and he certainly hadn't had a chance to talk with Shelly.

Every time he turned around, she was off getting another photo with the bride. Then when he thought he could finally catch her, Lena's parents had started talking to her, or someone from their work had pulled her aside. He was starting to think he wouldn't get the opportunity he so desperately craved.

Glancing around the reception area, Josh saw Shelly near the makeshift bar. He was about to make his way to her when he saw Rachel sitting at her table by herself, watching everyone dance. He had seen Mason chat with her and pull her into several dances. Rachel had smiled and moved to the music with ease, but there had been something off about her all day. Josh headed toward her table, deciding to find out what it was.

"Hey there," he said as he pulled out the chair beside her.

Rachel looked at him and smiled. "Hey. Nice night, huh?"

Josh relaxed into his chair, hoping to get a laugh from her. "I'll say. Have you ever seen a couple so stupid over each other?"

However, instead of the burst of joy he would have gotten from the usual Rachel with colored hair, he got a small grin from the new Rachel with black hair.

"They seem very happy."

Josh leaned toward her, reaching out to touch her shoulder. She looked at him, and Josh saw raw emotion welling in her eyes.

"You don't," he whispered.

"I don't what?"

"You don't look happy. In fact, every time I see you, I feel as though you look sadder."

She straightened her spine and blinked, clearly trying to hold back the moisture forming there.

"What's going on, Rach? You haven't been yourself lately."

She shook her head, smiling sadly. "It's nothing to worry about. I think I'm just a little out of whack. Not having Mom and Dad here today was hard."

Josh thought that might have been some of the issue, but for some reason, he felt it went much deeper than that. Obviously she didn't want to discuss it right now, so he squeezed her arm. "You know you can talk to me about anything, right?"

Rachel nodded but kept her mouth taut with tension. "Man-Eater is looking over here. I'm pretty sure she wants to get her hands on you."

Josh chuckled, looking over his shoulder. Shelly was indeed staring across the room at them. Looking at his watch, Josh nodded. "I think I've got time for one dance with her."

Rachel smirked. "Before what? You turn into a pumpkin?"

Josh stood and shook his head. "No. Before I hit the road."

Rachel tried for a full grin but once again failed. This sad version of her was worrying Josh a lot. "Drive safely, okay? And thank you."

"Anytime, Rach. You know I'm just a phone call away."

Then he turned, heading toward a certain blonde.

SHELLY WATCHED HIM make his way across the dance floor to her.

Mason and Lena had left half an hour earlier, and the festivities were starting to wind down. All night, Shelly had wanted to talk to Josh, but there hadn't been one moment where she could get away. But right now...well, she had nothing to do except watch him walk toward her.

He was dressed in a perfectly tailored black suit that molded to every tight muscle the man possessed. Under that, he wore the same crisp white shirt as Mason, and instead of the cobalt tie that Mason had worn, Josh's tie was a light blue to match the bridesmaids' dresses. The man looked sexy in a suit, and Shelly wanted to take it off of him, piece by piece.

When he stopped in front of her, holding out his hand, Shelly slipped hers into it, allowing him to pull her onto the dance floor. Tugging her toward him, he held her close as the music switched and Sinatra started singing "The Way You Look Tonight."

"I didn't think I'd ever get to speak to you tonight," he said against the side of her head, moving them gently around the floor with the other couples.

Who knew he could dance so well? Shelly held on and let him lead, loving the feel of his body as it swayed against her own. "I know. It's crazy how busy it was—all the photos and people and *food*."

"Oh God, yes, the food," Josh said with a false groan.

Shelly chuckled a little then looked up to see he was looking right at her.

"I love this song," she said with a smile.

His eyes crinkled at the sides as he stared at her while moving them in a slow twirl. When they were back to a basic step, he said, "Yes, it's one of those classics that's definitely stood the test of time."

Shelly felt his heartbeat against her chest, and she was starting to get nervous as he watched her with an expression she hadn't seen before. It was almost as though he was unsure of his next move.

Well, she could help that along. After all, she didn't want him to guess what she wanted tonight. She planned to make it crystal clear.

"Will you come home with me tonight?" Shelly licked her bottom lip, waiting for the answer she assumed was inevitable.

The one thing Shelly had not expected, however, was being taught the valuable lesson that one should never assume.

∽

JOSH LOOKED AT the beguiling woman in his arms and hated what he had to do next. He had no clue what her reaction would be. In fact, he was almost worried that she might tell him to go to hell and never talk to him again, but he had decided that this was what he needed to do if he was ever going to be more than a roll in the sheets to her.

"I'm leaving tonight," he said as the music stopped.

As they stopped swaying, hurt moved across her eyes and she pulled back a little, shaking her head. "I don't understand."

Josh followed as she moved off the dance floor toward the door to the front porch of the venue. When he got outside, she was making her way to one of the seating areas that overlooked Lake Michigan. She must have heard his feet crunching on the gravel because she turned toward him.

"You're running away," she accused.

Josh stepped closer to her and was about to reach out, but at the last minute, she turned away from him, crossing her arms. A light breeze teased through her beautiful curls, and Josh tried to remind himself that this was for the best.

"No, I'm running forward, Georgia. So catch up to me, would you?"

She spun around and moved up closer to him, pointing. "First you tell me I'm not ready and that you don't trust me." Her chest heaved as she bit her bottom lip, then she shrugged helplessly. "Yet now, when I try to tell you how I feel, you stop me at every turn." She sounded completely defeated.

Josh took the final step to her and gripped her shoulders. "Shelly, look at me."

She tipped up her head, facing him with huge cerulean-blue eyes filled with angst and tears.

He smiled sadly. "I don't want a girlfriend." He felt her stiffen and knew what conclusion she was jumping to. "I also don't want a woman who only decides she cares after a hot round of sex."

"That's not what happened," she whispered. "What would make you stay?"

Josh leaned in and kissed her forehead, knowing he was doing it. *This is it.*

She would either want what he wanted, or she would never talk to him again.

After taking a deep breath, he whispered against her hair, "This."

She didn't try to move away. She stood silently for a moment while he held her arms and kissed her hair. *God, she smells amazing.*

"What is *this*?" she asked softly.

Pulling back a little, he looked at her and tipped up her chin so their eyes met. "Everything that tonight represents." As the reality of what he was saying sank in, her eyes widened, and he felt his nerves bubbling up inside him. *Spit it out already.* "The music, the friends, the ceremony, but most importantly, the love. I want all of it. I'm *ready* for all of it, Georgia. And until you are too, nothing will make me stay."

Dropping his hands from her shoulders, he watched her take a deep breath and waited for anything she was going to say. But nothing came.

She just stared at him with eyes as big as he had ever seen them, and he felt as if he was being punched over and over again.

All right, man, time to leave. Turning on his heel, he made it three steps before he heard his name. Turning, he saw that she had moved, and she was facing him with the lake as her backdrop. The breeze had picked up, and it was whipping around her hair and dress.

She looks absolutely breathtaking.

He stopped and waited.

"How will I know?" she called.

Josh shook his head and shrugged. "I'm not sure, but one thing I do know is you won't have to ask."

With that, he walked away.

CHAPTER 24

October

September had been the longest month of Shelly's year. After Josh had left the night of the wedding, Shelly did something she had never done before. She went home and cried.

Never had she felt so helpless. She'd wanted to express the thoughts running through her mind when Josh had stood in front of her that night. But she couldn't.

Thinking you're in love with someone and just saying it seems so easy. However, the reality—a man telling you that he wants *you* to be everything that makes his world—was just completely terrifying.

What if I fail? That was all Shelly had thought about for days—hell, weeks now. What if, for some reason, she was like her father? It wasn't too far of a stretch. She obviously resembled him in many ways. *Why not personality flaws as well?*

Sighing, Shelly closed her eyes and pictured Josh as she had last seen him, standing in front of her with his heart on his sleeve, looking at her as though she had just let him down.

And she had.

She knew it, and he did too.

So what if I do that after we're committed?

Well, lying here isn't getting me anywhere, she thought as she climbed out of bed.

Booting up her computer, she went to her closet and pulled out a black satin robe. She sighed as the material slid over her bare skin. When the computer was up, she immediately went to her email, and there *it* was—the usual nightly letter he still sent her. This one had a subject header, *Halloween.*

Sitting in her reading chair, she placed the laptop on her thighs and clicked to open the message.

Georgia,

Mason is having a Halloween party at Exquisite on Saturday. I'll be in town. Do you want to be the Sandy to my Danny?

Josh

Shelly smiled and responded with seven words.

Yes. You're the one that I want.

After clicking Send, she was shocked when she got an almost immediate response.

You're awake early, considering you worked last night.

Josh

Shelly noticed he was online. Forgetting about email, she clicked the instant message bar and typed. **Couldn't sleep. Someone won't get out of my head.**

Josh: I'm annoying like that.

Shelly: Yes, you kind of are. Are you sure you want to go to the party with me?

Josh: I wouldn't have asked if I wasn't sure, Georgia. Nothing for me has changed. Just know that I'll be leaving after the weekend.

Shelly stared at the screen. *Nothing has changed for him.*

Over the last month and a half, this had been his approach, letting her know he still wanted to be with her and that it was *her* holding up this leg of the race. She also had a distinct feeling that her time would run out if she didn't *catch up.*

He had been clear in all their emails since the wedding. Until she was one hundred percent sure of what she wanted, he didn't want to hear it.

Shelly would like to argue that it wasn't fair. *But is it really fair to ask him to settle for anything less?* So there she was, stuck in a conundrum. She had a man who loved her and wanted everything, and she had a terrifying fear that she would fail him. *How do I get over that?*

Shelly: So at the party, am I allowed to touch you?
Josh: I'd be disappointed if you didn't.
Shelly: Well, that's something at least.
Josh: Don't mistake me walking away as me not wanting you. I'm just sure of what I want, and I have been for a very long time. I refuse to let you go on thinking this can't be more.

Shelly thought about that last sentence. *Is that what I'm doing?* She had been looking for the perfect man in so many places, yet it seemed he may have turned up in the last spot she would have thought to check.

Josh: So see you on Saturday? I'll be there around 4:00 p.m.
Shelly: Sounds good. Josh?
Josh: Yes, Georgia?
Shelly: I'm trying.
Josh: Try harder.

With that, she watched him sign off.

~

JOSH WAS SITTING on Cole's couch, staring at his computer screen.

Josh had known if he'd mentioned he was in town, Shelly would have invited him to stay at her place, and Josh was pretty sure his resistance was failing. Instead, he was going to let her believe he was arriving in two days. Meanwhile, he would hang out on his friend's couch.

Cole had gone out for the night and still had not returned. When Josh had asked where he was headed, he'd just said, "Out." Josh had decided not to push it further. He was just happy he could bum a few days on the man's couch. He was exhausted.

This new project had him working around the clock like a dog. He hadn't known at the beginning how much work it would take to make his vision come to life, but in the end, he knew it would fulfill a part of him that was gaping wide open. Just knowing that he could go to work and use his hands to create a perfect structure was so satisfying. He couldn't even begin to explain it.

He was also happy that the expansion on Exquisite was going as planned. It seemed they were on schedule, and within a few months, it would be ready to open.

Sometimes life handed you the perfect opportunity to do something vitally important, as well as the right thing, and for Josh, that had happened. It had also given him the perfect excuse to get away and think about what he wanted.

With Melissa, he had been so caught up in her that he had dropped all of his plans and followed her to LA. When he met Shelly, he felt himself doing the same thing. So he had decided to change tactics, switching gears in a sense. He left, knowing that he needed to sort out his own feelings without her clouding his mind.

She was scared. Hell, he was scared too, but he wasn't about to let her make their relationship less than what it was. As far as Josh was concerned, it was everything.

∼

SATURDAY AFTERNOON ROLLED AROUND, and just as the clock hit four, there was a loud buzzing through the condo. Shelly ran over and pressed the button to let Josh in, then she waited.

She sat on the couch, tapping her foot. She was nervous. The party didn't start until nine and Josh was here now. *So what does that mean?*

Every time Shelly had made a move on him recently, he had flat-out told her "no." But now that he would be here, she wondered if she was expected to just hold hands and watch TV with the man. She wanted him, and she wanted to know what he thought about that—or if he intended to *do* anything about it.

When the knock sounded, she made her way to the door, wiping her hands on her black leggings. Opening the door, she found him leaning against her doorjamb, looking more delicious than ever. He had a sports bag in one hand with his leather jacket draped across it, and Shelly assumed it held his costume.

Holding the door, she crossed one leg in front of the other, allowing herself to look him over. Her eyes traveled to the ripped knee of his overly washed jeans, then up to the nice display of tanned, bulging muscles where the midnight-blue T-shirt hugged his biceps. He had a blue baseball cap on backward, and as he raised his arm with the bag, slinging it back over his shoulder, Shelly was even more determined to convince him to let her touch.

"Hey, Georgia. Gonna let me in?" he asked in a voice so low and gruff, Shelly felt it rub all over her naughty bits.

Shelly nodded and moved aside. As he brushed by her, she took a deep breath and realized she had even missed how he smelled. He dumped the bag on the floor as she shut the door, and when she turned, he was looking right at her.

That was when he gave her a full-on DD smile. "You look really good, Shel."

Shelly finally found her brain *and* her tongue. "You look hot as hell."

He seemed shocked at first, then he laughed as he stuck his hands in his pockets. "Oh yeah?"

She licked her lips and moved toward him. When she got close enough to raise her palms to his chest, he took his hands from his pockets and gripped her wrists before she could touch him.

"Please don't stop me," she begged.

JOSH HELD HER by the wrists and looked into eyes that were pleading with him. *How can I continue saying no to her?*

The answer was simple. He couldn't.

Finally giving in to his own desire, he tugged her forward and dipped his head, crushing his mouth onto hers.

Immediately, she parted her lips, and he slid his tongue inside to taste her. *God, she's sweet.*

It had been too long. Months without touching her, kissing her, or even being near her had made him ravenous. With her hands trapped between their bodies, she could do nothing but go along with his demands. Taking the kiss deeper, he felt her sensuous tongue slip forward between his parted lips, flirting and tangling with his own, until she had him groaning.

Pulling his head back, he looked down at her. "Why can't you hurry up and decide what you want? It's killing me not having you with me."

As she was about to respond, he pulled her arms behind her back, arching her whole body toward him. Josh trembled as he looked at her. She was dressed in sexy black leggings and a cream sweater that was falling off her shoulder. Her hair was swept into a messy notch at the back of her head, and wisps of hair framed her face.

Her feet were bare, and as he pulled her forward, a little rougher than he had intended, she went up on her toes and those magnificent breasts were crushed against his chest. She gasped then pushed herself harder against him. Moaning, she tipped her head back, parting her lips.

Leaning forward so he was bending into her, he whispered against her mouth, "I *need* to be in you."

Her eyes tried to focus on his, but she seemed to be having trouble keeping them open.

"I'm going to pull you down onto this carpet, get rid of those sexy tights, then I'm going to bury myself so deep, you'll never *not* think of me again."

∽

SHELLY COULD BARELY BREATHE, let alone answer.

The man holding her arms behind her back and leaning into her was desperate. This man was strung tight on emotions, and he was going to consume her.

Licking her bottom lip, she watched his eyes focus on her tongue, then he released her and dropped to his knees. Reaching up under her loose sweater, he gripped the leggings and her panties, and with one smooth move, he removed them from her body. When they were at her ankles, she stepped out of them then dropped to her own knees, tugging the sweater over her head and throwing it to the floor.

He was kneeling opposite her, still fully dressed while she was now completely naked. His eyes couldn't seem to get enough of her as they looked her up and down, then up and down again. He finally lunged across the short distance to grip her face between his large palms.

Shelly let him push her onto her back, humming in sensual delight as he laid his fully clothed body against hers. *The friction is amazing.* She arched up and rubbed her aching breasts and pelvis against the fabric covering him.

"Oh fuck," he groaned into her mouth, pushing his denim-covered erection against her bare mound.

∼

JOSH WAS DYING. He could swear his blood was leaving his brain and going straight to his cock. And because it was confined behind his zipper, it would explode and he *would* die.

Beneath him on the carpet was a naked, writhing Shelly, and she was on fire. She made the sexiest noises he had ever heard as she arched against him, rubbing all of that perfect naked skin against his tense body.

Then her eyes snapped open, and she took his hat off before flinging it behind them. Running her hands through his hair, she gripped it tightly. She leaned up slowly to slide her tongue across the stubble on his cheek.

"I can feel your heart going crazy," she whispered.

Josh let out a puff of air. "That's because you're rubbing yourself all over me."

Shelly giggled. "Want me to stop?"

Pushing his hips down, Josh gently bit her grinning bottom lip. "Not even a little bit."

She moaned as he kissed her hard, rolling them so she was now straddling him.

∼

SHELLY WAS NOW SITTING astride a fully clothed Josh. She was completely naked, and as she rocked against the bulge behind his zipper, she unbuttoned and unzipped him. Shelly looked at his face and smiled slowly as she parted the jeans then smoothed her hands up under his shirt.

Pushing the blue material over all those tight muscles, Shelly couldn't help but lick her lips before bending down to drag her tongue over his impressive six-pack. She felt his abs quiver as she pushed the shirt higher, her tongue tracing every dip and valley along his ribs until she got to his nipple. She gently bit his solid pec.

Mmm...finally, she was tasting all of his warm, muscled skin, and she loved it.

Looking up at him, she watched his eyes darken. When his hands landed on her bare ass, he squeezed her flesh. Sitting up, Shelly dragged her palms down his body, and with her eyes on his, she slowly dipped them inside his parted jeans.

His eyes narrowed, and he focused on the hands now wiggling into his pants. She grazed her fingers against his boxers then winked. She started to move off of him so she could tug the jeans down.

However, as she moved from his waist, Josh jackknifed up and came for her, obviously thinking she was going somewhere. Giggling a little, Shelly decided to play and dodged his hands, which made his eyes take on a fiercer look. She got to her knees and was about to stand and run to the bedroom, but as she got one foot under her, two big hands grabbed her around the waist and pulled her back down to the floor.

He flattened her out on her belly and stretched over her. She heard him breathing a little harder while he rubbed against her ass.

"Where do you think you're going?" he growled in her ear.

Shelly smiled into the carpet and pushed her hips back. "I was going to pull off your pants, but you panicked."

Josh moved away then tugged her hips up and back until she was on her hands and knees. Looking over her shoulder, Shelly saw his eyes had zeroed in on her ass and between her thighs, where she knew she must be glistening wet.

"Well, do you blame me?" he asked as he slowly stood.

Shelly watched him, waiting for him to get behind her and take her. However, this view she liked too. As she watched, he pushed off his pants and shoes then removed his shirt.

Awestruck, she followed his movements with her eyes. He dropped onto his knees behind her, and before she knew it, she was whimpering as he slid his fingers between her thighs. He removed them from her heat and slipped them into his mouth for a taste.

"I have to be careful with you, Georgia. You often change your mind," he said.

Shelly moaned at the raw sex in his voice, then she dropped her head forward, presenting herself in silent invitation.

The man is insane. There was no way in hell she'd be changing her mind anytime soon.

∼

SHELLY ARCHED, PUSHING her ass back at him. He was so fucking hard, he thought he might physically hurt her when he finally got inside all of that waiting heat. Moving forward, he rose onto his knees and gripped her hips. He heard her breathy shudder as he moved the throbbing tip of his cock along her ass, sliding it against her wet, puffy folds.

"Now, Josh. God, do it now," she almost screamed.

He punctuated her request with a solid thrust.

Even though she had braced herself on her hands, when he thrust forward, he felt her slip a little. Her naked back arched, and he gripped her hips, slowly pulling his glistening erection out from her juicy wetness.

Watching his departure from her tight little body only served to spur him on further. So he tightened his fingers into her hips and slid them down to the sides of her thighs before thrusting forward again. When he heard her moan, he lost all control.

∼

SHELLY SWORE SHE felt every inch of him as he slowly withdrew the first time, only to drive back inside her time and time again. The sheer desperation in him pulled at Shelly more than any gentle lovemaking could have. His hand moved smoothly up her spine before gathering in her hair, and she felt her body contract around him. He thrust in hard and deep, then they both screamed.

Shelly thought they were lucky they didn't pass out from the sheer pleasure of it.

CHAPTER 25

*A*S SHELLY STOOD across the crowded room from Josh, three things occurred to her at the same time.

One, Danny Zuko had never looked so hot.

Two, she was a complete and utter moron.

And three, she was one hundred percent in love with Joshua Daniels.

It was funny, because she wasn't one to believe in "aha" moments, but this was most certainly one of them. He wasn't even looking at her or doing anything remarkably special. He was standing by the bar with Mason, laughing at something his friend had said.

But suddenly, every little piece of the puzzle finally shifted and locked together. Shelly sat down gingerly and watched the man she was finally *seeing* for the first time.

If she had to pinpoint the moment it had started to slide into place, it had to be the desperation in him that afternoon. When he had taken her with such raw passion, something had switched on inside her. It was as if he had lit a fuse, and the flame had spread like wildfire through her body, setting her heart ablaze.

Resting a hand on the table, she shakily held a glass of water in the other. *What the hell do I do now? Just go over and tell him?* After all, he hadn't been very receptive lately, always shushing her.

"Hey there."

Shelly looked up to see a little round peach beside her—Lena in costume. If Shelly hadn't known the story behind the outfit choice, she might have thought her friend was slightly insane. But the peach was a lovely nod to a creative date Mason had once come up with.

Shelly tried to smile but felt it came off a little strained. "Hey."

"Are you okay?" Lena asked as she tried—and *tried* was the right word—to sit beside her.

Shelly chuckled a little before nodding. "I think so."

Lena finally situated herself, even though the outfit had pushed up to just under her ears. It really was comical. She had on bright green tights and a little green cap shaped like leaves. The overall picture was downright hilarious.

"What do you mean you think you're okay?" Lena looked over to Mason and Josh. She turned back to Shelly. "Did you two have a fight?"

Shelly swallowed, shaking her head. "No, not at all. Just the opposite actually."

Lena frowned. "Opposite meaning?"

"I'm totally in love with him," Shelly blurted. She widened her eyes and clapped a hand over her mouth.

A wide grin split Lena's face. "Did that feel good? Or are you going to throw up?"

Shelly looked over at the guys again. This time Josh was staring at her, then he winked.

All of a sudden, Shelly felt just like Sandra Dee from *Grease*—and yes, she had gone as Sandra Dee. She was dressed in the white preppy sweater, red skirt, ponytail, and all.

In fact, Josh had taken one look at her and smiled before kissing her brains out. Dressed in Danny's black leather jacket, black shirt, and black jeans, he declared that he was *finally* the bad boy she had accused him of being.

Oh God, her heart *would not* calm down. It had kicked up and was thundering a deafening beat as he smiled in that devastating way that had first put him on her radar so many months ago.

Shelly turned toward Lena with a panicked expression. "I don't know what to do next."

Lena smiled and tried to reach across to Shelly, but the peach impeded her. It would have been ridiculous if Shelly hadn't been realizing that the next few hours would probably either secure her future happiness or commit her to a lifetime of heartbreak and misery.

No pressure though.

"How about you tell him?" Lena suggested.

Shelly gave her friend a deadpan look. "Wow, thanks for pointing out the obvious there, peaches."

"Hey. You asked," Lena said, pouting and sitting back the best she could.

She really did look beyond absurd.

"It was more of a rhetorical kind of thing. I know what I need to do." Shelly looked back at the man she now knew with certainty she wanted for the rest of her life. "Now I just have to convince him I mean it."

JOSH KNEW SOMETHING WAS UP. His spine had been tingling all night. He wasn't exactly sure what had happened, but Shelly had changed somehow.

"Earth to Josh. Hey," Mason said, waving a hand in front of him.

Josh turned his eyes to his friend and raised an eyebrow.

"Did the guys tell you they're ahead of schedule?" Mason asked.

Josh nodded, taking a swig of his beer. "Who the hell are you supposed to be again, man?"

Mason spread his arms out and did a mock bow, dressed in a white pirate shirt coupled with a black vest and cream pantaloons. "I'm Casanova. Lover of all women."

Josh shook his head, chuckling. "And douchebag extraordinaire? What on earth were you and Lena thinking? She looks so uncomfortable any time she tries to sit."

Mason chuckled. "I suggested it, and she liked the idea. Well, until I brought the costume home, but by then it was too late."

Josh shook his head. "Shocker, man, total shocker."

"Hey, that's my wife you're talking about. I happen to think she looks cute as a peach."

Josh looked at where Lena was squished up, seated with Shelly. "Okay, she does look cute."

Mason hummed his agreement. "And your Man-Eater looks downright tame, dressed as innocent little Sandra Dee."

Josh let his eyes wander to the perfect blond ponytail and the red-and-white get-up. He had to admit that he wished he was staying tonight, just so he could get under that skirt. "Yeah, well, maybe she isn't quite the man-eater I first thought."

"Oh yeah?"

"Yeah." Josh lifted his beer for another swig. "In fact, she's pretty fantastic—in every way."

Mason gave him a shit-eating grin. "In a forever kind of way?"

Shelly was now watching him. He winked at her then smiled, watching her pale a little before gathering her composure. When she turned back to Lena, he turned back to Mason.

"Oh yeah, man. In a forever kind of way."

~

SHELLY TOOK A deep breath and nodded. "Yep. I'm going to tell him tonight. Maybe he'll stay."

Lena nodded then grinned as Rachel appeared beside their table from the crowd. She was dressed as a ninja, wearing black skintight leggings that rode low around her waist and showed off her pierced navel, which, apparently, Mason knew about. She'd paired them with a slinky black top that clung to her every curve but left her arms bare. The black scarf wrapped around her head and neck revealed only her startling, now sad, blue eyes. The only reason Shelly knew what she was supposed to be was the fake sword on her side. *Oh yeah, I had to ask.*

"What's going on?" Rachel asked as she sat down beside the peach.

"Sandy over here is going to tell Danny that what they had over the summer really was true love."

Rachel snorted, and Shelly rolled her eyes.

"Ahh. So you finally worked out he's a keeper, huh?"

Shelly felt her spine straighten, as if she needed to defend herself. *Hang on, why should I?* She had just been erring on the side of caution.

"Fine. Okay, yes, you're right. I finally caught up." Like a teenage girl, she added on a sigh, "He's amazing."

Rachel let out a grunt. "Excuse me while I get a violin."

She turned to the left, pretending to get the fake violin no doubt, and froze. Shelly raised her eyes to follow Rachel's line of sight, and that was when she noticed him. *Isn't that...*

"What the hell is he doing here?" Rachel demanded in—*oh boy*—Super Domme's voice.

Lena struggled to sit up and peer across the crowd to where they were looking. When she locked on to who they were staring at, Lena turned to Rachel. "I thought you said you didn't know him."

Rachel's spine straightened, and her shoulders went back a noticeable inch. "I do *not* know him. I don't even know why he's *here*."

Shelly needed to try to calm her. Shit, she had enough on her mind without Rachel having an anxiety attack. "Look, if he's given you shit in the past—"

Rachel stood abruptly. "He hasn't done anything to me. *I. Don't. Know. Him.*" She turned on her heel before stalking off.

Shelly looked at Lena with wide eyes, then they both turned back to see the man from Whipped, whose eyes were on Rachel's retreating form.

~

MASON HAD LEFT a few minutes ago to go socialize when Josh got a text from Cole that he was just making his way in. He apologized for not dressing up, but he was coming from the office. Josh didn't think that was so unusual. After all, the guy practically lived there.

Scanning the room for his friend, he saw Cole stepping through all the colorful costumes. He noticed his lawyer and friend was looking at the table with Shelly, Lena, and Rachel. Josh smirked. *Hell, who can blame the guy?* They were a good trio to be watching, even though two were taken and the other one was more like a loveable sister.

Plus, Josh didn't think Cole dated. It wasn't as though he ever had time, considering the painfully long hours he put in on his job.

"Cole," Josh shouted.

His friend turned slowly on his heel, then he strode toward the bar. But he wasn't smiling or even grinning—he just looked serious with a frown. Cole came over and took the seat beside him.

"Want a beer?" Josh asked.

"How about a cognac?"

Josh chuckled. "Of course." After putting the order in, he looked back to Cole. "Another long day?"

Cole scratched his chin. "Yes. Long and tedious." He paused as the bartender passed him the lowball glass, then he gave Josh a thoughtful look. "However, I think it just got interesting."

Josh raised an inquiring brow. "Oh? Because of the party?"

Cole scanned the room then turned back to Josh. "Do you know the three women who were over there?"

Josh stiffened, immediately feeling the ugly green-eyed monster creeping into his gut. "Yes. Why?" His tone came out much shorter than he had intended.

Cole must have caught that because he narrowed his eyes on Josh, raising his glass to take a slow sip. "No reason. I thought I knew one of them."

Automatically, Josh thought the worst until Cole continued. "The one in black. She's not there anymore."

Josh's heart slowed to a normal rate. "Rachel?" Then he found himself laughing. "I doubt you'd know Rachel. She's a pastry-chef-slash-florist. Not really two things you have a lot of use for since you're married to your job."

Cole nodded slowly, tapping the side of the glass with his finger. "Perhaps I'm wrong. Maybe you could introduce me?"

Josh nodded. That would be great. After all, look how good his setup had turned out—well, almost turned out. "Sure, let me go get her."

Cole nodded. "I'll just wait here."

SHELLY TURNED TO LENA. "Okay, who's the guy with Josh?"

Lena shrugged as best she could. "Why don't you ask him? He's coming over here."

Shelly turned and saw that Josh was in fact making his way toward them. When he stopped, Shelly felt all the nerves from earlier come fluttering back. Forget the stranger at the bar—here was her man. *The man I want to spend the rest of my life with.*

"Hey there, Zuko," Shelly sassed, trying to hide her nerves.

He leaned down and pressed his lips to hers. "God, you're sweet."

She hummed then asked, "Can we talk?"

Josh grinned against her lips. "I'd love to talk to you. But first, where's Rachel?"

Shelly pulled back. "She left."

"Oh, that's a shame. My friend, Cole, wanted to meet her."

Shelly looked at Lena and widened her eyes. "That guy at the bar?" Josh nodded then twirled her ponytail.

"Who is he?" Shelly asked before she lost all focus.

"He's my lawyer and friend."

"Oh," Lena squeaked.

Josh looked over Shelly's shoulder at her. "What?"

"Nothing," they answered in unison.

So subtle. Shelly knew that she needed to distract him from Rachel. For some reason, this Cole guy was determined to meet the Super Domme, and Super Domme wanted nothing to do with him. Shelly stood, and Josh backed up a little.

"So? Can we talk?" she asked again.

Josh nodded and held a hand out to her. Shelly gripped it and was about to walk away with him. Before she did, he turned back to Lena.

"If you get a chance, go ahead and introduce the two of them. I think Cole's interested. It'd be funny to watch," Josh said.

Lena gave him a strained smile, and when Josh turned around, she looked panicked. Yeah, Shelly heard her loud and clear. *That would be one big hell no.*

JOSH HAD TAKEN S<small>HELLY</small>'s hand and tugged her into the newly renovated and empty space attached to Exquisite. He knew he had to leave soon if he wanted to make good time tonight, but as he stood with her in the silent room, he was finding it difficult to walk away.

"I love you," Shelly blurted.

There was no gentle delivery or buildup. Just straight to the point, like the bold, brave man-eater he had first met.

However, she was standing with her hands balled in front of her in a dark room, illuminated only by the passing taxicabs. She looked sweet, innocent, and full of love, and Josh was trembling with how much he wanted to believe her.

Taking a deep breath, he stepped closer and cupped her face. "Don't play with me."

"I'm not," she whispered. "I want everything you talked about. I'm ready."

Josh shook his head, not believing he was finally getting everything he wanted. He stroked a hand down her neck and cupped the back of it, tugging her closer to lean his forehead against hers. "You really mean it, Georgia?"

She blinked, and he felt her eyelashes against his skin. Then she looked at him. "Every single word. I want everything you said you wanted. I want to wake up with you in the mornings and fall asleep with you every night. I want you to stay."

Josh felt his heart clench. "I still need to go back tonight, Shel."

She stepped back and shook her head. "I don't understand. You still don't believe me?" Then she gripped his hands. "Because I mean it. I really mean it. With everything inside me. Just thinking about you leaving..." She sniffed a little, and he realized she was actually crying.

He pulled her into his arms. "You crazy woman." He hugged her tightly. "I have to go. I have responsibilities. But, Georgia, I believe you." Pulling back from her, he tipped up her chin and wiped a tear from her cheek. "Where's your brave face?"

SHELLY LAUGHED A little and tried for a smile.

"Still pathetic," he said and leaned in to kiss her.

His lips were so sweet and gentle that Shelly felt her heart crack even wider when he pulled back.

"I need to go. But, Georgia, if you mean everything you said tonight—"

She nodded. "I do."

A big grin crossed his face, and he squeezed her hand. "Then will you do me a favor?"

Shelly nodded before he even finished. He looked so sexy standing there, eyes and mouth smiling at her.

"If you mean everything you said tonight, next Saturday at four p.m., meet me."

Shelly cocked her head to the side as he dropped her hand. She frowned. "Does that mean you'll finally tell me where you've been staying?"

He walked backward toward the door, and Shelly literally felt her heart splitting apart the farther he moved away. *Saturday will take forever to get here.*

"Where, Josh?" She was almost afraid he would vanish before she knew where to find him.

Giving her the biggest grin she had ever seen, he shouted, "Saturday. Four o'clock. Where I once wished for you on a penny."

Shelly thought for a moment then gave him a huge grin of her own. "I'll be there."

When he opened the door, eyes still on her, he called, "Don't be late, Georgia."

All Shelly could think was, *For once, I plan to be right on time.*

CHAPTER 26

November

*I*T FELT AS THOUGH a year had come and gone by Friday morning.

Shelly had been anxious ever since Josh had disappeared on Saturday night. When Sunday evening rolled around, Shelly was woman enough to admit that she had checked her email at least twenty times.

Nothing.

On Monday, after a shift that had dragged forever, she upped her email monitoring to thirty times before reminding herself that she was acting like a complete idiot. The man had clearly stated he would meet her on Saturday, and just because he didn't send her an email every night did *not* mean he had changed his mind. She needed to stop worrying, stop obsessing over what may happen, and just trust him.

"Hey there, Dr. Monroe."

Shelly was standing just inside the doctors' lounge, and when she turned, she saw Dr. Robert McKinney strolling in. He smiled then made his way over to the coffee pot. Shelly returned the smile and approached the doctor she now considered a kind and friendly colleague who she had *once* dated.

"Good morning, Dr. McKinney," she said as he passed her a mug of coffee.

"I heard a little rumor that you're off to Georgia for the weekend."

Shelly grinned over the lip of her mug and nodded, feeling her heart squeeze. "Yes, that's right. I fly out at two o'clock."

McKinney nodded. "Going to see family?"

After taking another sip, Shelly lowered the cup and leaned against the counter. "Actually, yes and no. I'll see the family while I'm there, but I'm going to meet Josh down there."

McKinney frowned, then almost as if a light bulb had gone off, he nodded. "Oh, yes, Bob the Builder."

Shelly laughed at that image then thought of Josh that one time she had seen him with a tool belt around his waist. *Mmmm, maybe I'll have to get him to put that on again, so I can get on my knees and unzip—*

"Shelly?" McKinney asked, pulling her out of her fantasy.

"Oh, sorry. Yes, that's him."

McKinney looked into her smiling eyes and gave her a huge grin. "It's serious, isn't it?"

She thought back to the Halloween party and how Josh had smiled at her, telling her to come and meet him. *Meet him where he wished for me.*

She felt her heart melt as she said, "Yes. Very."

∾

JOSH WAS EXHAUSTED.

It was Friday night, and he and his crew had been working around the clock. Although the project was nowhere close to finished, they had gotten things to a point he was happy with. He had a couple of things to do tomorrow morning, but none of that came close to what he planned to do tomorrow afternoon.

Not emailing Shelly all week had been something he was unsure about at first. Ever since he had moved away, he had made sure to keep in contact with her, usually every night, just so he knew she was always thinking about him. And he also got a shot of adrenaline every time he opened his email and saw Dr. Shelly Monroe in his inbox.

However, this was different. He had laid down the rules this time, told her what he expected from her, and now it was *her* turn to show up and follow through.

Josh only hoped she didn't disappoint.

He looked around the cramped space he had lived in for the last several months. *If things go according to plan tomorrow, this will all have been worth it. If they don't, this sad, lonely room will be a fitting place for me to bury my broken heart.*

∼

SATURDAY MORNING HAD ARRIVED.

Shelly's flight had been smooth. Her father had been at the airport to pick her up. This time around, the drive back to the house wasn't in the least bit awkward, *and* they'd actually had a decent conversation. He'd asked her about work, how she was enjoying it, and even gone so far as to ask how she and Josh were doing. Of course, Shelly wasn't really comfortable divulging too much, so she just told him things were good then smiled and moved the conversation along.

Lunch that afternoon had been a civil affair as well. To Shelly, that was a huge step in the right direction. For as many years as she could remember, their family dinners had been awkward and strained.

Afterward, she borrowed her father's truck, put it in gear, and drove down the gravel driveway. As she pulled onto the main road, she was reminded of the day she had taken Josh to her favorite place—her dreaming tree.

She glanced at the clock by the rearview mirror and saw that it was two forty-five. She had plenty of time to stop by the river and take a moment to work out everything she wanted and needed to tell Josh.

But when she reached the right turn, she slowed down only to discover a huge red-and-white sign that read, *PRIVATE PROPERTY. NO TRESPASSING.*

Shelly stopped the truck and hopped out, making her way to the now-padlocked fence that stretched across the dirt road. *Well, shit.* She tried to look down the road, but she couldn't see anything.

That was *not* the way she wanted to start the day. The one place she had always found peace and solitude was now owned by someone who would never truly appreciate it.

Sighing because there was nothing she could do about it, she walked back to the truck. *Well, maybe it's for the best anyway.* After all, it could be a sign that it was time to actually live her life and quit standing under a tree and dreaming about it.

∼

IT WAS 3:50 P.M. As Josh stood in front of the fountain he had once visited with Shelly, he was nervous. *What if she doesn't show? What if this has all been for nothing?*

He took a deep breath and looked at the clear blue sky above him. Stuffing his shaking hands into his jeans pockets, he closed his eyes. *She said she loves me, and her eyes meant it. I saw it.*

Once he had calmed himself as best he could, he opened his eyes and stared at the white steeple of the Catholic cathedral, St. John the Baptist, where Shelly had told him she had been baptized. Reminding himself of everything he had put into this moment over the last several months, Josh was determined that nothing would deter him—nothing except for her failure to show.

∼

SHELLY FOUND HERSELF running through Lafayette Square at 3:57 p.m.

The stupid traffic had held her up. As she rounded the final bend in the path leading to *her* fountain, she slowed to a walk and took in the perfect scene before her.

Standing with his back to her was a man now so familiar, she would be able to pick him out of a crowded stadium, and beside that strong figure sat a dog. They were silent in their stillness, and as Shelly moved closer, she swore everything in the entire universe disappeared.

She had almost reached them when he turned, and she finally locked eyes with Josh.

Shelly stopped where she was, waiting to see what he would do, but Josh didn't do anything. He merely looked her over from head to toe, and when his eyes came back to hers, he smiled slowly. She could have sworn she felt that smile reach inside her and hug her heart.

∼

JOSH WASN'T SURE what he had been expecting, but as Shelly

stood in front of him, dressed in a billowy blue blouse and simple faded jeans, he knew his Georgia had shown up.

In a move so simple yet so incredibly important, he held out his hand to her. Then he took a deep breath and waited to see what she would do.

The woman he had fallen so deeply in love with stepped forward and took his hand without even a moment of hesitation. She gazed up at him as he squeezed her hand, tugging her closer. When Shelly put a hand on his chest to steady herself, he swore she must have been able to feel his heart beating a hundred miles an hour.

"You came," he whispered.

Those incredible eyes of hers smiled at him, and her mouth tipped up at the corners to match. "Nothing could have stopped me."

Josh finally let go of the breath he had been holding, and he shook his head. He stroked his free hand down the back of her head over her silky blond hair to cup the nape of her neck, bringing her closer. Then he did what he'd wanted to do all week—he kissed her.

SHELLY SIGHED AS his lips finally brushed against her own.

He was so gentle in his persuasion for her to open to him. He had no need to worry though. Shelly was ready to give herself to him, body and soul. And if he wanted anything else, he could have that too.

As he lifted his lips, he leaned his forehead against hers, and their noses brushed as he closed his eyes. He still had a hand on her neck, and the other one was holding hers. She felt his heart thundering beneath her palm.

"Josh?" When she got no response, she moved and kissed his cheek. "Josh?"

He blinked as though he was pulling himself out of some kind of daze, then he smiled at her.

"Stop it," she said.

"Stop what?"

She moved back and leaned down to pat Mutley's head. When she straightened, she bit her bottom lip and gave a nervous laugh. "Looking at me like that."

"Like what?" he asked as he stepped closer again. Before she could answer, he laid a finger across her lips. "Like I love you?"

Is that a question I'm supposed to answer?

Apparently not, because he continued. "Because I do. Love you, that is. I have never loved someone as much as I love you."

Shelly felt her heart starting that strong gallop, but she tried to remain steady as he cupped her face in his palms.

"I love the Shelly who made an outrageous deal with me one night in a club. I love the Shelly who brought me here to this very spot and showed me that she has a soft side that is so damn appealing, I would never be able to look anywhere else ever again. I love the Shelly who was confused and angry and who kicked me out of her life because she was honest. She didn't hold on to me and make me stay only to stray elsewhere." He kissed her nose before whispering, "But you know what, Georgia? I couldn't leave *you* behind."

Shelly looked at Josh with tears filling her eyes. *What a stupid woman I've been. Why did I wait so long to discover what kind of man he is?*

As she was about to speak, he stepped back and went down on one knee. Shelly felt her eyes widening and her mouth parting as she watched with something close to absolute wonder.

JOSH STARED UP at Shelly from down on his knee, taking her hand.

He had thought about this moment for months. He had gone over and over in his head exactly what he wanted to say to her. As he knelt at her feet, looking up at her shocked face, he felt a slight shiver of anxiety run down his spine.

Her eyes shifted to Mutley, who thankfully was sitting like an obedient dog, then they came back to rest on his.

Well, it's now or never. "Over the past ten months, I have met and fallen in love with three different women."

Shelly took a deep breath and swallowed.

"A man-eater, who is gutsy, bold, and so scary she *almost* made me walk away. A professional, who is so smart and sophisticated that her brains and sheer knowledge of certain things leave me breathless and in awe."

Shelly finally smiled at him, squeezing his hand. The shock had left her face, and he saw a tear sliding down her cheek.

That is definitely a good sign. "Lastly, Georgia. I met and fell in love with a sweet hometown girl who has a terrible brave face and sings the worst rendition of Shania Twain's songs I've ever heard. Yet she still managed to make me fall madly in love with her."

Josh kept his eyes on hers as he dug into his jeans pocket with his free hand and pulled out a small box. Looking at her, he let go of her hand, unsnapped the black velvet box, then looked once again at the most beautiful face he had ever seen.

"Georgia, will you marry me?"

SHELLY WAS FINALLY RENDERED SPEECHLESS.

Josh, down on one knee with his big beast of a dog beside him, was asking her to marry him.

As he waited patiently for her answer, Shelly kept running over all the important things she wanted to tell him. Like how much she had missed him since Saturday night. Or how hard it had been to see him with his ex-girlfriend all those months ago. Or how the thought of him leaving her life when he was planning to move away had ripped out her heart.

However, as she gazed at the man before her, holding out his hand with a little black box, none of that was important.

All Shelly could do was whisper, "Yes."

That sexy smile that was all Delicious Daniels spread across his lips, and those warm brown eyes lit up. He stood, and she wrapped her arms around his neck. He gripped her waist and hauled her up against his body, kissing her with a desperation born of fear and ending with sweet joy.

When Josh finally put her on her feet, he asked, "Yes?"

Shelly laughed and nodded. "Yes, yes, yes."

As she moved in close to kiss him, the huge bells in the church behind them tolled loudly. Both of them looked over their shoulders as the church doors opened, and a wedding party spilled into the street, making their way across to the park.

Shelly felt Josh take her hand, and she looked at him as he pulled it to his lips. He kissed her knuckles and slid the beautiful diamond onto her finger.

"I want that to be us. Whenever you're ready, I want to bring you back here and marry you in that church."

Shelly asked, "Why here? Why not Chicago? You are moving back to Chicago, aren't you?"

Josh kissed her softly. "I plan to be wherever you are so I can go to sleep with you at night and—"

"Wake up with me in the morning?"

Pecking her on the lips, he nodded. "Yes, and wake up with you in the mornings. This is who you are to me, Georgia. You're the girl in the faded jeans who grew up in a Southern town. The one who dreams under a tree. That's *my* Georgia, my little slice of heaven, and I want to marry you in the church you grew up in."

Shelly shook her head. "I don't need to dream anymore, and anyway, the dreaming tree has been sold."

To her surprise, a huge grin spread across Josh's lips. "Don't be too quick to throw it all away. Some dreams are meant to last." As Shelly quirked a brow, he leaned down to whisper in her ear, "I've been building a dream."

SHELLY TOOK A step back and tilted her head. "I don't understand."

Josh took her hand and whistled for Mutley, who trotted up along beside him. "Come with me. Trust me, and I'll explain it along the way."

EPILOGUE

*D*REAMS ARE FUNNY *things. They shift and morph as you grow*, Shelly thought as Josh's truck rumbled to a stop in front of the padlocked gate. He got out of the truck and walked around the front to unlock the gate.

On their way over, he had told her all about *his* dreams and what he'd been doing for the last few months. Quite honestly, Shelly was left speechless.

The man had bought her property.

Well, of course, it wasn't hers, but he had bought the place she ran to for comfort and solace.

As he climbed back into the truck, he gave her an almost shy grin. "You okay?"

Shelly nodded. "All this time, you've been here? That's what you're telling me?"

"Yeah." He put the truck in gear, and it lurched forward. "I wanted to get away from Chicago. It's never been for me. It's too cold, and when we came down here..." He looked to her, and Shelly smiled. He took her hand and touched the ring he'd just placed on her finger. "Well, when we came here, I fell in love. I fell in love with Savannah, with this property that has a river running down the back of it, and with a beautiful big oak tree where I made love to my fiancée."

Shelly brought his hand to her lips. She kissed his big knuckle then raised it to her cheek. "So then what?"

As the truck took the final bend in the road, she looked out the windshield and saw a small foundation and the start of walls and a roof right behind the large oak. Shelly gasped and looked at Josh, who had stopped the truck and fully turned to her.

"So then I started to build. I had no clue at first what I wanted to do. All I knew was I wanted to make something beautiful here—*for you*. I wanted you to be able to come back and visit your family and, if you wanted to, come down and stay by the river."

Josh grinned and jumped out of the truck, making his way around to her side. He opened her door, and she got out, taking his hand. They made their way over to the beginning of what looked to be a small cottage, then they stopped.

"It started as a hammock under this tree." Josh turned to her and took her hands. "In fact, it started as a kiss under this tree. A kiss from a sweet girl called Georgia, wearing nothing but a cowboy hat. But then, my dream changed. Every time we talked, every time I saw you and touched you, this grew in my head. I was building us a dream."

He pulled her in close, and Shelly felt tears sliding down her cheeks. *All of this is just too good to be true.* The man, the house, the place she felt most at home, and yes, even the damn dog.

"I know you live in Chicago. I know our lives are there." He kissed her nose. "But I want us to be able to come here whenever we want. Lie down on a blanket in the afternoon sun and make love. Unwind and dream together."

Shelly looked at the sweetest, sexiest man she had ever met and wondered how on earth she had ever let a day go by, let alone months and weeks, when he wasn't close enough to touch.

Wrapping her arms around Josh's neck, Shelly smiled into his warm eyes. "But what do you dream for when you have everything you want?"

His sexy smile widened across those delicious lips. "Good point."

Standing up on her tiptoes, Shelly kissed those lips and whispered in the best Southern accent she could dig up, "Oh, what a shame, sugah. Now it just looks like you'll have more time to unwind and make love to me in the afternoon sun."

Clutching her, Josh kissed her with a lot more force than she had.

"Oh, now, that is a shame, Georgia. When do you think we can begin?"

Shelly answered with a soft sigh. "I'm thinking now, sugah. I'm thinking right now."

With that, she found herself kissing her future husband under her dreaming tree and thinking of new dreams. She wondered, just for a moment, if it would shock Josh to know that the dream now held a dog and a toddler running around under a large oak tree.

As Josh picked her up and carried her closer to some shade and a blanket, he leaned down and nuzzled her ear. "I love you, Shelly Monroe. I can't wait to have a family with you."

"I love you too." Shelly turned her head and kissed him back, smiling.

This tree really does make dreams come true.

THE EXQUISITE SERIES

Exquisite (Lena & Mason)
Entice (Shelly & Josh)
Edible (Rachel & Cole)

***

Spin-Off Series
(Featuring Cole's half-brother Logan Mitchell)

Try (The Temptation Series I)
Take (The Temptation Series II)
Trust (The Temptation Series III)

Four Years Later...

Tease (The Temptation Series IV)
Tate (The Temptation Series V)
Untitled (The Temptation Series VI)

ACKNOWLEDGMENTS

I would like to take a moment to thank some amazing people, who have gotten to know my work and me over the past few months. It has been such a pleasure becoming a part of the wonderful indie-writing community.

First and foremost, I must thank my fantastic editor, Jovana Shirley, whom I was lucky enough to have found through Taryn Cellucci from My Secret Romance Book Reviews. What a great day that was when I saw a link to your site! You have been nothing but supportive and professional throughout our duration of working together, and I appreciate all of the time and effort you have put in to making Entice the best version of itself.

Second, I'd love to thank a few of the amazing bloggers that I have had a chance to work with: Shh Mom's Reading, TotallyBooked Blog, Scandalicious Book Reviews, Flirty and Dirty Book Blog, Reviews by Tammy & Kim, Zee Book Truth, Swept Away by Romance, Reality Bites! Let's Get Lost!, THESUBCLUBbooks, Romantic Book Affairs, My Secret Romance Book Reviews, Sinfully Sexy Book Reviews, Three Chicks and Their Books, Natasha Is a Book Junkie, and The Indie Bookshelf. All of these blogs offer some of the best recommendations in books, so if you're looking for some advice, I would go to one of these ladies straightaway. Thank you for all being so helpful with the Entice Blog Tour, and I look forward to working with you all in the future.

I also would like to thank Samantha Young, author of On Dublin Street, and Tiffany Reisz, author of The Siren, for writing two of my favorite reads of 2012.

ABOUT THE AUTHOR

Ella Frank is the *USA Today* Bestselling author of the Temptation series, including Try, Take, and Trust and is the co-author of the fan-favorite contemporary romance, Sex Addict. Her Exquisite series has been praised as "scorching hot!" and "enticingly sexy!"

Some of her favorite authors include Tiffany Reisz, Kresley Cole, Riley Hart, J.R. Ward, Erika Wilde, Gena Showalter, and Carly Philips.

For more information
www.ellafrank.com

Made in United States
Cleveland, OH
11 April 2025